The flashing ligh... ... ...
Judy's eye as she carried a bag filled with groceries into the kitchen. It was her day off and cleaning chores were next on the agenda. She pressed the message button.

"It's Kent, Judy. Don't get upset. We have to talk."

On hearing his voice, she dropped the sack, spilling its contents. Her mouth went dry and she leaned against the kitchen counter for support. *How dare he call me after what he put me through,* she fumed.

The message continued. "I've made a decision. Call me on my cell, five six one, two six eight six. I'm waiting."

"What decision?" she cried aloud. That decision had been made months ago. He started the affair and broke it off. When reality reared its ugly head, the promised divorce just melted away.

Repeated rings of the doorbell went unanswered until a loud knocking grabbed her attention.

"Kent!" she gasped on opening the door.

"Don't get upset, Judy. Before you say anything, hear me out." He entered and steadily advanced. "May I?"

She pushed him back. "Get out! There's nothing more to say."

"I deserve that, but give me a chance."

"You had your chance."

He reached for her hand. "I know I made a mistake, but I love you. Listen to me, Judy. I want to marry you."

She let out a scornful laugh. "Marry me? You're already married."

"But I'm miserable and never should have let you go."

"Too late, Kent, especially after all the hurt you caused me." Her eyes filled and she covered her face with her hands. "How could I be such a fool? What was I thinking of getting involved with a married man?"

Wings

BEHIND HOSPITAL DOORS

by

Dr. Richard Berjian

A Wings ePress, Inc.

Mainstream Novel

Wings ePress, Inc.

Edited by: Jeanne R. Smith
Copy Edited by: Joan C. Powell
Senior Editor: Jeanne R. Smith
Executive Editor: Marilyn Kapp
Cover Artist: Richard Stroud

Wings ePress Books
http://www.wings-press.com

Copyright © 2010 by Richard Berjian
ISBN 978-1-61309-933-9

Published In the United States Of America

May 2012

Wings ePress Inc.
403 Wallace Court
Richmond, KY 40475

Dedication

To my wife, Sally, whose devotion and technical support made this novel possible.

Hippocratic Oath

I SWEAR BY APPOLLO, the Physician, and Aesculapius and Health and All-Heal and All the Gods and Godesses that, according to my ability and judgement, I will keep this Oath and Stipulation:

TO RECKON him who taught me this art equally dear to me as my parents, to share my substance with him and relieve his necessities if required: to regard his offspring as on the same footing with my own brothers, and to teach them this art if they should wish to learn it without fee or stipulation, and that by precept lecture and every other mode of instruction. I will impart a knowledge of the art to my own sons and those of my teachers, and to disciples bound by stipulation and oath, according to the law of medicine, but to none others.

I WILL FOLLOW that method of treatment which, according to my ability and judgement, I consider for the benefit of my patients, and abstain from whatever is deleterious and mischievous. I will give no deadly medicine to anyone if asked, nor suggest any such counsel; furthermore, I will not give to a woman any instrument to produce abortion.

WITH PURITY AND WITH HOLINESS I will pass my life and practice my art. I will not cut a person who is suffering with a stone but will leave this to be done by practitioners of this work. Into whatever houses I enter, I will go into them for the benefit of the sick and will abstain from every voluntary act of mischief and corruption, and further from the seduction of females or males, bound or free.

WHATEVER in connection with my professional practice, or not in connection with it, I may see or hear in the lives of men which ought not to be spoken abroad I will not divulge, as reckoning that all such should be kept secret.

WHILE I CONTINUE to keep this oath unviolated, may it be granted to me to enjoy life and the practice of the art, respected by all men at all times but should I trespass and violate this oath, may the reverse be my lot.

HIPPOCRATES
460-377 B.C.

Prologue

6 AM, Florida Interstate Highway I-95

Olga Ottavio raced her black sedan south into Palm Beach County. A pang of fear surged through her body when her cell phone rang.

"Olga! Where are you? Time's running out."

"I'm afraid to go any faster, Ramon. Give me twenty minutes."

"You know if you're late again, they ask questions."

"*Aiee!* I'm past seventy already. Police will stop me."

"Don't worry about police. We got to get the money out quick. You know what happens if they find out."

Orange barrels dotting both sides of the road warned Olga of the 55-mile construction zone. But Ramon was right. They were more dangerous than the police.

Her heart pounded and she took in a breath, pressing harder on the pedal. "Okay, Ramon, I love you. Adios."

She turned off the phone, relieved this was the last trip transporting the Syndicate's money. She and Ramon had skimmed enough from earlier runs, and now they could escape to Costa Rica. They would marry and make a home for themselves and her teenage daughter, Carmella.

With the Jupiter exit behind, she balanced the risks taken during their long years of struggle. She trusted Ramon. They had met in Mexico and together crossed the sweltering desert with her four-month-old daughter strapped to her back. They picked crops, ran from Immigration and traveled the harvest trail from Texas to Florida. She felt committed each step of the way with Ramon at her side.

What chance did she have in Mexico? A single mother with no education? She did this for Carmella. Now her daughter would have a future and her own dream would become a reality.

With spirits climbing, she sped faster, humming *Little Bird* in her native tongue. A smile crossed her face at the thought of living in her own home. Over and over she planned it in her mind, visualizing every detail. Bright painted walls, ruffled curtains and brand new furniture.

Her eyes drifted to the ivory cross hanging over the dashboard, a gift from her mother on her twelfth birthday. She raised her hand to touch it for a sense of comfort and safety.

Not noticing the barrels narrowing the road, she clipped the edge of one, denting her fender. *"Dios Mia!"* she gasped, tightening her grip on the wheel.

She glanced into the rearview mirror and caught sight of a large gasoline tanker bearing down on her. Already speeding, she dared not drive any faster and pulled hard on the wheel to get out of the trailer's path. Unexpectedly, the tanker crossed into the same lane and to avoid getting hit, she made a sharp right.

She felt her body jolt from the seat at impact and heard the glass shatter and metal erupt. Suddenly, everything turned upside down as the sedan rolled over twice to rest on the grassy berm.

"*Ayuda me!*" she moaned in pain.

No one answered as the car lay on its roof, shrouded by a cloud of dust.

One

"Am I gutsy or just plain stupid?" Parker mumbled, shutting the buzzing alarm.

He threw off the flimsy sheet, turned on the TV and entered the tiny bathroom of his sparsely furnished apartment. Fresh out of training and single, he didn't need much room. Besides, he had no choice since his bank account hovered close to zero.

He stared into the mirror above the sink, stroking the stubble on his chin. Still uncertain about opening a solo surgical practice, his thoughts drifted to the ever-present risk of malpractice lawsuits as he shaved.

"Ouch," he grunted, nicking himself. "Screw the lawyers. Even if you do the right thing, you still can get nailed."

After sixteen years of college, med school, surgical residency and Fellowship, he was no longer protected by the womb of an academic center. But it was too late to change his mind, so he had to admit opening a private practice in Florida was probably a dumb move.

He heard the phone ring and dashed into the bedroom to answer.

"MCA Emergency Room, Dr. Dawson. You're on surgical call today and an auto accident is on its way in. How soon can you come?"

"Be there in fifteen minutes," he answered, toweling off the soapy lather on his face. The familiar adrenaline rush brought on by emergencies came over him. This first case was important. Hospital gossip was known to make or break reputations. Scrub nurses waited to see if the new surgeon would prove himself.

He returned to the bathroom and gave a final splash of water on his face, eager to scrub away any negative thoughts.

After quickly dressing, he turned off the small TV that sat on a wooden crate in the bedroom. The only other furnishings were a goose neck lamp and a telephone sitting on a battered nightstand beside the bed. Bargain Good Will purchases helped stretch his savings. Home decor had to wait. Most of his money went toward a one year lease for a modest office in the professional medical building located across from the hospital. It was only one of the many hospitals owned by the giant for-profit corporation, Medical Centers of America.

Dressed in a white coat, he grabbed his stethoscope and raced down the stairs to an aging but trusty Honda Civic. He took in a deep breath as he turned over the engine, ready to justify the promise of his long years of training.

~ * ~

Parker pulled into the doctors' lot adjacent to MCA's emergency room. A massive fire rescue ambulance parked

2

under the portico flashed its red and white lights, commanding a sense of urgency.

He left the car and sprinted toward the ER watching paramedics scramble to unlatch the doors. A stretcher emerged holding a woman strapped in a neck restraint. He followed the gurney through the open glass sliders and noted the patient appeared to be in her mid-thirties.

Endless possible injuries ran through his mind. A ruptured spleen, a torn aorta, who knows? He could tell by her soft moans and corpse-like coloring, she definitely had internal bleeding.

His heart pounded as he raced into the triage area, prepared for the worst. He watched as a nurse slapped on a blood pressure cuff, another drew blood and a third placed an intravenous solution into the woman's arm. Plastic prongs positioned into the patient's nostrils delivered oxygen.

"Pressure's eighty-four over sixty and pulse is thready," the nurse called out.

A paramedic held out a wallet. "Olga Ottavio is the name on her license."

"Thanks," Parker answered, cautiously lifting the blood-soaked gauze on her forehead. "Any family around?"

"No, she was alone," the medic replied.

Parker gazed down at the patient. "I'm Dr. Dawson, Olga. You're going to be all right. We're here to take care of you."

"*Que dolore*," the woman moaned, gripping her stomach.

He placed his stethoscope on her chest and listened to the rapid sounds of shallow breathing. "Oxygen's not helping." He then moved the scope to her stomach, causing Olga to let out a painful cry.

"She's guarding her belly, probably from internal bleeding." Turning to the nurse, he said, "Get the portable ultrasound."

"Sorry, Doctor, the unit is out for repair," the nurse replied.

"Son of a bitch," he muttered. "Set up for a peritoneal tap and get four units of blood ready for transfusion."

"No, no blood," the woman gasped, her dark eyes wide with fear.

Parker's voice rose. "Olga! Your life's in danger. You need blood."

"No, no blood," she repeated. "I'm Jehovah's Witness."

All activity stopped as everyone's eyes focused on Parker, who stood in disbelief.

A lab technician approached and handed him the report. "Doesn't look good, Doc. Hematocrit twenty-five, hemoglobin eight grams."

Olga's voice rose. "No blood, *Doctore, por favor!*

Frustrated by her demand, Parker searched the faces around him. "Great!" he groaned. " A bleeding Witness and no one here to sign a surgical consent." He knew he was facing a losing proposition and turned to the technician. "Start the cross-match, dammit. This woman's gonna need blood."

The nurse gave him a worried look. "Pressure down to seventy, pulse one twenty, Dr. Dawson."

No time to debate religious doctrine, he thought. With a belly full of blood and no transfusion, the moment he opened and released the internal pressure, she'd crash on the table.

"Forget the consent," he shouted. "Set up for a peritoneal tap. Once we prove blood in the belly, she goes to surgery."

He slipped on the sterile gloves he was handed. After a quick prep to the abdomen, he injected the anesthetic one inch below the belly button. A swift scalpel slit and a quick thrust of the plastic sheathed needle into the belly brought on a sudden spurt of bright red blood from the hub.

"Get her to OR," he shouted.

"OR is waiting," a voice replied.

He turned and froze in place, stunned at the sight of the slender blonde nurse standing before him. Memories flashed in his mind as he stood in shock, staring into her blue eyes. "Judy! "What in the hell are you doing here?"

"I'm nursing supervisor," she answered in a flat tone. "If this patient's a Witness, you can't give her blood."

"I know that!" he snapped with annoyance. "Don't you see the problem I have?"

She returned a stoic gaze. "We understand, Doctor, but you have a critical patient so don't waste time."

Olga let out another piercing cry. "I don't want to die."

Parker replied, "We won't let you die, Olga. Can we reach someone in your family?"

Olga reached into her bra, removed a key and pressed it into his hand. "Carmella, my daughter. Hold this for her if ..."

The nurse tending to Olga looked to Parker. "Pressure's dropping fast, Dr. Dawson."

Everyone could see Olga was slipping away, but how could he operate without blood? He had to act and turned to the nurse. "Get her to the OR and call Dr. Gold to assist me." As a new staff surgeon, he was required to operate under supervision and Morty Gold was that doctor.

"Who else should I call if he's not available?" Judy asked.

"See if Dr. Leader can come in."

Judy directed a nurse to tell the desk secretary to make the call and moved to Parker's side to help push the gurney. As they moved the cart, two men in business suits stood in their path.

Parker immediately recognized Eric Lindstrom, the tall hospital administrator he had met when applying for privileges. The stark fluorescent lighting on Lindstrom's pale face intensified the cold appearance Parker remembered at their first meeting. Beside him stood Henry Trask, Lindstrom's stocky assistant, writing furiously on a clipboard.

"Gurney coming through," Judy called out, but the men, engrossed in their business, didn't move.

Olga's sudden outcry caused Lindstrom to turn, step back and pull his assistant aside.

As they moved the cart through the doorway, Parker asked Judy, "What are they doing here so early in the morning?"

"No doubt looking to lay off more help. Lindstrom's been here a few months and he's already been named 'Mack the Knife.'"

"But I hear you're already understaffed."

"That's right, and if they cut any more, nurses will burn out and quit."

They rushed the cart carrying Olga to the OR entry and waited for the automatic doors to swing open.

Parker's eyes met Judy's. It had been close to three years since they separated and she was stunning as ever. "We have to talk, Judy. I've got to see you."

She returned a cool stare. "Take care of your patient, Doctor," and walked away.

After the OR circulating nurse maneuvered the cart into the operating room, Parker dashed off to change into scrubs. All his suppressed guilt flooded back with a vengeance. He had never forgotten her. The instant he saw her again, he knew he still loved her.

But right now, his feelings had to wait. His main responsibility was to save Olga's life.

~ & ~

Once inside the locker room, he spotted Rudy Catalano struggling to squeeze his portly frame into a green scrub suit. He liked the jovial Cuban anesthesiologist who had warmly welcomed him to the staff.

"Another highway accident?" Rudy asked.

"Yeah, and she's bleeding big time."

"You have blood ready?"

"Can't use any. She's a Witness."

A frown crossed Rudy's face. "Jesus, a bleeding Witness?"

"Don't panic, Rudy, we'll use the Cell Saver," Parker replied in an effort to sound confident.

"Shit! If she's hemorrhaging, that machine won't suck fast enough."

"Our hands are tied. We have no consent for transfusion so unless we want to get sued, forget the blood."

Once in the OR, Parker watched as Rudy took his place at the head of the table and passed an airway into Olga's trachea, flushing pure oxygen through the tube.

Rudy's brow wrinkled as he squeezed hard on the oxygen bag. "Damn it, Parker. I need blood. She has no pressure."

"Forget the blood," Parker answered, cursing under his breath. "There's no time to scrub. I'll open the chest and cross clamp the aorta. That'll stop the bleeding into her belly."

He donned sterile gloves over unwashed hands as the scrub nurse pushed the instrument table toward him. Making an incision into the left chest of the unconscious woman, he followed the edge of the fifth rib, widening the opening with a rib spreader. He inserted his gloved hand into the cavity, grasped the heart and forcefully pumped it.

"She's in V fib," Rudy yelled out.

Parker's eyes darted to the jagged, uncoordinated lines running across the monitor screen. "Keep pushing the fluid, Rudy, I'll shock her." He grabbed the paddles the nurse handed him and positioned them around the heart. "Set for three hundred Joules and everyone step back," he called out.

The charge jolted Olga's torso but the monitor showed no response.

"Raise to four hundred," he ordered. Another jolt surged through the body but this time the monitor showed a flat line.

"Adrenaline!" he shouted. He reached for the filled syringe and injected it into the heart. Still no response of life appeared on the monitor.

With eyes glued to the screen, he continued compressing the heart. "Atropine," he called out with panic in his voice.

"*Caramba*, her pupils are fixed!" Rudy bellowed. "She's flat lined. Call the code, Parker! She's *finito*, brain dead."

Parker pumped the heart more vigorously. "Don't die, you can't die on me!" he commanded. Beads of perspiration formed on his brow, and the circulating nurse gently patted it dry.

The room became still except for the hissing sound of suction.

"Call the code, Parker," Rudy pleaded. "There's nothing more we can do."

The circulating nurse tapped Parker's shoulder. "She's gone, Doctor."

All eyes rested on Parker as he fixed his gaze on the clock set on the tiled wall while still compressing Olga's heart.

Rudy continued to squeeze the ventilator bag, and after twenty minutes of pumping, injecting and shocking the heart, everyone knew Olga's time had come.

Parker bent over the motionless body and rested his bloodied hands on her chest. He looked up at the clock for the last time and spoke in a hoarse voice. "Time of death seven forty-eight AM. Thanks all for your help."

Stepping away from the table, he tore off his gloves and left the OR. *Son of a bitch* he swore under his breath. *What a way to end my first case.*

Two

It felt like the longest day in his life. Hanging around the hospital, hoping for a consultation and getting none. To waste time, he sat in the doctors' library for an hour reading medical journals. Hard as he tried, he couldn't concentrate.

On his way home, he picked up a frozen dinner at the local Publix market and once inside his apartment, sat before the television eating his meal. Even with the steady blare of TV noise, he became fully aware of his loneliness.

Judy was still on his mind. They had met at Ohio State Medical Center when he was chief surgical resident and she an intensive care nurse. At first they exchanged friendly banter which led to an invitation for coffee. They began to date and enjoyed being together. Even with his busy schedule, they managed to take in an occasional movie or go to dinner at Charley's, a mid-priced restaurant. It wasn't too long before their friendship developed into a passionate relationship.

In spite of his demanding schedule, he looked forward

to visiting her apartment whenever he had free time. There he could kick off his shoes and change into shorts and a tee shirt. They would eat dinner, listen to music and spend the night together. With Judy, life became more bearable, since he was able to share the challenges, successes and failures he endured as a surgical resident.

He loved her and wanted to get married but decided there was time for that after he finished training. His marriage wouldn't crash on the rocks like many of the other residents he knew. The grueling workload and hours away from home took a toll on married couples, making them drift apart. That wasn't going to happen to him.

Then everything came apart one night in her apartment. While lying in bed, he broke the news. "I applied for a fellowship in surgical oncology at Roswell Park. It's the cancer center in Buffalo." He still remembered her startled look.

"Another training program? For how long?"

"Two years and then..."

"Then what?"

"I'd like to try for an academic appointment at a major university medical center."

Her eyes flashed back in anger. "What about us?"

"I want you to come with me. You can easily get a job there."

"What about marriage?"

He remembered pausing before he spoke the fatal words. "We'll get married after I finish, but right now I think we should wait."

"Wait?" she cried. "You want me to follow you around like a puppy while you unravel your career choices? By the end of this summer, you'll have finished five years of specialty training and then another two years or more. When will it end?"

He took a hard swallow, recalling her how eyes had filled with tears and without saying another word, she had leaped out of bed and pulled on her robe.

He pleaded, trying to convince her. "Look, honey, this is very important to me. You have to pay a price to prepare for academic medicine. Lots of hours doing research, seeing patients, writing papers. We shouldn't rush into marriage at this time."

She glared back. "I love you, Parker, but there are certain things I need in my life."

He remembered how he had tried to explain they would get married after the fellowship, but all she did was calmly turn and walk into the bathroom to shower.

She finished, returned to the bedroom wrapped in a towel and looked into his eyes. "If that's your plan, do it without me."

No matter how he tried to reason with her, she remained cool and distant. He never returned to her apartment again.

He choked, recalling those painful moments. A week after their breakup, his adoptive parents died in a car accident. As their only child, he knew it was their unrelenting love and support that had guided him throughout his years of training. He owed them so much, but never had the chance to repay them.

But it wasn't until he accidentally spotted Judy having dinner with another resident that his already confused emotions dropped into a downward spiral. He really missed her, but by God, he told himself, she wasn't the only pretty girl on the planet.

Accepted into the fellowship program at the cancer center, he moved to Buffalo, hoping to leave everything negative behind. The loss of Judy as well as his parents hardened him and he threw himself into work. He compared the few girls he dated to Judy but it was never the same. Nothing in his life felt right.

His despondency over his personal life blocked the critical thinking needed for fresh research. After the fellowship, he looked for a change of lifestyle, away from academia and cold winters. It was time to make money to pay off school debts. Sunny Florida was growing, a good location to set up a private practice where he could apply his skills. He felt confident the move would open new horizons, but all that changed when he saw Judy again.

~ * ~

The following morning, Parker opened the door to his office, taking a long look at the empty waiting room. The furniture was simple. Eight vinyl cushioned chairs lined the walls, a neatly stacked magazine rack ready to serve and a tall brass lamp on a low table in the corner. A look through the open sliding glass window at the reception desk showed his newly hired medical assistant organizing papers.

"Hi, Gwen, swamped with referrals?" he joked, stepping through the door.

She shook her head and smiled. "Not yet, but don't worry, you'll be busy enough in a few weeks."

He liked her positive attitude and smiled back, hoping she was right.

Gwen Compton, a plump twenty-five year old mother of two, had been a hospital desk secretary at MCA. When she heard through the grapevine he needed a medical assistant, she approached him. "Give me the same wage I get at the hospital, and if I work out, pay me what you think I'm worth." That had clinched the deal.

He entered his private office with only enough room for a desk, swivel chair, small bookcase and a seat for visitors. He picked up a current surgical journal that Gwen had left on his desk which meant the mail was finally coming through. Halfway through reading an article, he heard a knock at the door and saw her standing with a troubled look.

"Two detectives are in the waiting room asking to see you."

"What would the police want with me? Bring them in."

As the men entered, Parker rose from his desk, noting their grim expressions. "How can I help you, gentlemen?"

The taller man responded by flashing his badge. "I'm Detective Cleary with the West Palm Beach Police Department and this is Agent Rucker from the Federal Drug Enforcement Agency. We'd like to ask a few questions about the woman you operated on after yesterday's car wreck."

"Her name was Olga Ottavio," Agent Rucker offered. "She's been under surveillance for some time regarding criminal activity."

Parker returned a surprised look. "She was in pretty bad shape when she came in. What do you need to know?"

Rucker asked, "Did she say anything to you before she died?"

Parker hesitated. "I'm not a lawyer, but I could be violating patient confidentiality if I answer your questions."

Rucker persisted. "Did you receive any information not related to her medical condition?"

Cleary cut in. "Doctor, we're asking about criminal activity, not medical data."

Parker paused, feeling uneasy. "She mentioned she had a daughter. I think the name is Carmella."

Cleary cleared his throat and looked directly at Parker. "Doctor, this is for your information as well as your protection. As Agent Rucker said, Ottavio was under surveillance for transporting illegal drug money. We found duffel bags stuffed with small bills totaling over one million dollars in the trunk of her car."

Parker's jaw dropped.

Cleary continued. "We got a tip she was moving it to a storage locker. It's what we call a stash house. Always at a different location, a hotel room, a place of business or as in this case, a rented storage unit. Did you find any keys on her?"

Parker blinked. "She did give me a key."

Cleary's eyes widened. "Why did she give it to you?"

"She knew her life was in danger if she didn't accept blood. That's when she handed it to me to give to her daughter."

"We suspected she had a key to the locker with her. Where is it? The hospital laundry's been checked and it's not there."

"Frankly, in all that excitement, I forgot about it." Parker slid his hands into his pockets. "These are the same pants I wore yesterday, but I don't have it."

"Time is of the essence, Doctor. That locker could be emptied in twenty-four hours. I hope temptation isn't blurring your memory."

"Look, Officers, I don't know where that key is. I must have dropped it when I changed into my scrub suit. With a Jehovah's Witness bleeding out on the table, what did I care about a key?"

"Well then," Cleary said, "we need to inspect your locker."

After a short walk across the hospital parking lot, Parker stood before his locker, turned the combination and opened the door. "Check for yourself," he said.

Agent Rucker flicked on a small pen light which illuminated the upper and lower compartments. Only a long white coat and stethoscope hung from the hook. He checked the pockets and shut the door. "It's not here."

"Satisfied?" Parker's voice carried a tinge of sarcasm.

Agent Rucker's eyes narrowed as he handed Parker his card. "Think about where you may have lost it. If it turns up, you'd better let us know. We'll be in touch."

Parker returned a nod, unconvinced the detectives believed he was telling the truth.

The overhead speaker paged him and he left to answer the phone. It was Gwen.

"Dr. Dawson, don't forget you have your first surgical department meeting this morning at eleven. Don't be late."

Three

Parker left for the meeting disturbed by Rucker's implication he might have the key. His student loan of $80 thousand had to be paid with interest, but the thought of stealing money never entered his mind.

The aroma of fresh coffee in the conference room drew him to the large urn. After filling a cup, he looked around the empty room and checked his watch.

Within seconds, Karl Lawton, Chief of Surgery, entered and waved a greeting. "Welcome aboard, Parker. Sorry about your first case. Not much you can do for a bleeding Witness," he said, filling his coffee.

While the words were comforting, Parker realized hospital gossip had already spread the news about Ottavio's death.

"I hear Morty Gold is your sponsor," the lanky Iowa transplant chuckled in a friendly manner. "Don't let him throw you."

"What do you mean?" Parker asked.

"You'll find he's pretty explosive. Wait 'til I tell him I'm putting a halt to all the arterial laser surgeries."

"The one opening blocked arteries? MCA is doing a

hell of a lot of advertising to sell that operation."

"That's the one," Lawton answered, taking his seat at the head table. "There was a third death this morning and I'm putting everything on hold until we review all cases."

Before Parker could respond, the door flew open and Morty Gold charged in holding a food tray. As he slid his lunch across the table, a gold Rolex glittered from under his shirt sleeve. He still carried a full head of hair for a man in his late forties, but the bulbous nose planted on a pudgy face failed to convey a strong masculine image.

"We gotta suspend Bob Meyer's surgical privileges," Gold huffed, stuffing a croissant into his mouth.

Lawton shook his head. "Not so fast, Morty. We have a more urgent issue to discuss this morning."

"Shit, Karl, this can't wait."

Lawton raised a hand. "Slow down, Morty. There was another laser death this morning so I'm putting a stop to the operation until all these cases are reviewed."

"Who's the surgeon?" Gold questioned.

"Paul Barco. The patient bled after surgery so he had to take him back to OR to stop it. The guy was only fifty-five. He died on the table at two this morning."

"Why blame Barco? These things happen," Gold answered.

The door opened and medical staff secretary, Anita Kralsky and Administrator Eric Lindstrom entered followed by his assistant, Henry Trask.

"Sorry we're late," Kralsky chimed. "We were held up by another meeting."

Parker could see Gold's face turn red with anger as he faced Lindstrom.

"Eric," Gold demanded, "Bob Meyer refused to come in to see a patient on his ER call. That's pretty serious, and I say we should suspend his surgical privileges."

"Hold on, Morty, I run this meeting," Lawton broke in. Turning to Lindstrom, he added, "It's more important we discuss this morning's laser death instead of arguing about a case that was properly managed."

"Bullshit," Gold shouted. "A gastro guy had to cover Meyer's ass. He came in and removed the open safety pin stuck in the kid's esophagus."

"And that was the right thing to do," Lawton replied. "Meyer explained he wasn't trained to use a rigid scope to do the procedure, but he was willing to come in."

Lindstrom interrupted. "As long as the hospital has no legal liability regarding that case, it's a moot issue." He then faced Lawton, his stoic expression turned into a glare. "What's this about canceling laser angioplasties? MCA trains our surgeons for this procedure at our Designated Center of Excellence in California."

Lawton's voice rose. "At a weekend course? What can you learn in two days about an operation that can kill you?" He looked to Parker, encouraging a response.

"Maybe Dr. Lawton is right," Parker answered softly. "It can't hurt to look into those deaths."

The administrator frowned with a detached calm. "As chief of surgery, you must have more important matters to deal with, Dr. Lawton. Dr. Gold and I will investigate the deaths. Any objections?"

Gold snapped, "Hell, no! But I still think Meyer shouldn't get away with what he did."

The cross conversation halted when two more staff

20

surgeons wandered into the room. Kralsky counted the number of doctors present and shuffled papers, waiting for more arrivals. A dim buzz of whispers filled the emptiness as she finally looked at her watch. "It's nearly noon and we don't have a quorum, Mr. Lindstrom. I'll have to reschedule this meeting."

The administrator nodded his agreement and rose to leave with Trask and the latecomers following.

Waving his hand in disgust, Gold remained seated and continued finishing his lunch. He then dabbed his mouth with a napkin, flung it on the tray and escorted Kralsky out of the room.

Once alone, Lawton turned to Parker. "Do you really think they'll do a thorough investigation?"

"I hope so, Karl," Parker answered, trying to sound diplomatic.

Lawton shook his head. "MCA made a big investment in that operation. How deep do you think they'll probe if it risks hurting corporate profits?"

"Then why didn't you challenge him? You're chief of surgery."

Lawton smiled. "Sure I'm chief, but patient referrals depend on hospital politics, not your title. In private practice, you have to be careful you don't piss people off if you want them to send you cases."

He rose from his chair and placed a hand on Parker's shoulder. "Glad you're on staff. If you need any advice or help in surgery, call me." He moved to the door and before leaving, turned. "You'll learn there's more to private practice than just good medicine."

Parker sat alone in the room reflecting on what had just

transpired. It was evident Gold was a hothead and an ally of the administrator. And while Karl was surgical chief, his power was limited by the hospital's political winds and corporate interests. After only two days in practice, Parker was discovering a world of medicine far removed from what he expected. *Did his support for Karl to review the deaths alienate him from Lindstrom?* He wondered about that.

But he also had staff privileges at St. Ann Community Hospital, and while he was new on staff, he didn't want to be new forever. It was time to meet potential referring doctors, so lunch at St. Ann was where he'd begin.

~ * ~

Parker flicked the radio dial to AM 815 on his drive to St. Ann.

Phil Bologna, the quick-talking host of a local weekly medical program came on. Today the doctor warned about the dangers of charcoal broiled meats causing cancer. His female co-host attempted to play down listener anxiety, but Bologna was unstoppable. Suddenly hope appeared. "Squeeze lemon juice on the meat to reduce carcinogens," Bologna said." Parker chuckled and wondered what scientific evidence Bologna used to make a statement with such authority.

Heading to the doctors' dining room, he noticed the patients at St. Ann represented a diverse mix of social and economic levels. African-Americans, Latinos and Caucasians could be seen in hallways and rooms dressed from high fashion to shabby chic or just plain shabby.

Unlike the Medical Corporation of America chain, St. Ann was a non-profit hospital, accepting the uninsured without question, thanks to the generous millions donated by wealthy Palm Beachers. Working here appealed to him, and he hoped the atmosphere would allow him to focus on medicine rather than politics.

Leaving the hot buffet, he carried his tray to an empty seat at a long table occupied by a number of doctors. The ongoing lively conversation dealt with bits of shop talk about malpractice, greedy lawyers or the punch line to a joke, causing an eruption of laughter.

"Is this chair taken?" he asked the doctor seated across from him.

The man wore a small goatee which appeared to further sharpen his craggy features. He studied Parker before answering abruptly. "It's yours now."

Parker gave a small laugh and extended his hand. "I'm Parker Dawson, new on staff."

"Phil Bologna, gastroenterology," was his curt response.

"Dr. Bologna?" Parker replied with surprise. "I just heard you on the radio."

Bologna smiled. "Did you like it?"

"Sure did," Parker answered, hoping to sound sincere.

Bologna bit into his roast beef sandwich, speaking as he chewed. "What's your specialty?"

"General surgery and surgical oncology," Parker answered, watching the doctor swallow his food with a swig from a Coke can.

"Great. I have a referral for you. Do you have time?"

Parker's pulse quickened, knowing he had plenty of that. "Sure do," he answered.

Bologna's speech was quick and short. "Good! Marsha

Hoffman at MCA. She needs gallbladder surgery. Forgot the room number, but check with the operator." He pushed his tray away and rose quickly to leave.

Parker could see Bologna was a man of action. The doctor was almost out the door when Parker called after him. "I'll see her today and get back to you."

After Bologna left, Parker rushed though lunch, unconcerned by the lack of cordiality from the other doctors at the table. He had his first consultation and eagerly dialed Gwen to let her know.

~ & ~

Arriving at MCA, Parker checked Marsha Hoffman's room number with the desk receptionist. He entered to find an elderly woman watching television from her chair. Her faded blue robe appeared several sizes too large, and the hollow sockets of her eyes, accented by protruding cheekbones, hinted rapid weight loss.

"I'm Dr. Dawson, Mrs. Hoffman. Dr. Bologna asked that I see you."

"Well, I've been waiting," she answered in a raspy voice. "Are you the surgeon taking out my gallbladder?"

Parker smiled. "Yes, but first I'd like to examine you. Could you return to the bed?"

Hoffman rose from the chair, giving him a harsh look before shuffling toward the bed in rubber-soled slippers. She slowly moved under the covers and asked, "Why do you need to examine me? Haven't you seen my x-rays? I have gallstones."

"I understand, but I see from the chart that you've been getting blood transfusions."

"Dr. Bologna says I'm bleeding from my gallbladder

and the surgery can't come soon enough."

Parker drew back the covers and probed for abdominal masses or areas of tenderness.

"What are you looking for, young man? You know I have gallstones," Hoffman insisted.

"Just making sure nothing is blocking your intestines to explain the bleeding," Parker answered.

"I told you Dr. Bologna said my gallbladder is the problem."

"I'll be done in a minute. Could you take a deep breath?" he asked, resting his stethoscope on her chest.

The woman responded half-heartedly by taking shallow breaths. After Parker finished, she pulled herself up in bed. "All right, now that you've poked me, when do I go to surgery?"

"I'd like to get a few more tests before I operate."

"Tests!" she cried out, pulling the sheets over her frail frame. "I've had enough tests. Tubes passed up and down, in and out. Enough tests. Take out my gallbladder!"

"Give me a chance to talk to Dr. Bologna, Mrs. Hoffman. I'll be back."

As he turned to leave, her grating voice called out to him. "You'd better reach him quick because he's on his way out of town."

When he called Bologna's office, he learned Hoffman was right. Answering service told him the doctor had checked out to another physician but there was a chance he could still be at home. After several minutes, the operator returned.

"I've patched him through and he's on the line."

"Hi, Parker, did you see Mrs. Hoffman yet?"

"I did, but I'm concerned about the source of her bleeding. It can't be coming from gallstones. I'd like to get a few tests before operating."

"Just schedule the surgery. She's definitely bleeding from the stones."

"How can you be sure?"

"I saw blood draining from the common bile duct into the duodenum when I scoped her. Go ahead and take out the gallbladder."

The conversation ended with a click of the phone.

Parker was thankful Bologna couldn't see his frown. Gallstones didn't cause bleeding from the liver. Only an arterio-venous fistula resulting from trauma or tumor could do that. At the least, a bleeding scan was needed to narrow down the source of the problem. But there was a risk. If he embarrassed Bologna by proving him wrong, it could result in losing referrals.

His thoughts were interrupted when Judy Keller approached him at the desk.

"Parker, I want to let you know how much the nurses appreciated what you did trying to save that young woman's life."

Her unexpected compliment was the lift he needed. "Thanks, Judy. It was hard losing my first case."

"Everyone understands, and the important thing is that you tried," she answered as she turned to walk away.

"Wait!" he blurted. "Do you have a minute?"

"Sorry, I'm too busy," she replied over her shoulder.

He stood, staring at her trim figure glide effortlessly down the hall. *I really hurt her*, he thought to himself. *But how do I fix things?* Not finding an answer, his attention returned to Hoffman's chart.

After re-reading the x-ray and lab reports, he knew Hoffman had problems much more serious than gallstones. No way would he be hustled into doing an unnecessary surgery. Picking up his pen, he wrote the order. 'Bleeding scan—STAT.'

Four

The next morning

After a leisurely breakfast with a few minutes spent watching news on TV, Parker left his apartment for MCA to see Hoffman and check on her bleeding scan. In the parking lot, he spotted two olive-skinned men standing by his Civic. The tall slim one sported a mustache and leaned against the car while his husky broad-shouldered companion stood peeling an orange with a sharp knife.

In his gut, Parker knew they had something to do with Olga Ottavio and the drug lords. He looked around, wondering if they had seen him and debated if running back into the building would risk getting shot.

"Are you Dr. Dawson, *senor*?" the taller man called out in a heavy Hispanic accent.

"Why do you ask?" Parker questioned.

As the man with the knife moved closer, Parker saw the jagged scar on his cheek. Two gold teeth glistened in the light when he spoke.

"Olga Ottavio was our friend," he said.

Despite their fancy jeans and western shirts, Parker could tell these weren't gentlemen farmers. "Do I know you?" he asked, fully aware they had never met.

"We look for the money you took from the 'storage locker," the gold-toothed man insisted.

"What money? I don't know what you're talking about."

The taller man with the moustache frowned. "Olga had the key to that locker."

"Now it's empty," his husky companion added.

"*Digame*, where is the money?" the mustache insisted.

Parker felt his heart pound, wishing Rucker and Cleary would suddenly appear.

"Don't play with us," the gold-toothed man growled in a deep guttural voice. "We know you have the key. You took the money."

"I have no idea what you're talking about," Parker answered in a firm tone to mask his fear. A hard object suddenly pressed against his ribs, and he went into a cold sweat, afraid to move. Next came a sharp punch to his chest and he grunted in pain.

"We want to be nice, give you time to think about where the money went," the man said, holding the knife against Parker's face. "When we come back, make sure you remember."

With that warning, they got into the silver Jaguar parked next to his car and drove away.

Numbed by the unexpected blow, Parker leaned against the Civic in an attempt to recover from the excruciating pain. Despite the warm morning sun, he couldn't stop shaking. *What difference who emptied the locker*, he thought? If they didn't find the money, he was marked as the fall guy.

He stood up and brushed off his white coat, wondering what he had done to deserve all this. *How in the hell could trying to save a patient end up with my life threatened and ass kicked in?*

~ & ~

Parker stared into the empty room at MCA when a passing nurse called out.

"Looking for Mrs. Hoffman, Doctor?"

"Yes," Parker answered, staring into the empty room. "Is she in x-ray getting the bleeding scan?"

"No, she's been discharged. Dr. Bologna transferred her to St. Ann yesterday."

"Why?"

"Don't know. I wasn't her nurse."

As Parker watched her walk away, he wondered why Bologna hadn't notified him. With no other patients to see, he headed to St. Ann to find Hoffman.

The moment he entered her room, she snapped. "You're no longer on my case. Dr. Morales is taking out my gallbladder."

Parker watched her lips purse for battle.

"You can leave now," she demanded.

Stunned by the intensity of her outburst, he replied, "Dr. Bologna never discussed this with me."

"Everything's arranged," she lashed out. "I have a weak heart and he transferred me here because this hospital has an open heart team."

Reluctant to argue, Parker gave her a polite nod. "That's fine, Mrs. Hoffman. I'll speak to Dr. Bologna."

Retreating to the nurse's station, he questioned Bologna's professional ethics for not consulting with him about the transfer. Did Bologna order the move because he worried that a medical review committee might question why a more plausible cause for Mrs. Hoffman's bleeding wasn't pursued?

He quickly flipped through the chart looking for any reference to his surgical consultation at MCA but there was none. The lab report showed her hemoglobin had dropped even farther. Convinced the blood loss was coming from somewhere other than the gallbladder, he pondered if he should make an entry stating that, but decided it unwise. Repugnant as it seemed, it was apparent he had to play the game if he was to survive private practice.

He picked up his pen and wrote in the chart. 'Hemoglobin 9.2 grams, dropped again. Patient requests another surgeon. Will be happy to review findings with new surgeon. No longer on case. Dr. Dawson.'

Given Hoffman's transfer to St. Ann, he was no longer authorized to write orders on her chart. The woman's gallstones might justify the gallbladder surgery even though her bleeding problem was more urgent. Frustrated by his analysis, he still gave the nurses a smile as he left, relieved he didn't have to perform the operation.

His name came over the speaker and he picked up the phone.

Gwen was on the line. "Dr. Lawton asked if you would assist him in surgery at two-thirty and I said you would because I knew you were free."

"Thanks, Gwen, good move. Tell him I'll be there."

"I told you things would pick up, and you've only been here a few days. What about the Hoffman consultation?

Are you going to do the case?"

He hesitated, not wanting to explain. "I turned it down. She didn't need the surgery."

There was no sound of disappointment in her voice. "Don't worry, there'll be others."

The thought of operating with Lawton brightened his mood. He needed friends and this man seemed like someone he could count on.

But the morning's threatening incident with the drug traffickers still darkened his thoughts. What kind of protection could he expect from the DEA? He lifted the phone.

~ * ~

"Look Rucker, they nearly killed me! What are you going to do about it!"

"Sure, Doc, we'll protect you, but you have to work with us to catch these guys."

"Hey, wait a minute, it's my neck on the line. These druggies think I took their money from that locker."

"We know that and we need you to lead us to them. They're pushing everything. Cocaine, heroin and the latest is Oxycontin."

"Forget it. I don't want to get involved. Just protect me."

"We'll keep you under surveillance."

"That doesn't sound very comforting."

"We're working twenty-four seven on this. They're moving stuff across our borders through foreign imports, phony wholesale distributors or anything that works."

"How the hell are you going to save me? These guys jabbed a gun into my ribs and next time they'll pull the trigger."

"Calm down, Doc, someone will be tailing you."

"I'm not convinced."

"When will you be in your office?"

"Probably by five."

"I'll send someone to give you a GPS transmitter programmed to your cell phone."

"What will that do?"

"It'll give us your location if you're in trouble. That locker held millions and they won't stop until they find it."

"Look, I'm just a poor doc who's scared for his life. Why do I want to get between the police and those drug traffickers?"

"Like it or not, we're doing the best we can. Once we find the kingpin, you're off the hook. An agent will come by and give you the GPS unit. We'll be in touch."

Parker's heart raced as he hung up the phone, wishing this nightmare would go away. He was now the bait and he wondered if the law could really protect him.

Five

That weekend

Gwen's Sunday invite for dinner was for 4 PM, but Parker was running late due to an emergency room consult. Although he wasn't on call, he volunteered to fill the spot, hoping to increase his surgical volume as well as income.

He drove the narrow streets leading to Gwen's home located in a development of low roofed stucco ranches built in the sixties. Narrow green lawns bordered crumbling asphalt driveways in front of the modest zero lot-line buildings.

He stopped at the house where a small open-bed pickup was parked before a one-car garage. The lawn was freshly cut and edged, and a lush flowering hibiscus bush shaded a wide picture window.

He stood at the entrance, holding a large stuffed teddy bear under one arm, a fire truck under the other, and rang the bell.

Gwen stood at the open door. "I worried why you were late."

"Sorry, Gwen, I went to ER to see a patient."

"Did you operate?"

"No, the guy didn't need surgery, and anyway, he had no insurance."

She chuckled as she closed the door behind him. "Well, that's good news. We already have quite a few no-pays on the books. Come in and meet Paul and the kids."

He followed her through the undersized living room and entered a small pool and patio area where a blonde young man sat with two children playing at his feet. Potted plants holding colorful flowers lined the small screened area, lending it an unexpected charm. It was evident Gwen took pride in enhancing the beauty of her home.

"Paul, meet Dr. Dawson," she said.

The man wore faded jeans and a University of Florida tee shirt. He rose to reach for Parker's hand. "Gwen's said a lot of nice things about you, Doc."

Parker grasped his hand and grinned. "She's just being kind."

"No, it's true," Gwen insisted, lifting the little girl who strayed too close to the pool. She held out the child. "This is Stacy. She's two and our son Ryan is three."

Parker handed the little girl the teddy which she eagerly grabbed with a squeal. When he offered the fire truck to the boy, the excitement in the child's eyes was well worth the trouble it had taken to buy it at Toys R' Us. Ryan energetically pushed the truck and Parker followed, causing excited outbursts of laughter from the child.

"Can I get you a beer, Doc?"

"Sure," Parker answered.

Gwen brought out a tray of cheese and crackers and placed it on the picnic table. The fire glowed and the burgers sizzled on the aged grill as the two men sat drinking.

Parker asked, "Did you grow up in Florida, Paul?"

"Gwen and I were both born in Palm Beach County at a time when everyone knew everyone and folks were neighborly."

"You mean immigrants from the North like me changed everything?"

"Some of it is for the better. I can't complain. I'm in construction and we haven't stopped building since the boom began in the nineties."

The three-year-old pushed his fire truck close to Parker who lifted him onto his knee. Ryan's laughter encouraged Stacy to waddle over. Parker grabbed and positioned her on his other knee, bouncing them both as they shrieked joyfully.

Paul leaned back in his chair, smiling while Gwen set the table under the covered portion of the patio. With Stacy sitting in a high chair and Ryan in a booster seat, dinner progressed uneventfully.

"You thinking of having a family, Doc?" Paul asked.

"Shush, Paul," Gwen snapped. "Give the man a chance, he's just started."

Parker gave them both a gentle smile. "I hope so, especially since I have none."

"Then you can adopt us, Dr. Dawson," Gwen replied.

"I'd be honored to be an uncle to your two adorable kids," he answered.

Gwen laughed. "Does that mean you'll babysit?"

"Anytime," Parker answered.

Paul piped in, "We couldn't do that to you, Doc.

Stacy's still in diapers."

"That doesn't bother me."

Paul rose laughing, "Let's have another beer, Doc."

Parker didn't want to blunt Paul's happy mood so he accepted. It was clear they were hard-working decent people. With Paul's warm reception, he felt a strong bond to both of them.

As the sun dropped down over the horizon, the children were ready for bath and bed.

"I think it's time for me to leave," Parker said, rising slowly from the table.

Paul asked, "You have an early start tomorrow?"

"I have no surgery, but I spend time at both hospitals in the morning. I like to be around to pick up cases." He looked to Paul. "What time do you go to work?"

"I'm up by six and on the job by seven."

"That's even more reason for me to leave, so I'll say good night. Thanks for a great evening."

Paul walked him to the door. "Come again, Doc. The kids like you."

Parker hugged Gwen. "I'll see you in the office tomorrow."

As the darkening shadows emerged, Parker drove back to his tiny apartment, happy he had met Gwen's family. After this evening, he knew she would always be there for him.

Six

The flashing light on the answering machine caught Judy's eye as she carried a bag filled with groceries into the kitchen. It was her day off and cleaning chores were next on the agenda. She pressed the message button.

"It's Kent, Judy. Don't get upset. We have to talk."

On hearing his voice, she dropped the sack, spilling its contents. Her mouth went dry and she leaned against the kitchen counter for support. *How dare he call me after what he put me through,* she fumed.

The message continued. "I've made a decision. Call me on my cell, five six one, two six eight six. I'm waiting."

"What decision?" she cried aloud. That decision had been made months ago. He started the affair and broke it off. When reality reared its ugly head, the promised divorce just melted away.

Repeated rings of the doorbell went unanswered until a loud knocking grabbed her attention.

"Kent!" she gasped on opening the door.

"Don't get upset, Judy. Before you say anything, hear me out." He entered and steadily advanced. "May I?"

38

.

She pushed him back. "Get out! There's nothing more to say."

"I deserve that, but give me a chance."

"You had your chance."

He reached for her hand. "I know I made a mistake, but I love you. Listen to me, Judy. I want to marry you."

She let out a scornful laugh. "Marry me? You're already married."

"But I'm miserable and never should have let you go."

"Too late, Kent, especially after all the hurt you caused me." Her eyes filled and she covered her face with her hands. "How could I be such a fool? What was I thinking of getting involved with a married man?"

"Just give me a chance."

"For what? More empty promises? Do you have any idea how it feels to be lied to?" she cried, wiping her tears.

He reached for her shoulders. "I never loved Sheila. I love you." His voice cracked as he spoke. "I just couldn't walk away from my boys."

She looked into his eyes and for a split second questioned herself. Was she still in love with him? The Kent Markman she had fallen in love with was sensitive and caring. She felt like a queen when she was with him. That's what hurt so much.

"I never knew I could love until I met you," he whispered. "All Sheila wants from me are the big bucks to climb the social ladder."

Her gaze never left his face. She tried to quell her tears, not knowing what to think. He looked lost, so pathetic, standing there pleading. How different from the photos printed in the Palm Beach shiny sheet, this handsome confident doctor clinging to his vivacious wife gowned in a silk Versace original.

Her eyes suddenly narrowed. "Are you sleeping together?"

"Only as a ritual obligation."

"What about your boys? They probably have no idea."

He smiled, hearing her concern for his sons. "They're the only good thing in my life." His eyes suddenly widened. "You're not seeing anyone, are you?"

"Hardly!"

"Sorry, I just panicked." He moved to her side and whispered, "Let me make it up to you, Judy."

"Don't!" she snapped, pushing him away. "You can't hurt people and think you can pick up where you left off."

Those biting words stopped him and he sheepishly turned to leave. Abruptly, he halted, pounded the door. "I've suffered too, knowing I turned my back on you after all we shared. I never realized how much you mean to me and hope it's not too late."

The melodic ring of his cell phone made him curse. "Dammit! I still need to make rounds."

The interruption sobered her. "You'd better go," she said.

He fumbled for the cell phone. "Give me a minute, please." He flipped open the phone to speak, keeping his eyes steadily focused on her. "Yes, this is Dr. Markman. Two West? Mrs. Pappas? No! Keep her NPO. No, in a half hour. Thank you."

Judy waited until he shut the phone. "It's late and you have patients to see."

He stood tall with a more commanding posture and

looked into her eyes. "Remember how it was, Judy. I can't undo the past, but maybe I can change the future. At least think it over."

She felt a lump in her throat and took a deep swallow, struggling to control her tears.

"I love you," he whispered and left.

Thoughts swirled in her mind as she leaned against the closed door. A pink tea rose resting on the entry console with an envelope beside it made her catch her breath. The scent of fresh petals recalled happier days, but she hesitated to read the letter.

"My God," she cried out. "First Parker and now Kent. What's to become of me?"

Seven

Carolyn Robertson, Lindstrom's secretary, circled the long board room table distributing printed handouts prepared for the meeting. Tall and lean to a fault, she wore a no-nonsense expression. A quick look at the clock made her frown. The meeting was scheduled promptly for 1 PM and it was already five minutes after, tardiness that warranted comment. Divorced at forty and now fifty-five with no family to keep her in California, she had joined Lindstrom when MCA transferred him to Florida.

A sudden onset of laughter broke the quiet as Judy Keller and six charge nurses sauntered into the room followed by the managers of X-ray, Laboratory and Purchasing. All seated themselves in the cushioned chairs and engaged in friendly chatter.

The scene annoyed Robertson, who felt excluded by the gulf separating administration from the medical staff. It was a fact of life she accepted and was happy to avoid any familiarity which could weaken her sense of executive power.

Within minutes the room grew quiet and the guests sat

at attention, eager to discover the meeting's purpose.

As Robertson took her seat, the ICU supervisor asked, "What do I do with the census figures and departmental costs?"

"Mr. Lindstrom will explain all that," Robertson answered crisply.

The side door opened and Lindstrom appeared with his assistant, Trask. All eyes fixed on them as they moved to the head of the table.

Equally tall as his secretary, Lindstrom remained standing. "Thank you for coming," he announced, turning to a tripod supporting an oversized pad. With a black marker, he scrawled, SUPPLIES, STAFFING, SERVICE. He put down the pen and turned to face those sitting before him.

"We need to do a better job to meet our goals," he announced. "Personnel must be cut, lab tests curtailed and the number of unnecessary instruments on surgical trays reduced. If a surgeon wants an instrument not on his tray, he'll have to wait until it comes from Central Supply. Limiting the use of disposable instruments is of utmost importance. Under managed care, we get paid according to diagnosis, not what it costs to do the job."

He pointed to Lonnie Martin and barked, "Purchasing!"

The manager bolted upright in his chair.

"Why are you ordering port catheter needles from Bartlett Corporation when cheaper ones are available from Asian suppliers?"

The manager leaned forward to answer, but Lindstrom fired, "We could save fifteen percent a year on just that item alone. Why isn't this happening?"

"But the doctors prefer the Bartlett needles," Martin blurted.

Lindstrom glared back. "Doctors have to understand that MCA isn't a country club. We're here to provide delivery of efficient medical service without wasteful spending."

The room became quiet. All department heads froze in their chairs as they watched the purchasing manager cringe in his seat.

"Mr. Trask will discuss the brands to purchase," Lindstrom continued. "Any questions?"

Martin shook his head, indicating no as he sank lower in his chair.

Lindstrom turned to the OR supervisor. "Miss Reilly, have you limited the number of instruments on surgical trays as we discussed?"

"Yes," Reilly answered. "I sent all the surgeons a list of instruments on their tray and asked them to delete what they didn't use very often."

"No, Miss Reilly. Each surgeon is to be notified which instruments will be placed on his tray. If they need a special one, they'll have to wait until the circulator gets it from Central Supply. Surgeons are not to be treated like prima donnas."

Nurse Reilly didn't appear cowered by Lindstrom's threatening tone. "But the circulators are unhappy about routine supplies like Foley catheters being stored at Central."

"Inventory control, Miss Reilly," Lindstrom replied with a wave of his hand. "Loss and waste by shrinkage or a better term, theft. We'll not have doctors and nurses walking off with supplies."

Nurse Reilly said nothing as the others waited their turn in the threatening silence.

Lindstrom stood tall, peering steadily into the group before turning to Trask.

"Will you say a few words, Henry?"

The assistant stepped forward to address the group. "In your handouts, you will find the number of positions to be terminated. Lab and x-ray will lose the most."

The manager for Pathology, Freddie Gonzales, raised his hand. "I see you cut the number of histotechs in Pathology from four to two, Mr. Trask."

"That's right, Mr. Gonzales."

"I hope that's a misunderstanding."

"A misunderstanding?"

"Yes." Freddy's response was hesitant. "The first histotech comes in at five-thirty AM to remove slides from the overnight paraffin bath. That allows the pathologist to read them when they come in by eight. The second tech is needed to prepare frozen sections from the operating room. If you cut two positions, who will prepare the emergency frozen sections that come in from OR after three?"

Trask returned an amused look. "I hope you know the answer."

Gonzales gave him a blank stare. "But with your plan, only the pathologist will be there after three."

"True, Mr. Gonzales, so the pathologist will cut, freeze and read his own slides."

Gonzales withheld any further questions, wondering

how to break the news to his already overworked staff.

Lindstrom stepped forward. "Cutting costs is a national urgency and MCA is leading the way. Managed care contracts pay a flat fee whether a patient stays five or fifty days. Discharges must be early and that goes for orthopedics, neurosurgery and maternity."

Judy raised her hand. "We're all aware hip replacements and lumbar disc surgeries can be moved to step-down units and discharged within seventy-two hours. But what about our cancer patients? We now have a surgical oncologist on staff, Dr. Dawson, and the medical oncologists are asking for a cancer wing to provide more intensive treatments."

Lindstrom frowned, fixing his icy blue eyes on her. "There'll be no cancer unit, Miss Keller. Oncologists should give chemotherapy on an outpatient basis, and we should treat only curable cases. We don't recoup the costs caring for terminal patients who require lengthy stays. Any other questions?"

No one answered.

"Then I suggest we meet again after Mr. Trask has had a chance to conference with each of you."

Carolyn Robertson rose first and looked across the table. The gold chains dangling across her blouse failed to enhance her bony frame. "This meeting started late. In the future, please be prompt," she announced.

After everyone left, she opened a folder and handed a sheet to Lindstrom. "These are the appointments I've arranged for the doctors you want to see."

"You made no mention about money arrangements?" Lindstrom asked."

"No. When they inquired what the meeting was about, I said it had to do with their patient census."

"As usual, Carolyn," Lindstrom winked. "I can always depend on you."

Eight

Morty Gold drove his red Mercedes convertible up to the front entrance of the Breakers Hotel. He stepped out and with a flourishing gesture, dangled the key before the valet. "Take good care of this baby. I don't want to see any dings on the door."

With an indifferent shake of the head, the parking attendant took the key and handed him a receipt.

Gold marched pompously through the impressive entry of the five star hotel, exhilarated by Lindstrom's invitation to a private dinner. Making his way through the marble lobby, he approached the main dining room with its vaulted ceiling.

An attractive hostess greeted him, and when he gave his name, she smiled. "Mr. Lindstrom is already seated with his guests, Doctor. Please follow me."

Plush carpeting muffled their footsteps as she guided him to the table. The walls of the dimly lit room were covered with fine gold damask accentuated with warm mahogany trim. Flickering candlelight illuminated each table, leaving the occupants' faces to one's imagination.

Gold sensed the presence of wealth and power surrounding him in this hushed atmosphere and decided to end the meal with an expensive cigar.

"Sorry I'm late," he said, approaching the table where Lindstrom and Trask sat with Vice Chief of Staff, Jack Fox. Sliding into the chair, he added, "This sure beats meeting at the hospital."

Fox, a family practitioner, leaned over the table, wearing a sport coat too small for his bulging waist. His bare scalp sported alternate rows of recent hair transplants and glistened in the flickering light.

"I know the food here will be better than the hospital menu," he chuckled. Noting Lindstrom's frown, his face reddened with embarrassment. "Excuse the joke," he added meekly.

Lindstrom ignored the comment and smiled back. "Dr. Gold, Dr. Fox, tonight you are the guests of MCA. Order whatever you please."

Gold's face brightened. "Miss Robertson said we would be discussing plans for the hospital's future growth."

Trask responded, "The reason we're meeting outside the hospital is to avoid any explanation to the Executive Committee."

Gold grasped the lavishly carved arms of the tufted chair, feeling empowered, knowing he was among the chosen. "There's nothing like enjoying oneself while doing hospital business," he answered.

"I'm glad you approve, and MCA appreciates your support of the hospital," Lindstrom replied, as the waiter handed him the wine list and menus to the others.

The two physicians grinned back, enjoying the compliment.

Throughout the evening, the waiter attentively refilled the wine glasses and by dinner's end, even Lindstrom had shed his usual cold formality.

Gold rolled an unlit hand-wrapped cigar between his fingers, relishing the thought of smoking it after the meeting. "This is a perfect example of hospital and medical staff working together. After all, we do share each other's interests."

Lindstrom's face turned serious as his piercing blue eyes focused on the two physicians. "Gentlemen, Mr. Trask and I are pleased with your leadership, but we need your help to secure MCA's financial future."

Fox scratched his head in wonderment. "But the hospital's never been busier and new doctors are coming on staff every month."

"True," Trask offered, "but because we made certain financial arrangements with a number of staff physicians, we must control the types of cases they admit."

Fox glanced around the table and his eyes widened. "But how can we control the type of patients we see? We treat whatever comes in."

"I agree," Lindstrom responded, "but if we are to continue with our success, we must admit cases that add to MCA's bottom line. Welfare, Medicaid admissions are money losers and so are certain operations."

"Okay," Gold asked impatiently, "What specifically are we talking about?"

Lindstrom leaned back in the chair, still holding his icy stare. "We want more hip replacements, out-patient plastic surgery and neurosurgical laser spine operations. These patients do well and are discharged within forty-eight hours. Bowel and chest cases stay in the hospital for too many days for which we don't get paid."

Trask leaned over his cognac snifter and spoke in a low tone, aware that what he was about to say was not for public knowledge. "Both of you, as well as other staff doctors, receive payments from MCA for each case you admit. That requires you to be very selective. We get a flat fee from insurance companies for each procedure performed. The sooner a patient is discharged, the more profit per admission."

Lindstrom cocked his head, adding, "That's why MCA is applying for approval to perform open heart surgery."

Fox blinked his amazement. "But open heart cases are sick and need a lot of care."

Trask interrupted. "However, that operation provides a high marketing profile and pays well. Within forty-eight hours, you know if the patient will make it or not."

Fox wrinkled his brow. "What about cancer cases?"

"That's a problem," Lindstrom answered, looking at both doctors. "Tell me whose name stands out in cancer research? None. The world connects DeBakey with heart surgery, that's why we're promoting laser angioplasties. It's a better marketing tool than advertising a dead-end disease like cancer."

"But breast cancer is always in the news," Gold interjected. "What about those cases?"

"Treating them is fine," Lindstrom answered. "After surgery, they're usually home by the second day and mammograms give repeat business. But patients with stomach, esophagus or pancreatic cancer do poorly and strain the nursing staff. Most linger on and are terminal no matter what heroic measures are used."

Fox turned to Gold with a look of disbelief.

"Then what about Dawson?" Gold asked. "He's a surgical oncologist. Is he costing the hospital money?"

"He's new and hasn't operated enough for us to get a good profile on him," Lindstrom answered.

Gold quickly cut in. "We better keep our eye on him. He had the balls to question the laser angioplasties at his first departmental meeting."

"Take it easy, Morty," Lindstrom cautioned, "we've handled that already. You don't want to be caught making libelous statements about him."

Fox straightened in his chair. "Yeh, Morty. Let's not stir up a legal battle. I get nervous when lawyers come snooping around." He looked to Lindstrom. "Are you sure the hospital kickbacks to the docs are legal?"

Lindstrom kept a steady voice. "Careful, Dr. Fox. The term is 'contracted payments.' Don't ever use that word again."

Fox stiffened in his chair. "I get the message," he mumbled.

Lindstrom gave an approving nod and waved for the waiter to bring the check. "Thanks for coming, gentlemen. You'll get the word out to the other doctors, won't you?"

"We will," Gold replied.

Lindstrom continued, "Now that our meal is over, I'm sure you're both ready to leave because you must have an early tomorrow."

"Thanks for dinner," Gold said, rising quickly and

signaling Fox to join him.

"It was great," Fox added as he stood up. They walked away with Gold still holding his unlit cigar before him as Fox followed.

Alone with Trask, Lindstrom raised his glass. "Here's to the future most successful hospital in the MCA chain. It's not where we'll make our fortune, but it will work very well for us."

Trask's head bobbed in agreement.

Lindstrom continued, "And by getting Gold and Fox in our camp, we own the medical staff."

Trask responded by giving him a thumbs up.

After signing the bill, Lindstrom raised his snifter, emptied it and looked to Trask. "Operation profit is now on its way. Shall we go?"

Nine

It was Sunday morning and with nothing planned for the day, Parker lingered in bed listening to the various TV commentators review the national politics of the week. Primary in his thoughts was the danger he faced from the drug traffickers. He had enough worries starting practice and paying bills and he didn't need any additional challenges.

Rising from the bed to head for the shower, he thought of Judy again and wondered if he should call her. As much as he hated being alone all day, he decided not to, rationalizing she needed more time. Although Gwen invited him for dinner last Sunday, he couldn't impose on her every weekend.

The steady stream of hot water beating down comforted him. As an only child, he felt blessed by his adoptive parents' unconditional love, never feeling the need to search for his birth mother. It was only after they died that he learned they mortgaged their home to pay for his education. His only inheritance was their love, but that was more than enough.

In their minds, there could be no more honorable profession than medicine. Remembering how proud they were the day he received his medical degree, he was determined more than ever to do the right thing and be a credit to their memory.

Back in the bedroom, he turned off the TV and dressed. With only a few checks coming in, he couldn't waste money in bars or discos and decided to lunch at MCA's cafeteria to fight his loneliness and hunger pains. A free meal for staff doctors was incentive enough to leave the apartment.

Alone in the empty cafeteria, he ate roast turkey smothered in gravy, and after finishing, made his way to the doctors' lounge. He checked his mailbox, sorting through hospital memos and commercial advertisements when the door flew open and Morty Gold appeared.

"Hey, kid, want to assist on an emergency surgery? Looks like all the surgeons are enjoying their day off."

"Sure," Parker answered. "What's up?"

"Got a sixty-five year old black gal with a colon obstruction, probably cancer."

"Are you going to give her a colostomy?"

"No, we have to resect her before she's completely blocked."

"Do you have a tissue diagnosis?"

Gold paused, giving Parker an annoyed look. "Don't need one. Bologna's biopsy showed scar tissue so what else can it be with that long, narrowed recto-sigmoid?"

Parker was disturbed by his answer, aware that colon cancer wasn't usually associated with long stretches of narrowed bowel. But before commenting, he decided to see how the case went.

As the two stood over the open belly, the only abnormality found was the lengthy thickened segment of the rectum seen on the patient's x-rays.

"I'm not convinced this is cancer," Parker said in a subdued voice.

Gold stopped conversing with the nurse and his eyes narrowed above his mask. "What do you mean you're not convinced? This has to be cancer."

"Wouldn't it be better to do another sigmoidoscopic biopsy to prove it?" Parker asked.

The room turned quiet as Gold stared back. After a long wait, he turned to the nurse. "Get me a sigmoidoscope and biopsy forcep. I'll get another specimen."

Guided by Parker's hand in the abdomen, Gold passed the scope into the rectum to reach the hardened area in question. Biopsies were taken and sent to the lab.

After a short wait, the OR intercom crackled.

"Pathology reporting on rectal biopsies for Dr. Gold. I can't confirm a diagnosis of cancer. All I see is fibrosis and inflammation. You'll have to wait until tomorrow for the permanent sections to be read."

"I have to wait till then?" Gold called back.

"Afraid so," came the pathologist's response.

Parker leaned close to whisper into Gold's ear. "We can't do a resection without a diagnosis."

Gold's eyes glared over his face mask. "Bologna scoped this patient and he says it's cancer. I say it's cancer. Are you telling us we're both wrong?"

Parker watched the nurses and anesthesiologist stiffen as they waited for his response. He took in a hard swallow. "Not exactly. What I'm mean is, check for other things, like AIDS or scleroderma."

"AIDS!" Gold bellowed. "Let's just cut out this damn thing and stop guessing."

"Sorry, Dr. Gold. If you want to do a resection, you'd better find another assistant."

"What?" Gold shouted back. "You young surgeons are all alike. It's easy to ask questions to make you look important, but I get the job done."

Parker felt the blood rush to his face. He didn't need enemies so early in his career but stood his ground. "I'll be happy to assist after the report is in," he answered firmly.

Gold, his brow beaded with sweat, fixed his eyes on Parker. "Shit! Let's close and get this god damned surgery over with."

Parker turned to the anesthesiologist and spoke in a low voice. "Make sure you draw blood for an AIDS test."

The surgery ended without conversation. Only the metallic sounds of instruments collected by the scrub nurse broke the forced silence.

After surgery, Parker followed Gold into the doctors' locker room and quietly dressed while the chief of staff dictated his surgical report in a muffled voice. Before he was able to place the last knot in his tie, he saw Gold bolt out of the door. He finished dressing and entered the hallway to see him standing before Lindstrom in the distance.

"Mark my words, Eric," Gold shouted, holding one finger in the air. "That fuckin' Dawson's gonna make trouble around here."

Ten

Following weekend, Saturday morning

Kent Markman felt energized as he steered his forty foot cabin cruiser, *The Lazy Lady*, along the Intracoastal Waterway in a southerly direction.

His eyes peered into the distance, watching the sun reflect on waves like sparkling diamonds dancing under a cloudless sky. The gusty winds buffeting his face felt invigorating, and his pulse raced with excitement. Judy had finally agreed to a secret meeting. Too many unresolved issues lingered, and she was giving him a chance to explain why he had broken off their affair without warning.

Dressed in tailored whites, Docker deck shoes and sunglasses, his body reflected the perfect nautical image. Friends often quipped he resembled the late President Kennedy when he dressed like that, a comparison he secretly enjoyed.

Piloting the *Lazy Lady* always gave him a sense of renewal, moments which allowed the luxury of introspection. While the trappings of success and security were important in his life, to get them he recalled the calculated moves he had to take.

Marriage to Sheila gave him instant access to the world of corporate power. Her father was Stan Glassman, the vice president of a giant insurance company that owned an HMO subsidiary. With Glassman's influence, he was able to land a 'full risk provider' HMO contract.

As an HMO gate-keeper, Markman controlled patient diagnostic testing, specialty consultations and hospitalizations. In return, he received a princely sum every month for each patient, whether they were seen or not. With close to four thousand assigned clients, he was able to leverage fees with hospitals and consultants. To fight off any sense of guilt, he constantly reminded himself that it was the same formula Henry Ford used to mass produce Model T cars. But with all his financial success, there remained a void in his life which Sheila couldn't fill.

As he approached the Royal Palm drawbridge, he stopped behind a majestic sailing ship waiting for the roadway to rise. Throttling down the engines, he waved to the crew, although his thoughts remained on Sheila.

He had long since stopped questioning who was to blame for the breakdown of their ten year marriage. Wearied by her obsession to rise in the social pecking order, he just wanted out. She was no longer sensitive to his needs and the demands of his professional world.

His attention returned when the hulking concrete and steel drawbridge rose gradually to rest at right angles to the roadway. Both vessels resumed their southbound journey, leaving the bridge behind.

Kent pushed the throttle and the engines responded,

causing water to spray on deck as the *Lazy Lady* surged past the sailing ship.

As the bridge disappeared in the distance, he enjoyed watching the stately ships and ocean sailing yachts lining both sides of the shoreline. Palm Beach was where a good number of his wealthy patients bedded in season. Marveling at the magnificence of one palatial mansion facing the Intracoastal, he pondered whatever one's financial worth, illness ultimately reduced everyone to the same risk of death, whether from heart, lung or kidney disease.

His cell phone rang and reluctantly he lifted it to his ear. "Hi, whoever you are, I hope you don't need me," he laughed. After listening a moment, he answered, "I don't care who she is. I'm off for the weekend and Dr. Crane's taking my calls. Good bye."

He leaned on the throttle and felt the engine respond to the power. No one was going to ruin what he had planned for today.

The waterway narrowed, and when Grundlach's Marina came into view, he slowed the craft. Checking his watch, he saw his timing was perfect. Judy would be waiting at the dock, a location where no one would know them. Getting her to agree to this rendezvous was his first challenge, but meeting on his boat posed even a greater hurdle. After persuading her it was the best way to avoid being seen together, she agreed. That convinced him she might still love him.

He cruised past a maze of slips occupied by yachts of various sizes. At the dock, two workers stabilized the mooring lines before he shut down the engines. As he jumped onto the pier, his eyes roamed in search of Judy. From the depths of the marina, he spotted her slender figure in white shorts, exposing her perfectly shaped legs. She wore dark glasses and a banded straw hat, and as she approached the dock, the workers smiled their approval.

Kent waved, "Right on time."

"I'm glad I found the marina," she replied, smiling with relief.

He helped her onto the boat and into the cabin. "It's eleven o'clock and I have a cab coming in five minutes to take me to the Ritz Carlton. I have to register for a medical meeting."

He saw her quick frown.

"Don't worry, I'm only signing in. Sheila and the boys are in Gainesville for a soccer meet this weekend, and this was a perfect time to get away. I'll only be twenty minutes."

"Things are getting complicated, aren't they?" she said.

"Please, Judy, I'll be right back. This is important to both of us."

She moved to the cushioned bench along the window. "I'll be waiting."

It was nearly forty minutes when Kent returned and jumped on the deck.

"Let's go!" he cried out with boyish excitement.

They left the harbor and returned to the Intracoastal Waterway to head toward the ocean. The sun climbed higher and a growing number of weekend sailors began to appear.

Although early in the day, they could see many partying as their ships moved closer in the narrow channels. Judy responded to their greetings with a carefree wave while Kent flashed a thumbs up sign and smiled. Despite the happy pretense, they knew this trip would determine if they had a future together.

As Judy sat upright in the deck chair, Kent piloted the ship, deep in thought. He was prepared to do whatever she wanted. If she became upset after they talked, they could return to land before sundown. But if she agreed they needed more time together, they would stay on board overnight and return to land on Sunday.

He took quick glimpses of her, hoping the openness of the waters would make her relax. When she tilted the deck chair back to sunbathe, he felt it was a good sign and struggled to fight the urge to hold her. But he knew that would have to wait.

The high-rise buildings facing the ocean were still in view when he decided to drop anchor. The afternoon sun beat its full intensity on the deck, and the *Lazy Lady* rocked gently as the waters lapped against her hull.

He led Judy back into the cabin and took out a bottle of champagne from the cooler, setting it on the table.

Before he could uncork it, Judy's voice lowered. "It's time you told me the truth, Kent."

He took in a deep breath. "That's all I've thought about, Judy. My attorney scared the hell out of me when I told him I wanted to divorce Sheila. He said she would ruin me."

After sipping from his glass, he shook his head. "All of my money is in her name, a legal protection in case I get sued. Honest, honey, he stopped me. I'll be forty in another year and he warned divorce would be a financial disaster."

"So what's changed?"

"I've changed!" He reached for her hand. "I know I can't live without you."

"Are you saying you filed for divorce?"

"Not yet, but I have a plan."

She pulled back her hand.

"Trust me, Judy. Without you, my life is empty."

She turned to look out at the water. "Why should I trust you? You string me along, promise divorce for over a year. Then without explaining, you dump me. Then you're back with another promise. Why should I trust you?"

Kent's shoulders sagged. "You're right, but if you're with me, I'm willing to risk it now. My lawyer has it all planned."

He read the painful thoughts exploding in her mind.

"Please, listen," he said, reaching for her hand again. "This lawyer says he will quietly transfer my assets to a dummy corporation which will dilute Sheila's part of the money. It's going to take time, but all I have to do is give him the signal, and he'll start the process."

"It sounds complicated, Kent, and I don't understand it. Can't Sheila's lawyers follow a paper trail? You can't hide everything."

Seeing he had captured her interest, he persisted. "He assured me it will work. Leave it to attorneys. They can plug square pegs in round holes. Believe me, Judy, I want that divorce more than you can imagine. There's got to be another chance for us."

The lines on her brow deepened as she studied his face. "I can't make the same mistake twice, Kent. You're still not free."

"Please, honey, I promise. As soon as my lawyer shifts the accounts, we file."

"Am I supposed to say okay? We pick up again just because you promise?" She glared back at him. "No, Kent, not this time."

He watched tears fill her eyes and run down her cheeks. "I deserve everything you say," he whispered, "but you're the most important thing in my life. I can't believe you don't feel the same."

She wiped her tears and turned away.

"I'll do whatever you want," he continued. "We can turn back or we can stay. You decide. All I ask is, do you feel the same?"

Judy rose from the table and crossed the cabin to look out the window. "I wouldn't be here if I didn't. It's just that I need more than a promise."

He moved to her side and held her waist from behind. "Help me, Judy. If we're together, I can handle this. If not, I don't think I can make it."

She sensed the warmth and the softness of his cheek against hers, and, for the first time, felt she was in control.

She kissed his cheek and whispered, "Let's stay on the boat tonight."

~ * ~

Judy awakened to early morning sunlight pouring through the cabin window as Kent slept by her side. His bare chest moved rhythmically with each breath as she studied his profile, following the clean lines of his straight nose and sculptured chin.

Slipping quietly from under the covers, she removed his terry cloth robe from the hook, wrapped herself and reached for the cigarettes on the nightstand.

On deck, she watched the sun rise, highlighting the whiteness of the clouds as they floated across the horizon. Immersed in the beauty surrounding her, she inhaled deeply on the cigarette with her thoughts drifting.

What attracted her to Kent? He was handsome, energetic and bright, but something else drew her to him, an untapped tenderness that seemed to have been hidden for so long. Yes, she thought, that's what fascinated her. Kent was like the orphaned little boy, looking to be loved, and she felt she could fill that void after her heart-rending breakup with Parker.

Single and alone in Columbus, she was intrigued when a nursing school friend invited her to interview for the position of supervisor at a hospital in Florida. It offered a higher salary, and most important, a change of scenery. Her parents were long gone and there was nothing holding her back.

Her first meeting with Kent was on hospital matters and purely professional. Complimentary and supportive, he boosted her confidence which had suffered after Parker's rejection of marriage. Eventually, he opened up to her, confiding about his marital unhappiness. She could tell he was in pain and it made her feel wanted. That's how it began. Kent had reached into the private recess reserved for only a few in a lifetime.

Suddenly she felt a kiss on her neck and turned to see him in his shorts. He took the cigarette from her hand, flipped it into the water and drew her up from the chair.

"If only this day could last forever," he whispered, embracing her.

She answered by holding him tight. "I want this to be our fresh beginning, Kent."

He kissed her and slipped his hands under the robe. "You can sunbathe in the raw. No one can see us out here," he teased.

"You're being naughty," she laughed, dropping the robe from her shoulders.

He caressed the fullness of her breasts, but stopped when he felt a firm ridge close to the hollow under her arm.

"You felt that last night, didn't you?" she asked.

"Yes, I thought it might be a lump in your breast."

"It's a scar from where Dr. Mehlman removed the mole. Don't you remember sending me to him?"

"Mehlman, the dermatologist? Yes. I remember now, but after everything came apart, I lost track. I don't think I read the biopsy report."

"Don't worry. Mehlman said the mole wasn't cancerous. Just hold me. I only want to think good thoughts."

After a leisurely lunch, the *Lazy Lady* made a slow return to Grundlach's Marina as the sun began its descent in the west. After Kent left, Judy stood on the dock and watched his boat disappear from view. It had been a long time since she felt positive about her future.

Eleven

Same day

It was dark when Kent returned to an empty house. Sheila and the boys were still away at the soccer match but he expected them soon. After a quick shower and change of clothes, he waited in the family room and read the Sunday paper. The quiet ended with the sound of Sheila's car pulling into the driveway. Stomping feet followed as the boys burst into the house.

"Hi, Dad!" Scott, the older son. called out, running into the room. "We won!" he shouted, flopping onto the sofa beside his father."

"That's great," Kent answered, joining in his excitement.

Nathan, the younger boy, entered, guiding a soccer ball with his foot. "Our team took first place!" he said and joined his father and brother on the sofa.

Kent embraced his sons, marveling at their boundless energy, but when he saw Sheila standing in the doorway, his smile vanished.

"Let's go, boys, upstairs to the shower," she said. "We're going out for dinner tonight."

"Good idea," Kent added as they ran out of the room. He returned to reading the paper, avoiding her icy stare.

"And where were you this weekend?" she demanded.

He studied the sneer on her face. "You know very well I was at a medical meeting at the Ritz Carlton."

"Then why weren't you registered at the hotel?"

"Because I stayed on the *Lazy Lady* at the marina close by."

"You took the boat? I don't believe you."

"Why? I miss running her."

She entered the room and placed her purse on the table, tilting her head as she stood over him. "Am I allowed to ask if you were alone?"

"Of course I was!" He knew he had to keep lying until his legal affairs were completed.

"I can't predict you anymore, Kent." Her hands moved defiantly to her hips. "If you wanted to take the boat, why didn't you tell me? Suppose I needed you. I couldn't reach you."

"You needed me?"

"Yes, I wanted you to congratulate the boys on winning."

Kent bit his lip. "Sorry, Sheila, I didn't realize."

She looked into his eyes, "If you're lying, Kent, be careful. Don't play cutesy with me. I don't intend to be the other woman."

He rose from the sofa and faced her. "I was alone, dammit! Don't compare me with your friends, hopping in and out of bed with each other."

"You know nothing about my friends so don't change the subject. I couldn't reach you on your cell or anywhere.

68

I had no idea where you were."

Kent let out a deep sigh. "Let's not spoil the evening for the boys. I was alone and I'm sorry I got you upset."

She gave him a frigid look and left the room.

To survive the evening, he realized a more convincing apology was needed for damage control.

The sound of running water echoed from the master bath as he entered the bedroom. He sat on the edge of the bed, waiting for the water to stop. Hearing the shower door open and then shut, he called out. "Come on, honey, don't be mad at me."

There was no answer.

"I know I should have told you I'd be on the boat. It was such a hectic day at the meeting, I turned off the cell phone just to relax."

Again he heard no answer except for the sound of a cabinet door slamming shut.

"Aren't you going to talk to me?"

"Be out in a minute," came her reply.

Relieved that she answered, he rose from the bed to wait, studying their framed wedding picture on the dresser.

He had been attracted to her the first time they met. It was during their first year at college when he considered going out for the football team. Everyone knew players drew women like magnets, but when he couldn't make the team, he settled for the job of manager.

Sheila was a cheerleader and he could still recall her best stunt, the human pyramid. She would perch on top and after holding that pose, leap into the air, falling gracefully into the arms of two guys at the bottom of the formation. The memory was still vivid—her skirt billowing up during descent, revealing those firm tapered thighs. Like most college men, it was natural for him to want her.

He never intended having just one relationship at college, but over time found himself constantly involved with her. One attraction that sustained his interest was her father. While his dad earned a good living as a pharmacist, he couldn't match the financial prowess of a corporate mogul like Mr. Glassman. The Markmans didn't have a second home at Cape Cod nor did they take family ski trips to Vail. Unlike the Glassman children, he wasn't sent to a private school. The Markmans may have been successful, but the Glassmans were wealthy which made Sheila very appealing.

The bathroom door opened and Sheila emerged, her face perfectly made up and her robe precisely belted.

He moved to her and touched her shoulder. "I'm sorry, hon. I wasn't thinking. Please forgive me."

She wiped away a tear. "You seem to forget your responsibilities, Kent. You do have a family, you know."

"You're right," he said, lowering his head. "I was wrong."

Her expression softened. "We owe it to the boys."

"Then let's celebrate their win tonight."

"I'd like that," she answered with a tense smile. "I'll get dressed."

Satisfied he was able to diffuse her anger, he kissed her cheek and left to wait in the family room.

Reflecting on their past, he recalled how she had hinted they share rather than keep separate apartments after they hooked up in their sophomore year.

When the large discount chains forced the Markman Pharmacy to close, the lack of money made marriage to Sheila an option. That's when Mr. Glassman offered to subsidize his medical studies.

After they married, the long hours on call as a resident made it easy for him to stray. There was an excitement with each new sexual partner, and it never challenged his conscience because he still believed he loved Sheila. After the birth of their first son, he knew the Glassmans would always be supportive of their union and his professional success.

When Glassman's company created an HMO division in Florida, he seized the opportunity to have his father-in-law arrange a full risk provider contract for him.

How Sheila objected. "Why should we leave? We have everything here—family, social acceptance, a successful practice," she argued.

But after telling her he resented the gossip of friends claiming his rapid success was due to her father's connections, she agreed to the move. It helped that her New York contacts arranged introductions to the social elite of Florida's Gold Coast.

The two boys stormed into the room shouting, "Let's go, we're hungry!"

Sheila followed with a smile, "So am I."

Kent walked over and kissed her on the neck, which caused the boys to giggle. Their enthusiasm had broken any lingering tension, and they were his strongest bond to Sheila.

"Let's celebrate, guys," he said.

The family trooped out the door to begin the victory banquet. He knew he had dodged a bullet but was determined not to turn back. His plan was to spend the rest of his life with Judy, not Sheila.

Twelve

After the Hoffman debacle, Parker never expected to see another referral from Phil Bologna, but he did. While the elderly woman finally had her gallbladder removed, he heard through the grapevine she still needed blood transfusions and was steadily failing. Obviously, her future was grim, especially in the hands of a medical cowboy like Bologna.

The new referral was a jaundiced sixty-year-old man suspected to have pancreatic cancer for which a Whipple procedure was needed. Parker assumed his advanced training as a surgical oncologist was the reason the patient was sent to him.

The operation was complicated, involving removal of the head of the pancreas, the common duct draining bile from the liver and duodenum, the first portion of the small bowel. In order to restore the common pathway of drainage into the digestive stream, meticulous reconnection and reconstruction of the remaining organs was required.

He needed a capable, motivated assistant for this

challenging operation, and Jason Tucker came to mind. The young black surgeon had joined the staff eighteen months earlier after finishing his residency. *Why not?* Parker asked himself. *He's focused and I like his serious attitude.*

Tucker was happy to accept and after six hours in the OR, they completed the surgery. The two entered the doctors' lounge and headed for their lockers, satisfied with what they had accomplished.

"Great job. Loved working with you," Tucker said, giving Parker a high-five.

"Thanks Jason, but sorry it took so long. If Bologna hadn't messed up the field by doing all those blind dye injections, the surgery would have gone smoother."

"I guess some docs have the knack of making simple things more complicated," Jason quipped. "Most of our time was spent searching for that damn bile duct. After that, the operation moved like a charm."

Kent Markman stood before his locker as they entered the dressing room. "What monumental procedure did you guys do today?"

"A Whipple," Parker answered.

Kent questioned, "What for?"

"For cancer, what else?" Parker shot back.

"See you guys later," Tucker said, sensing the tension and eager to leave.

Kent seated himself on the bench, facing Parker. "Of course Whipples are done for cancer, but these patients die within six months. Why even do it?"

Parker didn't answer. Instead, he opened the locker and dressed with his back to Kent. After a few moments, he turned around to look him in the eye. "You don't have to tell me the statistics, Kent. I know they're not good, but there's a chance twenty percent of these patients will survive five years."

Kent let out a boisterous laugh. "You're a dreamer, Parker. Of a hundred cases, only twenty are possibly operable. But of those twenty, only two might last five years. So why bother?"

Parker shut the locker door with a slam. "I bother because these patients get pain relief when the cancer's removed."

"What's the benefit?" Kent replied. "Shove a catheter into the liver, drain the bile and give them pain pills. They're gonna die anyway. It's a lot cheaper with less liability." He rose and placed a hand on Parker's shoulder. "I'd like to use you if you would operate only what is absolutely necessary."

Parker returned a stunned look. "What do you mean by necessary?"

"Like obvious emergencies, hot gallbladders, appendectomies, nothing fancy."

Parker tried to contain his anger. "Let's put it this way, Kent. You want me to give up on patients who are sick and deserve quality care? Well, I won't. In my opinion, HMO medicine can shortchange both the doctor and the patient. I'll have no part of that."

"Calm down, Parker. You've got to change your attitude."

Parker's eyes narrowed. "No, you do. You HMO docs are rationing medical care and that's downright unethical."

Kent took a quick step back, raising his hands in the air. "Fine, keep your principles. Times are changing, so you better change with them."

He stepped away to leave, and then turned around with a grin. "Remember how the story goes, Parker. The last buggy whip maker made the best whip ever, but unfortunately he had to go out of business. Call me if you decide to reset your thinking."

Parker stood deep in thought after Markman left, trying to calm himself. He still had the patient's family waiting to hear about their loved one and postop orders to write. He swung open the door and left, believing he had done the right operation for his patient. But he couldn't shake off his pessimistic thoughts. Physicians like Markman allowed themselves to be sucked into this wave of HMO mentality without even giving their patients a chance.

~ * ~

The following morning, Parker drove briskly through heavy traffic for his 8 AM hernia procedure at St. Ann Hospital. The OR supervisor was known to run a tight ship with surgical scheduling so he didn't want to be late and risk an argument.

As he weaved through the traffic, his thoughts focused on the surgical steps needed to perform a successful repair. The patient's large incarcerated hernia was filled with bowel, requiring precise steps to avoid intestinal injury.

Glancing at his rearview mirror, he noticed a silver Jaguar tailing him and changed lanes. When the sedan followed, he panicked and touched the GPS transmitter Rucker had given him. The thought of facing those narcos again disrupted his surgical thoughts.

He raced to the next exit, searching for a gas station and pulled up to the pump. Jumping out of the car, he looked around but saw no sign of the sedan. *Am I getting paranoid.* he thought, reaching for his cell phone to call Rucker. Before he could dial, his phone rang.

"Dr. Dawson, this is MCA emergency room calling. Hold for Dr. Baum."

A cold sweat broke out on his brow as he waited. *Where are the police? Even with the transmitter, I'm still at risk.*

The voice broke into his thoughts. "Dr. Baum, here. I have a forty-eight year old male who ran his bike into a truck and can't move his shoulder."

"When did he arrive? Are his vital signs stable?"

"Came in around five this morning and his numbers are normal."

"Are there any other injuries?"

"None that I can see."

Parker hesitated. "If it's only a shoulder injury, call orthopedics."

"I did, but Dr. Kern hasn't answered his page. I thought you could look him over. His name is Stanley Kingsley."

"But my shift doesn't start 'til eight.. Who's on call for general surgery before me?"

"Dr. Patel, but he refused to come in and said it was your call."

"Look at the clock, Doctor. It's not eight yet and your patient came in at five. Call Kern and if he needs me, I'll be happy to consult."

Parker closed the phone with mixed feelings, annoyed

that two surgeons refused to see the patient. He debated what to do, knowing his case was waiting at St. Ann. Lawton had warned him MCA's ER docs used general surgeons as a dumping ground when other specialists refused to answer their call. By responding, he'd only encourage the delinquency of those surgeons who didn't come in.

Since the patient arrived at 5 AM, he rationalized it absolved him of any responsibility because his shift didn't begin until eight. But those thoughts didn't soothe his guilt. As a physician, he sensed the moral obligation to see that patient.

The honk of a horn from behind signaled another car waited to reach the pump. Satisfied the Jaguar had gone, he decided to continue on to St. Ann. He'd go to MCA to check on the bike accident after the hernia repair.

~ * ~

The OR supervisor burst into St. Ann's operating suite. "Dr. Dawson, Dr. Gold is on the phone screaming you're on ER call at MCA. He says you better come right away."

"Tell him I'm in surgery and almost finished. See if he can pitch in until I get there."

The supervisor left only to rush back into the room. "He's mad, Dr. Dawson. He said you have to leave now if you know what's good for you."

Without looking up, Parker kept his calm and continued the repair. "Call Dr. Leader and ask if he can cover until I get there."

"Will do," the supervisor answered as she left in a hurry.

After completing the surgery, he raced his car to MCA,

angered by Gold's threat. *He's a surgeon and he's standing there. Why didn't he cover for me?*

Entering MCA's ER, he encountered a middle-age man lying on a gurney with blood and IV solutions dripping into a central venous line. A chest tube bubbled air into an underwater seal while a ventilator delivered rhythmic surges of oxygen through an airway.

Parker approached Baum and asked, "Is orthopedics here?"

The ER doctor stiffened. "No, Kern hasn't come in yet."

"But it's nearly ten o'clock. Where is he?"

Baum answered with an indifferent shrug.

"Is this the bike accident you called about this morning?"

Baum's reply was curt. "Yep, it is. My shift's over so I'm leaving."

Parker stood speechless as he watched Baum leave the room wondering when the orthopedist would arrive.

Within fifteen minutes, he saw Dr. Kern wander in followed by Judy.

The orthopedist moved to the X-ray view box and studied the films. "This guy has pelvic fractures and needs surgery. Call me when you get him to OR."

"OR is ready," Judy replied, handing Parker the lab slip. "I guess you're the admitting doctor and in charge, Dr. Dawson." Her warm smile was his first welcoming response.

The orthopedist left without comment which frustrated Parker because he wanted to coordinate their consultations.

Seconds later, Rudy Catalano charged into the room. The anesthesiologist huffed excitedly in his Spanish accent. "I gotta talk to you, Parker."

Parker read the anger in his eyes.

"I'm in surgery, see. Baum calls me to ER to pass an airway on this patient and I wonder why he doesn't he do it himself. When I get here, I find the guy's cracked ribs punctured his lung and air is leaking into his chest. I tell Baum the man needs a chest tube, not an airway, and he curses me. He says he's in charge and if I don't do it, he will."

"Then why did he call you if he said he would do it?" Parker asked. "Board certified ER docs are trained to pass airways."

"That's right," Rudy answered. "I've complained to Lindstrom because this isn't the first time he's done this."

Parker gave Rudy a questioning look. "I'm sure he's certified."

"Hell no!" Rudy growled. "That's the problem. He's not certified. He's just cheap labor. Medical staff doesn't do the hiring here, the hospital does." Seeing the gurney being moved to OR, Rudy said, "I better get back to surgery."

Parker heard his name paged over the speaker and reached for the phone.

"I have a federal agent asking to see you, Doctor," the operator announced.

Parker's heart sank. He had enough excitement for one morning, but maybe it was good news. "Have him meet me in the hall outside the ER," he answered.

After a short wait, he saw Rucker being ushered down

the hall by a Pink Lady volunteer.

Rucker walked up to Parker. "We know you were followed this morning."

"Thanks a lot. Where were you guys?"

"On their tail but lost them in traffic. They probably taped your calls and monitored your every move, hoping you'll lead them to the money."

"Dammit, Rucker, I need more security! I can't give those bums what they want and next time they'll do me in."

"Easy, Doc, we understand, but we need your help to get a line on this syndicate. We think they're part of a global crime ring that's also sponsoring terrorists."

Parker felt a chill, remembering the feel of the metal piece rammed against his ribs. "No way," he snapped, "I want no part of that."

"You don't have a choice, Doc. They think you stole the money and rest assured it's in the millions. Their code doesn't let anyone steal from the syndicate."

Parker shook his head, but Rucker persisted. "Look, we're talking about an annual thirty billion dollar industry for Mexico alone. And that doesn't even include the Colombians. The US government has thousands of sealed files listing people these trafficantes tortured and killed. Your only hope is to work with us so these local drug lords can be put out of business."

Parker read Rucker's grim look and thought, *If the Feds are trying to scare the shit out of me, they're doing a wonderful job.* "I guess you want me as bait to set up a trap?"

"Not exactly," Rucker answered.

"Are your supervisors in Washington aware of my situation?"

Rucker hesitated. "We report everything to them. But if it means involving the governments of Mexico or the U.S., don't count on the agency to take a position."

That wasn't a comforting answer for Parker. He was living a nightmare and it seemed Rucker was his only protection. Taking in a deep breath, he whispered, "Tell me what I have to do."

Thirteen

Same day, MCA Administrator's Office

Gold leaned his short trunk over Lindstrom's desk. "Dawson didn't answer his ER call. He abandoned an injured patient and broke the by-laws."

"Take it easy," Lindstrom cautioned. "He's new, just starting out."

"Makes no difference, Eric, he's a trouble maker."

Lindstrom gave a knowing nod and smiled. "Could it be you're worried about losing surgical referrals to him?"

Gold's face reddened. "Hell, no. Just because he did a Whipple doesn't mean he's a better surgeon. He had the balls to question my operation in front of the OR crew. And I thought I was doing him a favor by asking him to assist."

Gold read Lindstrom's unperturbed look and persisted. "Look, it hasn't been a month since he got here and already he's questioning the new laser procedure."

"But that's under control since we're reviewing the cases that died," Lindstrom replied. "Do you know what time our by-laws state emergency call begins and ends?"

"At seven AM."

"That's not so. I checked and discovered it's not documented. Whether ER call begins at six, seven or eight in the morning, it's not recorded. So what are you going to charge him with? Not responding to his call when you don't even know what time call begins?"

"Bullshit!" Gold shouted as he paced back and forth. "He abandoned a patient and that should be reported to the state. Who's to question the time ER call begins and ends when a patient's life's at risk?"

Lindstrom gave a frown. "What about the hospital's legal liability? Parker can sue us for wrongful prosecution."

Gold stopped pacing and placed both hands firmly on the desk. "What lawyer will represent a new guy in town? No firm will go against MCA and risk losing corporate business. Besides, Dawson's a pauper, no one's gonna take his case."

Lindstrom's eyes narrowed as he reflected on Gold's words. He had a point, and Dawson's willingness to question the vascular procedure could prove to be a thorn in MCA's side.

He gave Gold a wry grin. "Then you file the charges of abandonment with the hospital since you're chief of staff. I'll place those charges with the State Department of Professional Regulation, since by statute any violation of our by-laws is reportable. Just stick to that script."

"Good, then the government can take over from there."

Lindstrom frowned. "Before you get carried away, have you thought about your own liability? You were there and didn't offer to help that patient."

Gold halted his pacing. "Listen, if the hospital doesn't

complain, the state won't know a thing. They're only concerned with the guy on call. Let's not blow this."

"I'll also have to report this complaint to corporate headquarters."

"Why get the corporation involved?"

"Anything exposing MCA to potential liability needs to be reported. I know you're hot on this so I won't block you. Make sure the complaint states you were not a participant in the incident. Draw up the charges and I'll review it before filing it with the state."

Gold gave Lindstrom a broad smile as he moved to the door. "This'll stop him cold. If he tries to fight it, he'll be chasing his tail and drowning in legal fees."

Fourteen

One week later

The usual evening rush of activity in MCA's emergency room was evident as Parker scanned the occupied cubicles. Baum sat at the control desk, leaning back in his chair with both feet resting on the shelf. Two nurses burst out laughing at something he said and vanished when Parker approached.

After the mishandled bike emergency the week before, Parker regretted that Baum was the ER physician in charge. Managing a courteous smile, he asked, "Where's the possible appendicitis case you called me to see, Dr. Baum?"

"Perez, Stall three," Baum answered abruptly. He quickly stepped away to enter a cubicle and drew the curtain behind him.

Parker searched for Ms. Perez's chart at the desk, found it and entered her stall. The thirty-year-old Hispanic woman lay quietly on the gurney, her eyes filled with fear.

"I'm Dr. Parker, the surgeon called to see you."

"I hope this isn't serious, Doctor."

Parker looked at her white blood cell count taped to the

chart. "Your blood report isn't bad, but I can't tell until I examine you. Are you sexually active?" he asked.

She blushed, her embarrassment masked by her dark complexion. "You won't write it down, will you?"

"I'm sorry I must, but everything on your chart is confidential." He watched her turn her face away. "It's important, Ms. Perez."

She looked at him and whispered, "Yes, but only with one man. We hope to get married soon."

Parker smiled. "Let's keep it our secret. I need a nurse to help so I can do a pelvic exam."

He exited the stall to look for a nurse. Suddenly he heard a loud cry ring out.

"I'll be darned if I'm changing my plans!" Tessie Cashman, the charge nurse, stood outside the ER door, shaking her finger at Judy.

"If you can't find someone to cover me, I'll quit!" she said in anger.

"Just give me time to work it out, Tess. I'm sure I'll find someone to cover your shift," Judy pleaded.

Tessie drew back her shoulders in defiance. "I'm not married to this hospital, you know. If I don't hear by next week, I resign."

Parker watched Judy calmly pat Tessie's arm.

"I know how important this trip is for you, Tess, so I'll be in touch."

After Judy left, Parker called out, "Miss Cashman, could you please help me in this stall?"

He caught the look of annoyance cross her face as she approached to enter the cubicle with him. While he did Perez's exam, Tessie refrained from offering any support or hand holding women usually give one anther during such a personal procedure. As soon as he finished, she bolted from the room.

Perez's large dark eyes looked up at Parker. "What did you find, Doctor?"

"I think your pain is coming from a ruptured ovarian cyst. I don't believe its appendicitis."

"Will I need surgery?"

"I don't think so, but let's get a pelvic ultrasound and CT scan to make sure."

"But I don't have medical insurance and I can't afford it," came her timid response.

It was a familiar story with many patients that came through the ER. He didn't expect payment for treating Perez, but the hospital would certainly bill and pursue her.

He looked into her questioning eyes. "I'll skip the tests if you promise two things. Should your pain increase, call me. And see me in my office tomorrow so I can check you again."

Perez smiled. "I'll be there, I promise."

He handed her his card. "Remember, if your pain gets worse, call me, anytime."

Perez thanked him and Parker left to complete her chart at the control desk.

An attractive young woman dressed in a long white coat approached Parker as he sat at the desk. A stethoscope dangled freely from her neck.

Parker extended his hand. "I'm Dr. Dawson. Are you new on staff?"

"Gladys Albright," she answered sprightly, gripping his hand. "Dr. Markman's new physician assistant."

Parker smiled. "Welcome aboard. Haven't seen Kent around lately."

"Oh, he's away this week and I'm swamped. I already admitted four patients today. I can see why he needed another PA."

Parker didn't comment, fearful to show his disapproval of PAs treating patients in the ER without their doctor's supervision. It was clear why Markman could afford fancy cars and a high lifestyle. His formula was simple: be an HMO gatekeeper, hire physician assistants to see patients and then wait for the checks to roll in. He even got monthly payments for patients he never saw.

Not wanting to act unfriendly, he said, "I'm sure Dr. Markman appreciates how hard you're working, Miss Albright. Glad to meet you."

After the PA thanked him, he left for the X-ray Department to review some films. Heading down the corridor, he questioned how many of Kent's patients were aware they were being treated by a PA rather than a doctor. Diagnostic emergencies could be challenging to even the best of physicians, so his years of extra training had to account for something.

When he turned the corner to enter the Radiology Department, he saw Judy alone in the reception area placing files on the desk.

"What's going on with you and Tessie Cashman, Judy?" he asked.

"Just working on her schedule. She's planned a vacation with Dr. Baum and this trip is very important to her."

She gave him a frown. "It's no secret she's angry with

you, Parker. Baum's been bad-mouthing you for not responding to that bike accident."

"That explains her hostility when I asked for help."

"That sounds like Tess. She's known to be temperamental and quite a gossip. I'd keep my distance from her."

"Thanks for the warning, but Baum should have handled that case better."

"Try and tell him that," she replied.

He smiled at her. "Now that I have you trapped, how about dinner tonight?"

"I don't think so," she said, shaking her head.

He reached for her hand. "Come on. Judy. At least give me a chance."

"I'm truly sorry, Parker. It was great when we were together, but it's a different story now."

Tessie Cashman turned the corner and entered the suite. She froze when she saw the two of them facing each other.

"Excuse me, I hope I'm not interrupting anything," she warbled, strolling into the reception area with a faint sound of glee in her voice. "I'll only be a minute."

"Is there something you need, Tess?" Judy asked, pulling her hand away from Parker.

Tessie cooed "No" as she walked around them. "I just have to leave these requisitions here." She placed the file on the desk and left with a brisk gait.

Judy spoke first. "I hope she doesn't start spreading rumors around the hospital."

Parker laughed. "That wouldn't bother me."

"Well, it would me. I don't like to be the topic of useless conversation."

"Does that mean we can't have dinner, ever?"

"I have to go," she whispered and left.

He stood alone deep in thought. Judy had to be involved with someone, but there was little he could do about it.

Now Tessie Cashman was a different story. She was intimately involved with Baum and could become a problem.

Fifteen

Two days later, Parker's office

Gwen cleared her desk preparing to leave for the day when the phone rang. She reached for the receiver with the hope it held the promise of a new consultation.

"Yes," she answered, "but he's not on ER call today." As Parker approached from the hallway, she handed him the phone. "It's Supervisor Keller. She needs to talk to you."

Parker listened and then answered, "I'm on my way."

"What's that all about? Gwen asked."

"Judy Keller wants me to see her brother, Shawn. He was brought into the ER with gunshot wounds."

"It's great that she called you. Get moving," she chuckled. "You need to operate, not pontificate."

Parker made a hasty exit and sprinted along the path leading to MCA's ER. He wondered why Judy picked him rather than a senior surgeon, questioning if he should be flattered or worried.

Agonizing outcries greeted him once inside the triage area. Nurses struggled to hold the thrashing arms of a pale young man with a full head of blond hair. He was strapped to a gurney and a lab tech fought to draw blood.

"Glad you're here, Dr. Dawson," the ER physician said. "It looks like he took two bullets to the belly."

"What's his pressure?" Parker asked, moving to Shawn's side.

"He's stable, one hundred over seventy."

Parker slipped on rubber gloves and rested his hands on the crimson-smeared abdomen oozing blood from two holes. "The belly's rigid and he needs surgery. Why wasn't he taken to St. Ann's Trauma Center?"

"The paramedics were headed there but he kept screaming to take him to MCA where his sister works."

Just then, Judy rushed into the room. "Thanks for coming, Dr. Dawson. How bad is Shawn?"

"I can't tell until I take him to surgery."

She leaned close, whispering, "I need a favor, Parker."

He nodded.

"Please don't run a drug screen."

He gave her a questioning look. "Why? Is he taking any?"

"I don't know," she answered abruptly.

Her request was unexpected, but he rationalized that wasn't important. At this moment, the screen had nothing to do with saving Shawn's life.

He looked to the desk secretary standing by. "Call Dr. Leader to assist. We're taking him to OR and we'll get x-rays in there."

The look of horror on Judy's face made him reach for her arm. Encouraged she didn't pull away, he said, "I'll take good care of him."

"I know," she nodded, wiping the tears from her face.

Changing into his scrub suit, he again questioned why she chose him. It was clear she didn't want to resume their relationship, and what about the drug screen? Those questions needed to be answered.

Once in the OR, Rudy helped transfer Shawn onto the table, and the sudden move resulted in a sharp outcry.

"Your pain will be gone in a minute," the anesthesiologist responded in a soothing voice. He injected a sleep-inducing fluid into the IV tubing and a welcome quiet returned to the room.

After Parker prepped and draped the abdomen with the nurse's assistance, he looked at the x-ray hanging on the screen. "He's lucky. I don't see any bullet fragments in the belly, and the IVP shows no urinary tract damage."

The circulating nurse poked her head in the door. "Dr. Leader's on his way."

Parker made his incision, cutting through the peritoneum as bright blood spurt out the wound.

"You hit a gusher!" the scrub nurse gasped, holding a basin to catch the large dark clots Parker scooped out with his hands.

As he peeled away layers of plastered bowel loops, gaping holes appeared in segments of small intestine through which the bullets had passed. Blood surged from torn vessels in rhythm with Shawn's pulse.

Murray Leader charged into the room in greens, fully scrubbed with water dripping from his arms. "What did you find?"

"Thanks for coming, Murray. The bullets nailed the jejunum and must have passed out his back. I see no metal fragments on the X-ray. It's a wonder the shots missed the colon and pancreas."

Leader took his place at the table and together they clamped, tied bleeding vessels and resected torn segments of bowel. After they washed the abdomen with saline to remove blood and organized clots, Parker sutured the abdominal wall layers and closed the skin with staples.

Pleased with the outcome of the surgery, Parker couldn't wait to tell Judy the good news.

~ * ~

Judy sat waiting at the OR nurse's station, agonizing over the outcome of the surgery and Shawn's irresponsibility. She fumed over how her brother allowed himself to get involved in a shooting. They hadn't shared much lately since he never answered her calls. But as his big sister, she still felt responsible for him.

The outer door swung open and Wendy, the ICU supervisor, rushed in. "I just heard about your brother. What happened?"

Tears clouded Judy's eyes. "I don't know," she answered. "He was such a good kid growing up. Things changed after we were sent to boarding school."

"You mean you lived away from home?"

Judy nodded. "Both of us. Shawn was ten and I was thirteen."

"Sounds rough, leaving home at such a young age."

"It was. I can still hear Shawn begging Mom and Dad he didn't want to go."

"And how did you feel about it?

She paused, looking into space. "Our parents had problems and couldn't take care of us. Dad left for work every morning, but gradually returned home earlier and earlier. And Mom ..." She paused again. "She lost all her

95

sparkle. That's what alcohol does to you."

"I understand," Wendy answered with a sympathetic look.

Judy stopped talking, recalling the rank odor of whiskey and cigarettes greeting her each morning when she opened her bedroom door. Tears wet her face as she looked back at Wendy.

"Watching my mother struggle to make breakfast was painful. It was easier for me to do it so I took care of Shawn as well as myself."

Their conversation was interrupted when Parker walked through the doors in his scrubs. "They're moving Shawn into Intensive Care, but he'll need a ventilator."

Wendy gave Judy a hug. "Things will work out. I'll see you later," she answered, moving briskly in the direction of ICU.

"How's Shawn?" Judy asked.

"He's lucky," Parker answered. "The surgery went well. The bullets missed the pancreas and great vessels."

"That's wonderful news. What about the drug screen?"

"I didn't run one."

Her eyes lit up. "I can't thank you enough, Parker. Shawn's had some tough times lately, but I never expected this."

He still wanted to know why she called him, but when the outer door opened and Kent Markman appeared, that thought vanished. He noticed Judy stiffen as Kent awkwardly turned his gaze away from her.

Kent asked, "Hey, Parker, could you see a hot belly for me?"

"I'd like to, Kent, but I'm not on your HMO plan."

"Damn, I forgot, but it's about time you joined. You'll be swamped with referrals. No problem. I'll call Morty Gold," he replied and disappeared.

Parker approached Judy, whose eyes remained fixed on the closed swinging doors. He leaned close, fighting the urge to hold her. "Give me a smile, Judy. Shawn's going to be fine."

He caught her look of despair when she turned to face him. "Is something else bothering you?" he asked softly.

She shook her head.

"I know you better than that, Judy. Shawn's not the only reason you look so upset"

"It's nothing, Parker, just the shock of all this excitement. I'll be all right."

"Then, let's go see your brother in ICU." As they walked through the swinging doors, he placed an arm over her shoulder, pleased she didn't object.

On the drive home, he whistled along with the radio music, elated with Shawn's surgery and his new closeness to Judy. Bright lights suddenly flashed behind him, blinding his eyes when he looked into the rearview mirror. A car tailgated as his cell phone rang.

"*Doctore*, this is Ottavio's friend, keep driving. I want you to take us to the money."

Parker felt his heart pound and tightened his grip on the wheel. "I can't do that," he shouted into the phone. "I never took your money. Leave me alone."

"Okay, *Doctore*," the man answered in a cynical tone.

Parker's side view mirror shattered as the sound of a gunshot rang in his ears. He dropped the phone and raced the car to I-95. Time was running out, and where the hell was Agent Rucker?

Sixteen

MCA Hospital, 10 PM, same night

Morty Gold rushed out of the OR and into the doctors' lounge as the closing credits of the 10 o'clock news vanished from the TV screen. He frowned, realizing the late hour. Markman's case had taken longer than expected.

Grabbing his cell, he dialed his apartment. After the fourth ring, he heard her sultry voice.

"Yesss?"

"I know it's late, doll, but it couldn't be helped. I had a surgical emergency that turned into a disaster." Hearing no response, he groaned, "I couldn't help it."

"Then why didn't you call me?"

"I thought it would be a short case, but after I got into it, I lost all track of time. I'm changing now."

"Well, don't rush for me."

"Come on, baby, don't be angry. I know how much we counted on tonight, but this was an emergency."

"Doctors always have their excuses, don't they?"

Gold winced. "Please, honey, I'm sorry. I'm leaving now."

"Take your time. Dinner's cold anyway."

He knew he had to beg. "I promise this won't happen again."

"You'll call next time?"

"I will."

She let out a deep sigh. "I checked your answering machine to see if you left me a message. You didn't, but your wife did."

"Dammit, Bea, I don't talk to her. Anything she has to say, she can tell my lawyer."

"It's about your girls."

"What did she say?"

"Something about the orthodontist's bill. She wants you to call her back."

Gold gritted his teeth. "Screw her!" he shouted. "She's always calling for money. Let her bitch to my lawyer. If I get more custody time, I'll think about the money she wants." He shut the phone so hard it flipped onto the floor.

Quickly dressing, he relished the fact that Bea Stern was twenty-five years younger than her husband, Arthur, whose obsession for mergers and acquisitions was wrecking their marriage. The fact their interests were as wide apart as their ages gave him his opportunity.

The affair had begun when he sat next to Bea at a dinner party.

"It's not the men in my life that count, it's the life in my men that count," She joked, quoting Mae West. Leaning over to Gold, she added in a whisper, "I need a lover in bed, not a capitalist."

That gave him his chance. Whether it was Arthur's growing impotence or the drain of energy from business, it made no difference. Since he was in a divorce and

Arthur Stern was always away, what a better fit?

He pulled the gold Rolex over his wrist, slipped into his Gucci loafers and raced to the Mercedes in the parking lot. There was never a question of Bea having children. She couldn't and with his divorce underway, he didn't need a second family.

As he drove, he savored the gift of having Bea. The vision of her that first night in his apartment titillated him. When she appeared at the bedroom door, dropping the transparent plastic raincoat to her feet, it short circuited his brain. There she stood, all 5'4" of her in bare buff. With a narrow waist, shapely legs, a butt that curved gently and mesmerizing breasts, he questioned how Arthur Stern could waste all that for a business deal.

Recalling the smell of her white perfumed skin, sleek black hair falling to her shoulders as she crawled naked across the king-sized bed made his pants feel tight. He gunned the Mercedes faster. The vision of those bountiful breasts swaying with firm pointed nipples was embedded in his brain. Could things get any better, he thought?

A glance at his thickened waist made him decide weight didn't matter. She made him feel virile, something his wife never did. At this stage in Bea's unfulfilled life, he knew she just wanted good sex and he intended to be the guy to do the job. While he couldn't compete with Arthur Stern's income, hustling for surgical referrals would certainly improve his cash flow to keep her happy.

Feeling the growing hardness in his crotch, he sped through a red light. No matter what troubles he faced, he grinned knowing Bea would make the sexual part of his life more satisfying tonight.

Seventeen

MCA Hospital, the following morning

Brief showers gave way to a bright Florida sun that glistened on MCA's moisture-laddened walls. Parker could hear the energetic chirps of birds as he walked toward the ER entrance, his favorite portal of entry. After a sound night's sleep, he was eager to check on Shawn, so breakfast had to wait. Once inside the Intensive Care Unit, .he could smell the odor of aerosol deodorants failed to mask.

The desk secretary looked up from her notes. "Good morning, Dr. Dawson. Nurse Andrews has been waiting to see you. She's busy turning a patient right now."

Groans emanating from the cubicle adjacent to Shawn's room drew Parker's attention as he viewed the scene through glass partitions. Nurse Andrews and a male nurse struggled to turn a morbidly obese man over in bed. Any attempt to maintain the patient's modesty appeared futile.

Parker entered Shawn's room to find him in a drug-induced sleep. The peaceful scene was broken when Nurse Andrews rushed in.

She spoke in a whisper. "Mr. Keller has no motion in his legs."

"That can't be!" Parker replied. "I saw no spinal injury."

"I know, but check for yourself."

Parker drew back the sheet but, despite the movement, Shawn's eyes remained shut. He pricked both feet with a sharp needle and saw no response. Perplexed, he lifted each of Shawn's legs, only to watch them drop like lead weights. There was no doubt, Shawn was paralyzed.

He turned to Andrews. "Does his sister know about this?"

"No, we thought it best to wait until you came in," she replied.

Judy appeared in the doorway, witnessing the scene. "Is something wrong?"

Parker didn't respond. Instead he guided her outside the room and hesitated, not knowing how to tell her.

"Parker, how's Shawn?"

His eyes met hers. "Shawn has no feeling in his legs. He's paralyzed."

"How can that be? You told me the bullets missed the vital organs."

"I can't explain it. Hopefully it might be temporary. Right now we need a neuro consult and a CT scan to explain what happened."

"Why didn't you do the scan last night?"

"Last night he needed emergency surgery to save his life. A diagnostic CT would have been pointless."

Judy turned and rushed back into Shawn's room.

Through the glass partition, Parker could see her point

to Shawn's legs as Nurse Andrews stood by nodding her head. She left the cubicle and returned to Parker. "Why wasn't I told sooner? They know I'm his sister."

Parker placed a comforting arm over her shoulder and led her outside the ICU doors. What could he say? If he couldn't explain it to himself, how could he explain it to her?

He looked into her tear-swollen eyes and held her. "Judy, I need to figure out what happened, but in the meantime, you've got to stay positive for him."

He saw a flood of tears quench the fire in her eyes and embraced her.

Carolyn Robertson and Tessie Cashman suddenly approached, coming to an abrupt stop when they witnessed the scene.

Parker nodded awkwardly as Judy pulled away, giving them a weak smile.

After the two were out of sight, Judy whispered, "Sorry, Parker. I wasn't very professional."

"Don't apologize, just ignore them."

"I'll try, but I hope they will." She straightened up, wiping her eyes with a tissue. "Let me know what the CT scan shows."

He felt an overwhelming frustration as he watched her walk away. Getting a bad outcome after a good operation was a surgeon's nightmare. A painful reminder that surgery was a humbling profession. A successful surgical procedure didn't always guarantee a successful outcome.

Eighteen

The Markman home

It was nearly 11:30 PM when Kent reached home. He had purposely delayed his return, hoping Sheila would be asleep. After parking his BMW in their four car garage, he headed to the master bedroom.

Sheila lay nestled between satin sheets and when he approached, she rolled over to face him. "Kent, you're home. I just turned in."

"Sorry I'm so late. I got held up. Anything special with the kids?"

"The usual," she sighed. "They won their soccer playoff so both teams went out to eat. I didn't plan for dinner anyway."

"That's good," he answered.

"Good? I hope there's more to it than that. Aren't you proud of them? Why don't you show some excitement when I tell you these things?"

He caught the sarcasm in her voice. "Just what do you want me to say, Sheila?"

She sat up in bed and turned on the lamp. "I hoped you'd ask if the boys scored any goals, what the score was, anything that showed some interest."

Kent saw the fire in her eyes and let out a deep breath. "You're right, Sheila, but I'm just tired." He turned away and began to undress.

"Of course I'm right. You're always away; you never spend time at home. The boys hardly see you except at breakfast. What kind of a father are you?"

Kent braced himself. He was in no mood to answer at this late hour. His arms swept, pointing around the room. "Look Sheila, I have to work hard to pay for all this. That means I'm always on the go. If you think private school tuition is cheap, think again. It costs as much as college and they're not even there yet. Every time you accept a new committee assignment for another charity, it costs me. I have to sign those checks to support you in your social set so don't give me a guilt trip for not being a soccer dad."

Sheila raised both hands. "I didn't mean it that way. I know you're busy but it's something that had to be said."

He glared back. "Why do you do this to me, Sheila?"

"Because you're never around to share with us. I stayed up late hoping we could spend some time together."

He didn't feel like answering and continued removing his clothes. Sheila kept talking but he didn't listen as he made his way into the bathroom. He was glad she kept speaking because it avoided that deadly silence that develops when husband and wife can't communicate.

Hearing no response, she called out, "Don't back away from me, Kent." When he returned, she stood by the bed inviting him with both hands. She dropped a loose strap from her shoulder to display a good portion of one breast.

Moving to his side, she grasped his hand to cradle it onto her breast while searching for his genitals. She then led him to the bed, pulled him down and positioned herself on her back.

He was reluctant to disengage himself. At all costs, he didn't want to antagonize her. Any hint of an oncoming divorce would be costly and hurt him in court. *Oh what the hell*, he thought, *I'll just get on with it.*

Sheila removed her nightgown, exposing her shapely figure and generous breasts. Her breathing was heavy as Kent caressed her, and she yielded willingly as he penetrated her.

Although he climaxed quickly, she hadn't and continued to encourage him. Despite her failure to achieve orgasm, she held him tight, acting satisfied they had shared an intimacy after many months.

He kissed her cheek and whispered, "I've got a long day tomorrow, honey, and I need to get some sleep."

"I understand," she answered in a low voice as she rolled away from him.

His sleep was sound that night, although his thoughts were far removed from Sheila.

Nineteen

Days later, MCA Hospital

Judy joked lightheartedly with the nursing staff as she walked down the hall making evening rounds. She basked in the warm afterglow of Kent's passionate love-making the night before, more encouraged about their future together. A smile crossed her face as she lingered outside the ICU, recalling how he stuck his foot in the door and refused to leave her apartment. She had pushed him out with a laugh, knowing it was late and Sheila would be waiting.

On entering the Intensive Care Unit, she scanned the cubicles through the glass partitions. There were no empty beds for new emergencies and experience told her at least one would be needed before dawn arrived.

"Is there a chance a room will free up tonight?" she asked the charge nurse.

"Bed Three's a good bet," the nurse answered. "He stroked after a heart attack."

Judy glanced at the enclosure where a thin elderly woman sat at the bedside of a frail, pasty faced man connected to a respirator. Hanging bottles of dripping IV solutions surrounded him.

The woman gently caressed his forehead with her wrinkled hand, smoothing away the few wisps of gray hair on a bald head. She kept speaking to him in whispers, but his only response was the movement of his chest with each surge of oxygen delivered by the machine.

"May I get you some juice or coffee?" Judy asked on entering the room.

The woman smiled, her eyes lighting up through a veil of tears. "I'm fine, thank you. This is my quiet time with him."

"Just call if you need something," Judy answered as she moved slowly to exit the room.

The charge nurse at the control desk showed Judy the man's graphic chart, pointing to the blood pressure and arterial blood gas results. "Doesn't look good. His wife's been alone with him all day. It's sad because they have no children."

The woman's heroic vigil preparing to lose her only family stirred Judy's fears of being alone. She had just witnessed a love that lasted a lifetime and asked herself if she would be lucky enough to share that with Kent.

But tonight she didn't want to be burdened searching for an answer. Everything with Kent was positive so she turned her attention to reviewing another chart. The overhead page rang out her name and she reached for the phone.

"It's Kent, Judy. I gotta see you."

"You sound upset, what's wrong?"

"Where can we meet?"

"The cafeteria?"

"No, somewhere where we can't be seen together."

"What about my apartment?"

"Not tonight. How about my Escalade? I just picked it up from the dealer this morning. It's parked in the doctors' lot outside the ER."

"I can't leave the hospital, Kent. I'm on duty."

"Why? You're still on hospital grounds and carry a pager. Give me ten minutes."

He sounded threatened and she needed to learn why. She paused before answering. "All right, just ten minutes."

She quickened her pace as she entered the ER with fear blocking all reason.

Tessie sat alone at the ER central desk reading a magazine and forced a smile when Judy arrived.

"Everything okay?" Judy asked.

"Been quiet," Tessie answered.

"I need to get to my car, Tess. If I get paged, could you beep me?"

Tessie ran her hand lazily through her long hair and gave a slight nod before turning back to the magazine.

Judy exited the sliding glass doors of the brightly lit ER and walked into the darkness. At 8 PM, the doctors' lot was empty except for the white SUV. Before approaching the massive vehicle, she searched to make certain she wasn't observed. As she neared, the door swung open and Kent appeared.

"Good timing," he said, extending his hand and pulling her in.

"What's up, Kent?"

"It's Sheila, I think she's having me followed."

She read the panic in his eyes. "How can you tell?"

"I found a detective's business card on her nightstand. She probably got suspicious after that weekend on the *Lazy Lady.*"

"Kent, when are you going to tell her about us? If she's having you followed, isn't it time?"

He pulled her close, wrapping his arms around her. "Any day now, honey. My lawyer is still working on my financial affairs. Until then, we can't be seen together. If Sheila or anyone confronts you, deny it."

"You mean Sheila might come after me?" she questioned, raising fingers to her lips.

"I don't know, but anything's possible with her. No matter what, deny everything."

Judy sat stunned as tears filled her eyes.

He drew her close, kissing her gently to calm her fears. "Everything will be all right," he whispered.

She welcomed his words, though they brought little comfort. Was he getting cold feet, planning to back off from the relationship? It was clear, he was worried about Sheila.

She tried to pull away from him but his hold was strong.

"Don't ever doubt me, Judy," he said as his hands moved across her chest. He leaned her back on the bench, opening the top buttons of her uniform.

She felt the warmth of his hand slip under her bra. Her nipples tingled as he caressed them gently, but she knew she had to stop his advance before her defenses crumbled. A piercing sound of her pager interrupted their moment of privacy.

She pulled away, raising herself to grab her beeper. "I'm being paged, I have to go," she gasped. Scrambling out of the SUV, she turned to leave.

"Wait!" he shouted. "Button up!"

She glanced down and hastily buttoned her uniform before dashing into the bright lights to vanish behind the sliding glass doors.

Inside the building, a security guard sat facing a bank of video screens while another guard concentrated on eating a Hero sandwich.

"Hey, Joe!" the screener called out. "Take a look at this!"

Twenty

Leaving the glare of supermarket lights, Parker rolled the shopping basket filled with his weekly purchase of groceries into the parking lot.

Marie Callendar frozen dinners were the main evening staple since his other meals were eaten at the hospital. He moved the cart in the darkness between rows of parked vehicles. A short distance behind, the assigned police protection followed, giving him a sense of security.

As he stood before the trunk fumbling for his keys, he heard a sudden screech of tires. Blinding light beams followed with hands grabbing his shoulders and dragging him into a car. The door slammed shut and as the car raced away, he felt the cold barrel of a gun against his head. When he tried to get up, the sole of a shoe forcefully pressed on his back.

"Don't move," the raspy voice commanded.

Terrified by the loss of police protection, he knew they were out to kill him.

"Please don't hurt me. I'll take you to the money," he shouted, hoping this lure would give him more time.

He waited as a flurry of unintelligible Spanish ensued between the driver and the gravelly voiced kidnapper. Turning his head, he called out, "It's in a storage locker. Head for Forty-fifth Street and go west."

That caused another heated exchange between the two men.

At every turn, the hump of the drive shaft pounded his ribs. He tried raising himself again only to be forced down by a heavy boot.

"Let me get up so I can show you where to go," Parker said. A jab of the gun against his head was his answer.

When the sharp turns ended and the car moved at a steady speed, Parker guessed they had lost the police.

"*Doctore*, where to go on Forty-fifth Street?" the man holding the gun commanded.

"Drive north on Haverhill, you'll find a storage locker on the right."

The driver spoke rapidly in an agitated voice. The man with the gun responded in a flurry of Spanish that ended with "*Silencio*," which halted the exchange.

Moments later Parker felt the car make a turn and the driver shouted, "You lie! We see no locker."

"*Shit! I'm a dead man,*" Parker thought.

Suddenly sirens screamed and bright lights flashed. His body lurched forward as the car came to halt with the sound of shattered glass and crushed metal filling the air. Running feet could be heard with cries of "Stop or I'll shoot."

The man holding the gun was gone and a sheriff's deputy leaning over him asked, "Are you all right, Doc?"

"I think so but that was close," Parker answered as he

struggled to climb out of the car.

Surrounded by uniformed officers and the crackling sounds of two-way radios, he glared at the deputy. "Where the hell were you guys? They were going to kill me."

Agent Rucker approached holding a walkie-talkie to his ear. "Keep after them even if it takes all night," he bellowed.

Parker leaned against the bent fender sensing the rapid pounding of his heart. The drug traffickers' car had rammed into the side of the sheriff's vehicle which stopped them.

Rucker walked up to Parker with a smile. "We set up a road block, and you did the right thing getting them to where we agreed."

"Look, Rucker, those guys were going to kill me, GPS or not. The only reason they didn't was I promised to lead them to the money. I'm a marked man with no way out and it's the second time you guys dropped the ball."

"We did our best to keep you in sight, but they set up a trap to block your protection in the parking lot."

"Well there may not be a next time."

"We'll double the protection."

"Not good enough, Rucker. I nearly took the count."

"Easy, Doc. I know you're shook up, but these guys ain't gonna sleep. There's a turf war going on between the two narco gangs and you just happen to be an incidental problem."

"My life is just an incidental problem?"

"Not to us, but it is to them. That's why we have to cover you like a blanket from now on."

"From the way they set me up tonight, a lot of good that'll do. When this hits the papers, everybody will know my name."

"That won't happen because this is an ongoing investigation."

Parker shook his head. "Is this ever going to end?"

"It will once we get these guys behind bars or bury them in a box."

"Very reassuring, aren't you?"

"Look, you're tired, Doc. Two detectives will be tailing you from now on. Let's get you back to your car."

After the police escort dropped him off, the shopping cart loaded with his groceries was nowhere to be seen. He figured that was just another benefit of being used as bait.

~ * ~

Exhausted after a sleepless night, Parker paused to put on a bright smile before opening the door to his office. The paper made no mention of the attempted kidnapping, but he had to warn Gwen about the narco traffickers and the possible risks she might face.

He caught her troubled look as soon as he entered.

She held out a letter toward him. "It's a certified letter from MCA."

"More good news?" he quipped, quickly tearing it open. He didn't need another surprise after last night's close call.

"What does it say?" she asked.

"Hold on," he answered, his eyes widening as he read. With a stunned look, he replied, "I don't believe this!"

"What are you talking about?"

He stared back. "MCA is filing disciplinary charges

against me with the state."

"Why?"

"I'm being accused of abandoning a patient in the ER. It's about Stanley Kingsley, the guy who ran his bicycle into a truck."

"I remember that case. You weren't on call when he came in."

"That's not the point. They're saying I should have responded when ER called. I'll have to appear before Executive Committee to defend myself."

"What about Kern and Patel? You told me they were the ones on call and never showed."

"That's what I have to explain at the meeting."

Gwen shook her head. "Does Dr. Lawton know about this? He's chief of the surgical department."

"I have no idea," Parker answered, reading the unmistakable look of distrust in her eyes. "Don't worry. Once I present the facts, it'll all work out."

Gwen wrinkled her nose. "It makes no sense. Something about this smells."

Parker took in a deep breath. "Before you get carried away, there's something else you should know."

Gwen's eyes narrowed.

"Remember the Ottavio case? The Jehovah's Witness who died in the OR?"

"I sure do," she smirked. "We never got paid because she had no insurance."

"I've since learned she was a courier delivering drug money to a stash-houses."

Gwen's jaw dropped.

"Members of the gang have been chasing me. They

think I stole the millions she was delivering to the storage locker."

"Why would they think that?" she gasped.

"Ottavio gave me a key which I presume was to a locker holding the money. She said to give it to her daughter if she didn't survive the surgery."

"What did you do with it?"

"I can't find it. Last night, two hoods ambushed and dragged me into their car. I know they were out to kill me. If it hadn't been for Agent Rucker and the sheriff's department, I'd be a goner."

He paused, studying the horrified look in her eyes. "They got away but I'm sure they'll try again."

"You mean they tried to kill you?"

Parker nodded. "And I worry about those close to me."

Gwen slumped in her chair, her eyes fixed on Parker.

"Sorry I got you into this, Gwen. You should meet the DEA agent. His name is Rucker. He'll advise how to protect you and your family."

Gwen sat speechless, absorbing the dangerous conclusion to his warning. Suddenly she exploded. "Why should my family live in fear? We've done nothing wrong. We don't have their money. I like working for you, Dr. Dawson, but not at the risk of losing my life."

Her outburst didn't surprise him. He had exposed his innocent assistant to an international crime world that knew no boundaries when it came to murder. She faced the choice of risking her life over testing her loyalty to him.

"Agent Rucker assigned two detectives to shadow me," he said. "I'm sure he'll do the same to protect you."

Gwen rose from her chair. "I've got to think about this. I won't quit on you right now, Dr. Dawson. Maybe I'll feel safer after I meet with the agent."

Parker released a deep sigh and stuffed the letter into his pocket. "Thanks, Gwen. You don't know how much this means to me."

He headed to his office, leaving a confused Gwen to cope with her fears. "This can't wait," he grumbled, tossing the letter onto his desk. He had to confront Lindstrom about the charges.

~ * ~

With lips pursed, Carolyn Robertson looked up from her desk as Parker entered. "Mr. Lindstrom's very busy, Dr. Dawson. If you want to see him, you'll have to make an appointment."

Parker ignored her answer and flew past the desk, determined to press his complaint. He pushed open the door while Robertson rushed from behind to face a startled Lindstrom.

"Sorry, he just forced himself in," Robertson burst out.

Parker waved the letter in the administrator's face. "You damned well better explain what this is all about."

Lindstrom calmly leaned back in his chair. "That's quite all right, Miss Robertson. I'll talk to the doctor."

After Robertson left, Lindstrom faced Parker. "How can I help you, Dr. Dawson?"

Parker's voice rose. "Why was I charged with patient abandonment?"

"Because you neglected to respond to your ER call and failed to fulfill your ethical and moral responsibility as a staff physician."

"That's a lie! Kern and Patel were on call when Kingsley came in. They're the ones who should be charged."

"Sorry, Doctor. When the ER calls, you have to respond. It's my job to preserve the hospital's integrity and responsibility to this community."

Parker leaned over the desk and locked eyes with Lindstrom. "That's bullshit! These charges are all trumped up."

"Then let's see what the state decides. It appears serious enough to warrant an investigation. Don't you agree?"

Parker felt the heat rush to his face. "Not when the statements presented are false."

"Please don't make a scene, Doctor. Since this is a medical issue, I can't help you."

"Don't talk to me out of both sides of your mouth. The controversial laser procedure is a medical issue as well, and you're right in the middle of promoting that project."

Lindstrom leaned back and clasped both hands behind his head. "I trust this visit is over. You don't perform that surgery so any discussion about that subject is off limits."

Parker knew there was no way he could convince the administrator otherwise. It was clear the hospital was out to intentionally hurt him and he hoped the state would be more impartial. But how confident could he feel about that?

A knock on the door broke the tension between the two. Trask rushed into the room with a cell phone and handed it to Lindstrom. "It's urgent and he needs to talk to you."

As Lindstrom spoke into the unit, his expression hardened. "Yes ... no. The second airport sounds right. No, not Vero. Good-bye." He calmly returned the phone to Trask and with a firm look in his eyes, he said, "This time it's Wellington."

Without saying a word, Trask turned and rushed out of the office.

Parker remained seated, watching the interaction between the two men and before he could speak, Lindstrom stood up.

"Sorry I can't help you, Doctor. Is there anything else?"

Too angry to respond, Parker rose and walked out, slamming the door behind him. After this meeting, he knew he had the fight of his life on his hands.

Twenty-one

Parker waited anxiously for the chief of surgery to come on the phone. When he heard Lawton's voice, he couldn't contain himself.

"Tell me, Karl, how in the hell does a hospital administrator have the balls to file complaints against a physician? Lindstrom filed medical misconduct charges against me with the state."

"Hold on, Parker. What are you talking about?"

"I just received a letter from Lindstrom. Let me read it to you."

After Parker finished, Lawton replied, "I was never consulted about these charges."

"Look, Karl, I'm asking for your help."

Lawton paused. "I'll be at that meeting, Parker, but..."

"No buts, Karl. You have to defend my position to the other committee members."

"That could be politically sticky, Parker. People take sides and I don't want to ruffle any feathers."

Parker could feel his stomach turn. Karl seemed to be his only friend and should understand how unfair the charges were. A brief moment passed before he spoke into the phone. "At least you could explain that I wasn't on call when that patient came in."

"I'll review that detail," Lawton answered in a flat voice.

Lawton's reticence led him to believe the chief wasn't prepared to stand behind him.

"Then tell them the by-laws make no mention of the time ER call begins or ends."

"I didn't know that. Are you sure?"

"Yes, I checked it before I called you! I'd appreciate any help you can give me."

"I'll see what I can do," Lawton answered with slightly more conviction. "But I recommend you get an attorney. I've seen too many of these cases fall into the hands of the state and get out of control."

"Out of control? How do you mean?"

"The state investigators usually are retired detectives and policemen. People dealing with law enforcement have the habit of looking at everything as though you're a criminal. In their eyes, you're guilty until proven innocent. Look, Parker, you need someone who's medically astute, who knows the laws well enough to protect you. That's if you did nothing wrong."

"You're scaring me, Karl. You know I'm innocent. Who should I call?"

"There's a lawyer in Tampa by the name of David Fellini. It'll cost you, but I think it would be a wise investment."

Parker recorded Fellini's number, hung up the phone and sat immobilized at his desk. His fists tightened, ready to strike out, but who was his target? Medical politics had to be driving these charges. Gwen was right. Something did smell fishy. He dialed Fellini's number.

~ * ~

He could feel the moisture beading on his brow as he waited for Fellini to come on the line. What was he getting into by hiring a lawyer? But maybe Lawton was right. He needed legal protection.

"Fellini here," came the abrupt greeting.

Parker cleared his throat and decided to be direct and efficient in explaining his predicament.

"My name is Parker Dawson, Mr. Fellini. My hospital filed disciplinary charges against me with the state which are totally false. I think I may need your help."

"Who referred you to me?"

"Dr. Karl Lawton. He's chief of surgery at the hospital where I work, Medical Center of America in West Palm Beach."

"I see," Fellini answered. "And what's the basis for the charges?"

"I'll read the letter I received from Mr. Lindstrom, our hospital administrator. It's addressed to the Florida Agency for Health Care Administration in Tallahassee with a copy to me."

"Fine."

Parker cleared his throat and picked up the letter lying on his desk. He began to read.

'As per Article VI, Section I of the Medical Staff Bylaws, I am requesting disciplinary action be taken against Dr. Parker Dawson for two reasons.

First: Dereliction of Responsibility. On August 8, 2011, patient S.K. medical record #826196 was brought to the

Emergency Room of MCA Hospital, West Palm Beach, at approximately 7 AM. Dr. Dawson was on ER call and he refused to see the patient, stating his call did not begin until 8 AM. It is alleged Dr. Dawson left the hospital understanding a seriously injured patient was lying in the emergency room in desperate need of his skills.

Second: Unethical Conduct. Dr. Dawson's professional conduct does not meet the standards and aims of the professional staff. His actions were disruptive to the operation of the hospital and reflect unfavorably upon the reputation of the professional staff in the community. A copy of this request is being sent to Dr. Dawson notifying him of this action.' Sincerely, Eric Lindstrom, Hospital Administrator.'

After finishing, Parker waited for Fellini's response.

"And what's your position against these charges, Dr. Dawson?"

"The charges are without fact. The truth is the patient arrived to the ER before six AM and I wasn't on call at that hour."

"Have these charges been reviewed by your surgical department or the Executive Committee?"

"Not that I know, Mr. Fellini." There was a long pause until he heard Fellini's voice again.

"I'll need copies of the patient's emergency room record, your report on the ER sheet and a copy of the Medical Staff Bylaws. Can you provide me with these items?

"Yes I can, but..."

"You have another question, Dr. Dawson?"

"I'd like to ask what your charges will be."

"To start off, I'll need a six thousand dollar retainer fee to study the case so I can prepare a defense against the state."

"Should I expect any additional charges?"

"Probably. If I need to plead your case before the Probable Cause Panel, my hourly charge will be four hundred dollars. That includes the travel time I spend away from my office as well as the time needed to appear before the panel. It doesn't include office copying and mailing expenses, of course."

Parker could feel his heart sink. The $6,000 retainer was a gigantic burden for his budding practice. But the thought of additional payments for countless hours at $400 a shot scared the hell out of him. "I need to think this over, Mr. Fellini. I'm just starting out and I don't know if I can afford you."

"I understand, Dr. Dawson. But if the state should act unfairly against you, it might jeopardize your whole career. That's a risk you might not be able to afford."

"I hear you, Mr. Fellini, but I need time to figure this out. I'm really confused because I know I did nothing wrong that I have to defend."

"It's your choice, Doctor. If you decide to have me represent you, I'll be available."

"Thank you, Mr. Fellini. Good bye." Parker's emotions plummeted as he hung up the phone and thought, *No way can I afford that lawyer. I guess it's a risk I'll have to take.*

~ * ~

It was two days later when Karl Lawton stopped Parker in the hall. "Did you call the attorney I recommended?"

Parker hesitated. "Yes, but I'm not hiring him."

"Don't you realize how dangerous a state investigation can be, Parker?"

"But I did nothing wrong, Karl. Why should I have to pay a lawyer to defend me from some lousy trumped-up charge?"

"So it comes down to money."

"You're right. Fellini wants six thousand as a retainer just to start, and if he needs to prepare more material to attend hearings, it'll cost another bundle of money."

Lawton shook his head. "You have no choice, Parker. You're in this sinkhole and you have to get proactive. Go to your computer and Google the website for The Florida Agency for Health Care Administration. Look up and check where the Probable Cause Panel will hold its hearings."

"Why?"

"So you can see for yourself how they run these hearings."

"How is that going to help me?"

"It might convince you that you can't deal with the state without having a sharp attorney at your side."

Lawton's pitch truly scared him. He walked away even more anxious and confused than ever. A paralyzing panic suddenly gripped him and he stopped for a moment to ponder Karl's words. The only way he could fight this immobilizing fear, he concluded, was to figure out how to pay Fellini.

Twenty-two

One week later

Parker raced his car heading to Florida's west coast on Alligator Alley. Taking Lawton's advice, he checked when and where the Probable Cause Panel would meet. Although Naples was over two hours away, it was the most convenient location.

Gwen cleared the day's schedule, but a call from a postop patient who presented at the ER complaining of belly pain held him up. After he examined her, it took an enema and a laxative to correct her intractable constipation.

Parker arrived at the Five Star Registry Resort Hotel in Naples by 11 AM. As he dashed up the walkway, a uniformed attendant held open the massive door leading into the lobby. A quick glance at the day's events on the bulletin board directed him to the large partitioned section of the main ballroom.

He checked his watch and entered, aware that the meeting had been in session for over an hour. Five people seated at a long table in front of the room faced the audience. He assumed they were members of the Probable

Cause Panel but could barely read the names and titles on place cards before them. According to the website he studied, the five member committee was composed of three doctors from the Board of Medicine and two lay people to represent the public.

Parker took a seat next to a man in a pinstriped suit with an attaché case on his lap who sat completely absorbed in the proceedings.

When he turned and smiled, Parker asked, "Who are those people sitting at the two tables facing the panel?"

The man replied in a hushed voice, "The bald older guy on the left is the plaintiff who filed the complaint with the state. The man seated next to him is the state attorney."

Parker looked to the table on the other side where a heavy set man with a head of thick black hair sat with an open-collared shirt sporting tropical flowers. "I guess that's the doctor who's been charged," he said, pointing to the table on the right.

The man nodded. "Yep, and that's his attorney sitting next to him. They're just starting now. "

Parker watched the elderly bald man on the left wipe his brow nervously as he peered at the faces before him. The dark-suited state attorney beside him shuffled papers and appeared unperturbed.

When the chairman seated at the center of the long table lowered his glasses and rapped his gavel, Parker settled back in his chair, curious to listen to the proceeding.

"Let the record show we are prepared to hear the next case on the docket," the chairman announced, looking to the bald man seated on the left. "Mr. Kulas, since you filed the complaint against Dr. Paloma, you may address the committee regarding the proposed penalty. Please proceed."

Parker watched the old man suddenly straighten up in his chair, assuming a dignified air. The rustling of papers stopped as everyone in the room waited.

The man's resonating voice rang out. "I am the aggrieved father of a beautiful daughter who died due to Dr. Paloma's medical incompetence. Because of his negligence, my child, his long-standing patient with a known history of mitral valve prolapse, died because he ignored her symptoms. Twice she visited the doctor complaining of chest pain. All he did was to prescribe antacids and tranquilizers."

He paused, searching the eyes of the panel. "The next morning she called to say her chest pain had increased. After three long hours, a nurse finally called back to schedule a late afternoon appointment."

Parker listened in disbelief, glancing at the equally pained expressions on faces around him. In contrast, he thought the committee members sitting in front of him showed no outward signs of empathy.

Kulas' voice cracked and he stopped a moment to clear his throat before continuing. "My girl sat in the doctor's waiting room for two hours until she was seen. Even though her EKG showed evidence of a heart attack, the doctor diagnosed her as having esophageal spasm."

He stopped to wipe his brow with a handkerchief, and then continued. "My daughter was frantic and called me in hysterics, saying she wasn't receiving the correct treatment. I rushed over to the doctor's office and asked him to refer her to a cardiologist, but he refused. He said her EKG was normal and there was no need for a consultation."

Parker could not believe his ears. His heart went out to this father who spoke with such emotional eloquence. Suddenly, he saw Mr. Kulas jump up from his chair as if he no longer could stand the pain of telling the sad details of his story. The state attorney next to him quickly grabbed his arm, forcing him to sit again.

After the emotional outburst, Kulas appeared weary, his hoarse voice breaking the stillness in the room. "The next morning I called the clinic but Dr. Paloma was not on duty. Dr.Gomez was. I told him of my daughter's increasing chest pain but was informed by Dr. Gomez that he had no access to her records. He recommended she take another tranquilizer. One hour later, my only child collapsed and died from a massive heart attack."

Parker's face flushed with anger. This clearly was a case of medical incompetence. Again, he turned to the man beside him. "They should take that doctor's license away. His actions were reprehensible."

"Shush, settle down," his neighbor replied, causing Parker to sit sheepishly in his chair.

In spite of his tragic desperation, Kulas resumed a dignified posture and faced the committee members. His voice boomed across the room. "My complaint was filed over two years ago and to this day, Dr. Paloma still continues to practice. Due to his negligence, my beautiful thirty-eight-year-old daughter is dead. Therefore, I object to any agreement that allows Dr. Paloma to practice medicine. His license should be revoked."

The room remained quiet for a few minutes after Kulas finished. Parker could hear none of the usual chatter or shuffle of papers and felt certain the old man had made his point. For sure Paloma was in big trouble.

The bespectacled chairman was the first to break the silence and looked to the state attorney sitting next to Kulas. "What is the negotiated consent agreement?"

The attorney rose. "A one thousand dollar administrative fine and thirty hours of continuing medical education in cardiology."

"That's bullshit," Parker mumbled under his breath. He glanced at the man beside him who appeared unperturbed with the decision as if it were a mere fine for jaywalking.

The chairman turned to the five members. "Any comments from the panel?" he asked, tapping his pen on the table.

A physician member, who had left the table to fill his coffee cup from the urn behind them, spoke out. "Since this is the first complaint against Dr. Paloma, I feel the penalty is adequate."

Parker watched Kulas flinch and then looked to Paloma, who sat comfortably slumped in his chair. "What a scumbag," he swore to himself, hoping the man next to him didn't hear.

The chairman continued, "Thank you, Dr. Morningside." He then turned to one of the panel members seated at the table. "Do you have an opinion, Dr. Allea?"

The olive-skinned physician leaned forward to speak into the microphone. His voice carried the distinct trace of a middle-eastern accent. "We should spend more time discussing the medical implications of this case. I believe the conduct Dr. Paloma demonstrated by ignoring this woman's complaints warrants a more punitive fine. In addition, he should be placed on probation as one of his penalties."

Paloma's lawyer quickly rose to face Allea. "That will cause a hardship on Dr. Paloma. He's employed by MCA's HMO plan, and a probation penalty will result in termination of his position at the clinic. MCA does not allow doctors on probation to work for them."

The chairman turned to Morningside, who took his seat after filling his coffee cup. "Do you have any opinion regarding a probation penalty, Doctor?"

Morningside leaned back in his chair. "I still think the original proposed agreement is adequate."

The chairman nodded and then turned to the large dark-haired woman seated beside Morningside. "Miss Guittierez, as a lay member, do you have any comments?"

The portly woman shook her head, "No."

An attractive young African-American woman seated to the chairman's left raised her hand to speak.

The chairman nodded. "As our other lay member, Miss Warren, we would like to hear your comments."

Warren returned a friendly smile which lit up her face. She spoke with confidence. "I believe both doctors, Gomez and Paloma, should have listened more intently to this woman's complaint. We're not gambling with cards here. We're dealing with lives. Every complaint must be taken seriously, something the two doctors didn't do. The woman's repeated calls shouldn't have been dismissed so casually. I agree with Dr. Allea. We must look more critically at the infraction and the penalty proposed."

The chairman asked, "Dr. Allea, do you wish to make a further comment?"

Palermo's attorney shot up from his seat. "This court agreement is consistent with penalties rendered to other physicians who face the same complaints."

Allea gave Paloma a piercing look. "Was this an HMO patient, Doctor?"

Paloma returned a nervous nod. "Yes. All my patients are on MCA's HMO plan."

Allea pursued his questioning in a polite manner. "Dr. Paloma, I understand your practice is in Miami. You state your training in cardiology was outside the U.S. Are you Board Certified in cardiology in the U.S.?"

"No," Paloma answered meekly.

"And if you had referred your patient to a Board Certified cardiologist, would that have cost you and your clinic a reduction in HMO payments?"

Paloma hesitated and then answered, "No."

"That's a lie," Parker muttered, causing the man beside him to raise a quieting hand.

Allea's brow wrinkled, his voice more forceful. "This patient should have been admitted to a cardiac unit and not sent home to die. I choose not to accept the proposed agreement and recommend raising the penalty to ten thousand dollars. Also, Dr. Paloma should be given two years of probation and required to take sixty hours of Continuing Medical Education in cardiology."

Paloma's lawyer quickly answered, "The doctor has practiced as a respected physician for over twenty years. This is his first appearance before this panel."

"Yes," Kulas shouted into the microphone. "But most of those years were spent in Peru and only five in Florida."

Parker looked to the faces of the panel but only Morningside appeared eager to speak.

"I then recommend the fine be raised to three thousand dollars and a quality medical evaluation be done on the doctor's records. Probation should be dropped from consideration."

Allea shook his head in disgust but remained silent.

The chairman looked to the state attorney. "Does administrative counsel agree?

"We accept," the state attorney answered.

"Then I call for a vote," the chairman announced. "All in favor?"

Parker watched as only Allea and Warren failed to raise their hands.

The chairman slammed the gavel. "Dr. Morningside's recommendation carries with a three to two vote."

A background surge of conversation erupted as a weary looking Kulas rose to leave the room. Parker felt sorry for the hunched figure as he shuffled out, struggling to live with his loss.

The man beside Parker said, "You got pretty steamed up over this case, fella. Is the woman who died related to you?"

Parker shook his head. "No. I'm a physician and this man's story angered me. The panel is letting that doctor get away with murder."

"Don't let that throw you, Doc. This happens all the time. It shows you what a good lawyer can do. Here's my card. I'm Douglas Stern, Attorney at Law. Call if you need me."

Parker took his card with conflicting emotions. What he just witnessed told him that even if he were innocent, the outcome of his case could be unpredictable.

Stern gave Parker a friendly nod and appeared interested in carrying on a conversation. "Before you got here, a case was presented where the pathologist missed a breast cancer on a slide. They took that doctor's license away. Now here, you have a woman who dies after being ignored and the doctor receives only a slap on the wrist. So go figure it."

Before Parker could comment, the gavel struck again and the chairman announced, "It's nearly noon and the panel will resume hearings at one-thirty PM."

Stern asked, "Do you want to join me for lunch?"

"Thanks for the invite," Parker answered. "I've seen enough and I have to get back to my practice. I have your card if I need you." He shook the lawyer's hand and left the hotel.

Sitting in his car, he tried to analyze what to do. Until he experienced the Probable Cause Panel in action, he had no idea how easily his medical license could be snatched from him. He thrust the key into the ignition, turned over the engine and directed the car toward Alligator Alley. No matter what the cost, Lawton was right. The danger was real. He needed Fellini.

Twenty-three

Several days later

Parker walked the short distance that separated his office from MCA Hospital, dwelling on his unfortunate situation. *Could it get any worse?* he wondered. With only three months of practice behind him, he felt his whole life was in turmoil. Constant danger from unknown drug traffickers, the hospital's charges of patient abandonment and to add to his pain, Gwen could possibly quit. With his reputation in dispute, he was unable to attract surgical referrals which made him even more dependent on emergency room cases for financial survival.

It was after 5 PM when he opened the door to his office and walked in, expecting to see an empty waiting room. To his surprise, Gwen and her tousled haired husband Paul sat, waiting for him. She rose when he entered.

"Everything okay?" Parker asked.

Gwen returned a sad look. "Paul wants me to quit after he heard about the druggies."

"Yeh," Paul spoke out. "Gwen likes working here, but we have two kids and we can't take the chance."

"I understand your concern," Parker replied, "but I

only wanted to warn Gwen. It's me they're after."

"I don't know about that, Doc. For what she earns, putting her life in danger just ain't worth it."

Parker drew in a deep breath. "Did Gwen tell you I suggested she speak to Mr. Rucker, the DEA agent?"

"She did, but I'm against it. No one can protect you from these gangsters if you're in the way. Even if you're not the target."

Parker pulled up a chair to face them. "Look, Paul, I'd never endanger Gwen. Every precaution will be taken, and at this moment I need her. She understands my patients and the hospital politics I'm facing."

Paul rose and stared down at his wife. "I can't bear the thought of losing you."

"Please, Paul, don't get so dramatic," Gwen said. "Dr. Dawson's been honest. I like my job and he needs me."

"And I need you too, Gwen. If anything should happen..."

"You're such a worry wart, Paul. I've thought things through and I trust Dr. Dawson." She turned to Parker. "Tell him everything will be all right."

Parker nodded. "Gwen won't be at risk. These mobsters are following me for their money, not Gwen. I beg you, let her stay."

Gwen rose and kissed Paul's cheek. "Please?"

"If there's even a hint of danger, I promise she can leave on the spot," Parker added.

Paul hesitated as he looked at Parker. "You better be right, Doc. I'll hold you to your word."

Parker released a sigh of relief. "Now that it's settled, let's go out for dinner. The treat's on me."

Gwen giggled, "Sorry, Dr. Dawson, you may not have kids, but we do. Thanks for the invite anyway."

As Parker watched the couple leave, he felt he had just saved his sanity. While Paul was right that Gwen's salary wasn't worth the risk, he had learned something today. Gwen's job satisfaction was more important to her than the money she was making.

Twenty-four

Orlando Hilton Conference Center, one week later

The cancer meeting was well attended by a wide array of doctors from all over the country, but not every topic interested Parker. Still fuming over Lindstrom's phony charges and unable to concentrate, he left the darkened room while the lecturer continued to point to medical slides on the screen.

Passing by the ornate coffee urns stationed outside the conference room, he walked into the lobby to clear his head. At the newsstand, he paid for *USA Today* and strolled to a quiet corner sofa to read. Hopefully, the current news would distract him from his gloomy thoughts.

The registration desk was busy with new arrivals waiting in lines. Since it was late morning, the various meetings were breaking up. Clusters of people walked by clutching conference manuals, avidly engrossed in conversation. High-pitched voices echoed as women strolled by. Chatter and laughter broke his focus, causing his eye to catch the familiar walk of a woman in a group of three. Despite the streams of people obscuring his view, within seconds he recognized her. It was Judy.

As if drawn by a magnet, he rose, rushing in her direction. His sudden move toward the women produced startled looks until Judy spoke out.

"Parker, what a surprise!"

He broke out into a big smile. "It's pure luck I saw you in such a crowd, Judy."

She turned to her friends. "Ladies, meet Dr. Dawson, the surgeon who saved my brother's life."

Parker nodded with a smile. "I'm here for a medical meeting. What about you?"

"We're here as delegates to the State Nursing Association Conference," Judy replied."

One of her friends laughed, "But we're trying to convince Judy to join us for shopping instead of attending the afternoon meeting. They say Orlando has great outlet malls."

Feeling the urge to spend time with Judy, he blurted, "How about lunch before you ladies start your shopping spree?"

The two friends looked to each other. "It's awfully kind of you, Doctor, but that would hold us up," one of them answered. She turned to Judy and added, "You can stay if you want and we'll meet at the room before tonight's banquet."

Judy smiled at the girls. "Would you mind if I took a rain check?"

Both shook their heads and eagerly rushed off, leaving Parker and Judy standing in the midst of the traffic walking by.

"I guess I scared your friends away," he joked.

She responded with a laugh. "Nothing stops those two from spending money, especially since it's their first trip to Orlando."

As they walked toward the brass-trimmed eatery, her expression turned serious. "Shawn's still paralyzed."

Parker masked his concern over her brother's slow recovery. "Give it time," but before he could say more, the hostess welcomed and led them to a table.

While Judy scanned the menu, Parker wanted to stay positive by making small talk. After being served, her feeble attempts to finish a salad made him ask, "Not hungry?"

"I've had enough," she answered. "Wish I could smoke, it relaxes me."

"Am I making you uncomfortable?"

"No, I guess I'm bad company right now."

"Is it Shawn you're worried about?"

"Yes, but I hear you have your own problems at the hospital."

"You mean that ER incident?"

She nodded. "I was there, and I don't think Dr. Baum handled that case too well."

"It seems you're the only one who feels that way."

"Oh, there are others," she said, "but they won't talk. They need their jobs."

"I appreciate your honesty, Judy, but don't get dragged into this. Once I explain what happened, I'm sure they'll drop the charges. You have enough on your plate with Shawn."

"I know," her voice drifted, "among others."

The anguish in her voice seemed to convey a message.

"Want to talk about it?"

She shook her head.

"Try me. In spite of what's happened, I'm still your friend. Use me as a sounding board."

"Look, Parker, I appreciate it, but it's too personal. Sorry I even mentioned it."

After a minute of silence, he asked, "Of all the surgeons you know, why did you choose me to see Shawn in the ER? Was it because of the drug screen?"

A faint smile crossed her face. "No. I knew how good you were when I worked with you at the university. You proved it again when you did the Whipple. No surgeon around here would even attempt that operation."

"Thanks for the compliment," he said, reaching for her hand. "But what about the drug screen?"

She took in a deep breath and pulled back her hand. "I expected you to question where all that cash in Shawn's pockets came from."

"And?"

"As you guessed, he was dealing with the other side of the law. I guess it started with smoking pot at boarding school and from then on, to bigger problems."

"I see," Parker replied. "I always wondered where the money came from to send both of you away to private school."

She gave him a wistful look. "Grandpa left a small inheritance. After the money ran out, we had to fend for ourselves. I paid my way through nursing school with student loans and Shawn dropped out of college after two months."

Parker felt unsettled uprooting painful memories, but

being alone with her gave him a chance to reconnect.

"All that's behind you now, Judy. You have no idea how much I've thought about you. When I saw you again at the hospital, it was like a dream come true."

She lowered her head and closed her eyes.

"Did I say something wrong?"

"No, I just... I'm just a little confused right now."

"About what? You know how I feel about you. In all this time, that hasn't changed."

She turned her head away. "Things are more complicated now."

"Is there someone else?"

She nodded.

"I'm afraid to ask. Do you love him?"

"Please, don't go any further. I'll admit, now that you've come into my life again, nothing makes any sense."

"Christ, Judy. Open up, give me a chance."

She quickly rose and pushed back her chair. "I think I'd like to leave."

Parker could only nod, frustrated by an answer that left him in the dark.

The restaurant began to empty as most diners returned to their afternoon sessions. Walking into the crowded lobby, Parker tried to diffuse the tension. "Let's cut through the pool area," he said.

They entered into the bright sunlight bathing the pool deck and watched youngsters play at the shallow end. Mothers lounging in swimsuits focused on their children's every move. Splashes coming from a water battle between a young boy and two older girls made Judy and Parker step back. When the boy found himself losing the fight, he jumped out of the pool with sprays of water splattering Parker's pants.

"Hold on, little fella, don't hurt yourself," Parker chuckled, reaching for the boy's shoulder to stop him from falling.

The boy grinned back and then raced to the protection of his mother.

"I see you like children," Judy said. "You were so kind to him even though he soaked your pants."

"Reminds me of when I was a kid, just having fun."

"It must be great having happy memories of childhood."

Parker watched her serious expression return.

They walked the perimeter in silence, slowly returning to the lobby. It felt good being close to her again even if she was involved with someone else.

On reaching the hallway leading to their different meetings, she touched his hand. "Thanks for lunch, Parker."

He held her by the shoulders and looked into her eyes. "Do you love him?"

She looked away and whispered, "I made one mistake and I don't want to make another."

Twenty-five

Following week, MCA Hospital

A man's anguished cries filled the air as Murray Leader bolted into the ER.

"Glad you didn't waste time getting here, Doc," the ER physician said, unable to mask his excitement. "He was shot in the groin during a robbery and bleeding big time."

Leader's gaze froze on the steady stream of blood seeping through crimson-stained bandages. Even the nurse's gloved hands pressing hard on the dressing couldn't stop the hemorrhagic flow.

"Who put in the central line?" he questioned.

"I did and ordered six units," the ER doctor answered. "OR is ready for him."

Watching the victim writhe in pain, Leader quickly slipped on latex gloves to check the abdomen. The belly was hard and he could see he was dealing with a full blown peritonitis along with a major vascular injury.

A bolt of panic flashed through him when he realized the man could die. Recently out of training, he wanted no mortalities linked to his name. "Miss Keller, call Dr. Gold and tell him I need him in surgery STAT!"

"Will do," Judy answered and quickly left the room.

"Are we ready to move him to OR?" the ER doctor asked.

"I guess so," Leader answered hesitantly. With luck, Gold would arrive by time the patient was prepped and ready for surgery.

After the nurses transferred the multiple IVs onto the gurney stands, Leader helped roll the cart to the OR and spotted Parker heading in their direction. As they passed by, he couldn't ignore the wide eyed look on Parker's face focused on the trail of blood dripping to the floor.

Judy rushed up to Leader. "We haven't reached Dr. Gold yet, we're still paging him."

"You need help, Murray?" Parker asked.

Leader returned a blank look. "No thanks, I can handle this,: he answered, convincing himself his relationship with Gold would be jeopardized if he invited Parker to assist.

"Call if you need me," Parker replied as the cart rolled by.

Leader kept pushing the cart, reminding himself that Parker was definitely an outsider. Any collaboration with him would label him an outsider as well. so he wasn't going to take any chances.

Once inside the OR, Leader helped transfer the patient onto the table which evoked a sharp outcry of pain from the victim.

Rudy Catalano soothed the young man, speaking softly as he loaded syringes to administer the anesthetic. "You'll be asleep in a minute, sir."

Leader studied the colorless appearance of the patient's

injured limb intensified by the stark white florescent lighting. If he was to save the leg, circulation had to be restored pretty damned quick.

"Get him prepped while I scrub," he called out to the nurses, dashing to get to the sink outside the room. Upon returning, he found the patient asleep, prepped and draped under sterile sheets, ready for surgery.

"Has anyone heard from Dr. Gold yet?" he asked.

No one answered.

He moved to the OR table and waited for the instrument nurse to position her stand. He needed more time, hoping Gold would soon arrive, but the steady stream of blood from the gaping hole in the groin told him he couldn't wait.

He made an incision extending it through the wound where the bullet had entered. The blood gushed out and he shouted, "Push the transfusion, Rudy."

"What the hell do you think I'm doing?" Catalano called back as he watched Leader scoop away organized clots in an attempt to clear the field.

"Shit, I have no landmarks," Leader snarled, struggling to pack the opening to control the flow. He heard the circulating nurse on the intercom ask the lab for another four units of blood.

"Pressure's dropping," Catalano bellowed.

"Keep pumping," Leader answered.

"You gotta stop the bleeding!" Catalano insisted.

"I'm trying," Leader replied as he continued packing the wound.

Gold suddenly burst into the OR and looked down at the blood-stained floor. "What happened to this poor bastard? Christ! This room's a mess."

"Get scrubbed, Morty, I need help," Leader pleaded. Now that Gold had arrived he felt his confidence soar and waited for him to come to the table.

After scrubbing, Gold took his place and leaned over the table, giving Leader an arrogant wink. "Don't worry, Murray, this should be a piece of cake," he said, peeling away the blood-soaked packs. Fresh bleeding erupted and he shouted, "Extend the fuckin' incision."

Leader deepened the cut while Gold struggled to position a retractor to hold open the wound. Intestines poured out and the scrub nurse vigorously passed cloth lap packs to hold back bowels competing for the same space as the blood.

"The bullet must have nailed the hypogastric vessel," Gold growled. "Let's clamp the common iliac."

"I will after I find the ureter. I don't want to cut it by clamping blindly." Leader knew they had enough problems and he didn't need another. If he cut the ureter, he'd risk losing the kidney and have urine leaking all over the place.

"Fuck the ureter," Gold bellowed. "What good is a corpse with an intact ureter?"

"Pressure under seventy, pulse one twenty," Catalano called out nervously.

"Keep pumping," Leader answered.

"He's throwing PVCs," Catalano shot back.

Leader watched Gold's eyes drift from the operating field to the monitor.

"No way are we going to stop this bleeding," Gold snapped, loosening his grip on the retractors.

"We've got to!" Leader answered, forcefully repositioning Gold's hands on the blades. "Dammit, hold on and keep retracting, Morty! I need to get control."

"You're dreaming. This bleeding's not stopping for anyone."

"Get your god-damned paws in here, Morty, and help me."

Gold's attention returned to the operating field and after a few minutes, he looked up at the erratic lines running across the cardiac monitor. Once again his hands slipped away from the retractors. "Christ, Murray," he snarled. "It's all PVCs."

"I think I found the ureter," Leader shouted, hoping to encourage his assistant.

"Hell, that ain't gonna save this guy. No way can we stop this flood."

"We have to, Morty."

"You've got to be nuts, everything we touch bleeds. This guy's a goner."

Catalano called out again. "Pressure's barely sixty."

Gold grabbed Leader's hands and pulled them out of the field. "Look, this guy's as good as dead. Call the case and let's get the hell out of here."

"What do you mean call the case?" Leader lashed back.

"I mean it's all over."

"He's still breathing," Catalano gasped as he looked over the screen.

"There's nothing else we can do," Gold snapped.

"But he's still alive," Leader pleaded.

"Yeah, and a vegetable," Gold answered as he stepped away. "Face it, Murray, he's dead."

Leader's eyes widened as he stared over his face mask. "He's not dead, Morty. He still has a heartbeat."

Gold folded his arms. "Look, we're going into the lounge and calling the coroner to report an operating room death. That's the law."

"Are you crazy?" Leader screamed. "We can't leave him here to die!"

"Then stay." Gold turned and walked toward the swinging doors. "I'm outta here."

"Morty! You bastard, you son-of-a-bitch. Don't leave."

The doors closed behind Gold.

"Come back you fuckin' shit," Leader roared. He looked to Catalano as everyone in the room froze. "I need help, Rudy."

The anesthesiologist returned a stunned look, offering no reply.

Leader dropped his head and stepped away from the table.

"Don't leave, Murray," Catalano pleaded, but Leader continued walking out of the room.

"Call for a surgeon, any surgeon!" Catalano ordered the circulating nurse.

Leader could hear the urgent page over the loudspeaker as he entered the doctors' lounge. He saw Gold on his phone.

"Yes, Miss Keller, tell the coroner we have an OR death and they should talk to Dr. Leader."

Still wearing his blood-stained gown, Leader dropped onto the leather couch and cupped his bare hands over his face.

Gold rested a hand on Murray's shoulder. "Look, you

did your best. After all, you didn't shoot the guy."

"This is hard to take," Leader whispered in a hoarse voice.

"I understand, but these things happen," Gold answered. "Remember you're a surgeon and it'll happen again."

Leader stared vacantly at the floor as Gold left to change his clothes. The clang of the locker door closing symbolized the case had ended, yet his thoughts dwelled on the never-ending hemorrhage he couldn't control. Gold might have been right, he thought, but his conscience couldn't accept leaving the man to die on the table.

Minutes before, Parker had heard the panicked overhead page from OR,. He rushed, passing Gold in the hallway and changed into a scrub suit. With clean booties, cap and face mask, he dashed into the OR hearing the circulating nurse speaking on the phone.

"Yes, we have a patient on the table," she said, "but ... uh ... he's not dead." After listening, she whispered, "Maybe you should speak to Dr. Leader," and hung up the phone. She turned to Catalano. "The coroner thought we had a dead patient on the table, but I told him the patient was still alive."

"That's right," Catalano replied.

Parker studied the somber atmosphere in the room. The instrument nurse piled lap pads onto the wound while occasionally suctioning the overflow of blood. The agonal rhythm signaling cardiac death flipped across the screen as everyone watched for the appearance of the inevitable flat line.

"Time of death, four-ten PM," Catalano brusquely

commented. Noticing Parker standing in the room, he added, "Thank you for answering the page, Doctor, even if it's too late."

Parker quietly watched the nurses resume their procedural routine, counting instruments and lap pads although it made no difference. Despite the drama that had just taken place, he noted their eagerness to clean the room and have it ready for the next day's surgery.

~ * ~

The next morning, Parker sat alone in MCA's dining room reading the Palm Beach Post. He angrily flipped over the next page when Lawton slipped into the chair beside him.

"Christ, Karl, where's the honesty in the printed press? It says here yesterday's shooting victim died in the ER, but I know for a fact, he didn't. Gold and Leader left him to die on the OR table when they couldn't stop the hemorrhage."

"Hold on Parker, that's a pretty serious charge. The paper says he died in the ER."

"Look, I was there and saw it. As a surgeon, the one thing you don't do is abandon a patient on the table. I want to call the paper to set the record straight. Maybe I should talk to Rudy Catalano. He gave the anesthetic."

Lawton shook his head. "Rudy's hands may be tied, Parker. He holds the exclusive MCA contract for anesthesia, and if he blows the whistle, he'll be out on his ass. Check your facts and get the others involved in the case to agree with you before you shoot off your mouth."

"What, you don't believe me?"

"I believe you but the hospital gives the paper a lot of

advertising and Lindstrom's pretty cozy with the health reporter. Maybe the paper doesn't want to bite the hand that feeds it since this case sounds like a potential lawsuit. First talk to the nurses who were there and see if they'll support you."

"I think I will," Parker answered, rising abruptly with Judy in mind. He felt she was the one person whose honesty he could depend on.

Lucky to catch her alone in her office, he knocked on the partially opened door and entered.

"Oh, Parker, good morning. Can I help you?"

He gave her a serious look. "You were there, Judy. Isn't it true Gold and Leader walked out of the OR yesterday, leaving that gunshot victim to die on the table?"

"They sure did, but this morning, Mr. Lindstrom instructed the nurses involved to make no comments."

"And you went along with that?"

She wrinkled her brow. "What choice do I have? My personal situation doesn't allow me the privilege to question my superiors."

"Am I hearing right?"

"I know you're frustrated, Parker, but face it. We're only employees. None of us can afford to have any blemish on our records."

"As supervisor, didn't you notify the Coroner's Office?"

"No, Dr. Gold did. But the patient was still alive when the coroner called back. The office never followed up because it wasn't reported as an OR death."

"So when do you call the coroner's office?"

"Only for deaths that occur on the operating room table, or if there's evidence of foul play."

Parker let out a soft whistle. "Real sweet," he mumbled. "Administration plots a cover-up, nurses are silenced, afraid to lose their jobs, which lets Gold and Leader walk away unscathed."

"Won't Surgical Evaluation Committee review the case?" Judy asked.

Parker laughed. "With all the politics here, Gold's friends on the committee will agree it was a predictable death. Everything will be whitewashed."

Judy leaned back in her chair. "If you're interested in reforming hospital politics, Parker, shouldn't that come from doctors rather than nurses?"

"Is that a statement or a question?"

"Both," she answered, "but there's something else that concerns me."

Parker nodded.

"The drug Procrit."

"What about it? I use it all the time on cancer patients."

"A few nurses complained the drug isn't boosting the red cell count in patients receiving it. I asked Pharmacy to check with the manufacturer about its potency but was told Administration would take care of that."

"So we're back to the same roadblock, Administration."

"I guess so," she answered.

Parker let out a deep sigh and rose to leave. If he couldn't get the nurses to support him on the OR death, how believable would he be standing alone? Since hurting Judy or the other nurses was out of the question, it seemed wiser to let sleeping dogs lie.

Twenty-six

Following day, early evening

Parker didn't feel much like partying, but how often would he have the chance to mingle with the wealthy movers and shakers of Palm Beach? As he drove over the Flagler Memorial Bridge heading to the Island, he felt he was fighting an unwinnable war. The hospital's trumped-up charges along with Gold and Leader leaving a dying patient on the table angered him. But he realized it was time to give more thought to his social life than the ugly politics of medicine.

Tonight, he was invited to an exclusive party at the home of widowed Palm Beach socialite, Elise Linton, heiress to one of the big three auto makers. They met when she came into the ER one early morning hour complaining of severe abdominal pain. Although she first vigorously objected to surgery, his persistence saved her life when he operated on a ruptured ectopic pregnancy.

He slowed the car to get a better view of the ocean-crossing yachts moored on both sides of the Intracoastal Waterway. In his wildest dreams, he knew he could never afford a toy like that. Once over the bridge, he drove north on County Road until he reached the lofty shrub-encrusted walls of the Linton Estate. He parked his Honda between a sleek Jaguar and an imposing Bentley, hoping to hide it from view.

A white-jacketed attendant approached. "Welcome to Surf House," he said.

"Thank you. I'm Dr. Dawson," Parker answered.

"Mrs. Linton is expecting you. The guests are in the pool area. I'll show you the way," the man replied.

Parker followed him through tall iron-gated doors into a large sitting room leading to the pool. The glittering blue waters of the Atlantic viewed through an endless bank of open French doors stood in contrast to his small dark apartment. Stepping onto the verandah, he surveyed multiple tables abundant with food positioned under the shade of an enormous canopy. He guessed there were nearly forty people gathered around the pool and wet bar with no one swimming.

Elise Linton approached in a long, flowing, white chiffon dress. "It is so good of you to come, Dr. Dawson." The gusty winds caused her skirt to billow, enhancing the view of her slender legs and figure.

She took his hand. "Come let me introduce you," and marched him toward guests conversing with drinks in their hands. He was presented as the surgeon who saved her life, which had him field a flurry of medical questions.

After circulating and chatting with the many guests, he walked away from the crowd to stand alone at the stone balustrade railing facing the ocean. He sipped a glass of wine and watched the glowing red sun recede over the horizon, aware there was a limit to what he could share with Wall Street and Fortune 500 executives.

"May I watch the view with you?" a sultry voice came from behind.

He turned to face a slender young woman with long red hair, wearing a strapless emerald green dress.

"Elise told me what you're drinking, so I brought you the next round. By the way, I'm Marla Evans."

Parker studied the seductive sway of her hips as she spoke. Her silk dress clung to her body, inviting a long look at the contour of her exposed cleavage.

"Thanks, I think I've had enough already," he stammered as she handed him the drink. "But how can I turn down such an enticing invitation?"

She brushed up beside him and leaned on the railing, looking out to the ocean.

The fragrance of her perfume reached him as he searched for his next words. "I love watching the sun go down in Florida," he said.

She flipped her long hair away from her face and tilted her head toward him. "After you've lived here awhile, that can get boring." Her green eyes looked into his. "Besides saving lives of the rich and famous, what do you do for fun?"

"I guess I haven't had time to think about that, but I'm open to suggestions," he answered with a smile, aware that the wine had taken its effect. He took a long look at her and she stared back without flinching.

"Aren't you the Marla Evans who just divorced that prince from somewhere in Europe?"

"So you do read the social page," she replied raising one eye brow. She locked her gaze onto his eyes. "You still haven't told me what a busy young doctor does for fun."

A sudden outburst of voices from behind drew their attention to the open patio doors leading into the house. To Parker's amazement, there stood Eric Lindstrom greeted by a number of guests as though he were a celebrity. Not wanting to be recognized, Parker quickly turned to face the ocean and the growing darkness.

"See," she gushed, "the fun's about to begin."

"What kind of fun?" Parker asked.

"You'll see," she giggled. "Let's go meet him."

"I don't think so." Parker held her hand, restraining her.

"Why? Do you know the guy?"

"Yeh, but we're not the best of friends."

The sound of commotion died down and Parker turned to see Lindstrom enter the house with several people following.

Marla gave him a questioning look. "Are you afraid he'll bite you?"

"Sort of," Parker replied, shaking his head.

"Don't worry," she said, waving her hand. "I'll protect you from him and we'll still have fun."

She turned and called out to a friend. "Jessica, I need you. Could you please come here?"

Parker watched a dark haired beauty slither her way through the crowd to face Marla who whispered into her ear. He continued sipping his wine, unable to take his eyes off Marla's beautiful body. Whatever her secret, he might learn about it in time.

After Jessica left, Marla said, "Don't worry, he won't

see us." She took his hand. "Come, let's take our drinks and talk to a few people before we go in."

Slowly they made their way as Marla chatted with the few lingering guests on the verandah. Parker spoke sparingly to maintain social amenities but still remained uncertain about what lay ahead. His curiosity, along with his attraction to her body, made him follow. Hell, he thought, since I can't have Judy, you only live once.

"Are you going in?" Marla asked the couple closest to them.

Both shook their heads no.

"We'll see you later then," she replied, leading Parker into the house.

He followed her, and along the way she stopped and wrapped her arms around him. As she pressed her body against his, he knew she felt his growing hardness.

She gave a light laugh and pecked him on his lips. "I promise you a wonderful evening," she declared, grabbing his hand and pulling him down the hallway toward closed double doors.

She knocked before peering inside. "Here we are," she said, pushing it open to lead him in.

Jessica appeared and gave them both a grin. "I thought you'd never get here," she said. "Grab a straw."

In the dim light, Parker could see several couples standing around a table. Using straws, two inhaled the white powder laid out in strips along the glass top. His head floated with all the drinks but the sight immediately sobered him. "No, thanks," he said abruptly.

"Why?" Marla questioned. "It's pure stuff, the real thing.

"Excuse me, I don't want to interrupt your party so forget I was here." He turned to leave and Marla followed him into the hall.

"What's wrong with you? You know you upset everyone in there.

Her child-like pout caused him to shake his head. 'Look, Marla, this isn't my cup of tea. As for fun, I had other things in mind."

Her eyelashes fluttered, and her face softened. "We will, but later." She coyly placed a finger to the tip of his nose and smiled. "You're quite a guy and I could get interested in you. Come on, just try it."

Parker felt increasingly uneasy. This was one world in which he wanted no part. "No thanks, I appreciate the offer, but I have to leave."

"What a waste," she called after him as he made his way out of the building.

"Leaving so soon, Doctor?" the butler asked.

"Yes, got called to an emergency. Please thank Mrs. Linton and give her my apology."

Once outside, he spotted Lindstrom's white Mercedes in the parking lot. Everything was too bizarre to be real. *Where did that tight-assed Lindstrom fit into all of this?*

You're nuts, he told himself as he slipped into his car. I could have had her but not at that price.

Twenty-seven

One week later, MCA Hospital

Judy went to her desk and dialed Kent's office.

"Is this regarding a patient?" the receptionist asked.

"Yes," Judy answered. "He hasn't seen her yet but it's important I speak to him."

"He's with patients right now," came her bland reply. "I'll see he gets the message."

Judy hung up the phone, turned to memos piled on her desk and tried to blunt her disappointment. Hospital matters were far from her thoughts. Since Kent's warning that Sheila might have detectives spying on him, their meetings became less frequent. But her news couldn't wait much longer.

When the phone sounded, she lifted it on the first ring.

"Nurse Keller, please."

"It's me, Kent."

"What's up, Judy? My receptionist said your call was urgent."

"It is urgent, Kent."

"Has something happened? Were you approached?"

"No, I can't discuss it over the phone. Could you come

to my apartment tonight?"

"I'm afraid to do that, Judy."

"But this can't wait, Kent. I only need a few minutes and the hospital's no place to talk." Her heart raced as she waited for his answer.

"I have a meeting at seven and I'll try to be there by nine. But I can't stay long."

"I understand. Thanks for calling back." She closed the phone and sat frozen in a hypnotic trance. Maybe he wasn't ready to hear what she had to say, but there was no turning back.

The overhead page called her name for Intensive Care. Shrugging her shoulders to cast away any negative thoughts, she opened the bottom drawer of the desk and took out a mirror to examine her makeup. The reflection facing her confirmed the excitement she felt.

~ * ~

It was just before 9 PM when Kent entered Judy's apartment. He studied her smiling face as he closed the door behind him. "I swear I'm getting paranoid," he murmured. "Coming here scares the hell out of me."

Judy approached, wrapping her arms around him. "I've missed you, Kent."

"Me too, honey, but we have to be careful."

"I know, but something wonderful has happened." She leaned close, kissing him on the cheek and led him to the sofa. She looked into his questioning eyes. "I'm pregnant, Kent."

His body stiffened and he pulled back. "Are you sure?"

She nodded. "I did a home test and even checked it at the hospital."

"You used your name?"

She shook her head. "The lab tech did me a favor and ran it under an alias."

Kent sat speechless for a moment and then shot up from the sofa, pacing the room.

She felt her heart flutter watching his agitated moves. The fear she had submerged for so long surfaced.

"I didn't plan for this, Kent. Honest, I took my birth control pills. Can't you see how happy I am?"

She searched his eyes, hoping to find the answer she wanted but only saw a look of panic. Her face flushed with anger. "Call your lawyer, Kent! Sheila has to know. We're not playing games, this is for real."

Kent dropped back onto the sofa and rubbed a hand across his face. "Look, Judy, you can't be in the picture when I file for divorce." He watched her pleading eyes turn into a stony stare. "Don't get me wrong, honey. I'm happy too, but I need more time to arrange my finances."

"It sounds like you don't want the baby."

"I didn't say that. You're reading this wrong. Our timing isn't the greatest. I just can't go home and tell Sheila I'm leaving until legal matters are in place."

"You make everything sound so awful. This is our baby, Kent. Can't you be just a little happy?" The lurking fear of abandonment suddenly overwhelmed her and her eyes filled with tears. "You walked out on me once. I guess you can do it again."

He raised her chin and drew her close. "I'm doing no such thing, but it's just that you caught me off guard. I love you, Judy, and believe me, I am happy."

She hugged him back. "I had to tell you."

"I know, but we must keep it quiet." He looked at his watch. "I'll talk to my lawyer tomorrow to speed things up."

She studied his worried brow and wanted to say something to comfort him, but her only response was to kiss him on the cheek. "Go home. You've had enough excitement for today. Call when you can. I'll be waiting."

He gave her a peck on the cheek before shutting the door behind him.

She remained standing at the door, feeling the return of that familiar rush of anxiety. He agreed to the divorce, but when would he tell Sheila? The next step was his.

~ * ~

Judy awakened to the chatter of birds as sunlight streamed through the bedroom blinds. She found it difficult to sleep and the ring of the alarm brought a welcome interruption to her dark thoughts.

It had been two weeks since Kent assured her the plan for his divorce was moving ahead, but she wasn't so sure. Why hadn't he told Sheila yet? And was it true that Sheila had hired a detective to follow him? Those questions rattled about in her brain but she had no answers.

She wearily raised herself from the bed but a wave of nausea made her stop. Even though she ached all over, her promise to visit Shawn meant she had to act upbeat.

Moving to the fridge, she poured coke from a can and took small sips, hoping to settle her stomach. More from habit than hunger, she scanned the shelves. Her thoughts returned to Shawn and her heart skipped a beat picturing him trapped in a wheelchair. Of course she'd help, but could she raise a baby, hold a job and care for him, all at the same time?

An overwhelming frustration urged her to slam the door shut until she spotted ripe strawberries hidden behind a bowl of unfinished salad. She sat at the table, biting into the cold meaty freshness of the fruit, pondering the lonely world her brother faced with his dismal attitude.

After emptying the bowl and still with no solution, she rose to fight her growing lethargy. Returning to the bedroom, she dressed and painfully concluded she couldn't depend on Kent's promises any longer. The baby was on its way and time was running out. With or without Kent, having this child was her choice, not his. No matter what lay ahead, she had to plan for her future.

~ * ~

She walked the halls of the rehab center, waving to patients who recognized her from frequent visits. Reaching Shawn's room, she peeked in and saw him sitting in bed smoking a cigarette.

He quickly crushed the lit end when she entered.

She shook her head as she approached. "You know you're not supposed to smoke in here, Shawn."

"Cut the sermon, sis. I'm in no mood for a lecture." He gave her a troubled look as she sat in the chair beside him. "You look like hell, Judy."

"I'm fine. Just a little tired."

"Don't con me, sis, you look sick."

"There's a good reason for it, Shawn, and I've been meaning to tell you the news."

"What news?"

"I'm pregnant."

He flinched. "You've got to be kidding."

"I'm not kidding and I'm happy about it." She paused.

"But I'm very tired."

"Jesus," he gasped, "and who's the father?"

"I don't want to deal with that right now, Shawn. Just be glad you're going to be an uncle."

"Yeh, and how could a cripple like me play with a kid?"

"Stop talking like that."

"Good advice," came a voice from behind. A slender young woman in white entered sniffing the air. "You know the rules, Keller, no smoking in the room." She turned to Judy and extended her hand. "Good morning. I'm Kathy Sommers, the new charge nurse for the Center."

Judy immediately liked the assertive demeanor of this attractive brunette. "I'm glad to meet you, Kathy. I'm Judy, Shawn's sister."

"Shawn should be thinking about his future instead of moping around and smoking," Kathy continued. "Has he said anything to you about our pep talks?"

Judy shook her head.

"Stop, it!" Shawn snapped. "I don't need you both ganging up on me."

Kathy's face turned serious. "I've been telling him there are programs for careers in real estate, insurance sales, computers or just about anything that interests him."

"That sounds wonderful!" Judy replied with excitement.

"He can still live a full life, marry, have children, the whole works as long as he sets his goals." She turned to Shawn, throwing him a penetrating look. "As they say, you can lead a horse to water but..."

"You're relentless," Shawn scoffed.

"Listen to her, she's right," Judy insisted.

"What a lot of crap," Shawn muttered. "And thanks for reminding me I'm a cripple."

"Still not getting the message, are you," Kathy shot back. "Working in rehab, I've seen it all. The maimed, the amputees and the paralyzed. Only those who want to, will make it, and Shawn, you can make it if you try."

"Easy for you to say," Shawn replied. "You're not paralyzed."

Kathy stared down at him. "You're not the only one with problems, Keller. The only difference is that yours shows."

Judy watched Shawn's eyes shift to the ceiling, avoiding Kathy's gaze. "Are you listening, Shawn? She's trying to help so don't turn her off."

"I heard her," he answered indifferently. "But I don't want to talk about it anymore."

"That's fine," Kathy answered. "Let me know when you're ready." She turned to Judy and smiled. "It's nice meeting you and I don't give up easily." She waved and walked away.

Judy watched her brother with his eyes still glued to the ceiling. "Listen to her, Shawn, and give her a chance."

"Get off my case," he muttered, turning away from her.

The unmistakable sound of despair in his voice made her feel helpless. "I guess I'll go now," she said softly, leaving him alone in the room.

As she walked the corridor, she suddenly felt faint. A cold sweat broke out on her brow and she leaned against the wall for support. An aide walking by stopped to ask,

"Are you all right, Miss?"

Judy wiped her face dry with a tissue and straightened up. Taking in a deep breath, she replied, "I'm fine. Thanks for asking."

Leaving the building, she was fully aware that she had her own decision to make. Whatever it was, it would affect her for the rest of her life.

~ * ~

Exhausted, Judy steadied herself on the handrail outside the building. A blast of hot air hit her as she opened the car door. Slipping inside, she quickly started the engine, eagerly waiting for the cooling stream from the air conditioner. When it came, the welcome chill relieved the heat but not her worries.

I'm at least two months along, she thought. *Maybe this baby wasn't meant to be. An abortion would solve everything, but destroying a life is too painful to consider.* Tears filled her eyes as she put the car in gear and drove out of the parking lot with no destination in mind.

Aimlessly, she followed the traffic north on Interstate 95, pulling into the middle lane. As cars raced past on both sides, she grabbed a tissue and wiped her eyes. "Forget everything," she muttered, "Just drive."

As the traffic thinned and the open road appeared endless, her thoughts remained on her dilemma. If Kent denied this baby, what were her choices? Envisioning a fight in court to prove paternity would be too traumatic and embarrassing.

And there was Shawn to think about. The abortion would give her the freedom to help with his medical problems, but how would that enrich her life? The instant recall of Kent's shock when she told him about the pregnancy made her curse the day she had gotten involved with him again.

With no idea of time, hunger motivated her to leave the highway. The exit ramp led to a McDonald's and she found herself standing in line behind a mother and her three children. She watched as the woman discussed the menu with the older two while the youngest looked up at her with a blue-eyed innocence.

Straight blond hair framed the little girl's pixy face. "I'm getting chicken nuggets with a toy," she beamed at Judy.

"You are?" Judy answered with a smile that broke into her somber mood. "That sounds yummy."

The girl reached for her hand and held it.

Judy felt a surge of warmth. "How old are you?" she asked.

The child raised three small fingers.

"Three! Aren't you a big girl," she burst out, gently patting her head. She caught the mother's eye as the line moved forward. "I couldn't resist,." she said.

"That's quite all right, she's a very friendly child," the mother replied, directing the youngster toward the counter. "Give the man your order, Samantha."

Judy watched the child gaze at the colorful pictures of food menus above the counter. *Could I destroy a life like that?* she asked herself.

The attendant's voice broke into her thoughts. "Your order, Ma'am."

Leaving the restaurant, Judy resisted going home to face her problems in an empty apartment. She headed the car down the narrow road leading away from the Interstate. Whatever unknown community lay beyond was not important.

At the intersection, she came upon the usual cluster of gas stations and a 7-Eleven. The road led to rows of modest homes sitting on neatly trimmed lawns.

An old wood-framed church with a cedar shake roof surrounded by an expanse of green stood at the corner. It was small and inviting. She read the faded gold letters on the simple pine frame. 'Our Lady of Lourdes Roman Catholic Church.' It had been so long since she had been in a place of worship.

At its peak, the overhead sun beat down as she walked the stone steps to enter through the carved weathered doors. Once inside, she felt the cool air against the moisture on her skin. Adjusting to the darkness, she viewed the regimental rows of empty pews standing before a few burning candles at the altar. Her footsteps echoed on the tile floor as she moved to sit in a pew.

Gazing at the gold crucifix above the Sacristal Table, she sensed a peaceful calm and suddenly felt drained. Nothing was left within her to give, neither to Kent, nor to Shawn. Now she was the one who needed help and she dropped to her knees to pray. An uncontrollable anguish came over her and she let out a sharp cry. Each sob released her pent up emotions with enjoyable relief.

Hearing the sound of weeping, the parish priest moved quietly into the pew behind her. "Relieve your soul of its burdens, my child," he said in a soft voice, patting her shoulder.

Judy turned to face a portly middle-aged man dressed

in a white collar and dark suit.

"Oh, Father," she gasped. "It's so peaceful, I couldn't help it."

The round-faced cleric smiled. "Don't apologize. Meditate all you like, but if I can be of some assistance."

"Sorry, Father, I'm not Catholic."

"You don't have to be Catholic to speak to me."

She looked to the altar. "I would like to talk to someone if it's possible."

The priest nodded. "Let me introduce myself. I'm Father O'Toole." His Irish brogue charmed Judy's ears. "Why don't we go to my office where we can talk?" He led her down the short corridor and once in his office, invited her to sit.

Taking his place behind the desk, he asked, "Now, what is your name and how can I help you?"

"I'm Judy Keller, Father, and I must make some decisions. Frankly, I feel trapped."

"Why don't you start from the beginning," he replied with a gentle smile.

"My brother's twenty-seven and he's paralyzed. He's at a rehab center just now."

Father O'Toole raised his eyebrows with a serious look crossing his face.

"He was shot in the back," she added timidly, "and I'm the only family he has."

The priest filled his pipe without lighting it and listened as Judy went on to explain her involvement with Kent. She stumbled over telling him that he was married and admitted her pregnancy. When Father O'Toole showed no reaction, she added, "I'm thinking of having an abortion."

A moment of silence followed as she looked out the window.

"Will the smoke bother you?" he asked, holding out his pipe.

"No, Father," Judy answered, eager to hear his comments. She watched him strike the match and puff as he lit the tobacco. The ease of his manner lent him an air of wisdom.

"I know it isn't easy to face all your problems, my dear, but let's explore certain aspects."

Judy slipped back in the chair, feeling more at ease having told him her secret.

"The teachings of my Church state that a child is a gift from God. Please search your conscience. Destroying this life may cause more pain than you're facing now." He rested his pipe on the ashtray. "You can support your brother through his transition," the priest continued. "Keeping him with you will allow him to get an education. If he's as smart as you say, he'll find his way and need you for only a short time. I don't see that as a problem."

As he leaned forward, the penetrating look in his eyes signaled the seriousness of his words. "But should you persist in seeing this married man while carrying his child, you will only complicate the resolution of your own problem. Not only will his harbored frustrations harm your association, but it will destroy his relationship with his family."

The priest clasped his stubby fingers before him. "As you know, my religion prohibits abortion. While you've sinned in the eyes of the Church, all of us have sinned at one time or another. But your life shouldn't be destroyed because of this one transgression." He heaved a deep sigh. "Whenever I face a dilemma, I say, it's how one looks at a problem that can determine its outcome."

Judy nodded, waiting to hear more.

"You must ask yourself what emotional scars aborting this child will leave."

Judy's mind raced, recalling the little girl who held her hand at McDonald's. A rush of guilt ran through her as she envisioned tearing life from her womb.

Father O'Toole read the intensity of her thoughts. "If you terminate this pregnancy, you will always carry that scar." He watched Judy's hands tighten her grip on the arms of the chair. "However, if you raise this child, even as a single parent, the joys and blessings you'll receive will outweigh any personal suffering."

Judy stared at the priest, unable to respond. The sudden roar of a lawn mower outside the window broke the silence.

Father O'Toole continued. "As a priest, I cannot support this man leaving his wife and breaking apart his family."

Judy turned her head away as her eyes filled.

Not hearing a response, the priest continued. "I understand the difficult choice you must make."

Judy covered her face with her hands, and Father O'Toole waited until her sobs ended.

"You're young, and if you keep this child, you can still find marriage with someone worthy of you. The decision is in your hands. If you need to talk, I will always be available."

Judy released a deep sigh, looking up to the bronze

figure of Christ on the cross hanging on the wall. "I know I have a lot to think about, Father." She smiled and rose. "You've been a great help."

The priest left his chair to walk her to the door. "Remember," he said, "the right decision is usually the most difficult one to make."

Judy left Father O'Toole standing in the doorway. Driving home, she reflected on his words. An abortion would end all her entanglements with Kent. But if she had the child, would he be there for her? She couldn't answer that. With all this love to give, if not for Kent, why not the child? By the time she reached home, she had made her decision.

Twenty-eight

Kent sat at his desk, took in a deep breath and dialed his attorney. Gerald Wolfe was his closest friend and confidant, the person he trusted whenever he needed advice.

The receptionist recognized his voice immediately. "Mr. Wolfe is at a meeting, Dr. Markman. Can he call you later?"

"No! This is urgent and I need to speak to him now."

The woman hesitated. "I'm not sure..."

"Just tell him I'm waiting on the line."

In a cool voice she replied, "Please wait, Doctor."

The silence added to his frustration. Before the pregnancy, he felt no urgency to talk to Wolfe about the divorce. But now, he was desperate.

After a five minute wait, Wolfe came on the line. "What's the emergency, Kent?"

"I'm in a jam, Gerry."

"You dragged me out from an important meeting. What are we talking about?"

"It's about a nurse at the hospital. I got her pregnant." Wolfe's silence threatened him. "Talk to me, Gerry."

"What do you want me to say?"

Kent's voice dropped. "I really have strong feelings for this girl."

"You're sure she's pregnant?"

"I'm certain she's telling the truth."

Wolfe sighed. "First, you must keep the news from Sheila." He paused. "Does she know?"

"No."

"That's good, because she owns most of your assets and she'll win everything in a messy divorce." He hesitated. "Unless you.re looking for a divorce."

"No. Right now, no divorce. There's too much at stake with everything in her name."

"Will the woman agree to an abortion?"

"I don't think she'll go for it."

"Why?"

Kent paused. "There's that question of marriage."

"You mean you promised marriage?"

"Well, yes."

"Come on Kent, I know you too well. You actually proposed marriage?"

Kent's grip on the phone weakened as he struggled to answer "Yes."

Wolfe let out a whistle. "Now I understand. Here's my advice. Do nothing that will raise Sheila's suspicions. At all costs she mustn't know. We need time to set up something to transfer your investments out of Sheila's name."

Kent broke in. "But how do I handle the girl?"

"You have two options. First, ask her to get an abortion."

"And if that doesn't work?"

"See if she'll take money."

"Look, money is out of the question. And if she doesn't go for the abortion and files a paternity suit, Sheila will take me to the cleaners."

"Don't get too far ahead of me, Kent. Just keep Sheila out of this and try to get that abortion. If it doesn't work, get back to me. I gotta go."

Kent hung up the phone and wiped the sweat off his brow. He had to convince Judy to make a date with Planned Parenthood.

~ * ~

All week Kent plotted the best way to approach Judy about the abortion. Wolfe was right. That would solve all his problems, so what was he waiting for?

The next morning, he decided to talk to Judy at MCA after making rounds. He visited his last two patients, headed to the nursing supervisor's office and knocked on the door.

Judy answered. "Come in."

He pushed open the door, let himself into the tiny office and put a smile on his face, wanting to appear relaxed. "Got a few minutes?"

She beamed back, "Sure."

"Are you free tonight? Can I come over?"

"Of course. Come for dinner."

"I can't. Sheila has the boys at a school function and she'll expect me at home when they return. Is five-thirty all right? I'd like to talk about us."

Judy's smile faded. "What about us? Is something wrong?"

"No, I can't talk now, but I'll see you tonight."

Judy nodded and without speaking, Kent let himself out.

As he walked the corridor to the nursing station, he told himself she had to agree to the abortion. He lifted a chart from the nursing rack and sat at the desk. After flipping it open, he stared at a page, emotionally distracted.

A nurse walked by and gave him a friendly laugh. "Are you able to read that chart upside down, Dr. Markman?"

He flinched and forced a smile. "Thanks, just lost in my thoughts." He replaced the chart into the rack and walked away, reminding himself that Judy had to be convinced or else his life would turn into a disaster.

~ * ~

Kent's pulse raced as he waited for Judy to open the door to her apartment. He thought about Wolfe's suggestion Before he approached Sheila for a divorce, Judy had to get that abortion.

The word 'divorce' rankled him, recalling horror stories from doctors who went through the emotionally and financially exhausting process.

The door opened and his tension suddenly melted away. Before him stood Judy in a tight sweater and slacks. Her hair fell to her shoulders, framing a welcoming smile. Without a word, he held out his arms and embraced her with a kiss. She responded with such intensity, his only thought was to take her to bed.

Instead, she led him into the living room and drew him next to her on the couch. Ice, two glasses and a bottle of scotch rested on the coffee table.

"You look like you can use a drink." she said.

He nodded, aware that he needed one.

She handed him the scotch and filled one for herself. She raised her glass to his and said, "I hope it's good news."

He gazed back at her expectant look, feeling a lump rise in his throat. He sipped his drink, set it on the table before him and looked into her eyes. "Now Judy, you know how much I love you." He paused. "But this pregnancy..."

She stared back but remained silent.

His voice wavered. "This is something I would never ask, but you must realize the consequences if it's not done." He watched her eyes narrow. "You know what I mean, don't you?"

"No, Kent, I don't know. Say it."

He took in a deep breath and replied, "An abortion."

For a few moments, Judy sat without responding. Then she placed her drink on the table and stared him in the eyes. "What if I want this baby, Kent?"

"Oh, I want it too. But what will happen if you're alone raising a child?"

"Why should I be alone, Kent? You promised marriage."

"I know I did, but I just can't divorce and risk everything I worked for. I need time to settle my legal affairs."

"Then how long will that take? Babies deliver in nine months and I'm already eight weeks along."

His eyes drifted upward. "Oh, God. I don't know if I'm saying this right. I just want to make things easier for both of us."

Judy gave him a hardened look.

"I didn't mean it that way, Judy. I only meant we have to plan this carefully so everything will be in place when we marry."

Judy stood up from the sofa and stared down on him. "I thought you came here tonight to tell me that Sheila agreed to a divorce. You forget, Kent, we went through this once before, so where are we now?"

He rose and wrapped his arms around her. "Don't panic, honey, just forget I mentioned it."

She pulled back to search his eyes. "Are you sure?"

"Yes, I'm sure. I just can't bear the thought of losing you."

She kissed his cheek and whispered, "I want to believe you, Kent."

"You can. This won't come up again." He looked at his watch. "I better get home before Sheila and the boys get there."

Judy looked at him as they stood at the door. "When can we be together again? Not just to talk."

He shook his head. "I'll let you know. Remember, I love you."

He walked back to his car with a heavy heart, torn between two conflicting desires. Wanting her and the fear of losing everything.

Twenty-nine

Following day, rehab center

Slumped in his wheelchair, Shawn gazed out the lobby window with a distant look. Still coping with his paralysis after two months of therapy, he couldn't shake the feeling of helplessness. His whole world had crumbled, so what did he care about the future?

He yanked at his shorts and poked a finger into his thigh. *God damn, soft as pizza dough. Don't feel a thing.*

Hearing movement behind him, he turned and caught sight of an attendant pushing a wheelchair. It held an elderly man, dribbling saliva. Shawn turned away in disgust. *Christ,* he mumbled, *I gotta get out of here before it's too late.*

"Hey, Keller, why aren't you in rehab?"

Shawn turned to see Kathy Sommers march into the room. "What for?" he answered.

"You know what for. Therapy says you're not even trying."

"Excuse me, General, let me spell this out. Frankly, I don't give a fuck."

"Still feeling sorry for yourself?"

"What's it to you?"

"Everything. It's my job to get you better, but you have to help."

"Look Sommers, I'm paralyzed, so nothing you say can change that."

She leaned close. "Right, Keller, and only you can do something about it."

He tried avoiding her look, but the scent of her cologne and her closeness made his gaze linger. When she straightened up, he stared back. "You go home when your shift is over. How the hell do you know what I feel?"

"Can the self-pity. We all have problems, so start doing something about it."

He let out a soft whistle. "You are a hard-nose, aren't you?"

"Like a rock, so get used to it. If you want to make it in this world, you gotta hang tough. I've made my share of mistakes but I refuse to whine about it."

He studied her pursed lips but caught the flicker of pain that flashed across her eyes. "Since you know about my problems, what's your bitch?"

"I'm past analyzing. I've gotten on with my life."

He raised his brow, looking up at her. "Afraid to talk about it?"

"You're getting too personal, Keller."

"Right, Sommers, maybe I am. Why not get to know each other before I take your advice?"

Her gaze locked onto his, but she didn't answer.

He gave her a broad grin. "Just humor me. I've made my share of mistakes, so why don't you stop me from making another?" He saw her face soften, interpreting a glimmer of understanding in her eyes. "Talk to me," he whispered.

She broke her silence and took in a deep breath. "It's too long a story."

"I have the time." He reached for her hand and held it with a firm grip.

She tried pulling away, but he still held on.

"You are serious, aren't you?"

"Yes," he murmured, "I really am."

She sighed. "Then where do you want me to start?"

"From the beginning. Where did you grow up?"

She wheeled his chair toward the sofa and sat beside him. "I was raised in a small town outside of Jacksonville. My father would get drunk and beat me. My mother died when I was sixteen. That's when I left home."

"Where did you go?"

"Went to Jacksonville. Got jobs at burger joints but my life was crap. I was going nowhere."

"What about school?"

"Never finished. Got involved with a guy but that didn't last."

"So?"

"So I worked as a checkout clerk at a supermarket where I met an older man. I was eighteen then. We lived together and I went along with everything."

"What do you mean by everything?"

"Drugs and all."

"You got hooked?"

"You could say, but the worst was yet to come." She shook her head. "The next thing I knew, I lay in bed in excruciating pain, pouring out sweat. I had a full blown pelvic abscess."

He read the look of anguish on her face as she relived the experience.

"They called it a sexually transmitted disease and I had to have a hysterectomy. The surgery saved my life but I ended up extremely depressed."

She rose and walked to face the window. "I wanted to end it all so I overdosed on sleeping pills."

Shawn sat listening in a state of shock. Suicide was definitely on his mind, and the hollow sound of her voice only intensified the apathy he felt.

"You don't have to go on with this," he insisted.

She turned and gave him a determined look. "I know, but I want to."

He shifted uncomfortably in his seat with his eyes never leaving her face.

"Luckily, when they found me, I was still alive and was rushed to the hospital. That's when I met a nurse who talked to me like a mother. She arranged shelter, treatment and inspired me to go on with my life. Because of her, I finished school. So here I am."

She looked away with tears filling her eyes. "But what hurts most is that I will never be the mother that my mom couldn't be."

He watched her dry her eyes and the strong urge to hold and comfort her came over him. Instead, he straightened up in the chair and whispered, "Thanks for your honesty. Please don't give up on me."

Her smile warmed his heart and as she walked away, he thought, *God, what a woman. I think she just saved my life.*

Thirty

MCA Executive Suite

Carolyn Robertson took the call and transferred it to Lindstrom.

"Okay, Otto, tonight at eight, at the Breakers. Ask for Edward Jansen," Lindstrom replied. Hearing Otto's voice opened a rush of memories.

Robertson made the reservation at the Breakers Hotel without asking any questions. She understood Lindstrom and his situation. After all, she was with him in California. When he and Trask brokered the first deal, she knew all about it.

Evening had already settled in as Lindstrom drove his white Mercedes through the side streets of West Palm Beach. He pressed the lock button for protection as he passed through the seamy side of the city. The last thing he needed was a car-jacking by some street hood.

Quickly driving down 45th Street, he turned south onto Australian Avenue and then left onto Okeechobee Boulevard toward Flagler Drive. Disregarding the poverty he had just passed, he looked to the glittering lights of Palm Beach across the Intracoastal Waterway blazing in all their splendor. He sped over the bridge separating the City of West Palm Beach from Palm Beach Island, eager to leave behind the haven for drug pushers and street gangs.

The Breakers Hotel security guard welcomed him and when he drove up to the front entrance, the valet took his car.

Walking up to the registration desk, he signed under the name of Edward Jansen, and after giving the clerk the name of his guest, he went to his room. He slipped off his jacket and tie, made himself a Scotch and soda from the mini-bar and sank into a comfortable lounge chair.

Tonight he needed to entertain, but most importantly, put out any fires. He admitted his relationship with Otto was fiery enough in California, and if legal, they would have married. But Otto left for someone else, so what had brought him to Florida?

He appreciated Carolyn Robertson's sense of discretion. Aware she was attracted to him when he first hired her, he knew it wasn't too long before she got the message. For some reason, she remained loyal, enjoyed working and even protecting him. Maybe she had a girlfriend in Florida, he thought, but that was her business.

He poured another Scotch and soda since there was nothing else to do but wait. By the time his drink neared the bottom of the glass, a knock sounded at the door and he rose to open it.

He greeted the tall statuesque blond man dressed in a light tan summer suit. "Otto! Good to see you."

Otto hugged him, pressing his face to both sides of Lindstrom's cheeks. "Yes, it's been a while," he replied, taking in a long look at Lindstrom before sauntering into the room.

"Have a drink and make yourself comfortable," Lindstrom said.

"Don't mind if I do," Otto answered as he approached the bar. He filled gin and tonic into a glass and sat down opposite Lindstrom, crossing his legs.

Lindstrom focused on Otto. "Are you still with him?"

Otto avoided Lindstrom's gaze. "Not any more. I was wrong leaving you, Eric."

"So now what?"

"I think we should get together again."

Lindstrom shook his head. "Things are different now, Otto. I have other friends, other entanglements."

"But, Eric, you must have some room left for me, old friend. After all, remember what we meant to each other."

Lindstrom stroked his chin, his eyes glued on his guest. "Do you have a job, Otto? Do you need money?"

Otto gave Lindstrom a sorrowful look. "I'm not working, but that's not why I left California. The reason I'm here is to be with you."

Lindstrom rested his glass on the small coffee table. He didn't feel comfortable taking Otto back. "I can help you. If you need a few thousand to get you on your feet, I can do that."

"It's not money I'm asking for, Eric. I want us to be together."

Lindstrom's face remained flat. "Understand, Otto. Things aren't the same. I can't connect with you."

Otto's jaw tightened, his eyes narrowed. He rose and paced around the room, finally turning to face Lindstrom.

"I know all about your funny drug scheme in California."

Lindstrom sat, unperturbed.

"Maybe I should tell the authorities about it."

"I wouldn't do that, Otto," Lindstrom answered. "That has nothing to do with our relationship."

Otto grimaced. "Oh yeah? I ask you for help and you hurt me? You're wrong. It is all about us."

Lindstrom rose and spoke in a businesslike tone. "This is what I'll do, Otto. You can stay here tonight, the room is paid for."

He took out a check from his pocket. "Here's five thousand dollars made out to you. Our relationship is over. Don't ever threaten me again. Go back to California, find a new friend and get a job. If we ever cross paths again and you try to hurt me, you'd better worry about every turn you make, every car or stranger that crosses your path. There are people who take care of things like that."

Otto's jaw dropped, his eyes widened with fear.

Before he could respond, Lindstrom put on his jacket, picked up his tie and walked out the door. *If Otto didn't leave for California in twenty-four hours, he was going to have an accident.*

Thirty-one

Several days later

After the attempted kidnapping at the supermarket parking lot, Parker routinely drove a different route each day on his way to the hospital.

It was Sunday, the one day of the week he felt the loneliest. Practice was demanding enough, but the added challenge of watching out for the druggies plus fighting the hospital's charges left little time for romance. Especially not the Palm Beach type. But whenever he thought about a woman, it was always Judy.

Why was she so upset when they talked in Orlando? Who is she entangled with? Frustrated by the question and lacking an answer, he blocked those thoughts and peeked into the rearview mirror to make certain no one was following.

His gas gauge rested on empty so he pulled into a station with only two pumps adjacent to a small convenience store. While filling his tank in the rundown neighborhood wasn't too appealing, what choice did he have? He slipped his credit card into the slot authorizing the sale and squeezed hard on the handle to speed up the process. As the tank filled, he kept a close eye on those entering and leaving the weathered shack that housed the station office. The pump failed to print a receipt, so he headed for the building.

Inside, two olive-skinned men stood before the register speaking in Spanish. Their frayed Levis and torn tee shirts suggested they worked as laborers or farm workers. They smiled when the clerk came from the back and handed them an amber vial filled with pills.

The clerk raised one finger and said, "Just one tablet tonight, no more."

"*Esta Veeagra?*" the man closest to the register asked.

"Yeah, Viagra. But if it doesn't work tonight, you can take two tomorrow."

The men nodded their agreement and rushed out the door.

Parker realized he had just witnessed an illegal prescription drug sale. He wanted to question the clerk but thought it unwise to linger in such an unsavory neighborhood. "I need a receipt for my gas," he said nonchalantly.

After asking for his credit card, the clerk handed it back with a receipt from the register.

Curious, Parker wanted to learn more about the drug sale, but who could he approach? As he slipped into his car, his thoughts strayed to Shawn Keller. The guy was street wise and if anyone knew about this stuff, he'd be the one.

It was 9 AM when Parker headed to the rehab center. As he entered the room, Shawn called out, "Hi, Doc. Why aren't you in church?"

Parker returned a quick smile and moved to the chair beside the bed. "Something came up and I figured you could give me the low down."

"On what?" Shawn questioned.

"I just saw two guys purchase Viagra at a small convenience store. Since when does a gas station sell prescription drugs?"

Shawn let out a healthy laugh. "Are you kidding? You can get anything outside of the legitimate market. Antibiotics, heart medicine, Lipitor, you name it."

Parker was stunned by the response and lowered his voice.

"I don't mean to probe into your personal business affairs, Shawn, but I know you got shot because of hard stuff. Did you deal in prescription drugs too?"

"Fuck no!" he snapped. "Half the shit they sell is bogus. It's mostly counterfeit and peddled to those poor Latinos."

"Counterfeit? Where does the stuff come from?"

Shawn shook his head. "You're so naive, Doc. Let me clue you in." He took a quick look into the hallway and whispered, "Keep this between us."

Parker nodded and leaned closer.

"They approached me to peddle drugs to stores catering to Latinos. But when I learned they were counterfeit and some of the stuff was poisonous, I wanted no part of that."

"Who makes them? Where do they come from?"

"From overseas. China, Mexico, India, Nigeria, you name it. Some of the phony copies are so good, even the experts can't tell the difference."

Parker's voice rose in anger. "What a scam! Taking advantage of people who can least afford it."

"But think of the profit," Shawn replied. "If the prescription costs ten dollars a pill, and the counterfeit costs peanuts, millions can be made by selling just one case."

"This has to be a big operation."

Shawn's eyes widened. "I spent a lot of time digging into this. You contact an overseas manufacturer by Internet who sends a representative based here in the States to take your order. Then you set up a dummy corporation calling yourself a drug wholesale distributor. You sell the stuff to offbeat convenience stores or you can go legit."

"What do you mean legit?"

"By selling to pharmacies that supply nursing homes and hospices. The discount prices are so attractive and the meds look so real, even the big legitimate wholesalers buy them. How can a company refuse to purchase these phony drugs when they're so cheap and look so real?"

"What a rip-off."

"When I was approached," Shawn continued, "they told me everything could be arranged so that the money made could be transferred for deposit overseas."

"Why overseas?"

"To pay for the drugs without being questioned by the Feds. Any check for over ten grand sent out of the country by a bank sets off the alarm bells in Washington."

"Who arranges this overseas banking?"

"Lawyers set you up with a structured Cook Island Protection Trust which owns one hundred percent of a

Nevis Island Trust. Although you have two Trusts, you control the day to day activities of the second Trust without ever exposing your identity."

"Where's Nevis? I never heard of it."

"Neither did I. It's close to Puerto Rico. The beauty of this deal is that the Nevis Limited Liability Corporation owns one hundred percent of the Cook Island Trust. No outside court has any jurisdiction over it. And in addition, the Trust doesn't recognize judgments originating from any foreign country including the U.S."

"What if the money is gained fraudulently?"

Shawn laughed. "That's the catch. The Cook Island Trust statutes for fraud have a time limitation of one to two years. By then, the offshore jurisdiction limit to file will have expired."

Parker's eyes widened. "But what if the government pushes the clock and files an action before the time limit runs out?"

"No problem. Proving intent to defraud means the government has a high legal hurdle to cross." He paused and smiled. "But then the Nevis Trust kicks in."

"And who manages that Trust?"

"Any U.S. resident, but when things go bad...

"What do you mean bad?"

Shawn smirked. "When the courts get close to grabbing the money."

"Then what happens?"

"You temporarily appoint a bonded licensed Trustee as manager of the offshore Nevis Corporation accounts. But that's only when your assets are at risk. By doing that, you don't own the accounts, the Trustee does. That's why you're paying him to protect your money."

"But if in the end, you don't own the money, why protect it?"

"Gosh, Doc," Shawn answered, shaking his head. "The point is that the Trustee does everything you ask. When the bad thing goes away, you again become manager and you're always in control."

"Don't the officers of the first Trust have to identify themselves?"

"No! Everything is done by account numbers, no names."

"How does the money get credited overseas without IRS scrutiny if every transaction over ten thousand is questioned by the Feds?"

"By using Western Union to wire money orders or by sending checks under ten thousand dollars. But the sophisticated way is to use a courier or Fedex to get checks to the overseas bank. Believe me, if the numbers are big, it's easy and no one asks questions. I checked it out and it all works."

"Do you know who's moving these drugs into our area?"

Shawn shook his head, "No, and I don't want to know. Selling sick people fake pills made up of sugar isn't my bag."

Parker let out a deep sigh and rose to leave.

"You're square, Doc. Think of all those billionaires floating fancy yachts across the ocean. They'd never be able to do that by swinging a pick and a shovel. The drug companies know all about this scam, but they don't want to talk and scare the public."

"You're probably right, Shawn. I'm glad you didn't get involved in such a dirty scheme."

Shawn let out a deep yawn. "Yeh, even a crook can have principles."

~ * ~

After Parker left, Shawn felt restless and rolled his wheelchair out of his room. With Kathy's encouragement, he now religiously attended physical therapy six times a week, feeling the strength return to his arms and even some to his legs.

Using braces to straighten his limbs, he was able to suspend himself on parallel bars intended for walking assistance. He couldn't walk, but it felt good standing upright while developing his upper torso. His goal to independently transfer himself from wheelchair to the bed finally became a reality.

He felt more in charge of his life and optimistic about his future. With Kathy's guidance, he filled out applications, submitted resumes and waited to hear from brokerage houses for a job.

But today was Sunday and the therapy department was closed. He decided to roll past Kathy's office and was surprised to see the door open. He peeked in to see her totally absorbed, writing at her desk with two stacks of papers piled on either side of her. He sat for a few moments, studying the gentle curve of her chin and her delicate features before knocking twice on the door.

She turned with a startled look. "Oh, Shawn, can I help you?"

"I see you're busy. Do you have a few minutes?"

"Sure," she replied, rising from her chair. "Just

catching up on paper work, but a break sounds good right now. This office is too small, so let's go to the dining room."

"Fine, follow me," he answered and turned the wheelchair around. He looked forward to seeing her whenever they passed in the hall. She always made a point to stop and chat, making him wonder if it meant anything more than a nurse-patient relationship. He hoped it did, but no matter what, he had to tell her the good news.

Once they were seated, she with coffee and he with a Coke, she asked, "Have you heard from Merrill Lynch yet?"

"Believe it or not, I did. Got a letter a few days ago," he answered. "They reviewed my resume, interviewed me by phone, even arranged a training class. I start next week working for my certifying exam."

"Great!" she said and bent over, giving him a bear hug.

He laughed, enjoying the fresh scent of her perfume. "Thanks for the faith you have in me." He read the joy in her eyes and felt it was too personal to ignore. "I'm taking too much of your time," he stammered, struggling to find the right words.

"For an occasion like this, I have all the time in the world. I'm so proud of you, Shawn." She paused for a moment as her expression turned serious. "I'd like to know more about you, not as a nurse, but as a friend."

Shawn felt a flush cross his face. "And what could I tell you about my lousy life?"

"Your family, your mom and dad and Judy."

He sat back in his chair. "You think your father was an alky? My mom and dad drank themselves to death. I'm only telling you this because you can understand."

Kathy let out a long sigh. "Then it happened to you, too?"

"Yeah," he said. "My grandfather set up a small trust fund for me. That's what got me into a fancy boys' prep school. That part of my history must have impressed the Merrill Lynch guy."

"What about Judy?"

"Oh, that was tough. She went to a girls' boarding school a few miles away. The separation didn't make it easy for me. We were really close as kids when we lived at home. She always was there for me, more than my mom."

Kathy sat without speaking for awhile and then looked Shawn squarely in the eye. "I'm curious, Shawn, and this is not to condemn you. Where did you get off track?"

"Tough question," he answered. "I think about it a lot lately. I guess I felt abandoned by my parents when they sent me away. I was around ten and cried my eyes out, pleading I didn't want to go. Dad dropped me off and left the same day, rarely coming to visit. I just wanted to strike back. Always feeling like a loser, no mother and father on Parents' Day. Got mixed up with some rich kids smoking pot. You learn a lot at private boarding school and it's not all in the classroom."

He laughed, wanting to lighten up a bit, but noticed Kathy's brown eyes, wide and serious. "Want to hear more of this crap?"

She leaned over and said "Yes, I do."

He sighed and continued. "Mr. Yancy, Dad's close friend at work, drove Mom and Dad to the school to spend

Parents' Day that first year. But after that, it became obvious they were in no condition to travel."

"Didn't you get a chance to go home and visit?"

Shawn shook his head. "We did, but they were so sick, we spent the first Christmas visiting them in the hospital. They died in a nursing home within a day of each other a few years later. We had no relatives to speak of, so the Yancys became our guardians. Mom and Dad had no brothers or sisters."

Shawn cleared his throat, reaching for a napkin from the table to blow his nose. "I still remember the day Mr. Yancy came to school to take us back to Columbus for the funeral. The only people at the burial were Yancy, who was the Executor of Grandpa's trust fund, his wife, a couple of neighbor ladies and the minister."

Shawn looked at Kathy and could tell by her face, she understood his pain. He took a deep breath and continued to speak.

"I kept thinking, is this all there is to life? What an empty world. When I saw the two coffins stacked on top of each other sinking into the pit, I realized I was on my own." He grabbed another napkin and wiped his face.

"And you were how old?"

"Nearly seventeen. I finished my last year at prep school, but I flunked out of college the first year. That was fine with me because the money ran out anyway. I ended up with friends in the fast lane, and you know the rest."

"And you paid a price for that, didn't you?" she whispered.

He nodded. "Yeah, I sure did."

She stared back. "That gunshot was your wakeup call,

Shawn. You have a second chance at life now."

He leaned forward, reached for her arm and squeezed it gently.

She didn't pull away, instead placed her hand on his. "Thanks for letting me in your life, Shawn." She rose and said, "I have to go now."

Shawn watched her leave, amazed how he had opened up to her. *Yes, I could have a second chance at life, but only if it's with her.*

Thirty-two

Doctor's office, two months later

Judy pondered her future as she waited in the obstetrician's office. Convinced her fatigue was due to the approaching fourth month of pregnancy, with or without Kent, she had to face the future.

Their last meeting had ended up in a heated argument. Over the past few weeks, the larger her belly grew, the uglier their talks became. Deep down, she always knew he wanted her to get an abortion. But that illusion shattered when she told him about today's visit.

This was her first appointment with Dr. Shoup. She delayed picking a doctor from the HMO Provider List, blaming it on a number of things. Whether it was Kent's indifference to her advancing timeline, her heavy work load or Shawn's problems, it was her bulging waistline that forced the decision.

She heard her name called and followed the nurse into an examining room.

The nurse instructed, "Please remove your clothes and wear this paper gown. After I check your pressure and draw your blood, leave a urine specimen in there." She pointed to the bathroom, completed her tasks and left.

Judy sat on the edge of the gyn table between the stirrups and waited for Shoup. Stark, cold fluorescent lighting bathed the room which intensified her feeling of isolation. Covered with only a paper gown, cool air from an overhead vent gave her goose bumps. Any possible joy over her pregnancy was tempered by a feeling of frustration.

When the door opened, Judy faced the balding obstetrician followed by his nurse. A large man with broad shoulders, the circle of gray surrounding his scalp lent him a grandfatherly appearance.

"Good morning, Miss Keller, I'm Dr. Shoup."

"So glad to meet you, Doctor. You might recognize me as one of the nursing supervisors at MCA."

Shoup peered over his half glasses and grinned. "Of course, it's your pretty face I recognize, not that shapeless gown they put you in." He studied her chart and then looked up. "I see you're into your second trimester. Do you have any complaints?"

"Yes, I'm always tired. Even after a full night's sleep, I have to drag myself out of bed."

"Let's wait for your blood count report. Have you had a mammogram or breast exam lately?"

"No," she replied.

"It would be a good idea to have one now," he said.

After Judy nodded in agreement, he lifted the gown from her shoulders.

As he probed her breasts and checked under her arms, Judy studied his quizzical expression. He then measured the height of the uterus and listened to the baby's heart tones.

After the exam was completed, he asked her to sit up. "Your chart shows there's no history of breast cancer in your family, but I feel something in your right arm pit."

Judy felt her heart drop and tightened her grasp on the table's edge. "What are you feeling?"

"I can't say, but there's a fullness under your right arm. I see a small scar there. Did you have a breast biopsy?"

Judy laughed with relief. "No, it's from a mole that was removed. It's reported as benign."

"Good, but just to be safe, I'd like you to see a surgeon for a breast exam."

Judy read the serious look on his face and the longer she stared, the faster her heart pounded. Cancer quickly jumped into her mind.

Shoup noticed her frown. "It's only a precaution, Miss Keller. I didn't mean to alarm you."

"You can tell I wasn't ready for that, Doctor, but what about my pregnancy?"

"Your baby is fine."

The door opened and a nurse handed Shoup the lab report.

He looked at the numbers and glanced at her. "You're anemic, Miss Keller. That's why you're so tired. We'll give you samples of prenatal vitamins and iron and I want to see you again in two weeks. By then you should have seen a surgeon and I should have his report."

As he turned to leave, Judy called out, "Shouldn't I see a surgical oncologist?"

Shoup stopped to face her. "Well, yes, but a general surgeon would be easier to find."

"Dr. Dawson is a cancer surgeon. Will he do?"

"If he's on your HMO list, of course. I'll see you in two weeks, Miss Keller," Shoup answered and left the room.

The nurse handed her two packets of pills and before leaving she said, "Please schedule your appointment at the front desk."

Alone in the room, Judy tried to unravel the thoughts swirling about in her head. What if it was cancer? It was too late to terminate the pregnancy. Had she made the right decision?

~ * ~

She reached home and opened her HMO provider manual but saw no listing for Surgical Oncology. There were four names under General Surgery, and she recognized three. Morty Gold, Murray Leader and Jose Morales. A fourth surgeon was a distance away in Broward County with two offices located miles apart. None of the three names she knew was acceptable so she dialed the HMO plan. After listening to an endless series of recordings, she finally reached a live female voice.

"How can I help you, Ma'am?"

"I need to see a surgical oncologist and there's none listed in my provider's manual."

"What's a surgical oncologist?"

"That's a subspecialty for surgeons trained to treat cancer."

"Well, if you need a surgeon, pick one from the list under General Surgery."

"But you don't understand. I might have breast cancer and I want a surgeon trained to best perform that procedure."

"Sorry, Ma'am, general surgeons perform breast surgery."

"Obviously, you don't understand. There is a difference. Is there a supervisor I can speak to?"

"Sorry, Ma'am, you'll just have to pick from one of the general surgeons listed. Is there anything else I can help you with?"

Judy sat silent.

"That's all I can recommend, Ma'am. Thank you for calling."

Judy heard the click of the phone and it angered her. She needed a cancer surgeon and her plan denied her access to that specialty. Parker was the only surgical oncologist she knew, but he wasn't a listed provider on her plan. Would he agree to see her and accept whatever the plan paid? That was another hurdle she'd have to jump. Without hesitation, she dialed Parker's office.

~ * ~

"This is Judy Keller, Gwen. I need to see Dr. Dawson."

"Is it about Shawn?"

Judy hesitated. "No, it's for me. Dr. Shoup wants me to see a surgeon, but Dr. Dawson is not on my HMO plan. Will he accept me?"

"For you, I know he will."

"As soon as you can, Gwen. I'm pregnant and Shoup found a lump in my breast."

Gwen was quick to respond. "Don't concern yourself. I'm putting you in as the last patient today. Be here by five."

Judy hung up the phone with a sigh of relief. Whatever the outcome, she knew she could trust Parker.

It was 5:10 when Judy sat on the exam table and waited for Parker. She wondered if she had done the right thing by choosing her ex-lover. The last thing she wanted was to send mixed signals.

Within minutes, she heard a knock on the door and Parker entered, leading Gwen into the room.

"It's good to see you, Judy. Gwen tells me you're pregnant."

She flushed and nodded, "Yes, I am."

His look softened. "You say you feel a lump in your breast?"

"Dr. Shoup felt something by the scar where I had a mole removed. He wanted me to have a breast exam."

"Is there a history of breast cancer in your family or immediate relatives?"

"I don't know. Mother died in her forties and I have no other living female relatives."

Parker made an entry into the chart and then proceeded to slip the paper gown off her shoulders.

Judy no longer felt awkward having Parker examine her and pointed to the scar. "That's where the dermatologist cut out my mole about a year ago. He said it wasn't cancer."

Without commenting, Parker began to examine her breasts, gently probing in a circular motion. His fingers traveled under her armpits, leaving no area untouched.

It was strange to discover she enjoyed his tender touch. The intimate moments they once shared flashed into her mind. But he no longer was her lover. He was her physician who she hoped would carry her through this potentially life-threatening journey.

His eyes narrowed into a squint when he paused at the

same spot where Shoup felt the lump.

"What is it, Parker?"

"I'm not sure," he answered softly, replacing the paper gown over her shoulders. He turned to Gwen. "Could you please give us a few moments alone?

"Sure," Gwen answered and left the room.

Judy tried to read Parker's thoughts while he entered a note in the chart.

He finished writing and looked up, his eyes fixed on hers. "Judy, I know you're scared, but I agree with Dr. Shoup. There are no masses in the breast, but I definitely feel lymph nodes under your right arm."

Her voice trembled. "What does that mean?

Parker spoke in a professional tone, his eyes still focused on her. "The swollen lymph nodes are close to the scar and they need to be examined. Before we do any x-rays or biopsies, I'd like to review the tissue slides of the mole you had removed. We should have no trouble retrieving them."

His words pierced her heart like a dagger. The fear she dreaded since Shoup's visit was becoming a reality. "It's cancer, isn't it?" she gasped.

"Please, Judy, don't make snap judgments until we know."

She gazed back at him. "I trust you, Parker, and I know what you're saying is right. But I'm pregnant and really worried what it could mean to my baby."

"Your baby should be fine, Judy. Right now we have to concentrate on you."

"What should I do?"

"Give Gwen the name of your dermatologist so we can

get the slides. Leave the rest up to me."

Her eyes filled with tears. "You have no idea what it means to have you by my side, Parker."

"I wouldn't want it any other way."

He smiled and paused for a moment as if he had something difficult to say.

"Judy, I'm really glad we caught up with each other again. We shared wonderful days together, didn't we?"

She felt a lump in her throat and extended her hand to him. He reached for it and drew her close. She didn't know if it was fear or gratitude that caused her to hold him tight. Kissing his cheek, she whispered, "I'll wait to hear from you," and then pulled away.

Parker studied the worry lines on her face and lifted her chin with his fingers. "Could you at least give me a little smile?"

She forced a distorted grin as tears welled in her eyes again. Dabbing them with a tissue, she mumbled, "I'm sorry, Parker. I'll be fine. Thanks for everything."

"Remember, I'll always be here for you." With that, he turned and walked out of the room.

In the deafening silence, thoughts of Kent flashed into her mind and her heart raced. Breaking out into a sweat, she asked herself, *why isn't he here with me?* Not having an answer, she stepped down from the table to dress.

Gwen came back into the room. "Are you all right, Judy? Dr. Dawson really wants those slides right away."

"Sure thing, Gwen. I'll meet you at the desk and give you the info you need."

Judy finished dressing, left the room and walked to the front desk. She opened her purse and gave Gwen the dermatologist's telephone number. Still fighting her fears, she forced a smile. "Thanks for all your support, Gwen. I'm lucky it's Parker who's taking care of me."

~ * ~

After Judy left, Gwen dialed Dr. Mehlman's office only to hear an answering machine. She looked at Parker, who stood by anxious to pick up the call.

"Dr. Mehlman's office is closed, Dr. Dawson, but I'll try first thing in the morning." She knew her boss well enough to know he was worried. "You think it's cancer?"

"I don't know until we look at those slides. If the nodes show cancer, it means it's already spread. And with her pregnancy, it'll be a real complication."

Gwen sat still, absorbing the implication of his words. She looked at him and could see his mind occupied, analyzing what course of treatment to take.

She broke into his thoughts. "She's not just another patient to you, is she, Dr. Dawson?"

"You're right, Gwen. She was a nurse while I was a resident at the university in Columbus."

"You mentioned that when she called you about Shawn."

"Yeah, what a coincidence that we ended up at the same hospital in Florida."

"I'll need to get approval from her HMO provider to clear her for treatment."

"That won't be necessary, Gwen. We're not going to charge her."

Gwen tilted her head. "Dr. Dawson, she'll need a biopsy. Her HMO won't pay for any diagnostic and hospital costs if you're not approved to treat her. That's how these HMOs work. Even if your surgery is gratis, the

HMO won't cover any of the other medical bills if you're not cleared first."

"Then get HMO approval for me. I need to be the one to take care of her."

"The HMO will try to get you on their plan. Do you want to be a provider?"

"No, just clear me for her case only. Who's her gatekeeper?"

"Dr. Markman."

Parker shook his head, recalling his earlier argument with Kent about HMOs. "Then call his office to get me approved and accept whatever her plan pays."

"And if he won't approve you, then what?"

"That shouldn't be a problem. I'll talk to him."

"I'll call first thing tomorrow to get clearance," Gwen replied.

Parker glanced at his watch. "I'm glad you got her in, Gwen and thanks for staying late. Go home. Paul and the kids are waiting."

Gwen gave him a quizzical look. "I don't want to probe, Doc, but I have a feeling you and Judy shared more than just a working relationship."

Parker smiled. "It shows, doesn't it?"

"Yes, I have a nose for things like that. I could feel the chemistry in the room."

"The breakup was all my fault, Gwen."

"Maybe so, but I'm certain it isn't your fault that she's pregnant."

He paused for a moment. "Unfortunately it's not, but I wish it were."

Thirty-three

MCA, Department of Pathology, five days later

Parker paced the floor as John Boyd peered into his microscope studying Judy's slides. He had selected Boyd, who was a well-trained, meticulous pathologist.

"Gwen had a hard time tracking down the slides from her HMO, John. What do you see? They diagnosed it as benign, noncancerous."

"Take it easy, Parker, and give me a chance to review it," Boyd replied as he continued to look into the lens.

"I really appreciate this, John. She's very special." He stopped pacing and dropped into the chair next to Boyd. To occupy his mind, he concentrated on the pathologist's desk, cluttered with trays of glass slides, an open pathology text and a small stack of mail.

Boyd spoke as he looked through the lens of the microscope. "Did you feel a mass in the breast when you examined her?"

"Not in the breast. But I feel large nodes in her arm pit close to the scar."

Parker leaned over the desk to watch Boyd flip different magnifications as he studied the tissue. "Does it look like breast cancer?"

After a few minutes, the pathologist broke the silence. "It looks bad, Parker. This isn't an innocent Spitz nevus or low grade breast cancer. It's the worst you can imagine. What I see here is an aggressive malignant melanoma."

Parker felt the blood rush from his face and slumped back in the chair. "Dammit! They missed it. I had a feeling those swollen lymph nodes weren't coming from her breast."

Boyd shook his head. "The cut of the specimen is inadequate. Only one corner shows the full thickness of the mole. Under low power, it looks like an innocent benign Spitz, but under high power, if you study all of the area carefully, it's malignant melanoma. It's also very advanced, a Clark's Level IV with a Breslow's thickness of two point five millimeters."

Parker felt his mouth go dry. "With measurements like that, you're giving her a death sentence."

"Sorry, Parker, but that's the reality. I realize how serious this is."

"But how could they have misread the slides?"

"It can happen. Because of the volume of path tissues sent to central HMO labs each day, pathologists no longer cut their own gross specimens. Technicians do it, and if they don't sample the area of most interest, the pathologist can only read what's given to him. I happened to catch the malignancy on a small corner of the cut."

"So the pathologist depends on a technician who doesn't read the tissue?"

"You got that right."

Parker looked into Boyd's eyes. "Are technicians

slicing your specimens?"

"Hell no, I cut my own. That's why I'm always here so late."

Parker pulled a tissue from his pocket and wiped the moisture off his brow. "I didn't tell you but she's four months pregnant."

He saw Boyd's jaw drop. "Even if I do a regional node dissection, there's a high risk of distant spread. She doesn't have much of a chance."

Boyd released a deep sigh. "How will this affect the baby?"

"From what the literature reports, the placenta is the favorite site for spread."

"Then what happens to the fetus?"

"For some reason, it doesn't seem to affect the baby."

"Forever?"

"No one knows. The few cases reported aren't very conclusive."

A technician suddenly entered the room holding a tray of slides. "You need to read these frozen sections, Dr. Boyd. They're waiting in OR."

Boyd shook his head. "In a minute." He swiveled in his chair and peered into the microscope again. "The truth isn't always easy, is it, Parker?"

"You're damn right, especially when it's someone close to you."

After Parker left, Boyd slipped the glass slides the technician gave him under the microscope. "This biopsy is malignant," he said. "Which OR is waiting for the report?"

"Room four," the technician answered.

He read the name on the slide holder, pressed the button and spoke into the speaker connected to the OR. "Pathology calling room four on ovarian biopsy for patient Peterson."

"What's the diagnosis?" a voice crackled back from the two-way system.

"Melinda Peterson, ovarian biopsy malignant. Please repeat."

Boyd listened to the surgeon restate the name and diagnosis to confirm the patient's identity.

Suddenly a loud voice rang out across the room. "When do I get my bone marrow done?" Kent Markman marched in with chin raised for battle.

Boyd looked up. "As soon as I finish these frozen sections, Kent."

"That's not soon, enough. My patient's dying from AIDS and I need that report pronto."

Betty, the chief technician, interrupted. "But the request only came in an hour ago."

Markman glared at her.

Boyd turned from his microscope. "I'll get to it, Kent, but I'll need some extra time. AIDS patients are so sick, it's hard to get them to cooperate. Punching a biopsy needle into bone is painful, so I have to take precautions."

"Yeah," Betty followed, "the last AIDS case flew off the bed with poor Dr. Boyd hanging onto the needle for dear life."

Markman scowled. "Look, doctors and nurses have to deal with that."

Boyd raised his hand. "I promise to get to it soon, Kent. Let me finish these frozens and I'll get back to you with the report."

"I'll be waiting," Markman grumbled as he walked away.

"Gosh," Betty muttered, "if he wants that damn bone marrow so bad, why doesn't he do it himself? No, he wants us to risk getting stuck with a needle full of AIDS, that's why."

Boyd returned to the slide under the microscope. "Easy, Betty, he's just covering his ass. Probably afraid the AIDS lobby will criticize him if he doesn't go all the way."

"But it's your butt on the line," she replied. "I'm ready whenever you want to do it."

"I'll finish this slide and then we'll go." He turned back to the microscope. "This is a cancer specimen, too. I'll call the OR and the next frozen section should be processed by the time we get back."

~ & ~

The floor charge nurse led Betty and Boyd into a room where a gaunt, emaciated male lay motionless, staring at the ceiling. A beard coated his face and his eyes sank into two hollow sockets. Bags of intravenous solutions hung on poles dripping fluids into his veins.

As Boyd leaned over the motionless figure, he questioned what this poor soul had done to deserve this. A once vibrant human was now helpless because of a submicroscopic virus.

"Mr. Puleo," he said, "I'm here to do your bone marrow biopsy."

The man turned his gaze to him but gave no response.

The charge nurse held the patient's hand. "Everything will be all right, Mr. Puleo."

The patient reacted with an increased rate of shallow breathing.

"We're going to need your help," Boyd continued. "Do you understand, Mr. Puleo?"

"Yeah," the patient gasped.

"We have the consent, Dr. Boyd," the charge nurse volunteered as she moved to the other side of the bed to help turn the man face down.

Boyd prepared the skin over the lumbosacral area with an antiseptic and draped the field with sterile towels. After gloving his hands, he said, "You'll only feel a small stick when I freeze the skin, Mr. Puleo. But when I take the biopsy, you might feel a sharp pain, but only for a second.

The man gave an inaudible response.

"Now hold still, Mr. Puleo." Boyd injected the local anesthetic causing the patient to pull up and shift the drapes.

"Stop! That hurt!" Puleo shouted.

"Easy," Boyd cautioned. "The anesthetic should take care of that pain."

"But I felt it," he groaned.

"That part's over now," Boyd continued. "You shouldn't feel the cut I'm going to make in the skin." He made a small stab which Puleo didn't seem to mind. "Brace yourself. I'm going to take the biopsy now." He looked to the nurse. "Get ready to hold him down."

As the charge nurse pressed on the man's back, Boyd plunged the large bore needle into the bone, advancing it with a rotary motion.

"Stop!" the patient shouted as he bolted upright and pushed the nurse's hands away.

Boyd jerked his right hand, pulling out the needle. He tried holding Puleo down with his gloved left hand, but the man thrashed his body, deflecting the bloodied needle deep into the pathologist's palm.

"Ouch," Boyd cried out. A look of horror crossed his face. He had just injected himself with a needle coated with AIDS-contaminated blood.

Betty and the charge nurse froze, afraid to utter a word.

"Shit!" Boyd grunted.

"No more! No more!" the patient shouted as he rolled from side to side.

Betty took the needle from Boyd's hand. "Let's get some Clorox on that wound," she demanded.

"We might have some on the floor," the charge nurse offered.

"What?" Betty snapped back. "This floor has AIDS patients. It should be everywhere!"

Boyd kept squeezing his palm but the wound was too deep to make it bleed. It was as though his whole life flashed before him. What else could he do to reduce the viral load? Clorox couldn't reach into the depth of the wound and the virus was now flowing into his venous tree, the gateway to his entire body.

The patient continued to mutter incoherently as he lay staring at the ceiling.

Boyd looked down at Puleo and a cold shiver ran through him. Would he look like that in ten years?

"He's in and out of it most of the time, Dr. Boyd," the charge nurse whispered. "He's really not aware."

Betty collected her slides, the solution bottles and directed Boyd out of the room.

"I'm glad you're back, Dr. Boyd," the other technician stated as they entered the lab. "Another frozen section is waiting to be read and biopsies from a pelvic case are on the way."

"Tell them to wait!" Betty insisted. "Hurry up, Dr. Boyd, let's wash that wound."

"But the biopsy's waiting," the technician pleaded.

"Let them wait," Betty shouted. "Where's that bottle of Clorox?"

~ * ~

It was nearly 8 PM when Boyd walked into the doctors' parking lot adjacent to the Emergency Room. Only three cars remained in the area reserved for thirty. Bright lights from the ER entrance penetrated the darkness, beckoning new arrivals.

The ritual was the same. Press the remote button on the key, open the door, slide onto the seat, buckle the belt. But he stopped after inserting the key into the ignition. Going home tonight wouldn't be the same. What happened today would change his life.

He followed the protocol and had blood drawn to prove he was free of AIDS. An infectious disease nurse counseled him on Florida statutes legislating confidentiality. AZT was prescribed by an infectious disease specialist with the hope it would prevent him from converting to HIV positive. He accomplished all this while still working in the lab.

Driving out of the parking lot, he entered the northbound ramp to I-95 and cruised at a speed slower than usual. He debated what to tell his wife. After ten years of marriage, she could read him like a book.

Masking his panic would be difficult, but then to suddenly dump his fears on her was cruel. He could be positive, telling her the treatment had already started. But that didn't comfort him, so how could it convince her?

An engine roared from behind as a bus the size of a Greyhound, cut into his lane, forcing him to brake. None of the familiar dog markings could be seen, but emblazoned on its rear was the familiar 'Balance Scale of Justice' and in large letters, *Beigleman and Associates—Attorneys At Law*. In smaller print, he read, *"Have you been injured? Protect your rights—we will come to YOUR home for a free consultation."* An 800 number followed.

Sure he'd been injured, but how could a lawyer protect him from AIDS? He risked his life every day at work. *All a lawyer risked was losing a case,* he thought and mumbled, "But where is the justice for me."

Unleashing his anger into action, he accelerated and pulled ahead of the bus, waving his fist at the driver. His hands trembled and he gripped the wheel tighter as a wave of nausea hit him. Easing the car onto the soft shoulder, he watched the bus move on. Tears clouded his vision as he slumped over the wheel.

Good God. We'll be living with this for the rest of our lives.

By the time he opened his front door, his mind was numb until he heard his wife call out. "I was wondering what kept you, John. Is everything all right?"

Thirty-four

Parker didn't waste any time scheduling Judy for an appointment. It was painful but he told her the truth. Boyd's review of the pathology slides confirmed her mole was not benign but showed evidence of malignant melanoma.

Once Judy heard the news, Gwen watched her face turn white with shock and moved to her side to comfort her. She could see this tortured woman was in no condition to interpret all the information and motioned for Parker to leave. Placing her arms around Judy's shoulders, she whispered, "Cry all you want. I'm here for you."

Judy left Parker's office, running frantically to her car. She thought she had prepared herself to hear the C word, but the moment Parker said "malignant melanoma," nothing else registered. As a nurse, she knew her condition was extremely serious.

Sitting at the wheel, she felt her heart pound and a dampness on the back of her blouse. She inserted her key, kicked over the engine and raced home.

Once inside the apartment, she flung down her purse,

rushed to the bathroom and splashed cold water over her face. Staring at her reflection in the mirror, she wondered if she should tell Kent about the news. His calls were rare and visits even less frequent. How much longer could she keep pestering him about the divorce without losing all dignity?

Anger welled up within her as she grabbed a towel, wishing it would wipe away every bit of her past with him. She dried her face, moved to the computer and Googled *'Pregnancy and Malignant Melanoma.'* The screen lit up multiple articles reported by researchers from various cancer centers. She felt the tightness in her chest increase as she read. Two facts stood out that determined survival: the thickness of the malignant mole and the extent of cancer spread.

She remembered Parker's opening comments. Her mole was thick and certainly the count of palpable nodes in her armpit numbered more than just one. When she screened the staging classification measuring tumor size, node count and distant spread, she learned her condition fit Stage III, very serious.

Her breathing became more rapid as her fingers eagerly ran over the keyboard, opening the National Cancer Institute website. With widened eyes, she reviewed the statistics. Patients with Stage III malignant melanoma or higher had very low five year survival rates.

"My God," she cried out. "I'll never see my child grow up."

Breaking through her paralysis, she searched for articles that included information on cancer spread to the fetus. The few studies she found indicated that in the majority of cases reported, there was little evidence the fetus developed cancer in utero. But it went on to state the studies were few and inconclusive.

She clicked the link to '*Treatments for Malignant Melanoma*' and waited for the study to come on the screen. The news was disappointing. Reports showed treatments, such as radiation, biotherapy, chemotherapy and Interleukin proved to have poor response rates with unlikely cures. When she reviewed the high dose Interleukin data, she read how toxic it was and rejected any consideration.

But there was some glimmer of hope. Two new biotherapeutic drugs were going through the approval process. One showed a certain percentage of patients carrying a specific genetic mutation could benefit for the treatment of metastatic disease, although it offered no hope for cure. A second biotherapeutic drug had just completed the approval process and showed an arrest to disease progression although it also suggested cure was unlikely.

It was 7:30 PM when she looked to her watch. She couldn't contain herself and dialed Parker's number. His answering service responded and she waited for his call.

The phone finally rang and she heard Parker's voice.

"Do you want to talk, Judy?"

"Yes. I apologize for leaving the office so quickly. I was in no condition to understand what you said."

"I'm sure it was a shock. But here's what I plan."

"Surgery?"

"Yes. We need to remove the metastatic lymph nodes under your arm, and after that we do some tests."

"What kind of tests?"

221

"Blood tests, ultrasound, an MRI. We can't do a CT scan because the radiation could hurt the fetus."

"Exactly," she cut in. "We'll do nothing that will harm the baby."

"I understand, but those lymph nodes have to be removed."

"What good would that do?"

"To reduce the tumor burden and hopefully remove all cancer. It'll also help verify your stage of disease so we'll know how best to treat you."

"Look, Parker, you know the statistics. Even without the pregnancy, I have no more than a ten percent chance of surviving five years. All the treatments you could propose offer no possibility of a cure at my stage. Can't we wait until I deliver? I don't want to hurt my child."

"Please, Judy, we shouldn't wait. The surgery poses very little danger to the fetus."

"Let me think it over."

"Do that, but talking on the phone is no way to discuss such a serious issue. Let me see you in my office."

"Whatever you say. But even if I only have five years, I want them to be spent with my child so I'll consider the surgery."

"Good. I'm glad you're thinking clearly."

Judy sighed. "My research might not be as expert as yours, but deep down we both know the facts. That's why I have the right to question any treatment. If I can't save myself, at the least I'll do everything to save my child."

Thirty-five

Two weeks later

The call came to the apartment at 10 PM and by 10:05, Parker was in his car, headed to MCA's ER. Emergency Medical Services was transporting a gunshot victim, and no way would he again be accused of delaying his response to an emergency.

He entered the unit, relieved Baum wasn't the doctor on duty. Weaving his way through the cluster of attendants, he approached the gurney to see a dark-skinned man gasping for air despite oxygen running through a nasal cannula.

The moment he spotted the scar on the man's left cheek, he froze. It was the drug runner who had kidnapped him. *Was fate putting him to the test?* As a physician who took the Hippocratic Oath, he had no other choice. He had to save this man's life.

The x-ray technician rushed in and placed a film on the view box. "We don't see any bullet fragments, Dr. Dawson. The shot must have passed through his chest."

Parker could see the bullet had collapsed the left lung. Air leaked into that side of the chest and the distended neck veins confirmed the patient had a tension pneumothorax. The increased pressure in the chest cavity was squeezing and collapsing the right lung.

"I want a sterile tray, a thirty-two French chest tube and a Pleurovac," he called out. "We need to release the air trapped in this guy's chest."

The supplies arrived and Parker prepped the patient before injecting a local anesthetic into the fifth rib interspace. After making a quick slit, he thrust a Kelly clamp into the chest cavity. To confirm that the pleural lining of the chest wall was free of adhesions, he poked his pinky finger into the wound before plunging in the tube. Trapped air bubbled into the underwater seal and the man's breathing eased as his color returned.

"Great job, Doc," the nurse assisting him commented.

Parker nodded his appreciation and ordered the technician, "I want to see the tube position so shoot another film."

A nurse handed him the clipboard with the patient's record. For the first time he read the man's name.

Looking down at him, Parker spoke in a firm voice. "Ramon Lopez, do you recognize me?"

Lopez stared back with widened eyes.

"You tried to kill me, you son-of-a-bitch."

Lopez flinched, causing his respirations to increase.

Parker's voice rose. "Don't worry, I'll still take care of you, but I never touched your damned money." He looked up, realizing he had caught everyone's attention. Before another word was spoken, he heard his name and turned to see Rucker standing in the doorway. A sheriff's deputy stood by the agent's side.

Parker burst out. "That's him! He's the one who ambushed me."

"We know," Rucker answered calmly, as the deputy cuffed the man's wrist to the gurney. He took Parker's arm and led him into the corridor. "Lopez was caught in a turf battle. Colombian coke is moving into Cuban territory along with Mexican Meth trafficking and it's all heading here."

Parker responded, "I know your job is tough, but now that you have Lopez, do I still have to worry about getting killed?"

A frown crossed the agent's brow. "Can't say, since you're not their only target." He leaned close and lowered his voice. "We don't want to panic the hospital personnel so a guard will be posted outside Lopez's door."

"Why? Where can he go with that chest tube connected to the suction?"

Rucker paused. "He'll be a good source of information, so we have to make sure he's protected. We're in a gang war and we can't take any chances he'll be rubbed out by the mob."

"What about me, Rucker? Looks like he's getting more protection than me."

"It may appear that way, Doc, but you have to understand how violent these thugs are. They just shot an attorney who was subpoenaed to testify in a drug case. He was found dead in his office. The same day, a liquor store at the mall was riddled with machine gun bullets but we don't know what triggered that party."

"Then I'm still a target?"

"Afraid so, Doc. Things are heating up. A major drug shipment must be on its way because the Coast Guard intercepted floating bales of contraband that washed onto the beach. Nobody steals from these cartels. They knock people off just to show their muscle."

"If they still think I stole their money, I need police protection more than Lopez."

"Don't kid yourself, Doc. Because he knows so much, he's at a greater risk. When can we grill him?"

"With chest tube in place, he should be fine, but I'll know by morning," Parker answered, checking his watch. "By the way, when do you sleep, Rucker?"

The agent smiled. "Whenever I can. As the officer in charge, I have to know all the players and everything going on."

"And when does this nightmare end?"

Rucker shook his head. "Maybe never. Miami is the command center for worldwide cocaine trafficking. It's also a hub for laundering drug money."

"Is the Mafia involved in this?"

"Yes, along with world terrorists who use drug profits to support their global activities. You'd be surprised how many political groups depend on that money to undermine the governments they attack. The Irish Republican Army, the PKK Kurdish revolutionaries, the Taliban, the Asian Tamil movement, and the al-Qaeda. Some you've never even heard about."

Parker raised his hands. If Rucker was trying to make him feel secure, he certainly missed the mark. Maybe the way out of this mess was to leave south Florida, but that wasn't possible just now.

The sheriff returned with two cell phones. "We found these in Lopez's pocket."

Just as Rucker took the phones, his own cell rang. He listened and replied, "I'm on my way."

"What's happening?" Parker asked.

"Lopez's partner died in the shooting and they found an address in his wallet. The sheriff's office checked it out and they think it's a stash house. The SWAT team's getting ready to raid the place."

"I'm coming," Parker spoke out.

"No, Doc, it's too dangerous and you have your patient to watch."

"The patient is taken care of, but it's my ass on the line. I have a right to see the hoods targeting me."

Rucker's eyes narrowed. "I'm ordering you to stay away."

Before Parker could reply, the emergency room doctor approached. "Dr. Dawson, will you write the admitting orders?"

Parker eagerly grabbed the chart. "Put him on my service and get him to ICU. Make sure his hands are cuffed. I don't want him pulling out that chest tube."

"I'll call for the bed," the doctor answered picking up the phone.

Parker watched Rucker and the sheriffs move quickly down the hall. He scribbled the ICU admitting orders in the chart, handed it to the nurse and said, "I'm on my cell. If ICU runs into any problems, call me."

~ * ~

Although Parker knew he was going against Rucker's order, he decided to follow without being noticed. He trailed the sheriff's caravan of cars from a distance, always keeping them in sight.

When they exited the I-95 ramp onto Blue Heron Boulevard in Riviera Beach, he followed, driving around side streets lined with modest homes. Finally the deputy cars stopped before a cinder-block house sitting on a small patch of shaggy lawn. The lights were on, indicating it was occupied.

The moon illuminated the rundown residential area, making it possible for Parker to see shadowy figures around the bungalow. He parked his Honda away from Rucker to avoid being noticed but still in position to view the action. Slipping out of the car, he edged closer and watched two SWAT team deputies approach the targeted building. The bulk of their uniforms indicated they wore bulletproof vests.

With the house surrounded, one deputy pounded the barrel of his automatic weapon against the wooden door and shouted, "Police, open up!"

Parker watched the front lights in the house go out as the deputy again beat on the door, bellowing, "Open up or we're coming in." Getting no response, the officer aimed his weapon at the lock and fired. Parker jumped on hearing the shot and saw the officer kick open the door.

An exchange of automatic weapon fire pierced the darkness while the officers crouched on both sides, avoiding the line of fire. The shattering of glass erupted and the hissing of tear gas could be heard as smoke billowed from the house.

After a short wait, he saw two men stagger out the doorway, coughing uncontrollably. One in cut-off jeans held a towel to his face while the other used his torn tee-shirt to dry his eyes. With guns drawn, deputies rushed up and cuffed the two.

Parker hid in the shadows as the neighborhood lights came alive. People from surrounding homes emerged in their night clothes and watched the deputies run a yellow tape around the property.

Amid the smoke and confusion, Parker thought he caught sight of a slight figure slip out the side door and run into the bushes toward an adjacent house. With his vision obstructed by tall shrubs, he gingerly moved in the direction of the shadowy form. As he neared, a slight breeze caressed his cheek. The smoke cleared and for a split moment, he noticed the shrub move, suggesting someone was hiding there. He quickened his pace and cautiously spread the limbs of the bush. In the moonlight, he confronted a whimpering young girl sitting in a stooped posture amid the lush foliage.

Tearful oval brown eyes stared back at him. "Please," she cried, "don't hurt me."

He gently extended his hand to coax her out. "Don't be afraid. No harm will come to you," he assured her.

She appeared to believe him and with the innocence of a child, she clasped his hand and emerged out of the bushes.

Just a kid, no more than thirteen, Parker surmised. Suddenly the vision of Olga Ottavio on that first fateful day in the OR came into his thoughts. This girl had to be Olga's daughter, the one who was to get the key.

He watched the tears run down her face and comforted her with an embrace. "You must be Carmella."

Thirty-six

Parker turned off the morning alarm and lay in bed trying to make sense of his situation. A week had passed since he witnessed the raid on the stash house and he wondered why Rucker never let him know what had happened to Carmella.

The hospital's charge of patient abandonment kept most doctors from referring cases to him. But thanks to the few who appreciated his surgical skills, he was able to pay most of his office expenses. The mounting college loan was another question, and he would deal with that when his income increased.

The GPS monitor lay on the night stand, a constant reminder that the drug traffickers were still out there. He strapped the unit on his ankle, recalling the newspaper report describing the Mexican drug cartel's savage retaliation against law enforcement. Three policemen on the Mexican border town of Nuevo Laredo were beheaded by the syndicate. The chief of police quit in fear he was their next target and left the community in a state of criminal anarchy.

He rose from the bed and dialed the phone. "Rucker,

what's happened to Carmella?"

"She's in custody as an illegal alien."

"Does she know anything about the key or the money?"

"The kid's scared. All she could tell us was that Lopez and her mother planned to marry and fly with her to Costa Rica to live."

"Why not Mexico where they're from?"

"Probably because Costa Rica has no extradition treaty with the U.S. We figure Olga and Lopez corralled enough money from the syndicate to quit the mob and live well."

"But if they're Illegals with no identification, how can they board a commercial flight?"

"Sorry to say Illegals, drugs and cash are smuggled in and out of this country every day. They use private planes or power boats that can out-run most Coast Guard vessels to get to the Bahamas. With enough money, it's easy to get to Costa Rica."

"What about the two cell phones you found on Lopez?"

"We're working on that."

"What did you find in the stash house?"

"A little money, not more than three thousand dollars. But the jackpot was the ton of cocaine and cases of prescription pills packed in plastic packages. They look like counterfeit blue Viagra tablets with the Pfizer label. We're sending them to the company for analysis."

"That fits with what I saw," Parker replied. "A clerk at a convenience store sold Viagra to two guys while I was standing there. I couldn't believe it. Where's the stuff coming from?"

"The last batch we confiscated were sugar pills and

they came from China. Until the drug company analyzed it, they said they couldn't tell the difference between the real tablets or the bogus ones."

Parker whistled. "With Viagra costing five to ten bucks a pop, it has to be a hell of a lucrative operation."

"Peddling counterfeit drugs is getting to be more profitable than hard drugs. But our real challenge is to follow the money trail and how the mob launders the profits. We estimate the local syndicate deposited billions in cash in more than eighteen banks over the past two years."

"You're talking big money. I know nothing about that stuff."

"Look Doc, laundering money is complicated. You've heard of the Costa Nostra and the Bonnano Family, haven't you?"

"Yeah, the Mafia."

"They've even used pizza parlors to distribute smuggled heroin coming from the Golden Triangle of Asia. All that money has to be washed."

Parker paused, taking in a deep breath. "Look, Rucker, this is way above my head. I'm just a simple doctor trying to save a few lives. Remember, I'm scared as hell every time I see a car follow me or some stranger loiter outside the hospital. Just find the money and get me out of this fucked up mess."

Thirty-seven

Days later

Rucker led the sheriff's patrol cars into the upscale gated community of PGA National, stopping in front of a two story house on the quiet tree-lined street. The telephone number retrieved from Lopez's cell phone, alias Cougar, led them to the home of Henry Trask, Lindstrom's assistant administrator. At 10 PM, most homes on the block were dark except for the targeted house.

After his discharge from the hospital, Lopez became a wealth of information for Rucker. The trafficker used the code name Cougar as a cover in the shadowy world of drug pushers and money launderers. His sincere concern for Carmella's welfare as well as his own made him an extremely cooperative witness, especially when facing charges of kidnapping and money laundering.

Rucker, along with deputies, approached the front door while two lawmen took positions in the driveway and two in the back of the home. He pressed the buzzer and waited a few moments.

The door opened and the thick-set administrator wearing glasses appeared in his bathrobe.

Rucker held out his badge. "Good evening, Mr. Trask. I'm Agent Rucker of the DEA. We have a court order authorizing us to enter and examine the contents of your home."

Before Trask could answer, Rucker pushed open the door and the deputies followed.

"Wait!" Trask objected. "You can't just walk in here."

"Sorry," Rucker answered, handing him the court order. "Read it!" He then told the deputies to search the first floor as he climbed the stairs to the master bedroom.

On entering the brightly lit room, he saw the computer on the desk displaying a screen filled with data. He moved closer, sat down and read the display.

Trask rushed into the room. "That's private, you can't do that!" he shouted.

The two deputies following grabbed and restrained him.

Rucker chuckled with a broad smile. "Thanks for opening the page we need." He studied the screen and picked up an invoice marked Reliant Drug Distributors laying on the desk.

"Now this looks interesting," he said. "I wonder where this company is headquartered?

"You have no right!" Trask bellowed.

"Unfortunately we do, sir. The judge agreed we had enough evidence for probable cause to justify a search warrant. Your computer represents material evidence and if we can track illegal money transfers to offshore bank accounts, you're in big trouble."

"I have to speak to my lawyer," Trask demanded.

"You will," Rucker answered. He began reading Trask

his Miranda Rights while the deputy clasped handcuffs on his wrists.

"There's nothing of interest in the other parts of the house," a deputy said, entering the room.

Rucker faced Trask as the deputies continued to restrain him. "I believe we have what we're looking for." Seeing the panic in Trask's eyes, he added, "If you agree to tell us who else is involved in this operation, we might make a deal."

Trask glared back at Rucker, saying nothing.

"Take him away," Rucker ordered. "Shut down the computer and take it for evidence. It's probably got the information we're looking for."

Another deputy came into the room pulling a large roll-on piece of luggage. "Look what I just found," he called out. "There's enough cash in here to buy a private jet."

Rucker smiled. "Good work, guys. We're going to play it straight and count all of it together."

~ * ~

Parker heard the news of Trask's arrest through the gossip channels of MCA. Opinions ranged from shock to ridicule. The story was withheld for a few days, but the press finally reported it when Trask was arraigned.

The nursing supervisor for the floor approached Parker at the control desk just as he finished writing orders. "Could I have a word with you, Doctor?" She motioned him to follow her into an empty room.

"This is just between us," she whispered. "I've noticed something disturbing. With Mr. Trask's arrest, I wonder if it's related."

"What do you mean?"

"I wonder if there's something strange going on. The Procrit and Epogen we're giving our cancer patients isn't boosting red blood counts. More alarming are the adverse reactions we're seeing. Patients are experiencing painful muscle spasms, something I've never seen."

Parker frowned, recalling Judy's complaint about Procrit. "Have you told anyone else about this?"

"I told Dr. Gold because he's chief of staff, and he said he'd check into it but nothing's happened." Lowering her voice, she added, "I hope you could talk to Administration."

"You're questioning the purity of the drugs?"

"Yes," she replied softly.

Parker took in a deep breath, remembering one of his patients who failed on Procrit. "Are you sure the bottles are labeled properly with the same official logo of the companies?"

"Yes, I checked it myself. They look completely identical to what we used in the past."

Parker shook his head. He had enough problems and didn't need another battle with Lindstrom. "This could be serious. Maybe someone else should bring it up to Administration."

"Dr. Dawson, I asked you because nurses know you listen. I'm afraid Dr. Gold didn't take what I said very seriously. Frankly it's what I would expect from most of the staff." She shook her head. "They don't want to get involved with Administration."

He read the determined look in her eyes. "I'll talk to Pharmacy."

After the nurse thanked him, he walked down the hall

with his thoughts mired in conflict. At the moment, Judy was his most urgent concern because she was having second thoughts about the surgery. So what options were left, chemotherapy, biotherapeutics? Both of them had serious side effects and could risk the pregnancy.

But with all of her hormones raging in the third trimester, he worried the cancer was on the verge of exploding. He needed a quiet period of uninterrupted time to convince her she had to have her lymph nodes removed. Making an abrupt turn, he headed to Pharmacy.

The technician let him pass through the locked door and when he entered, Fred Russo, the head pharmacist, greeted him. "Hi, Dr. Dawson, what can we do for you?"

Parker smiled. "I'd like to know the name of the drug distributor supplying our Procrit."

Russo gave him a quizzical look. "I've never had a request like that."

"Just curious. It has nothing to do with the pharmacy."

Russo rose from his chair. "The invoice is in our file. I'll pull it."

Parker became increasingly uneasy as he waited. Word about his probe into pharmacy matters was bound to reach Lindstrom, so he hoped it was fruitful.

Russo returned holding the invoice. "Here it is—it's Reliant Drug Distributors." He watched Parker check the address on the invoice and added, "Lonny Martin from purchasing said Trask instructed him to buy from Reliant because their prices are lower."

"How long have they been supplying you?"

"Maybe about three months."

"Look, Fred, I'd like a copy of the invoice."

Russo gave him a doubtful look. "You know I'm not authorized to do that. Are you on to something I should know, Dr. Dawson?"

"I hope not, Fred. Maybe I'm just a little paranoid, but I need to track down the source of our Procrit and Epogen."

Russo studied Parker's grim expression. "I haven't been too happy about changing our pharmaceutical suppliers, so if there's a problem, I'd like to know."

He left to make a copy and returned, handing it to Parker. "I trust you won't say who gave this to you."

Parker shook his hand with a firm grip. "Let's just say this never happened."

Thirty-eight

Following day

Parker left his office early and headed to the bank to sign for the loan covering Fellini's legal fee. With no assurance from Lawton that the hospital's abandonment charges would be dropped, an investment in lawyer protection was the only way to retain his sanity. If things were going to get ugly, he wanted an experienced attorney on his side.

The paper work with the bank manager was interrupted by the ring of his cell phone. It was Gwen.

"Dr. Dawson, Elise Linton, that wealthy lady from Palm Beach called. She wouldn't tell me anything but insisted she needs to speak with you right away. She sounded really upset."

"I'm still at the bank, Gwen. Give me her number." He jotted it down, excused himself from the banker and dialed.

Elise answered on the first ring. "Dr. Dawson, you must come to my house immediately!"

"What's up, Elise?"

"It's Marla. I think she overdosed on drugs."

"Is she conscious?"

"I'm not sure. When I shake her, she mumbles to leave her alone. Her eyes are closed and she's shaking. I'm worried she might not wake up."

"Call nine-one-one right now and get her to MCA's emergency room. I'll call the hospital to let them know she's coming in."

"But if nine-one-one reports she overdosed in my house, my name will get in the papers."

"That can't be helped, Elise. Marla's life is in danger and you've got to act now."

"You'll be there when she arrives?"

"Yes, and I'll speak to you after things are under control. Talk to you later."

He turned to the startled bank officer. "Sorry, I have an emergency, but I'll be back. Just hold on to those papers."

He rushed to his car, hoping it wasn't too late for Marla. A traffic jam in the parking lot forced him to wait, wasting valuable minutes.

Frustrated by the delay, he dialed MCA's Emergency Room. "Dr. Dawson here. The rescue team's transporting a patient who appears to have overdosed on drugs. Her name is Marla Evans. Tell the doctor on call I'm on my way in. Good bye."

The cars ahead finally moved into the street and he pressed on the gas, driving into the flow of traffic on Northlake Boulevard. The vision of Marla in her sexy gown standing next to him on Linton's verandah made him shudder. He had a hard time figuring why a beautiful woman with everything to live for would want to trash her life on drugs.

He debated why he hadn't called Rucker to let him know that Lindstrom was at Elise Linton's party. The administrator might be a link to the drugs used that night. But at this moment, his hope was that Marla would pull through and identify the pusher.

The late morning flow of drivers frustrated him so he quickly cut around the slower cars, moving into open lanes. He finally reached the hospital and ran up the walk that led to the ER, hoping it wasn't too late.

Once inside, he dashed past the control desk and entered the triage area where the ER physician hovered over Marla's limp body.

Parker asked, "What's her pressure?"

The ER doctor looked up, shaking his head. "She has none."

The sound of a ventilator delivering surges of oxygen into Marla's lungs filled the silence in the room. Parker's eyes widened as he approached the gurney with its hanging bags of IV solutions dripping fluid into her veins. But the flat line on the monitor screen told the whole story. Marla was dead.

"Sorry, Dr. Dawson, she got here too late," the ER doc said.

Parker stared down at Marla's motionless body. Her clothes had been cut, exposing her chest. The stark contrast of her black bra against a colorless skin conjured up a ghoulish image in contrast to the vibrancy she exuded that night on the verandah.

What a fuckin' waste, he cursed to himself. *Those drug-pushing, money-hungry bastards don't give a shit about the lives they wreck.*

The urgent sound in the desk secretary's voice broke into his thoughts. "The coroner's office is on the line and someone outside is asking about the patient's condition, Dr. Dawson."

The ER physician moved to the phone. "I'll talk to the coroner," he said.

Suspecting Elise was the person waiting, Parker entered the nearly empty reception area. An Hispanic couple wearing thread bare jeans and faded tee shirts conversed openly in Spanish. Elise sat opposite them, dressed in a finely tailored designer blouse and pants, probably purchased from an upscale store like Saks.

The irony of the scene struck Parker. Illegal drugs grown south of the border contributed to the corruption and poverty from which these poor souls escaped. The same drugs caused Marla's death which was the reason why the two divergent social classes were now sharing the same waiting room.

Elise rushed up to him. "Marla looked dreadful. Is she all right?"

Without answering, Parker took her arm and led her inside the ER. He drew back the curtain to the cubicle where Marla lay. "I'm so sorry, Elise. She's gone.

Elise burst into tears. "It can't be! How could this happen?"

Parker drew her close, holding her until the sobs diminished. "There's something I need to know," he asked.

Elise nodded, wiping her face with a handkerchief.

"Can you tell me who supplied Marla with the drugs?"

She pulled away. "What's the difference? Marla's dead."

He looked into her eyes, gripping her shoulders. "It's important, Elise. I must know who she was dealing with."

"You're hurting me!" she cried, pushing his hands away. She rubbed her shoulders and returned a questioning look.

"I apologize, Elise, but I need your help."

"I know nothing about what you're asking," she answered in a defiant tone.

Realizing she was struggling to cope with Marla's death, his voice softened. "Let's not talk here," he said. "We can both use a cup of coffee."

She nodded and Parker led her to an empty doctors' dining room.

"Elise, I saw drugs at your party and I also saw our hospital administrator, Eric Lindstrom, there. Do you know him?"

He paused, noticing her lips tighten. "Why was Marla at your house today?"

She let out a breathy sigh. "Marla's like a wandering kitten. She comes and stays with me whenever she's depressed. Sometimes for a week at a time. She went through a horrendous divorce and needed someone to be with her."

Parker persisted. "Did you see her taking drugs?"

"No. I saw nothing like that around me. All I can say is that Marla was at my house for lunch. Someone came to the door and she answered it. I don't know who it was."

Parker didn't want the trail to go dead and tried to contain his excitement. "How long have you known Lindstrom?"

"I really don't," Elise answered. "He just seems to

show up at Palm Beach parties and I guess everyone accepts him."

Parker studied her bewildered look of confusion. He felt she was telling the truth and thought it wise to stop pummeling her with questions. But it was time to tell Rucker about this connection.

They sat without speaking as they sipped their coffee when Elise broke the silence.

"Excuse me, Dr. Dawson. I have a question for you. The painful look on your face makes me think you were in love with Marla. Were you?"

Parker smiled. "Did she say I was?"

"Not directly, but I know she was attracted to you."

"That's flattering, Elise. Maybe it could have happened at another time. But what she needed was the kind of help I don't think I could have given her."

Elise dropped her head. "Maybe I let her down."

Parker reached for her hand. "You were a good friend to her, Elise. You did nothing wrong."

As he watched the tears fill her eyes, he pondered who really was to blame for Marla's death. Was it the drug pushers or Marla herself? In the end, it seemed everyone profited along the trail of distribution except the victim. And this time the victim was Marla.

Thirty-nine

One week later, 9 AM, Parker's Apartment

With no surgery scheduled for the day, Parker sat at his kitchen table and reviewed the Reliant Drug invoice Freddie had given him. Procrit and Epogen, expensive drugs used for treating cancer patients, were listed on the form. If the purchased drugs were bogus, he needed proof before confronting Lindstrom. If his accusations proved false, he could face a lawsuit.

He put down his cup, rubbed his face and began to question his situation. He had to be clear about his decisions. It already cost $6000 for Fellini's retainer to defend him against the state, not to mention the added cost if they had to appear before the state's Probable Cause Panel. And who knew how the Executive Committee would decide about his charges of abandonment? Those thoughts kept him up at night.

One problem at a time, he thought to himself, as he picked up the phone and dialed Rucker. "I need your help," he pleaded.

Rucker's voice was firm. "Were you threatened again?"

"No, something else came up. I need an undercover investigation."

Rucker cut in, "Hold on, Doc. I can't do anything illegal."

His response startled Parker. "You know me better than that. Let me explain. I'm holding an invoice from Reliant Drug Distributors. They supply MCA with certain meds and I'd like you to check to see if this company is legitimate. I suspect they might be selling counterfeit drugs."

Hearing no response, Parker wondered if it meant Rucker was acquainted with the company. He continued, "Trask instructed MCA's pharmacy to buy from Reliant. With his arrest, I thought there might be a connection."

"I can't comment about Trask, Doc. That investigation is in progress, but I'll run a check on Reliant. Trask's computer printed all the invoices that were laying on his desk and I have them."

"Then you won't need my copy?"

"I want it to compare with the one I have."

"I'll have it at my office but don't say who gave it to you."

"I can live with that. We'll be in touch."

Parker shut the phone and dialed Gwen at the office.

Her voice sounded strained when she answered. "You just received another registered letter from MCA, Dr. Dawson."

"I expected it. Read it to me."

"You want me to open it?"

"Sure, I tell you everything."

"Fine," she replied.

He heard her slit open the envelope followed by a pause.

Her voice was steady as she read.

"Executive Committee of MCA has scheduled a meeting to formalize charges of patient abandonment against you. You are to appear before the Committee, however you may not be represented by legal counsel, only by another member of the medical staff."

She stopped. "Do you want me to continue?"

"No, hold on to it and I'll deal with it later." He shut the phone, feeling a sharp pain in his chest. Wiping the moisture off his brow, he reasoned he was too young to have a heart attack. It was time to talk to someone wiser than himself, so he dialed Fellini.

The receptionist put him through immediately.

"I have another problem, Mr. Fellini."

"Why? Has the state Investigator contacted you?"

"No. I just received another certified letter from MCA. The Executive Committee has ordered me to appear before them to face charges of patient abandonment."

"If that's what the by-laws say, then you have to abide by the process."

"But it won't be a fair hearing."

"Why do you say that?"

"At least five of the members on that committee have a financial involvement with the hospital. I think that's a conflict of interest."

"How so?"

"They all have sweetheart deals with MCA that can be terminated at any time without cause. For instance, the chief of cardiology holds a contract that pays him to read all the hospital EKGs. The chief of family practice holds the contract for the corporation's HMO plan as well as the chiefs of radiology and neurology. Need I say more?"

"But isn't that true at all hospitals, Dr. Dawson?"

"No," Parker answered. "Most hospitals spread their contracts around to more than one physician in each department. That's not the case here."

"What you're telling me is that the doctors who are on the Committee to judge you are beholden to Administration."

"Exactly! And to top it all off, MCA aggressively markets Dr. Barco as their premier surgeon performing a dangerous laser operation. He is also a member of the Committee."

"I understand what you're telling me, but according to the by-laws, those are the facts you have to live with."

"Dammit, Mr. Fellini. What really bothers me is that I'm not allowed to bring an attorney to the meeting. I feel my rights are being jeopardized."

There was a long pause before Fellini spoke. "Unfortunately, Doctor, my practice doesn't permit me to deal with local hospital litigation. I only handle state actions against physicians."

Parker took in a deep breath. "Excuse me, Mr. Fellini. What's all this bullshit about procedure when the deck is loaded against me?"

"I understand your frustration, Doctor, but you have to play out the process. Can you bring in a staff physician to defend you?"

"Yes. The letter states a staff member can represent me, but how does that protect me legally?"

"If you decide to sue MCA for these allegations, you must follow the by-laws."

"Even if the process is fixed?"

"Yes, because no court will look favorably on your complaint unless you follow the procedure. Is there a friendly staff member you can ask to speak for you?"

"That's a problem. Everyone is afraid to go up against the hospital. If they stand up for me, they know the hospital will give them a hard time, especially if a case of theirs goes sour."

"I sense your hospital's politics are heating up."

"Then you understand."

"I do. I've seen many a hospital trash good doctors, but the best advice I can offer is that under no circumstance should you go into that meeting without representation. Alone, you'll never prevail. This doesn't constitute a legal opinion, Doctor, only a suggestion."

Parker hung up the phone with his spirits dropping even farther. Little did he realize when he began his career, the struggles during his years of training were tame compared to the pot holes of private practice.

Forty

"Sorry I couldn't get here sooner, Mr. Lindstrom," Judy apologized. "It's been busy on the floors today."

The administrator sat erect in the tufted leather chair behind his desk, taking in her worried expression. "Quite all right, Miss Keller. I called because questions have been raised concerning your professional judgment. I'd like you to think clearly before you answer." He watched the nursing supervisor squirm in her chair.

"If it's regarding the transfer of ICU patients to a controlled ward, I had to do that because we ran out of beds."

The administrator shook his head. "No, I need to ask about an Emergency Room incident that involves Dr. Dawson. You may recall he was late to respond to an ER accident involving a biker, Stanley Kingsley. You were present, were you not?"

"Yes," she answered softly.

Lindstrom nodded. "Dr. Dawson is to appear before Executive Committee to explain his delayed response to the emergency. You will also be asked to appear before the Committee. You will be questioned who was called first, Dr. Patel or Dr. Dawson."

"Neither," she shot back. "Dr. Kern, the orthopedist, was contacted first, then Dr. Patel and finally, Dr. Dawson."

"You're sure about that?"

"Yes. That's what Suzy, the desk secretary, told me when I arrived to the ER. At first she couldn't reach Dr. Patel or Dr. Kern, but when she got to them, they wouldn't come in."

Lindstrom rose from his chair, turning to face the window behind his desk. "I don't want you to mislead the Committee, Miss Keller. It could hurt you."

"I have no intention of misleading anyone, Mr. Lindstrom."

"Let me be clear. It's come to my attention you were involved in an immoral act with one of our married staff physicians."

He turned to face her again, his eyes locking onto hers. "It took place in an SUV parked in the doctors' lot. Isn't that so?"

Judy's voice dropped. "I can't imagine what you're referring to, Mr. Lindstrom."

"If you insist." He slid into his chair, rested his elbows on the desk and clasped his palms as if in prayer. "A parking lot security camera videotaped you and the doctor. The infrared camera catches everything, even in the dark. Does that refresh your memory, Miss Keller?" He watched her face turn pale, and when she didn't respond, he added, "Do you have anything to say?"

"No." Her voice was faint.

"Let me be clear. You violated your professional responsibility by leaving the premises while on duty. That compromises the integrity of this hospital and it is reportable to the Florida Board of Nursing and Department of Professional Regulation. Your license and career could be in jeopardy."

Judy froze, casting her eyes downward.

"But perhaps that can be avoided." He paused, watching her stare at her hands clasped in her lap. "It would be to your advantage to not recall which surgeon was called first."

"But I can't lie, Mr. Lindstrom."

"I'm not telling you to lie. Maybe you're uncertain. You can't remember. I'll be attending the meeting so we needn't speak again. Think of the consequences your answer will incur. Thank you for taking the time to come in."

Lindstrom watched her dart out of the office past Robertson's desk. Her eagerness to leave told him his proposal had made its mark.

~ * ~

Later that evening, Judy paced restlessly in her apartment waiting for Kent's call. It was 7 PM when the phone finally rang, and she dashed to grab the receiver. She debated if she should tell Kent about her malignancy, but decided she would first see how the conversation unfolded.

"Give me a break, Judy. My lawyer's already finalizing the arrangements for the divorce."

"It's not that, Kent…"

He cut her off. "Then what else should I worry about?"

252

"Mr. Lindstrom called me to his office today. An infrared video camera recorded us in your SUV and he's threatening to report me to the nursing board."

"What video? What are you talking about?"

"Remember the night you called me to the parking lot? The security cameras filmed us in the dark."

"You've got to be kidding! What did you say?"

"Nothing. What could I say? I'm to appear before Executive Committee that's investigating Dr. Dawson and he wants me to lie."

"About what?"

"He wants me to forget Dawson wasn't the first surgeon called to see an emergency in the ER."

"So what's the problem?"

"It's not true, Kent! Dr. Dawson was called last after the first two surgeons refused to come in."

"Don't make this into a crisis, Judy. Say whatever Lindstrom wants."

"I can't do that to Dr. Dawson."

"Look, Judy, this is serious! Just say you can't remember, then we're both off the hook."

"I'm scared, Kent."

"We have too much to lose. Don't worry about Parker. He'll come out okay."

"I'm so confused."

"There's no other choice! You're not lying, just say you can't remember. If I'm dragged into this, it'll screw things up." Her silence made him call out. "Speak to me, Judy!"

"I don't know if I could do that."

"You must, so don't complicate our lives. Remember

how much we mean to each other and the baby."

Words about the baby stopped her. "I'll have to think about this," she answered stiffly.

"No, Judy, don't think about it. Just do it!"

The commanding sound of his voice angered her. "Don't talk down to me, Kent! I'm the one carrying the kid and I'm the one on the line at work, not you. Good bye!"

She slammed down the phone, feeling the moisture on her brow. How much more could she commit to cover up for him? She had to think about the baby. It was obvious telling him about her cancer wasn't going to change their relationship for the better. Kent was of no help, and as far as the cancer, she had to put her trust in Parker.

To clear her mind, she felt the need for a hot shower and moved to the bathroom. After bathing, she reached for the toothpaste in the medicine cabinet. An unopened package of birth control pills on the shelf triggered a sudden wave of guilt when a thought surfaced from her subconscious. *Did I miss taking the pill on purpose?*

Forty-one

Parker stepped away from the operating table and casually flipped his rubber gloves into the hazardous waste basket. Blood on his gown, drapes and floor gave evidence to the excessive bleeding due to the patient's ruptured spleen.

"There goes my weekend in the Bahamas, Rudy," he sighed.

"You planned a vacation?" the jovial anesthesiologist asked as he worked to awaken the patient.

"Yes, combined with a medical meeting at Paradise Island. But after this emergency, I can't go. There's no one to cover for me."

Rudy lightly patted the sleeping patient's cheek. "This *hombre's* damn lucky you came to check him. ER was ready to send him to the floor."

"Can't take anything for granted," Parker answered, carefully removing his wet gown. "Even a fender bender can cause severe injuries."

Rudy removed an empty blood pouch and shook his head. "This here fella's a big shot Wall Street lawyer with

255

mucho dinero. He lives in Loblolly, that fancy golf club, so you better watch him good."

"You worried about getting sued?"

"All the time," Rudy chuckled. "Play safe. Don't send him to the floor yet. Get him an ICU bed."

Parker smiled, aware that the Intensive Care Unit provided the best care in the hospital. "You're right, Rudy. Then we both can get some sleep."

He headed to the doctors' locker room to change his clothes, confident he had just prevented a possible medical disaster.

Despite Gwen's repeated prediction his surgical referrals would pick up, the cases were not rolling in. Hospital scuttlebutt fueled gossip about his disciplinary charges, and most staff doctors were reluctant to take sides or buck Administration. Now more than ever, he was dependent on the Emergency Room for new cases.

Standing before his locker, he dried the bloodied moisture off his waist.

The outer door opened and Karl Lawton walked in. "Working late?" the chief of surgery asked.

"Not by choice," Parker replied. "Are you operating tonight?"

Lawton shook his head. "No surgery, just a vascular consult."

Parker knotted his tie, looking into the mirror on the locker door as he spoke. "Not my lucky day. I have to cancel my trip to Paradise Island for a meeting tomorrow because of this emergency."

"That must be the same conference Morty Gold's going to. Did you ask Leader to cover for you?"

"He said he had to take his wife out of town."

"Your meeting's paid for?"

"The hotel and airfare, too."

Karl sat down on the bench, looking up at Parker. "What time is your flight?"

"Three o'clock tomorrow."

"Tell you what. Introduce me to your patient in the morning and then take off. I'll cover you."

"I really appreciate that favor, Karl."

"No problem. When you get there, keep an eye out for Morty."

"Why?"

"I saw him there at the crap tables one weekend, betting pretty heavy with a hot babe at his side. No question it wasn't his wife."

"Did he see you?"

"Hell, no. His eyes were glued to the dice and the chick's cleavage. Didn't look like he cared about how much he was losing. I guess that's why he operates on anything that crawls. Spends money like water."

"Call me square or stupid, Karl, but why is it that guys who break the rules always look smart and seem to get away with it? Leader and Gold let a patient bleed out on the table and I'm the one facing disciplinary charges."

Karl rose and before leaving, he turned. "It ain't a fair world, is it?" he replied, closing the door behind him.

~ * ~

Parker's Friday night flight to Nassau from Fort Lauderdale was short, smooth and relaxing. He had to be available night and day, seven days a week since the start of private practice. Taking this short break felt like a luxury.

He reached the Atlantis Paradise Island Coral Towers after a short ride from the airport. By 6 PM he sat in the conference room listening to the keynote speaker talk about the same cancer Judy faced.

The lecturer reviewed the snail-like progress made in the treatment of incurable metastatic melanoma. He discussed the disappointing failures of chemotherapy and the minimal benefits from immuno and hormonal therapy. Finally he approached the main thrust of his talk, targeted therapy. This newest treatment stalled the growth of the cancer. The complex scientific data of melanoma germ cell mutation, protein kinases and a host of growth factors was presented, which only scientists dedicated to that narrow area of research could understand.

But as a clinician treating patients, Parker had to decide which of the cytokines would benefit Judy. The lecture focused on two possible treatments he would consider. This was her best hope.

Once outside the room, he went to a large table spread of appetizers. He filled his plate, searching the room for Morty Gold, but he was nowhere to be seen. Finishing his meal, he decided to explore the resort's plush surroundings.

It was past 8 PM when he walked over the bridge leading to the casino which proudly advertised its one hundred crap tables. Sauntering the lengthy aisles among energetic gamblers, he finally spotted Gold rolling the dice. To avoid being noticed, he stepped back and watched the chief of staff throw the cubes, shouting, "Be there!"

The striking brunette beside Gold shrieked a piercing

"Yes," wrapping her arms around him. With every bob of her head, dangling earrings flipped wildly as she squealed, "We won!"

Parker watched the croupier's stick guide Gold's winnings toward his stash. No doubt, the chief of staff had registered for the meeting to get continuing medical education credits, but Parker could see this trip was only an excuse to party.

He moved to the opposite side of the table behind a group of gamblers. Karl's description of the babe was accurate. Big breasts, a plunging neckline and a tight waist. She was a hottie, all right.

Tired of people watching, he tried his luck at the slot machines, reinvested his winnings and stopped when his twenty dollars disappeared. The odds were in favor of the house and long play put you into a sucker's game.

Reggae music drifted out from the Dragon Night Club adjacent to the casino. The driving beat drew him through the doors and his mood lightened. He walked beside the long black granite bar, watching couples drink, laugh and talk while colorfully dressed natives pounded their music and rhythm on steel-rimmed instruments.

Two enormous dragon sculptures dominated the room and in a dark corner he saw a most unexpected sight. There sat Lindstrom in a bright tangerine linen shirt, leaning his head against the shoulder of a younger man. The hardnosed administrator, totally out of character, let out a maniacal laugh.

Convinced that this tight-assed hospital administrator lived a double life, Parker suspected Lindstrom not only peddled drugs to Palm Beach society, but probably collaborated with Trask to profit from counterfeit drug trafficking.

He moved to a remote table where he could observe the two without being seen. When a waiter approached, he ordered a glass of Merlot which he nursed while listening to the music. Before he finished his drink, he watched Lindstrom and his friend rise and stroll together toward the exit. Just as they walked out the door, Parker froze when he saw Lindstrom grab his companion's right butt.

~ * ~

Gwen greeted Parker as he walked through his office door Monday morning.. "How was your weekend in Paradise Island?"

"Very interesting," Parker chuckled. "Gold and Lindstrom were there, but certainly not for the conference."

Gwen broke out in a broad smile. "Oh goodie, what were they up to?"

Their conversation halted when the door opened and Rucker walked in.

"Good morning, Doc. Could I have a word with you?"

It was unusual to see the agent in his office. "Sure thing, Rucker." Parker turned to Gwen and whispered, "Tell you later."

As they sat in his office, Parker felt unsettled by the agent's penetrating look. "You have some information for me, Rucker?"

Always neat, the agent's dark blue suit hung comfortably tailored with his tie never out of place. His jaw remained firm as he sat erect in the chair opposite Parker.

"I see you visited the Bahamas this weekend."

"Yes, I went to a medical meeting. How'd you know?"

"We're protecting you, aren't we?"

"So you know the druggies are still on my tail. Most times they use a different car."

"We know. The syndicate is still waiting for you to lead them to the money."

"Then they have a long wait."

Rucker shifted in the chair and gave him a questioning look. "We found the locker that goes to your lost key."

"Fantastic! So you got the money and I'm off the hook?"

Rucker shook his head. "Not so fast, Doc. The locker was empty."

"Wait a minute. How do you know that was the right locker?"

Rucker's voice was curt. "We canvassed all the storage facilities in the area. Olga Ottavio and Ramon Lopez were the ones who rented the unit. We identified them by their descriptions and confirmed it by the surveillance videos."

"So where did the money go?"

"We thought you could answer that."

Parker clenched his fist, his eyes narrowed. "What do you mean by that, Rucker?"

"Whatever you think, Doc, just giving you the facts."

The agent's steely look told Parker there was still a glimmer of doubt in his mind.

"Get off my back. You know damn well I don't have the money, so look elsewhere. What about Reliant Drugs? Is it legitimate?"

Rucker shook his head. "It's a dummy corporation.

Trask is President and CEO, but they have no building or staff."

"I thought so," Parker shot back excitedly. He slammed his fist on the desk. "What about Ramon Lopez? How does he fit into this?"

Rucker straightened his tie, maintaining eye contact. "We know he's distributing hard drugs to street peddlers along with counterfeit prescription medications to pharmacies, nursing homes and Mom and Pop convenience stores."

"Then it fits. MCA's chief pharmacist told me Trask pushed Lonnie in Purchasing to buy drugs from Reliant. So Lopez works for Trask?"

"Yeah, he named Trask as his connection."

"How did you get Lopez to spill the beans?"

"He's cooperating to protect Olga's daughter, Carmella. By providing state's evidence, he hopes to get hit with a lesser charge."

"Did he say anything about Lindstrom?"

"Doesn't even know who the guy is."

"There has to be a connection with Trask. What about Carolyn Robertson? Does she fit into the Reliant Drug scheme?"

"Can't say. She worked for Lindstrom in California and that's where the first counterfeit drugs from China made it to the U.S. We know she's single and has no police record."

"Could she be a cover for Lindstrom? Running his errands, fronting for his transactions?"

"We suspect something like that because she deposits Reliant money into the bank and draws a cashier's check on the amount. We have no idea where the money ends up because we can't trace the payment from a cashier's check."

Parker let out a whistle as he leaned back in his chair. "So the cartel is involved with trafficking hard drugs as well as counterfeits."

Rucker nodded. "Unfortunately, yes. But I don't think Trask is connected to the cartel. He makes the contracts for Reliant's counterfeit drugs with various outlets and Lopez is the delivery man. It's not that big an operation but it appears to be very profitable."

Stunned, Parker rose from his chair, leaned over the desk and focused on Rucker's eyes. "Are you admitting you can't stop this drug-running operation?"

Rucker's face hardened. "It's a tough nut to crack, especially when there's so much profit."

Parker's voice rose. "How do you think that makes me feel?"

"We're doing the best we can and keeping a close eye on you, Doc."

"Some protection. These men are ruthless. Politicians, police, nothing stands in their way. Thanks for the assurance."

He studied the look of despair in Rucker's eyes. Given the danger these lawmen faced, he was sorry for what he said. His voice lowered. "I wish I could help, but I don't know how."

Rucker leaned back in the chair and his tone softened. "I understand your frustration, Doc, but that's why we follow the money trail. If you have any idea where that cash is hidden, I'd like to know."

A sudden grin came over Parker's face. "I can't help

you on that, but I saw something interesting in the Bahamas."

Rucker's eyes lit up. "Like what?"

"Lindstrom was at the casino with a younger man. The guy was a real flamer, an obvious homosexual."

"That's fine, Doctor, but I'm not interested in social partnerships, only criminal activity. We know the Islands are active conduits for illegal drug and money transfers between the States and offshore banks. I trust the medical meeting was your only purpose for the trip?"

Parker released a long sigh as he searched the lawman's face. Until now, he felt Rucker might believe him. But his question made Parker wonder if the protection offered was only an excuse to see if he had stolen the money.

Forty-two

Parker's office, same day

As Fellini recommended, Parker knew he had to have a doctor represent him at the upcoming hearing before Executive Committee. He re-read the certified letter from MCA ordering him to appear.

His pulse quickened as he paced around the desk, dwelling on the written words: '*unethical conduct ...action disruptive to the operation of the hospital unfavorable reflection upon the reputation of the professional staff.*'

Outrageous lies, his inner voice cried out. Fellini was right. He couldn't go into that meeting alone. But who could he ask? Who would be willing to take that risk?

He sat in his chair and reviewed the names of staff doctors listed in the hospital's directory. After the third search, he finally dialed Lawton's office.

The receptionist informed him Dr. Lawton was seeing patients but would call back. After a painful twenty minute wait, the telephone rang.

"What can I do for you, Parker?"

"Thanks for covering for me and you're right. Morty Gold was with that babe at the crap tables."

"I knew he wasn't going there to broaden his medical knowledge."

Parker's voice turned serious. "But that's not what I'm calling about. You're aware Executive Committee has set a date for me to appear before them regarding the disciplinary charges."

"Yes, I heard."

"I need you to represent me at that hearing."

There was a long wait before Karl answered. "I know what you're asking, Parker."

Parker's voice rose. "Well, will you?"

Another pause followed before Karl spoke. "I went through a similar experience years ago when I was on staff at a hospital in Iowa. False accusations were leveled against me."

"Then you understand."

"I do, but after expensive lawyers to clear my name and a divorce, I vowed never to get involved in hospital politics again."

"Please, Karl, I'm begging."

"Did Morty Gold place the charges?"

"No, Lindstrom did, which surprised me. Since when does a layman have the right to make medical judgments against a physician?"

"That is strange because this is a medical staff matter," Lawton replied.

"Well, will you defend me?" Parker broke out in a sweat, waiting for Karl's answer.

"You realize if I side with you, I'll make enemies on staff."

"I know." Parker's voice dropped. "But if you think

I'm being railroaded, you can't turn me down."

Another pause followed and then a sigh. "I'm just one vote on that committee, Parker."

"But you're chief of surgery. Your opinion should carry some weight."

"You're forgetting something, Parker. This no longer is a medical issue, it's political, and that's dangerous territory."

Parker's pulse raced as he searched for a meaningful answer.

Before he could speak, Lawton replied, "I've purposely stayed away from this issue because it's gotten so loaded. I can't promise anything, but let me look over the charges and any information you have. When's the meeting?"

"It's scheduled for 7 PM tomorrow."

"You aren't giving me much time."

"I know, Karl, but I appreciate it. I've written a summary of the event as it happened."

"Get it to me right away."

"Gwen will bring it to your office in twenty minutes. There are copies of documents I can't trust to the FAX machine."

"Enough said. See you at the meeting."

Parker hung up the phone, feeling the moisture in his palms. The cards were stacked against him, and Karl was his best hope.

~ * ~

Parker paced outside the MCA board room the following day, panicked that Lawton hadn't arrived. In five minutes, he was to stand before Executive Committee to defend himself and where the hell was Lawton? When his cell phone rang, he picked it up and shouted, "Karl! Where are you?"

A female voice replied, "This is Nurse Callahan from St. Ann operating room. Dr. Lawton ran into complications and wanted you to know he'll be late."

"When will he get here?"

"He said try to stall the meeting. Hopefully, he'll be there within the next half hour."

Parker broke out into a cold sweat, knowing Gold and Lindstrom were out to nail him. The only thing left was to march in and fight.

Stern looks from the department chiefs greeted him as he entered and took his place at the long conference table. Gold, Fox and Lindstrom seated at the opposite end, faced him. He felt a chill in the somber atmosphere as he looked around the table, alone in the lion's den.

Gold raised his gavel and rapped it as the diamond ring on his pinky flashed in the light. "I call this meeting to order," he announced.

A legal stenographer hovered over her machine close to Gold. Gray roots peeked out from under dyed red hair rolled up in a bun. "Please, everyone spell out your names for the record," she requested.

After the formality ended, Parker raised his hand. "Mr. Chairman, I'm requesting this meeting be rescheduled. The physician to represent me is held up in surgery."

Gold threw Parker a frown. "You had plenty of time to prepare for this hearing, Dr. Dawson. This meeting will proceed as scheduled."

Parker felt an adrenaline rush and took in a deep breath. *Dammit,* he thought, *I'm not taking this lying down*. He spoke out in a firm voice. "I have the right to be represented, Mr. Chairman."

Gold ignored the comment and began to read the charges.

Parker winced as he heard the familiar words once again. *"...patient abandonment...unethical conduct...action disruptive to the operation of the hospital...unfavorable reflection upon the reputation of the professional staff."*

Gold concluded and looked up. "Dr. Dawson, do you have a statement for the Committee?"

All the physicians sat in a piercing silence, waiting for an answer.

Parker replied, "These charges are false and groundless! I wasn't on call when the patient was brought to ER."

Gold slammed the gavel. "Dr. Dawson, you were called to see a seriously injured patient and you didn't respond. That's patient abandonment."

Parker's eyes showed fire. No question, Gold was out for blood. The wisdom of Fellini's advice not to go into the meeting alone instantly became apparent.

Vice-Chief Fox cleared his throat, his eyes peering over his spectacles. He spoke over the low din of incoherent discussion. "How do you plead to these charges?"

Parker stared back at Fox, whose tight smile infuriated him. As angry as he was, he almost laughed when he imagined the Vice Chief's hair implants resembled rows of cultivated corn stalks.

He refused to answer Fox. Instead he shouted, "Why isn't Baum here? He was the ER doc that day. It's his incompetence that caused this problem."

Fox rose with a grin on his face, apparently enjoying his position of power. "You're here to answer questions, not ask them, Doctor. Are you denying you refused to take your call?"

"Yes, I am," Parker answered.

Paul Barco shot up from his chair and pointed at Parker. "Stop ignoring your responsibility! My God, you were close to the ER. Why didn't you see that patient?"

Parker looked into Barco's eyes, stunned by the hateful sound in his voice. He wondered if his support of Lawton's investigation into the laser deaths was the reason. Why not? Barco was already on MCA's payroll.

Parker answered Barco firmly. "Stanley Kingsley came in as an orthopedic case. I don't do orthopedics and wasn't on call when he arrived to the ER."

Fox's eyes darted around the room. "Mr. Chairman, I say we should call for a vote."

"Not so fast!" Lawton's voice rang out as he marched into the room. "Sorry I'm late, but as Dr. Dawson's representative, I'd like to ask some questions."

Parker watched Gold's jaw drop and Lindstrom's eyes narrow. A wave of relief flowed through his veins as he sat down in his chair.

Lawton stood tall, his voice commanding. "I understand Dr. Dawson has been reported to the state for patient abandonment before having his right to due process." He stared directly at Lindstrom. "Does this mean he's been charged, sentenced and set up for execution without the safeguards provided in our by-laws?"

Lindstrom leaned forward. "By law, I'm required to report any disciplinary action to the state within thirty days."

Gold rapped his gavel, "You're out of order, Dr. Lawton."

"No, Mr. Chairman," Lawton replied, "this hearing is out of order. What MCA has done is like sending someone to the gallows, hanging him and then telling the family to begin the appeals process."

An explosive eruption of voices followed as Gold kept rapping his gavel.

The stenographer called out, "One at a time! I can't tell who's talking."

Karl spoke out over the uproar. "I still have the floor, Mr. Chairman, and as chief of surgery, I'm appointing a committee from my department to investigate this matter. I have that power and no other committee can override that. I'm leaving now since I doubt my presence serves any further purpose." He spun about and headed out of the door.

"You can't leave," someone shouted as Gold kept pounding the gavel to quiet the uproar.

Parker gloated inwardly as he watched Lawton disappear. The astonished looks on the faces of the committee members warmed his heart. Maybe now he had a chance.

Forty-three

Karl Lawton strode into the OR holding area and passed between sedated patients lying on gurneys prepared for morning surgery. He entered the doctors' locker room, changed into his scrubs and waited for his 7:30 case. With a good twenty minutes to spare, he sat in the lounge and picked up the *New England Journal* laying on the table.

The OR supervisor poked her head into the room. "Sorry, Dr. Lawton, your case is held up. Dr. Tucker is finishing an emergency in your room."

"How long will he be?"

"He's closing now and with cleaning the room, I figure another thirty minutes."

"I'll be waiting," Karl answered as he moved toward the coffee urn. He filled his cup and flicked on the TV with the remote. Stock market gurus pontificated over the significance of yesterday's precipitous rise in the Dow following the lowering of interest rates by the Fed. The droning boredom of their meaningless projections failed to interest him. His mind was occupied with other matters.

Who would he ask to be the fifth member of the committee to investigate the charges against Parker? He already chose the chiefs of urology and orthopedics in addition to Bob Meyer, the thoracic surgeon who had his run-in with Gold. These three doctors had no reason to have any bias against Parker. But to give balance, he relented and asked Paul Barco even though he was a strong ally of Lindstrom.

As the chairman, he couldn't vote. Since the fifth member would cast the deciding ballot, he needed a surgeon who had the strength of character to be impartial even if it meant fighting the hospital's political machine.

The thought came to him instantly. What better choice than Jason Tucker? The young conscientious surgeon worked long hours to attract his share of referrals. Most appealing was his integrity and ability to distance himself from hospital entanglements.

Satisfied with his choice, Lawton returned to the couch to gaze at the TV screen and waited for Jason to walk in from the OR.

After twenty minutes, the door opened and the tall black surgeon entered. His firm muscles bulged through the short-sleeved shirt of his green scrub suit.

"Sorry my case held you up, Karl. I had to explore a pelvic abscess."

Karl nodded. "No problem. Glad I caught up with you because I need your help."

Jason tore off the paper mask hanging from his neck and gave Karl a questioning look.

"Jason, I want you to serve on my committee investigating Parker's ER incident."

273

Tucker's chiseled face hardened. "Do you realize what you're asking? This panel hasn't even met and already the hospital feels like a ticking time bomb."

"I need someone like you to give Parker a fair shake."

Jason's voice rose. "Hey, man! Nobody wants to get in the middle of that mess. Gold's ranting that if any surgeon wants to protect his ass, he'd better stay away from your committee."

"Are you going to listen to threats or facts, Jason? Don't let Gold scare you."

"Easy for you to say. I don't want to be the next victim, someone who doesn't make it because he crossed the wrong people. I learned at an early age what you can and can't do so I want no part of that committee."

Lawton rose from the sofa to fill a second cup of coffee. "You're a damned good surgeon, Jason, and you know it. That's why I need you to see if Parker's being railroaded."

"You may think so, but there are others who figure I got to where I am by the color of my skin. I've lived poor all my life and I can't risk taking chances with a committee that has nothing to do with me."

Karl returned a soulful look. "Sorry you feel that way, but haven't you been treated unfairly sometime in your life?"

"Everyone's got a story about getting shafted," Jason snapped.

"You gotta realize your input is your protection, Jason. Suppose the hospital filed trumped up charges against you? How would you like to face the state alone with no one on staff giving a damn? Everything the hospital does

274

isn't always legal, but it flies because it carries the power of an institution."

"I don't want to hear about that!"

"It hurts, doesn't it," Lawton sighed, tossing his Styrofoam cup into the wastebasket.

Jason flipped open the chart that lay on the desk in front of him. "I got orders to write. I don't want to do anything that makes me vulnerable."

"Everybody's vulnerable, Jason."

Jason stopped writing and stared Lawton in the eye. "We have over two hundred docs on staff and less than five are black. What happens if one of my cases goes sour? Do you think a committee will say 'tough case, we understand?' No sir, they'll go for my ass to prove they're doing the committee's work. Then they'll talk about all the lucky breaks I got and how I didn't have to work to get through med school. In the end, they'll say, let's just watch this guy."

Lawton remained silent, studying Jason as he returned to his chart again.

Jason could feel Lawton's eyes on him and finally broke the quiet. "I just got off supervision and I like it that way. I don't need another surgeon looking over my shoulder, checking me at the operating table. Why should I risk bucking Administration?"

Lawton shook his head. "Everything you say might be true, but if you want to protect yourself in the long run, you should serve. I need you on that committee, Jason."

"Hey, I'm married with my first kid and I'm not looking for trouble!"

"Think it over, Jason. It's your choice."

The overhead page called out Karl's name and he pushed open the door. "Let me know what you decide."

The door closed, leaving Tucker staring after him.

Karl waited, but at the end of the day there was no call from Jason Tucker.

Forty-four

The call came from Fellini several days later.

"Dr. Dawson, I received a call from David Reese, the state investigator for the Florida Agency for Health Care Administration. He had some disturbing news."

Parker took in a deep breath. "What is it?"

"He said the agency received a scathing letter about you from Mr. Lindstrom. Did something new happen to turn him on?"

Parker tightened his grip on the phone, angered by what he heard. "Give me a minute, Mr. Fellini. I'm in the hospital and I need a private place to talk."

Two nurses walked by, giving him quick smiles which he returned as he hurried down the corridor deciding where he could find some privacy. The library was his best choice, since physicians rarely congregated there during morning rounds. Rushing down the stairs, he entered the small room with its limited selection of journals and medical texts. Good, no one was there.

"I'm back, Mr. Fellini. What did the letter say?"

"In a nutshell, he accused you of being emotionally

disturbed, causing you to act in an irresponsible manner. He said you were a danger to your patients."

"That son-of-a-bitch! What else could he conjure up?"

"Easy, Doctor. Do you know what's going on to justify such a letter?"

"Possibly because I followed your advice and had my department chief speak for me at the hearing."

"What did he say to upset Lindstrom?"

Parker grinned. "Dr. Lawton blasted the committee. Told Lindstrom he had no right to report me to the state before I was given due process."

"Good move!" Fellini interjected.

"Then he told them he'd appoint his own committee of surgeons to investigate the incident and stormed out, leaving everyone in an uproar."

"Now I understand," Fellini answered. "Let me deal with Mr. Reese, and I'll be in touch."

Parker sensed a wave of relief as he pocketed the phone. He was glad to have Fellini on his side.

A second later, his phone rang again and this time it was Gwen.

"Dr. Lawton's trying to reach you. He's at his office and said to call back."

Parker hesitated for a moment, wondering if Lawton had changed his mind. *Did Lindstrom's letter to the state open a new bag of worms?* There was no point in delaying the call so he dialed.

Lawton's voice sounded upbeat. "Thought you should know the five man committee has been appointed. The good news is that Jason Tucker agreed to serve."

"Great. All I want is the chance to clear my name."

"That's why I'm calling. Questions are being mailed to all the nurses and doctors involved. With those answers, we cut through a lot of wasted time. Then the committee can make its decision based upon the facts and not opinions."

"Karl, do you think I have a chance?"

"That depends upon the committee."

"I understand and want to thank you for trying to set the record straight for me."

"It's not only for you, Parker. It's for any other doctor who has to face the same situation."

Parker hung up the phone and for the first time, felt he might be playing on a level field.

~ * ~

Judy fidgeted as she sat outside the MCA conference room waiting to appear before Lawton's committee investigating the charges against Parker. Well into her third trimester, she shifted uncomfortably in an effort to relieve the pressure on her legs caused by her pregnancy.

Clicking sounds of high heels down the hallway made her look up. Only Tess Cashman dared to wear such a revealing scooped-neck sweater which was certain to attract the attention of any warm-blooded male. Tess flopped down on the chair next to Judy, pulled out a file from her red mini-purse and hummed as she swept her fingernails in long strokes. "This meeting's really screwing up my night off. Hope these guys don't keep us too long."

Although Judy was in no mood to chat, she replied, "Who knows? They just interviewed Suzie, the desk secretary. I haven't seen any doctors show up yet."

She saw Parker approach and noticed Tess suddenly stiffen. She knew Tess was Baum's live-in girlfriend and certain to lie, providing damaging evidence against Parker.

"Good evening, ladies," Parker said, taking a seat next to Judy.

Although Tess didn't respond, Judy returned a weak smile. She sensed Tess suspected her relationship with Parker was more than professional.

Judy could feel Parker's frustration as he sat quietly without saying a word. In spite of all his persistence to have her start treatment, she stood steadfast in her decision not to pursue anything that possibly could harm her pregnancy. I have incurable cancer, she stoically convinced herself, and accepted the inevitable.

Before Parker could speak, the door opened and Judy was called.

She entered the Conference Room to face a display chart standing on an easel. A constructed flow sheet taken from the medical records showed the time of each documented vital sign and each physician-nurse interaction. She sat and faced the committee, squirming nervously in the chair, trying to compose herself.

Lawton gave Judy a warm smile. "Thank you for coming, Miss Keller. We have a few simple questions to ask you in order to clarify some confusion regarding what happened the day Stanley Kingsley arrived to the ER. Could you tell us if there was any sense of urgency regarding his condition at the time of admission?"

Judy paused, and then answered. "You realize the patient had a fractured arm."

Lawton replied, "Yes, we know, Miss Keller, but it's important to know if the patient was stable when he arrived. Just answer yes or no."

"Yes," she answered timidly.

"Now, can you tell the committee which surgeon was called first?"

Her voice lowered to a whisper. "I can't say."

"Is there a reason, Miss Keller? You were the nursing supervisor in charge."

"Dr. Lawton, the only thing I can tell you is that Dr. Baum was attending Mr. Kingsley. I was only coordinating the nursing."

"If I may," Jason Tucker interrupted.

Lawton nodded.

"This patient came in around six AM with only Dr. Baum in attendance. Did you see any evidence there was an immediate need for a surgeon? And if there was, which one was called first?"

Judy's voice quivered. "I can't say. My shift begins at seven and I was not involved in the patient's clinical assessment."

Tucker persisted. "But if your shift begins at seven, Miss Keller, and an hour had passed since the patient arrived, didn't you question why the orthopedist hadn't been called in since the patient had a bone injury?"

Judy's voice rose. "I told you. My attention was turned to coordinating the nursing support and helping Dr. Baum in any way I could. I was not involved with contacting the specialists."

"So, I presume you don't know which surgeon was called first."

She paused before answering. "If I did, I don't remember."

Lawton turned to his colleagues. "Are there any other questions for Miss Keller?"

There was no response.

Lawton shook his head. "Thank you, Miss Keller. The committee had hoped you could provide us with more information. But under the circumstances, you're excused for now. Please be available if we should need you again."

Judy rose quickly and rushed out through the door. Tears rolled down her face as she quickly passed Tess and Parker sitting outside the conference room. She knew she hadn't helped Parker, but hoped what she said didn't hurt him.

~ * ~

Tess Cashman was next to appear before the committee. She gave each member a broad smile as she entered, relishing the thought of being the center of attention.

Lawton asked the first question. "Miss Cashman, when Stanley Kingsley arrived to the ER, who was the first surgeon called?"

Without hesitation, Tess replied, "Dr. Dawson, of course."

Lawton's eyes remained fixed on the nurse. "Now what prompted the call to Dr. Dawson if the patient wasn't in shock and only suffered a fracture?"

"But Mr. Kingsley was in shock, that's why."

"When did Dr. Baum call the orthopedist?"

"I can't answer that. But I know Dr. Dawson was needed because the patient was hypotensive."

The chief of orthopedics then spoke. "Dr. Gold is a general surgeon and was present for a short time. Did he participate in treating the patient who you say was in shock?"

She was quick to respond. "I don't know."

Paul Barco called out, "Miss Cashman, it's not necessary for you to justify the actions of any physician. It's not your job to interpret facts."

Lawton gave Barco a stern look. "I think the nurse involved should be able to document her assessments if a state of urgency exits. If this patient was truly in shock, Dr. Gold could have helped. However, the record shows he failed to intervene at any time."

Tess raised her voice. "They put in a central line which shows Mr. Kingsley was in shock."

Jason called out. "Yes, but Dr. Baum didn't do it. Dr. Rico put the line in hours later when he came on duty after Baum's shift ended."

Dr. Strauss then commented, "The record shows Dr. Leader arrived to cover for Dr. Dawson. He did not intervene in Mr. Kingsley's care, which indicates there was no need for a general surgeon. How can you say with such certainty that a surgeon was needed by seven AM?"

Tess's eyes widened, but she said nothing.

Paul Barco jumped up and shouted, "Don't answer that, Miss Cashman."

Lawton turned to Barco. "Please don't raise your voice. We're here to discuss, not badger."

Jason Tucker remained silent.

When Tess was dismissed, she straightened up and took in a deep breath, allowing a full view of her contoured chest. Every eye followed her swaying hips as she sauntered out of the room.

Parker was called next. As he entered the room, he

studied the grim faces staring at him, but his mood perked up when he saw Lawton's smile. He sat in the chair before the committee.

Lawton cleared his throat. "Dr. Dawson, this committee has reviewed the testimony of nurses and personnel involved. We are searching for one fact. What time were you called to see Stanley Kingsley?"

"It was after seven. I feel certain of that. I was heading to St. Ann for a scheduled case at eight in the morning."

"Were you aware of the time Mr. Kingsley arrived to the hospital?"

"Baum told me he came in at five. He said he called Dr. Patel who refused to come in."

Lawton turned to the committee. "Does anyone have any questions for Dr. Dawson?"

"I do!" Barco cried out. He leaned forward in his chair. "Dr. Dawson, were you not asked by Dr. Baum to see this patient in the emergency room?"

"Yes, but I wasn't on call. Dr. Patel was on call when Mr. Kingsley arrived."

"Excuse me, Doctor." Barco paused. "You were minutes away from this patient and you refused to see him?"

"I chose not to see him because Baum told me Mr. Kingsley was stable with a fractured arm. I'm not an orthopedist."

Barco shot up from his chair. "That's no excuse!"

Lawton slammed down his gavel. "Control yourself, Dr. Barco. That's the doctor's testimony. We're only here to get the facts." He scanned the other faces of the committee, wondering why Tucker was remaining silent and continued. "If the committee has no other questions, you're excused, Dr. Dawson."

Parker felt his heart pound, preparing to do battle, but Lawton's dismissal meant he had to calm down. He rose, stared at Barco and then faced the committee. Before walking out, he said, "Thank you, gentlemen."

After all the individuals involved in the incident had been interviewed, Lawton knew the hard work was yet to come.

"Let's take a ten minute break," he announced.

The surgeons moved to the coffee urn except for Jason Tucker who remained seated and focused on the timeline chart before him.

He revisited the red markings of Kingsley's vital signs and the hour each doctor was called. After listening to the differing testimonies of the ER nurses and doctors, he searched for the kernel of truth lying somewhere in the records. Any decision regarding Parker's guilt or innocence had to be based on fact.

When Lawton announced, "Let's get back to the matters on hand," Tucker nodded in agreement.

Strauss, the orthopedist, was the first to speak. "Parker didn't do anything wrong by not responding to a call outside his specialty."

Tucker watched Barco shift restlessly in his seat and then rise abruptly.

"God dammit!" Barco shouted. "Dawson was obliged to go to the ER to see that patient!"

Strauss answered, "But the record shows it was only an orthopedic case at the time of admission."

Barco shot back. "That may be, but when ER calls, you go."

"Now, now, Dr. Barco," the urologist responded, pointing to the chart. "Not only was a general surgeon not needed, but I believe Dr. Dawson honestly thought his surgical call began at eight AM instead of seven."

Barco's contorted face showed his anger. "You don't ask questions when ER calls."

"Stop making doctors criminals," the urologist replied. "This isn't a question of medical misconduct. It's only a problem of miscommunication."

Jason watched with a pensive look during the heated discussion.

Lawton finally broke in and asked, "Dr. Tucker, could we please hear from you? We'd like your opinion."

Aware of Barco's intense anger, Tucker spoke firmly, "First I'd like to say I have no ax to grind. I've listened to all the witnesses, reviewed the medical record and followed the timeline chart. Since the first two consultants refused to come in, I don't believe a surgical emergency existed when Dr. Dawson was called."

Barco objected, "I disagree!"

"You don't have the floor, Dr. Barco," Lawton insisted.

After a pause, Tucker continued. "It bothers me that Dr. Dawson was so quickly charged with medical misconduct. Baum's medical management appears slipshod, and it seems to me that everyone is covering up for him by dumping on Dr. Dawson."

He turned away from Barco, directing his attention to the other surgeons. "I must question the motives here. Why did the hospital report Dr. Dawson to the state so quickly?"

Barco jumped up, his face red with anger. "It's the law, that's why! Any infraction has to be reported to the state. Dawson refused to come in and the patient crashed. He ducked his responsibility."

Tucker replied, his voice steady and firm. "The record shows the patient was stable, Dr. Barco. At the time of admission, there's no evidence Mr. Kingsley's life was in danger. I believe the hospital was unfair to Dr. Dawson."

Barco slammed his fist on the table. "Unfair? Who are you, a newcomer, challenging the decision of Executive Committee?"

"Easy, Barco," Lawton cautioned, "let's not fight among ourselves."

Barco could not be contained. He rose again and glared down at Tucker. "Unfair? he repeated. "You've been marching to that drumbeat for so long, whenever you don't get your way, you shout foul. I'll bet affirmative action got you into medical school."

Tucker stood up to face Barco as a rush of silence filled the room.

"I serve on this committee in good faith and don't deserve your personal attacks, Dr. Barco. Are you judging my ability and accomplishments? For your information, I never checked the race box on my application to Yale."

"Take it easy, gentlemen," Lawton pleaded. "Let's not make this a personal issue. Just stick to the facts."

Tucker released a deep sigh as he watched Barco sit down and nervously tap a pencil on the table top. He looked to Lawton and said, "I'm ready to vote whenever you are, Mr. Chairman."

Forty-five

Parker nervously waited for Lawton's committee to render a decision. Concerned as he was, he still had to continue working and entered the elevator for the second floor to check on his post-op patients.

He walked to the nurses' station where the first shift was going through its early morning rituals.

A plump desk clerk sat inserting lab reports into patient charts as a medication nurse hovered over her cart punching data into a laptop computer mounted to its side.

Suddenly, a nurse called out in an urgent voice. "Over here, the medicine room, Dr. Dawson! Come quick!"

Looking in her direction, he saw Judy slumped on the floor and quickly rushed to her side.

"It happened so fast, Doctor," the nurse said with panic in her eyes. "She just fainted and her pulse is real thready."

Parker reached for Judy's wrist and felt her weak pulse. He brushed away the wisps of blond hair clinging to her moistened brow. "Judy, can you hear me?"

Her eyes opened slowly, and in a low voice, she answered, "I'll be all right."

"She's not all right!" the nurse snapped. "I tried to grab her before she collapsed. It's her eighth month and she's looking worse than ever."

Parker opened Judy's palm and studied the crease lines. They were blanched white. "No wonder you're tired, you're anemic," he said and looked to the nurse. "Get a wheelchair and take her to the lab for a stat CBC."

The nurse nodded and rushed away.

Parker stroked Judy's face, gently smoothing the hair from her temple. Even in her weakened state, she looked beautiful.

"It's about time you stopped working, Judy."

Her eyes lit up with fire and her voice grew stronger. "No, I can't afford to."

He embraced her. "Please, Judy, don't get upset. Let's wait for the blood count."

"Dr. Shoup sees me tomorrow. I'll be fine."

Parker felt the warmth of her cheek. He rocked her gently in his arms, realizing the depth of the love he felt for this woman who suffered from incurable cancer.

When the nurse returned, he helped Judy into the wheelchair and she was taken away. He remained deep in thought when another nurse entered.

"Is everything all right, Dr. Dawson?"

"Everything's fine," he replied. "After I get the blood count, I'll check on her."

He lingered over the chart rack as a horrendous thought crossed his mind. Judy's blood count was still low despite the Procrit injections. There was a good possibility she was receiving a counterfeit drug.

He picked up his cell and dialed Gwen. "Track down

the Procrit sales rep and see if the company finally analyzed the vials we sent them."

"Funny you ask," Gwen replied. "I just got a call from the regional sales manager. He's in town and wants to see you."

~ * ~

Parker rose from his desk and greeted the pharmaceutical sales representative Gwen ushered into his office. "I hope you have an answer for me," he said.

The man wore a stern look. Before sitting in the chair, he rested his sample case on the floor and held out his card.

"Glad to meet you, Doctor. I'm the regional rep for Procrit hospital sales. Sorry to say we found that the vials you sent for analysis contained only two thousand units of Procrit instead of the forty thousand labeled on the bottle."

Parker knew his suspicion was on target. "So the drug's been diluted! Did you trace the source?"

"We're working on it, but we have our hands full. Federal investigators confiscated thousands of counterfeit Procrit and Epogen vials from wholesalers in multiple states, including Florida. The batch they intercepted in Miami contained only tap water."

Parker sat dumbfounded. "How the hell can I depend on your drugs?" He rose from his chair, leaned over the desk and looked straight into the representative's eyes. "Right now I have a young pregnant woman dying from cancer. Her anemia is getting worse because of that bogus Procrit. Do I tell her the truth?"

"That's a legal question I can't answer, Doctor, but the company's doing everything it can."

"Like what?"

The representative released a wistful sigh. "I'm no authority, and the company is very tight-lipped. But let me tell you what I do know."

The man leaned back in his chair. "All the pharma companies sell their drugs to three large national wholesalers. These companies then sell to regional wholesalers. From that point on, things get murky. It's a gray zone where a lot of transactions occur, which can allow counterfeits to co-mingle with legitimate products."

Parker's voice rose in anger. "How can that happen?"

The sales rep flinched at his outburst. "It starts when the wholesalers sell overstocked items to other wholesalers who need to fill shortages. Multiple transactions can take place and items can be moved from bulk into single-unit blister packs. That's when counterfeits can be mixed successfully into the drug supply because it's easy for the seller to conceal the origin of the drug he's supplying."

Parker shook his head. "So the counterfeiter profits and the unwitting patient suffers."

"It's an ugly story, Doc, but when money talks, morality walks. That's why we need patients and doctors like you to tell us if a drug isn't working."

"What about the drugs being ordered on the Internet? How can you tell if they're legitimate?"

"That's a problem, and it's even worse in third world countries. Ten to fifty percent of prescription drugs sold in Africa, Asia and South America are estimated to be counterfeit. It's so bad in India, they want to pass a death penalty for drug counterfeiters."

"Where are these counterfeits made?"

The agent took in a deep breath. "The likely sources are countries with loose government controls. China, India, Nigeria and who knows."

Parker shook his head. "Christ! Then once the drug gets out of the manufacturer's hands, you have no control. And with Internet counterfeits ordered from abroad, what can we trust?"

The rep gave Parker a sympathetic look. "The major U.S. pharmaceutical companies are trying to push a radiofrequency identification tag on medications that carries an electronic code. It's one way they can verify authenticity."

"Yeah, and in the meantime, criminals profit at the expense of patients."

"Sorry, Doc, but those are the facts. The pharmaceutical companies are working hard to combat this. In Africa, we've intercepted drugs to treat AIDS and malaria and found them to be phony."

"What could be more heartless," Parker muttered.

The rep continued. "You can say that. We face the same problems here at home. We've intercepted counterfeit Viagra, Lipitor and Zyprexia, all looking identical to the legitimate drugs, even to the trained eye."

The sudden knock on the door interrupted their discussion as an excited Gwen rushed into the room. "The hospital called, Dr. Dawson. Judy just had a convulsive seizure."

~ * ~

It was the following day when Parker left the X-ray Department to head to Judy's hospital room. He heard his own footsteps echo down the hall, feeling he was marching to an executioner's cadence after learning the radiologist's grim report showed what he most feared. Judy had multiple tumors spread to her brain which explained why she collapsed. Unfortunately they were too numerous to operate so her immediate treatment had to be radiation therapy to the brain to control further seizures.

He paused at her door, debating what to say. He knew she was terminal but he had so much to tell her and time was running out.

Knocking on the door, he entered wearing a smile. The room was darkened by the drawn shades except for the flashing scenes on the muted TV screen. Her eyes were closed but she didn't appear to be in a deep sleep. It had to be the sedative effect caused by the Dilantin he had ordered to control the seizures.

He leaned over the bed, speaking in a whisper. "Judy, are you awake?"

Her eyelids fluttered for a few seconds before opening. She focused on his face and gave him a weak smile. "Oh, I'm so glad you're here, Parker. The nurses told me what happened. The only thing I remember is going for a CT scan."

"Has Dr. Shoup seen you yet?"

"Yes, he just left and said the baby's fine. Did you get the CT report?"

His voice cracked as he reached for her hand. "Judy, you have to know. The cancer has spread to your brain."

Her stoic look upset him. *My God, she's already accepted her death sentence. I've got to tell her now.*

He sat on the edge of the bed and caressed her

shoulder. "You know I've always been in love with you." The back of his hand swept a tear from his eye and he decided to lighten up a bit and gave her a smile.

"Remember the first time we met? It was in the hospital parking lot in Columbus. You looked so helpless staring down at your flat tire. That was the day I fell in love with you."

Her face lit up and her lips quivered. "You saved me. I don't know how I would have gotten to my nursing exam if you hadn't changed it." Her smile disappeared and her eyes filled. "But that was so long ago and now it's too late."

"It's never too late," he said.

She opened her arms and he readily locked into her embrace.

"Just hold me," she said tearfully as the wetness on her cheek pressed against his. "I've always loved you, too."

Every fiber within him resonated its message. Hold on to her, don't let her go. He drew back and gazed into her eyes. "I was too stupid to understand the meaning of what we had. I don't want to lose you again."

Judy raised herself up from the bed and gently placed a finger on his lips. "Stop," she cautioned. "Let's enjoy whatever moments we have together."

He wrapped his arms around her, and they kissed as she brought her lips to his. *I'm not giving up hope. I've got to convince her,* he told himself.

He pulled away, giving her a serious look. "Right now, it's urgent you receive cranial radiation to control the seizures and protect your chances of having a safe delivery."

She squeezed his arm. "Will it hurt the baby?"

"No, the baby will be protected. After the delivery, we'll treat you with the newest biotherapeutic drugs."

She raised her hand. "I'll take the radiation, but nothing further. Whatever strength I have must be left for the baby."

"But we have to try. We can't just give up."

She shook her head. "Please understand. Until I make arrangements for the baby's adoption, I can't be weakened by drugs that could blunt my decision-making. I owe that to my child."

The reality of her words sobered him. "Have you talked to Shawn about this?"

"No, and I can't expect him to take on this burden. I'm going to ask Social Services to contact an adoption agency so I can interview prospective parents."

"I see," he answered softly.

The sounds of footsteps interrupted them as Kathy wheeled Shawn into the room.

"Hi, sis. Are you okay?" her brother called out.

"Just fine," Judy answered in a strong voice.

"We got here as soon as we could," Kathy said as she wheeled Shawn closer to the bed.

Parker rested a hand on Shawn's shoulder. "You folks have a lot to talk about, so I'm leaving."

Shawn searched Parker's eyes. "She'll be all right, won't she, Doc?"

"Yes, she's a fighter, and the best medicine for her right now is her family."

Forty-six

Three weeks later, Parker's apartment

The persistent rings of the phone awakened Parker from a deep sleep. Instinctively, he reached for the receiver and glanced at the illuminated face of the clock. It was 2 AM and he heard the urgent sound in Shoup's voice.

"Sorry to get you up, Parker, but I just examined Judy. We have to deliver her baby."

Parker rubbed his eyes. "Did she have another seizure?"

"No," came Shoup's quick reply, "but she will if we don't deliver her now. She's in severe eclampsia. Her pressure shot up to one seventy-six over one-twelve with mild contractions. Although she's nearing thirty-six weeks, I'm inducing labor. I want you here in case she needs a Cesarean."

Now fully awake, Parker understood the seriousness of Shoup's call. Eclampsia was life-threatening to both mother and baby, and the melanoma was another unknown.

"Start the induction, I'm on my way."

"It's already started," Shoup replied. "Let's hope I don't need you."

As Parker raced his car to MCA, he worried about the complications vaginal delivery would pose. Pulling on a placenta riddled with cancer was fraught with danger, possibly resulting in uncontrolled hemorrhage. The worst complication would be for Judy to need an emergency hysterectomy. She wouldn't tolerate that operation in her weakened condition and she could still lose the baby.

A cold chill ran through him as he envisioned the scene. With all she'd been through, her only hope was to stay alive to hold her child before leaving this world.

After changing into a scrub suit, he froze at the door before entering the delivery room. This is it, he murmured. If Shoup needed him to operate, he'd be performing it on the woman he loved. The thought of losing her on the table made him break out into a cold sweat.

Taking a deep breath, he entered the delivery room to see Judy in stirrups covered with sterile sheets. Shoup stood between her legs and a pair of delivery forceps rested on the surgical table behind him.

"Good, you're here, Parker," Shoup called out. "She's just starting to dilate."

Shoup's words broke into his thoughts and he quickly moved to Judy's side. He reached for her hand and whispered, "I'm here, Judy. Everything will be fine."

She gave him a gentle smile and released an exhausted sigh. "I know I'm in good hands, but I feel so tired." She suddenly let out a sharp cry, tightening the grip on his hand. After the contraction eased, she gasped, "That was a rough one."

He held a firm grip on her hand. "Hang in there, Judy. I'm with you every step of the way."

Shoup looked to Parker. "The epidural catheter's in place, but we won't administer the anesthetic until she's nearly fully dilated."

Since this was Judy's first delivery, Parker realized giving the anesthetic too early would block her contractions. He looked to Shoup and asked, "Are you planning a forceps delivery?"

"Most likely," Shoup answered, "she's too weak to push."

Suddenly a piercing cry rang out from Judy as another contraction took hold.

Everyone in the room listened to her exhausted grunting and panting.

"She's dilating nicely," Shoup stated, as Parker watched the obstetrician sweep his fingers around the cervix.

"You're coming along great, Judy," Parker said in a low voice. "It won't be long before they give you the anesthetic."

Judy gave another outcry of pain as a longer contraction took hold, making Parker tighten his grip on her hand. Seeing her contorted face released all his pent up anger. *Where the hell is this baby's father,* he thought to himself. *The girl's dying of cancer and he should be with her.*

After two more strong contractions heralded by Judy's painful outcries, Shoup nodded to the anesthesiologist. "Start the epidural block."

"It's on its way," the doctor answered as he injected the

drug into the epidural tubing.

Parker could see the drug taking hold as Judy's pants and groans subsided and a peaceful expression emerged on her sweat-beaded face. He wanted to kiss her cheek and tell her how much he loved her. Instead he drew her hand and pressed it to his lips.

Shoup broke the silence and called out, "What's the reading on the fetal heart tones?"

The nurse answered, "They're good now but during the contractions, they drop down to around seventy."

"We can't wait much longer, even though the head is fairly high. I can't take the chance of having fetal distress. I'm putting the blades on now."

Parker watched the obstetrician insert the forceps, locking them onto the baby's head. "Isn't it too dangerous to do a high forceps delivery?" he asked.

"Don't worry, I'm from the old school," Shoup answered. "We trained in forceps to avoid Cesareans." He began a gentle, steady pull on the blades. "Young docs rely on Cesareans because they're afraid of malpractice lawsuits if the kids they deliver aren't geniuses."

Parker caught the wisdom of Shoup's comment. A mid to high forceps extraction in experienced hands was less dangerous than an emergency Cesarean. He watched the obstetrician exert steady traction, carefully following the direction of the birth canal. After each slight advance of the head, Shoup released the compression lock on the blades. With a slight rotation, the dome of the baby's skull began to appear.

Shoup looked to the anesthesiologist. "What's her pressure?"

"One seventy-six over one-ten, but it was higher before I administered the spinal block."

"Good," Shoup said, continuing his traction on the head. "We're in the last stage."

Slowly the head emerged and Shoup slipped off the blades with the baby's face staring down in the correct position.

The nurse suctioned the infant's mouth and nose, and within seconds, the shoulders and body followed. Suspense in the room was broken and everyone smiled as raspy, bellowing wails filled the air.

Shoup then clamped and cut the cord. "It's a girl," he called out, holding the baby high for Judy to see.

"She's okay?" Judy asked in a weak voice.

"Looks fine, with all toes and fingers in place," the nurse answered, carrying the baby to place her on Judy's chest.

"She's beautiful," Judy sighed.

"And so perfect," Parker added.

"I'm delivering the placenta now," Shoup announced.

The obstetrician kept steady traction on the clamp holding the cord and after constant tugging, the placenta finally emerged as both surgeons stood in amazement. Hemorrhagic grape-like clusters of tumor interrupted the smooth surface of the shiny placental membranes.

"My God," Parker gasped. "I've never seen anything like that!"

Shoup pointed to the placenta embedded with the malignant growths. "The good news is that it's intact and no cancer's left behind." He turned to the nurse. "Send the specimen to Pathology for gross and microscopic examination."

The circulating nurse approached Judy. "May I take the baby now?"

Tears ran down Judy's exhausted face and she said, "Take good care of her."

"We certainly will," the nurse answered, cooing down at the child. "You're such a little sweetie."

Shoup called out suddenly as he pressed on Judy's abdomen to massage the uterus. "We got a problem, Parker! She's bleeding real heavy and not clamping down."

Parker anxiously watched Shoup sweep the uterine cavity with a sponge, pulling out large clots. "God, she's losing a lot of blood and she can't afford that," he cried out.

"We gotta stop it. Start the Pitocin," Shoup ordered.

The anesthesiologist started the infusion and the room remained quiet as the drip flowed into Judy's veins.

Shoup continued massaging the dome of the uterus while his gloved hand swept the uterine cavity with multiple gauze sponges, removing large clots. "What's her pressure now?" he asked.

"Down to one-ten systolic, but her pulse is racing and she could be going into shock," the anesthesiologist answered.

"Start the transfusion!" Parker ordered, feeling the blood rush from his face. "We can't take any chances. She's pale and hemorrhaging."

"There's blood cross-matched and waiting in the bank," Shoup answered.

Parker was relieved at having an experienced obstetrician in the room. With the blood infusing and a

Pitocin drip running, after forty minutes, Judy's bleeding gradually abated.

Tears filled Parker's eyes watching Judy sleep with the innocence of a child. Her eyes were closed and full lips slightly parted. The bleeding had stopped; she had her baby and was at peace. But he realized any happiness with her child would be short-lived by the prospect of her inevitable death.

Forty-seven

The Sunday morning sun lit up the horizon when Parker finally returned to his apartment. Exhausted, but emotionally relieved Judy's delivery went better than expected, he climbed the stairs. All he wanted was to get some sleep.

That hope vanished the moment he put in the key. The door was unlocked and he wondered how he could have forgotten such a normal ritual. He braced himself for the unknown. With the money still missing, his life remained in danger.

Carefully, he pushed the door open and peered inside. Everything appeared in place. Moving into the kitchen, he slid open the utensil drawer and pulled out a long bread knife. Gripping it like a weapon, he made his way gingerly into the bedroom. The moment he entered, a jab of cold steel pressed against his temple.

"*Buenos Dios, Doctore.* Drop the knife, *por favor*," a gruff voice demanded.

Parker felt the gun barrel press harder against his brow and let the knife drop to the floor.

"*Bueno*, now the money," the man said.

Numbed by fear, Parker decided he was a dead man and surprise was his only weapon. In a flash of rage, he spun around with elbows flailing, smashing his right fist into the intruder's crotch as he deflected the gun with the other hand.

The bearded man doubled over, moaning as a shot rang out.

Parker grappled for the gun the man gripped in his hand.

As they struggled, the intruder's gun fired again.

Parker watched with astonishment as the man crumpled to the floor with a soft gurgle coming from his throat. He reached for the gun laying on the floor and stared down at the motionless body. Kneeling to check for a pulse, he knew the intruder was no longer breathing. The bullet wound was directly over the heart.

Horrified, he flung the gun across the room and staggered to the phone to dial nine-one-one.

"I just shot a man in my apartment. Come quick."

The operator asked a flurry of questions, but all he could give was his address. His next move was to call Rucker.

"Are you all right?" the agent asked.

"I guess so, but shit! Where the hell were you guys?"

"Stay put, Doc. I'm coming right over. We're in the middle of a drug war and we can't tell who all the players are."

"Well, get your ass over here fast. I'm scared." Parker slammed down the phone and threw himself on the bed, wondering when this bad dream would end.

~ * ~

Agent Rucker and the sheriff's deputies filled his tiny apartment. When the medical examiner and crime scene investigators arrived, it was standing room only.

Parker sat in a corner watching Homicide go through its ritual investigation. Intruder or not, his thoughts were deadened by the knowledge he had almost gotten murdered, no less killed a man.

A yellow tape marked the periphery where the sprawled body lay. After the Medical Examiner declared the man dead, photographers took pictures from all angles. The detectives in the outer room directed each other as they dusted the door and all surfaces for fingerprints.

Rucker approached. "You constantly amaze me, Doc. You just took down a hardened criminal."

Parker, still stunned, nodded without taking his eyes off the dead body.

"After we run down our findings, the D.A. will need to ask you some questions."

Parker felt his body shake as he stared aimlessly at the floor.

"You're as white as a sheet, Doc. Don't crucify yourself until we check this guy out."

Parker felt his anger rise and looked up at Rucker. "You cops can't stop these fuckin' drug traffickers. This shit is all over the place. On the streets, in the schools, even in the homes of the wealthy. What makes you guys think you can control anything?"

The agent paused and his voice hardened. "What do you suggest? Cops are killed every day, trying to keep drugs from poisoning our society. I understand you're pissed because you just had a brush with death, but sometimes we do win."

Not hearing a response, he continued. "We just caught the two murder suspects who engineered the turnpike execution of the Rosales family. Their syndicate controls the cocaine ring that runs along the east coast. Because Rosales and his wife peddled for another drug lord, they got shot. Even blew away their three-and four-year-old sons."

Parker returned a blank stare. "Sorry, Rucker, I'm just upset and feel helpless right now."

Rucker patted his shoulder. "We're on top of this, Doc. We're not your enemy. These drug lords have a pipeline that runs from Mexico to Miami and Dallas and throughout the whole country. It's an unending battle. You're just one cog in the war."

Parker released a deep sigh. "If you're trying to comfort me by saying these guys are heartless and I'm still a target, it's not working."

"Look, Doc, with Lopez in jail and two suspects under arrest, we have a good chance of breaking up this local cell. That could put an end to you being a mark."

"Yeah, until another gang takes over."

"We're nearly finished," a detective called out to Rucker, donning rubber gloves. "I need to check the body for I.D."

"Good," Rucker answered. "But most prowlers leave their wallets at home."

Parker watched the detective search the front pockets of the dead man's plaid flannel shirt and jeans.

"Nothing here," the detective responded as he rolled the body over. He saw a bulge in the right rear pocket, pulled out a thick envelope and looked inside.

"Pay day!" he whistled, fingering a thick wad of bills circled with a rubber band. He pointed to a white slip of paper on top. "And look at this. A telephone number."

"Read it to me," Rucker replied. "I don't want my prints on the paper." He scribbled the number on his pad and smiled at Parker. "It's kind for our friend to be so helpful, Dr. Dawson. Let's see where this leads us."

Forty-eight

Judy's hospital room

The nurse entered and announced, "Feeding time." She held the infant bundled in her arms and handed her to Judy. "As soon as this little darling reaches five pounds, she can stay in your room."

Judy eagerly held the child and attempted to place the nipple into her mouth. "She didn't finish her last formula. I hope she does better this time."

"She'll get the hang of it before long," the nurse chuckled, giving her a motherly smile.

Judy stroked the baby's lips, enticing it again with the nipple. "I hope my milk starts soon. It must be a wonderful feeling to breast feed your child."

"Don't be too concerned, dear, as long as she takes the bottle," the nurse replied and left the room.

Judy smiled with relief when the baby latched on to the nipple. She watched her take a few sucks and then fall asleep. Carefully she raised the child, patted her gently on the back, enjoying the scent of a newborn. She waited for the first burp, but the joy of the moment was brief, knowing this little one would grow up without her.

Who would raise her child? She had her genes, her blood, and she couldn't just hand her over to strangers without question. Her eyes filled and she told herself the decision had to be made. Because she opted for an open adoption, the agency informed her she could select the couple.

She heard the infant finally gave a gentle burp and kissed her head. *Could an adopting mother be as committed as me?* she wondered. Breaking into tears, she fought the thought and dried her eyes. With so much love to give, she longed to guide this innocent newborn through life's pitfalls. But that wasn't going to happen.

Shawn insisted on being present at the interviews but he didn't approve of either of the first two couples. One appeared too materialistic rather than loving, and the other seemed desperate to hold their marriage together using the child as a bond.

The third couple was to arrive soon and she hoped Shawn would not be late. Before the baby finished the bottle, her brother wheeled himself in with Kathy at his side.

"Hi, sis, how's Mama doing?"

Before Judy could answer, Kathy approached the sleeping infant. "Oh look, Shawn, isn't she precious?"

"Gorgeous and every bit a Keller," he replied. He rolled close to Judy and gave her a peck on the cheek. "I want to see the agency report on the couple coming in."

Judy pointed to the nightstand. "It's the Ackerlys and they should be here any minute."

While Shawn read through the papers, a knock sounded on the door.

A tall attractive woman with red hair stood at the entry. She wore a kelly-green suit and a wide smile. The man at her side projected a corporate image. Dressed in a dark suit, white shirt and striped tie, he carried a serious expression. According to the agency records, he was thirty-nine and she thirty-seven.

"Please come in, folks," Judy announced, giving a welcoming smile.

"Just call me Cheryl," the woman beamed, "and this is my husband, Bob."

Judy felt the woman's friendliness appeared genuine. "I'm Judy, and meet my brother Shawn and our friend, Kathy."

"We're so happy to meet all of you," Cheryl gushed as she pulled her husband into the room.

"Yes," we're thrilled," Bob added.

Cheryl's eyes sparkled, approaching the baby for a closer look. "Oh, she's so tiny!"

Judy laughed. "They all are at this age, but she'll grow."

Bob's eyes scrutinized the infant. "What's her name?" he asked.

"Haven't decided yet," Judy replied. "We're just getting acquainted." She looked to Cheryl. "Would you like to hold her?"

"Could I?"

Judy was touched by Cheryl's radiant smile as she reached for the baby and cooed sweetly. But she felt Bob's intensity made him appear that he was searching for the slightest imperfection.

The nurse returned and checked the nearly empty

bottle. "She did real good this time. May I take her back?"

After Cheryl returned the baby to the nurse, she squeezed her husband's arm. "Oh, Bob! Don't you think she's perfect?"

"Yes," Bob answered with a forced smile.

Judy leaned forward in the bed. "Tell me, Bob, I understand you're in banking. Just what do you do?"

"I deal with mortgages and arrange loans."

"How long have you worked for your present employer?" Judy watched his smile turn to a frown.

"About six months."

"And where did you work before?"

"I did the same thing at a bank in Atlanta."

"Was it longer than six months?" She noticed Cheryl bite her lip.

"Around a year," came his quick response.

Sensing her questions disturbed him, Judy turned to Cheryl. "And what about you? The agency says you're a Human Resource Manager. Is it a nine to five job?"

"Yes," Cheryl answered softly.

"Do you plan to leave work and stay at home with the baby?"

"I will, but..."

"You see," Bob interrupted, "Cheryl eventually plans to be at home with the baby, but for now, we'll make arrangements."

Judy watched Shawn shift uncomfortably in his seat. "If I may ask, is there a reason you can't have children?"

Cheryl flashed a sharp look at her husband. "We're not sure. Bob has a low sperm count and there's no explanation for me."

Bob broke in. "We've tried everything. Hormones, artificial insemination. Nothing's worked."

Judy watched Cheryl's eyes moisten.

"But even if we adopt, we won't stop trying," Cheryl replied.

"Good," Judy answered. "Now do you have any questions for me?"

Cheryl hesitated. "Your illness. It's cancer, isn't it?"

Judy nodded. "Malignant melanoma. Do you know much about the disease?"

"Only that it comes from a mole," Cheryl replied. "Can it affect the baby?"

"We don't know," Judy answered. "Perhaps you should speak to my obstetrician, Dr. Shoup."

"We'll do that," Bob cut in, "but we're told the baby's fine."

"That's correct," Judy replied.

Shawn sat up in his chair and finally spoke. "Excuse me, folks, if Cheryl works, who takes care of the baby?"

Bob gave a nervous flinch. "We planned for a day nursery when Cheryl's at work."

"Then you need her income?"

"Only temporarily, until I get better situated at the bank," Bob answered.

Shawn felt uneasy and directed his question to Bob. "I've heard stories about negligent child abuse at these centers. Are you concerned about that?"

Judy interrupted to break the tension. "Where did you two grow up?"

"I'm from Detroit and Cheryl, St. Louis," Bob replied.

Shawn wouldn't give up. This time he addressed

Cheryl. "So you'll leave the baby in daycare?"

"Oh, I wouldn't at first."

"No?"

"Not at first."

"Then when?"

"The company gives me four weeks of paid leave." She looked to her husband. "And I can take another two without pay."

"I see," Shawn answered as he turned to Bob. "What did your father do for a living?"

"He was a stockbroker," Bob replied.

"Did you go out for sports in school?"

"No, but I follow them."

"Then I gather you weren't in Little League. Did you play baseball with your dad?"

"He was quite busy, but he took me to a Tiger game once." Bob waited for Shawn's reaction but saw none, and then asked in an irritated tone, "So Shawn, what did your father do?"

Judy realized Shawn's questions reflected his own frustration of missing a close father-son relationship. Raising her hand to stop a possible argument, she interrupted, "We want this to be a family decision. That's why Kathy and Shawn are here."

"We understand," Cheryl answered, her face flushed with excitement. "Whatever you want, Judy, we agree."

"You realize no money changes hands with this adoption," Judy responded.

"Yes and we appreciate that," Cheryl answered.

Judy turned to take a sip of water. "I'm really getting tired. Maybe after you speak with Dr. Shoup and you're still interested, we can meet again."

"No question we're interested," Cheryl answered with an earnest look.

"We'll leave now so you can rest," Bob replied, guiding Cheryl to the door.

Judy could see Shawn's eyes narrow as they exited. When they left, she asked, "What do you think?"

"I'm leery," Shawn answered. "He's no prime mover at the bank and she's never going to leave work. He looks like a control freak and who knows what their future holds?"

Judy looked to Kathy. "And what's your opinion?"

"I think Cheryl is the one who wants the baby. I'm not sure about Bob because I don't think he's comfortable with the cancer."

"Even if they come back," Shawn said, "I don't like the idea Bob didn't spend time with his dad. Big deal, he once went to a Tiger game. Kids need their dad. His father didn't play a big part in his life, so why should he be any different?"

"Let's wait and see if they come back," Judy said. She looked to Kathy. "Could you call Dr. Shoup's office to tell them it's all right to discuss my case?"

"Sure," Kathy answered, "but think it over, Judy. I know time's running out, but maybe Shawn has a point."

"I understand," Judy murmured, releasing a deep sigh. "A decision has to be made soon." She lay back on the pillow and closed her eyes. "I just want to bond with the family that raises my child."

Forty-nine

Following day

Parker rushed down the steps of the West Palm Beach Police Station, eager to leave behind the dingy cubicle he had sat in for three hours of questioning. He didn't need any more legal entanglements and hoped the district attorney would rule the intruder's killing a justifiable homicide.

His cell phone rang just as he reached his car.

"This is MCA, Dr. Dawson. Judy Keller's blood count dropped again even after her transfusion. She's below eight grams."

"I'm on my way in to write orders," he replied.

Judy was slipping away. More than brain radiation, she needed pure Procrit to raise her blood count so she could enjoy what little time she had left with the baby. He drove on to MCA, anxious to check with the pharmacist.

As he approached the pharmacy window, he heard loud voices arguing and rang the bell.

In moments, Russo appeared. "Come in, Dr. Dawson," the pharmacist said, pushing a button to open the door.

Parker entered, surprised to see Trask present, glaring at Russo.

"Sorry, Mr. Trask," Russo snapped. "Baxter Labs wants all our heparin returned and that's final."

"But what you have didn't come from Baxter," Trask objected.

"More reason why they should check our stock for purity as well as origin. Over twenty heparin deaths have been reported nationwide, and I can't take the chance the shipment you ordered through Reliant isn't tainted."

Trask's face flushed when he spotted Parker in the room. Without saying a word, he rushed by and left the department.

"I see Trask's back," Parker said.

"He's out on bail," the pharmacist replied.

"So the Heparin as well as the Procrit came from Reliant Drugs?"

"That's right," Russo said, shaking his head. "There's well over seventy deaths reported globally caused by tainted heparin. The source is coming from small unregistered workshops in China. That's why I'm returning all my stuff to Baxter."

"What's in it that's causing the deaths?"

"The government found the contaminated heparin contained a toxic chemical called oversulfated chondroitin. It's not made from natural pig intestine like the real stuff, but imitates it. I'll never order anything from Reliant again, even if it risks my job."

Parker gave Russo a smile. "I'm glad you have the balls to stand up to Administration."

"Yeah, especially when it's backed up by government recall."

Parker chuckled, "You have a point. But I came to ask

if you received a new batch of Procrit from Johnson & Johnson. Judy Keller needs it desperately."

"Just write the order, Doc. I have it in stock."

"Thanks, Fred." Parker turned to leave and then stopped and looked squarely into Russo's eyes. "Your profession should be very proud of you."

"Just doing my job," Russo grinned.

Parker's steps quickened as he made his way to Judy's room. As he exited the elevator, high pitched shrieks and bellows resonated down the corridor.

Changing direction, he followed the uproar leading to the medicine floor. The scene was unbelievable. An angry Morty Gold stood at the desk tugging on a chart which a nurse held firmly in her hand. At the far end of the station, a wide-eyed desk secretary sat with the phone to her ear.

Parker watched as Gold ripped the chart from the nurse's hand, rushed to the opposite side of the station and wildly flipped the pages. He suddenly stopped and froze as he read a report.

"Oh God!" he moaned.

The nurse ran over, retrieved the chart and frowned. "You have no right to look into that chart, Dr. Gold. It's privileged information."

A dazed Gold stepped away and staggered down the corridor without saying a word.

"What was that all about?" Parker asked.

"I can't tell you, Dr. Dawson," the nurse replied, putting the chart away.

Parker decided to go about his business when the secretary who still held the phone to her ear, shouted, "That's right! It's Mr. Stern's chart. Dr. Gold was looking

317

for the HIV report."

"Quiet, Mary," the nurse shot back.

"Sorry," the secretary answered timidly.

Parker sensed Gold was up to no good and turned to the nurse. "You should report this to Administration."

The nurse wrinkled her nose and returned a cynical smile. "That's who Mary was calling but I doubt anything will come of it, knowing how much clout Dr. Gold has around here."

Although reluctant to get involved with another battle, Parker offered, "If you need an eye witness, you can call on me."

After the nurse thanked him, he retraced his steps to Judy's room when Karl Lawton approached.

"Hi, Parker. How did the police questioning go?"

"Oh, you heard about that?"

"I called the office to talk to you and Gwen told me what happened."

Parker shook his head. "It's in their hands now until they let me know what they decide."

As Karl began to walk away, Parker stopped him. "You'll never believe what I just saw. Morty was in a tug of war with a nurse over a chart. He was searching for an HIV report on a Mr. Stern."

"That's Bea Stern's husband."

"Who's Bea Stern?"

"The gal you saw in the Bahamas that Gold's been screwing. My patient was in his room and had to be moved because the guy's dying from terminal AIDS."

"So that's why Gold was in shock."

"Well he ought to be. Bea Stern's husband is a wealthy

developer and travels all over the world. Who knows how many strange ink wells he's dipped his little pen into?"

"Then if Morty's having an affair with Bea, that means he's at risk for AIDS."

"I hate to say this, but the son of a bitch deserves it."

Parker shook his head. "A bittersweet justice. If Gold's infected, politics can't help him now."

Fifty

Next morning, Parker's apartment

The *Palm Beach Post* carried the story. What appeared at first to be a routine home fire alarm suddenly emerged into the discovery of another marijuana grow house. Inside, sheriff's deputies found almost a hundred plants growing in individual pots. For the year, it was the sixty-sixth such house discovered in the county.

The blaze was set off by an overheated extension cord diverting power from a meter. Dripping molten metal and plastic falling onto cut dried marijuana leaves caused the overwhelming acrid smoke and fire which alerted the neighbors.

Parker studied the picture posted above the article showing the foil-covered pots with irrigation pipes leading to each plant. It was mind boggling to see what extent traffickers would go to meet the demands of a drug dependent society.

But he smiled when he read the news report on the next page. The U.S. Attorney General announced he was seeking the death penalty for the murderers of the Rosales family. *That should send a warning to those bastards who kill innocent kids,* he thought.

He recalled his own harrowing experience with the home intruder and thought about moving. But a change of address would do little to protect him since he was so visible at the office and hospital.

Frustrated by all the criminality surrounding him, he threw down the paper and entered the bedroom. As he dressed, he reflected on all the counterfeit overseas drugs coming into the hospital. He felt he should complain to Lindstrom about ordering from Reliant, but most likely the administrator was involved with Trask in that deal. Rucker had already linked Trask to Reliant but could he find proof Lindstrom was profiting from the arrangement as well.

He left the apartment determined to confront Lindstrom, hoping to uncover information for Rucker. As he drove to MCA, his cell phone rang. Hearing Rucker's voice, he pulled into a Wendy's parking lot.

"I got some good news, Doc."

"That's a new twist," Parker answered. "Did the DA render an opinion about my home break-in?" He couldn't bring himself to say the word 'killing.'

"Yes, and I'm happy to say he's decided to not press charges."

"Well that's a relief."

"They traced the guy's rap sheet through his fingerprints. He was one tough hombre, involved with multiple murders, serious acts of violence and the shooting death of a Broward County sheriff's deputy. All in all, he's had thirty-five arrests. including burglary and has been deported multiple times, but none of the counts stuck. I guess this time you accomplished what law enforcement couldn't."

"I'm not proud of that. Killing isn't my forte. Did you track down the number you found in the guy's wallet?"

"Yes, and it led right to Lopez. He's probably a member of that same mob."

"Then if that hood was looking for the money, it means I'm still a target."

"We think so because we're talking millions. But there is a bright side to my call."

"Don't stop now. What is it?"

"Ramon Lopez, alias Cougar, is facing a whole lot of charges. Drug trafficking, cocaine possession, peddling counterfeit drugs, shooting another gang member and possible attempted murder. We're learning more each day. He's a career criminal but we think he knows where the stolen money went."

Parker's throat tightened, unable to ask a question.

Rucker continued. "We got the first clue from Olga's daughter, Carmella. She let out that Lopez planned to take her and her mother to settle somewhere in the Caribbean. We suspect he's been skimming from the mob for that purpose."

"Did Lopez admit to that?"

"Not at first but since he's facing enough charges to spend his retirement in prison, we thought we'd offer him a deal."

"What kind of a deal?"

"If he came clean about his connection with the Mexican cartel kingpins and his links to the overseas counterfeit drug operation, we'd consider allowing him to leave the U.S. with Carmella and go to whatever country he could get into."

"What about the money?"

"That's the hook. He'd have to cough up the money."

"Did he bite?

"Not yet, but we're waiting."

It was clear to Parker where the missing money disappeared. Lopez and Olga were stashing it somewhere.

"Doc, you still there?" Rucker called out into the phone.

Parker felt the beads of sweat on his brow. "I can hear you, Rucker. Just give me a minute to recover."

"Take your time, Doc. It's the first time I'm bringing you some good news."

"And I have some information for you. Trask may be out on bail but his counterfeit drug business is still flourishing."

"What is it you know?" Rucker's voice was low and sharp.

"Baxter's recalling all heparin that came from Reliant Drugs. A number of deaths have been reported with its use and the stuff from Reliant might have come from China."

"As you know, we're working on that."

"Well I'm going to see Lindstrom and bitch about using Reliant."

Rucker snapped, "Don't do that! We've got Lindstrom in our sights and we're close to building a case."

"Does he suspect?"

"He might, because..." Rucker stopped. "I can't say any more. Just go to work and say nothing."

"That's easy for you..."

Rucker cut him off. "You'll be hearing some news soon. Bye, Doc."

Parker hung up the phone, occupied with a flurry of concerns. He had enough on his plate. Keeping Judy alive, waiting for Fellini's answer and getting the drug ordeal behind him were enough to keep him jumping.

As he left the parking lot, the thought occurred to him. If he spent as much time on medicine as he did on crime and politics, he would have received a Nobel Prize by now.

~ * ~

Parker read 3 PM on the OR wall clock as he placed the last skin clip on the patient's mastectomy wound closure. On his earlier visit to Judy, he was encouraged by how well she was tolerating her radiation therapy. Given her medical situation, the hospital allowed her to have an extended stay to receive the treatment which relieved his concern about sending her home too early.

"Call your office, Doctor," the circulating nurse said, tossing piles of blood-stained gauze sponges into the red biohazard waste receptacle.

He nodded his thanks, peeled off his gloves and headed to the doctors' lounge. After talking to the patient's family and dictating his operative notes, he finally dialed the office.

He heard an urgency in Gwen's voice.

"Mr. Fellini needs to talk to you, Dr. Dawson, but he wouldn't say what it's about."

Parker quickly hung up the phone and dialed the attorney. "I can't take any more bad news," he said when Fellini came on the line.

The lawyer laughed. "Not this time, Doctor. I'm happy to inform you that the state found no grounds to pursue disciplinary action against you. You're cleared of any wrongdoing and no record of the complaints will be documented anywhere."

Parker could feel the tightness in his chest fade, absorbing the attorney's words. A surge of euphoria flooded his brain and he impulsively replied, "And I owe it all to you."

"Thanks for the compliment, Doc, but the facts spoke for themselves. I was only the messenger. The person you should thank is Dr. Lawton. His surgical committee wrote a powerful piece clearing you of any wrong. They actually did the work for me."

"Does that mean I have a case against the hospital?"

There was a moment of silence.

Fellini hesitated. "Yes, but a word of caution. If you sue MCA, what are you looking to accomplish? A financial settlement, an attempt to hurt the corporation, revenge? Think about it."

"But they tried to ruin my reputation. Shouldn't they pay for that?"

"That's for you to answer, Doctor. But if you feel that strongly about it, you'll need outside counsel. As you know, I only deal with state disciplinary actions."

Fellini's unenthusiastic response dampened Parker's fervor.

"Then that's the thanks I get for taking care of the state's social problems. The indigents, the uninsured, all the emergencies that show up in the ER?"

"That's right," Fellini answered. "But consider that a

privilege the state grants you."

"That's bullshit, Mr. Fellini and you know it."

Fellini's voice hardened. "Look at it this way, Doctor. You don't make the laws. The politicians do. If you want to play the game, you have to do it by their rules."

Parker's voice softened. "I think you're sending me a message, Counselor."

"In a way I am. Concentrate on your career. You're young with a long horizon. Don't get bogged down with legal battles and court appeals that can only drain your pockets and surgical energies. No matter how bitter you feel about businessmen corrupting medicine, it's nothing you can change."

Parker's voice rose. "But if MCA is not held accountable, what will stop them from doing this again?"

"I hear what you're saying, but there's a little known fact we all have to live with. In general, it's the institution and corporation that survives. The individual is expendable. It's all a matter of money and the simple fact is that they have more of it than you do."

There was a moment of silence as Parker reflected on the wisdom of Fellini's words. Maybe it was time to accept reality. "I hate to admit it, but you might be right. As you can see, this subject was never taught in medical school."

Fellini chuckled. "Get on with your life and enjoy your victory, Dr. Dawson. I'm sure Lindstrom and Gold are going to get ulcers over this ruling."

Parker gloated inwardly, picturing the two administrators running for the Alka-Seltzer. But it still didn't seem right after all the sleepless nights and money they had cost him. Suing was a question he would have to think about.

"Do I owe you another payment, Mr. Fellini?" he asked. He could hear a chuckle at the other end.

"You've taken enough hits, Doctor. No, there's no additional charge."

Parker shut the phone and sat, lost for words. Fellini proved that this lawyer did have a heart.

Fifty-one

Despite Fellini's advice not to sue Lindstrom and MCA, Parker had difficulty overcoming the anger that stirred within him. He struggled to control his bitterness and ultimately came to the conclusion he needed to confront Lindstrom to set things straight.

He dialed the phone. "I need your help again, Karl. I can't let Lindstrom get away with what he did. I've decided to sue him, along with MCA."

"Slow down, Parker. Do you realize you'll be taking on a national corporation if you sue MCA?"

"I know that."

"Even if you could afford the attorneys, what important firm will take your case?"

"I'll find one."

"You're dreaming, Parker. What will you sue for? Lost income? What? Fifty, a hundred thousand? That's peanuts. No firm will take that challenge for such a small amount."

"Come on, Karl. You know what they put me through. I could have lost my license."

Karl sighed. "Not likely, Parker. The hospital never

took away your surgical privileges, so any issue regarding lost revenue is irrelevant."

"I can't stand the thought of Lindstrom and the hospital getting off scot free."

"You'll have to live with it, Parker. What choice do you have?"

"I want to meet with Lindstrom and I want you to go with me."

"What's that going to accomplish?"

"I've got to tell him how I feel. Let him worry about getting sued."

Lawton laughed. "Do you realize how many lawyers MCA carries on its payroll? A lawsuit from you is the last thing the corporation would worry about." He paused. "Besides, I don't want to be labeled a trouble maker."

"If you won't go with me, I'll go alone."

"Don't be such a hothead, Parker." Lawton's voice was firm. "You'll only create hard feelings and alienate the medical staff."

"Maybe so, but what the hell. I have to get this off my chest."

"No, Parker. That's no solution."

"Look, Karl. It's the principle of the thing. It's not just for myself. What about the next young doc who comes along and doesn't play the game? Lindstrom can and will do it again to some innocent victim."

"Dammit, Parker. There you go again."

Parker spoke over him. "Karl, I've made up my mind. With you or without you, someone has to stop unscrupulous businessmen from abusing physicians."

"I don't know, Parker. Your intentions are good, but

arguing with the hospital doesn't sound like a solution. Cool down and think about it before you go saying something crazy."

"Maybe you're right. Forget the lawsuit. I just need some closure. I want Lindstrom to know he's playing a dangerous game poking his nose into medical matters. I want him to know how he hurt me."

"He knows what he did. What makes you think he'll listen?"

"If I go alone, he might not. But if you go with me, I'll bet he will."

Lawton remained quiet while Parker continued speaking into the phone. "I'll be clear and to the point without showing any hostility."

Karl sighed. "One way or another, you're determined to go, aren't you?"

"I've got to have my say and speak for anyone else who might face the same problem."

There was a long silence until Lawton responded. "You're a good man, Parker, but somewhat naïve. Don't hurt your career by doing something stupid."

"Then you'll go with me?"

"Only if you promise to be civil. Express your concern and warn him this should never happen again. No noise, no rancor, just set the record straight."

"I promise."

"I must be nuts to do this, Parker. Go ahead and set up the appointment."

~ * ~

Parker watched Carolyn Robertson's body stiffen as he and Lawton walked past her desk to enter Lindstrom's office. She reminded him of a lioness ready to pounce in order to protect her cub from danger.

Once inside, they were greeted by a young man dressed in a dark suit who rose from his chair.

"Good, morning, Doctors. I'm Lawrence Hicks, hospital attorney for MCA's internal affairs." He handed them his business card.

Lindstrom's penchant for neatness annoyed Parker. He sat at his sleek desk, devoid of papers, and motioned them to sit in the two chairs before him.

In his usual cold tone, he asked, "What can I do for you, Doctors?"

Lawton spoke first. "Since Dr. Dawson has been cleared by the state, he wants to express his feelings about the hospital's actions against him."

Lindstrom gave Parker a puzzled look. "If you've been cleared by the state, Dr. Dawson, what is your complaint?"

Parker worked hard to remain calm as he spoke. "Mr. Lindstrom, you and MCA have caused me irreparable harm, not only to my reputation but financially."

The attorney chimed in, "No by-laws were violated, Dr. Dawson. Mr. Lindstrom acted in accordance with state law and corporate advice."

Parker's voice rose. "I disagree, sir. I believe Mr. Lindstrom acted with malicious intent to harm me. He took advantage of a mishandled emergency room situation to improperly charge me."

"I'd be careful making such a claim." Hicks responded.

"Easy, Parker, you promised." Lawton cautioned.

Parker turned to Lawton. "Sorry, Karl, they don't

realize they're risking a potential lawsuit."

Hicks shot up from his chair. "You're planning to sue MCA?"

Lawton broke in. "No, that's not what this meeting's about."

"Then exactly what is this meeting about?" Hicks demanded.

"Medical honesty!" Parker shouted.

The attorney returned to his seat. "What does that have to do with Mr. Lindstrom? He doesn't deal with medical decisions."

"Oh yes, he does," Parker shot back. He watched Hicks flinch and decided it was time to expose Lindstrom's dirty tricks. He felt his face flush as he spoke.

"Two surgeons left a gunshot victim to die on the operating room table when they couldn't stop his bleeding. Mr. Lindstrom ordered the staff and involved doctors not to discuss what happened. That's a cover-up, Mr. Hicks. No investigation, no mortality review. Who says this administrator doesn't deal with medical decisions?"

Hicks's eyes narrowed. "Careful, Dr. Dawson, you're making a slanderous charge."

Lawton cut in. "That's not what he meant."

"That's exactly what I meant," Parker answered. He rose from his chair and faced Lindstrom.

"It seems to me that MCA doesn't have as much interest in quality care as it does to the bottom line."

"Easy, Dr. Dawson. You're treading on thin ice," Hicks replied.

Parker gave up all hope of keeping cool. *Dammit,* he thought, *I'm just going to let it all out.*

His voice rose. "I know the scenario too well. Your HMO signs up a gatekeeper, usually a family practitioner who's the least knowledgeable in the chain of medical expertise. The patient is handed a limited list of providers with lots of hidden restrictions. Controlling choice and cost is your goal, not quality. It sounds like post office medicine to me, Mr. Hicks."

Hicks's cool demeanor vanished. "I see your bias, Dr. Dawson. Who are you to question the medical standards set by our HMO panel?"

"I question with medical integrity on my side, Mr. Hicks. After finishing a five hour Whipple procedure on a patient with pancreatic cancer, one of your HMO gatekeepers told me I shouldn't have performed the operation."

"Why?" Hicks questioned.

"According to him, the patient would die within the year. He said it's too costly to waste money and time on that kind of treatment."

Lawton pulled at Parker's sleeve, forcing him to sit down.

In spite of Karl's effort, Parker continued. "That's medical dishonesty, sir. My patient is now free of pain without narcotics and has a chance to live for more than a year. Don't talk to me about your HMO standards."

Hicks's cool detachment returned and he gave Parker a smile. "How old are you, Dr. Dawson? Thirty-one, thirty-two? Can you afford the time and money to file a lawsuit against MCA?"

He paused to cross his legs and leaned toward Parker. "And could you stand the stress and strain of legal filings and counter filings that will tie you up in court for five to ten years? In the end, what point will you have made?"

"To defend medical integrity," Parker replied.

Hicks chuckled. "Grow up, Doctor. Medicine is changing faster than you can imagine. In a few years, just a handful of companies will manage America's second largest industry. How important can your concerns be to the overall problems of delivering massive healthcare to a nation? Your complaints pale in face of the complexity of issues we must address. Unfortunately, Dr. Dawson, you're just a single fly in the forest."

Parker shook his head in defeat. It was clear listening to Hicks, doctors were no longer in charge of medicine.

Lawton broke the silence. "I think we should go, Parker."

Hicks responded with a grin. "I hope this meeting has sobered your thinking, Dr. Dawson."

"We'll see," Parker answered. As he rose from the chair, he noticed Lindstrom's lips had never lost their tight smile throughout the meeting.

Once outside in the hall, Karl said, "Are you satisfied, Parker? You were a real hothead in there."

"I guess I lost my cool but seeing that smug look on Lindstrom's face drove me nuts."

"That's nothing new. You know how superior he acts around doctors. He must be feeling pretty cocky these days. I read a financial review of MCA's new business plan. They call it 'strategic repositioning.'"

"Sounds ominous."

"And guess who was listed as one of its star performers in generating income? None other than Lindstrom when he was at the California hospital."

"So what's new, Karl? Everyone knows Lindstrom was sent here to beef up MCA's profits."

"That's true and the corporation gave him a fifty thousand dollar bonus to boot. It's a far different world for us doctors, isn't it?"

Parker's voice turned wistful. "Yeah, and even more different for patients lost in the shuffle."

Fifty-two

Kent's guilt took an emotional toll with Judy's pregnancy. But now that she faced a life-threatening cancer, it was too much for him to handle. Deep down, he believed he was partly to blame for her misdiagnosis. She was the woman he loved, not just another one his HMO patients. When he walked out on her that first time, he totally forgot to check the pathology report. He suspected the mole could be malignant. Had he read the report that said it was benign, he would have asked for a second opinion.

Now he had to bear that responsibility. Whether to soothe his guilt or to alleviate the fear that she would expose his paternity, he needed to see her. He tussled it over in his mind and came to the conclusion that Judy was dying. If he couldn't be with her, to safeguard everything he worked for, staying with Sheila had to be the lesser evil.

He entered the darkened hospital room, approached Judy's bed and stood over her as she slept. Despite the illness, her striking beauty made his heart sink.

She opened her eyes and looked up at him. "Kent, it's you."

He stammered. "Are you feeling better? I heard about your seizure."

She didn't answer. Instead she closed her eyes again.

He knew she was not asleep so he touched her arm. "They say the baby's fine."

She raised herself in bed, more alert. "Yes, Kent, the baby's healthy. That's the good news. But the bad news is that her father abandoned us."

Kent's voice rose to a sharp pitch. "That's not true!"

"Really?"

"I came here to see how I can help."

"Isn't it a little too late, Kent? By now you know my mole wasn't benign. They gave it a new name, malignant melanoma."

His voice was barely audible. "I know."

"So Kent, there's nothing you can do for me or the baby. In all the time we spent together, you took from me. You gave me nothing. So what can you offer now?"

Her words cut through him and he searched for an answer. "You're exhausting yourself, Judy. Please don't waste your energy."

"Then why did you come?"

"I just wanted to see you."

"What for? To tell me you're taking my baby after I die?"

He raised his hands. "No, Judy, nothing like that."

"Of course not. Why disturb your happy life with Sheila?"

The mention of Sheila's name brought a pang of fear into his heart. "Judy, you're saying things you don't mean."

"Then why are you here if it's not for your daughter?"

"Shssh!" He raised his fingers to his lips. "Not so loud."

"Oh God, that's why you came!" She covered her face with her hands and fell back on the raised head of the bed. "You want to make sure I didn't tell anyone you're the father!"

Kent could feel the blood rush from his face, aware that's exactly what he wanted. "Does any one know?"

He read the distrust in her face and instantly knew it was the wrong thing to say.

Judy curled her lips into a smirk. "Keep guessing, Kent. That should drive you crazy."

Fifty-three

Parker had a hard time digesting the exchange he had with Lindstrom and attorney Hicks. It rankled him that corporate interests seemed more protected than the individual. Karl was right. Medicine was changing and there was little he could do about it. Those thoughts rang in his mind as he walked out of his last case.

Judy would be discharged soon and there was one question that nagged him. He hoped she would answer it but he wasn't sure.

He found her resting in bed with the baby asleep in an adjacent bassinet. The sound of his footsteps caused her to look to the door as he approached. A smile broke out on her face.

"Ready to go home?" he asked.

"Yes, I think it's time," she answered.

He stroked her head and studied the puffiness of her cheeks. The Decadron prescribed to reduce the swelling of her brain contributed to her facial edema. He bent over, kissed her brow and said, "I don't do this with all my patients."

Her response was faint, almost a whisper. "I hope not, but it feels wonderful."

A more serious look crossed his face. "After your radiation therapy is over, we'll start the new biotherapeutic treatment I spoke to you about."

She returned a hollow stare. "I'm too weak to argue. I just don't want to get so sick I lose time with the baby."

He felt his heart sink. There were severe side effects associated with all of the treatments, but he couldn't leave any stone unturned. "Just do it for me," he insisted. "We're in this together and we can't give up."

"I'm not giving up. I just want to be well enough to spend quality time with little Judy."

Deep down, he knew she was right and decided to change the topic. "Have you made a final decision on the adopting couple?"

She shook her head. "Shawn is against all three we interviewed."

He reached for her hand. "Judy, I think it's time you told me. Who's the father?"

She looked away, shaking her head.

He felt a sudden flash of anger. "Dammit! It's his child and his responsibility, too."

He watched her eyes fill, her lips quiver. "Forgive me," he whispered. "I want so much for you."

She extended her arms to hold him. "I know you mean well, but how could I allow him to be a part of my baby's life? He has no love for either of us."

He held her tight in his arms as she broke into convulsive sobs. "I'll always be there for the baby," he whispered. "If ever the child needs to know, only then will I reveal it."

He dried her tears with a tissue. "I have my own suspicions, so tell me."

She pulled away and hid her face in the pillow. "Don't push me. I've made up my mind and that's the way it's going to be."

He heard the knock on the door and turned to see Kathy and Shawn at the entry.

"We're all set to go," Shawn said, wheeling himself into the room. "A nurse is coming to help."

Parker rose from the bed, somewhat relieved to have ended a possible argument and looked to Kathy. "Judy tells me you'll be staying with her and the baby."

"That's right," she answered. "And Shawn's moving into an independent living facility, ready to start his new job."

"Congratulations, what's it to be?" Parker asked.

Shawn gave a broad smile. "You're looking at the next multimillionaire hedge fund manager. I just passed my certifying exam to become a stockbroker."

Judy raised herself up in bed. "That's great, Shawn. You have no idea how happy that makes me."

Shawn laughed. "Well, someone in this family has to make a living."

The nurse entered with a wheelchair and assisted Judy with the transfer.

Parker stood by as they all prepared to leave with Judy holding the baby. He touched her shoulder. "See you later."

He wanted to kiss her again, but understood she knew how he felt. His heart ached and he choked up. That should have been his baby. That moment, he made a promise to himself. Before she left this earth, she would have no doubt that he was her true soul mate.

~ * ~

It was after 10 o'clock that evening by the time Parker walked out of MCA's Emergency Room. He was tired and relieved the patient he was called to see didn't require surgery. It had been a busy few days. With the grueling police questions, operating emergencies and the emotional exchange with Judy, he felt totally drained and ready for sleep.

As he walked the quiet halls toward the doctors' lounge, he felt bothered by Judy's persistence to keep the baby's father a mystery. It was unfair for her to assume this burden and risk the child's welfare by absolving this man from his fatherly responsibility.

Once inside, he dialed the code on his locker and hung up his white coat, weighted down with a handy Washington Manual he used for quick medical reference.

The clatter of his locker door closing was followed by the sound of the outer door opening. When he returned to the lounge, he faced Kent Markman.

"I need to talk to you about Judy Keller, Kent."

Markman's face tightened and he gave Parker an icy gaze. "Talk about what?"

"I need approval from the HMO to get a gene assay of her tumor. The biopsy specimen is in the lab."

"A gene assay? What in the world for? I've already cleared her for radiation therapy."

"The assay is the one shot she has to get a good response or hopefully a cure. The information we get will help tailor her treatment to select the best new biotherapeutic agent available."

"Why don't you try chemotherapy?"

"Chemo at her stage offers a less than a 10% response without cure. A University of Chicago researcher has shown the expression of melanogenesis in the assay will identify whether the fighting T cells can attack the cancer."

"And if it doesn't?"

"Then we can try the vaccine."

Markman gave him a disparaging look and sank down on the sofa. "Look, Parker, the HMO won't approve it. It's all experimental."

"It's not experimental, Kent. With these results, we can decide if she'll respond to this new approach."

"Sorry, Parker, as her gatekeeper, I can't approve it."

Parker felt the heat rush to his face as he prepared to argue but stopped when his cell phone rang. He heard Judy's voice.

"The father is Kent Markman." A click followed.

Parker's jaw dropped. His face flushed with rage as he pointed to Markman. "You're the father!"

"What in the hell are you talking about?"

"Judy's baby! You're the father!"

Markman's face turned white and he jumped up from the sofa. "I don't know where you're getting your information, but I'm not listening to this shit any longer."

"No, you don't, you son of a bitch." Parker grabbed Markman by the jacket lapels and pulled him close. "I had a hunch it was you but until now she wouldn't say. That girl suffered all alone and you, you bastard, you abandoned her."

"Get your hands off me, you're crazy." Markman grunted. He pulled away and rushed out of the door.

Parker shouted after him. "You can run away, Kent, but your DNA can't."

Standing alone in the room, he could hear his heart pound. He sat down, trying to collect his thoughts. It was pointless to run after him because a lab test would prove paternity, a fact Kent couldn't erase. But right now he had to concentrate on Judy's treatment.

As he left the lounge, he reasoned why she finally revealed the father's name. Since she wasn't happy with any of the prospective adoptive couples, she put her trust in him to protect the baby's future.

Fifty-four

Kent sat at his desk, pulled out a handkerchief and wiped the sweaty beads off his brow. Now that he was exposed, God only knew who else besides Parker was told he was the father? All he envisioned on the horizon was divorce, financial ruin and the distasteful obligation to support an unwanted child.

He grabbed the phone to dial Wolfe, but before he could press the last button, a knock sounded on the door.

His nurse stuck her head in the doorway. "Dr. Markman, are you ready to see patients?"

He slammed down the phone. "Not yet. I need some time."

"How long? The waiting room's jam packed."

"I don't know. If they can't wait, just reschedule them. I'm busy right now." He caught the deep frown on her face, but that didn't stop him from motioning her to leave.

After she closed the door, he opened the bottom drawer of his desk, removed a flask and took a long swig. Sitting quietly for a minute, he felt his heavy breathing subside. His fingers trembled as he redialed Wolfe.

"Dr. Markman here. I need to speak with Mr. Wolfe right away."

This time the receptionist answered with a twinge of panic. "I'll see if I can find him, Dr. Markman."

"Is he in?"

"Yes. Let me check for you."

"This is urgent, so please hurry."

He shifted restlessly in his chair, drowning in all his negative thoughts. The fact that Judy had told Parker about his involvement made him pound the desk in anger. *Why did she do this to me? And why is Parker sticking his nose into my life?*

Wolfe finally came on the line. "Hey Kent, you frightened the hell out of my receptionist. What's going on?"

"A lot. Judy told her doctor that I'm the father."

"Calm down, Kent. You gotta settle down to think this out."

Kent took another swig from the flask. "How are the transfers coming along?"

"Fine. I have the dummy corporation set up and you're the president. Some of Sheila's accounts have already been transferred."

"She signed the agreement without questioning you?"

"Yes. I told her it was for tax purposes."

"Good. Then all of the accounts have been transferred?"

"No, the rest have to be moved slowly. We don't want to raise any suspicions."

Kent's voice rose. "But there's no time. Judy's already delivered, and when she passes..."

Wolfe didn't answer immediately. "I know what you're thinking, Kent. When she dies, we can expect a legal paternity action against you."

"And you know what that means. You know what will happen when Sheila and her big shot father find out."

Wolfe released a deep sigh, but didn't answer.

Kent continued. "Gerry, I'm at my wits' end. There has to be a way to avoid all this shit. I'm a dead man if this comes out."

Wolfe let out a nervous laugh. "Look, Kent. We've been friends since college. Have I ever let you down? Right now, let's just hope her doc doesn't spill the beans. I'll figure something out."

Kent felt his chest pound and eyed the flask resting on his desk. "I get crazy thoughts in my head, Gerry. Like getting rid of the baby."

His hand tightened on the phone, frustrated by the silence from the other end and his voice dropped. "I can't believe I'm talking like this."

Suddenly, Wolfe broke the quiet. "I may have a solution. Can you afford two hundred thousand to solve this problem forever?"

"Sure. That's peanuts to what I could lose to Sheila."

"I want you to put the cash in two envelopes. Twenty-five thousand in one and a hundred twenty-five thousand in the other."

"What about the other fifty thousand?"

"I'll need that paid separately to my office. Hand deliver it directly to me."

"You sure this will work?"

"Trust me. I'll tell you about it when you come here. I

have a few details to work out yet, but I think we can kill two birds with one stone."

"You're really a life-saver, Gerry. I'll have it all in your hands by tomorrow."

Kent shut the phone and leaned back in his chair, feeling a sense of relief. That extra $50 thousand, whether into Gerry's pocket or where ever, was worth it. For the first time, he might have a way out.

~ * ~

Parker checked his watch all during office hours, anxious to see Judy after the last patient left. She was at home and steadily weakening. Even though Kathy kept him posted on her progress, he visited every day to see for himself. Her weight loss and low hemoglobin concerned him. Tonight he would draw blood to see if she needed another transfusion.

He toyed with the idea of flying her to the National Cancer Institute at Bethesda, Maryland to receive the toxic Proleukin regimen. But in his gut he was realistic enough to know she was too weak to travel or tolerate a procedure that carried such a high mortality. No matter how dismal the outlook, he wanted to keep hope alive.

Kathy greeted him at the door. "I have to run out for groceries. Shawn should get here soon if county transport isn't late again."

"Don't rush," Parker replied, eager to be alone with Judy.

After Kathy left, he entered the bedroom to see her cradling the infant, making baby talk in a soft breathy voice. Makeup covered her pale skin but the steroid-induced roundness to her face failed to define the familiar high cheek bones. It didn't matter what she looked like. To him, she was as beautiful now as when they first met.

"I prayed you wouldn't get stuck with an emergency," she said giving him a radiant smile.

"Not a chance, I take no calls tonight." He bent down to gently embrace her and the baby.

She held the infant with outstretched arms. "Just look at her, she's beautiful."

"Without a doubt," he agreed, sitting on the edge of the bed to rub her back. He felt each bony rib poke through the thin fabric of her nightgown, a grim reminder of her deteriorating condition.

He fought back his tears. If he hadn't put his needs before hers, things could have turned out differently. She wouldn't have been involved with Markman and his damned HMO that botched the diagnosis of her mole. In the end, it was Judy who was suffering for all of it.

"Why so quiet? What are you thinking about?" she asked.

"Just a little daydreaming." He leaned over and kissed her as his cell phone rang.

When he didn't answer it, she asked, "Aren't you going to take the call?"

He shrugged his shoulders with annoyance and flipped open the phone.

Rucker's stern voice came through. "I thought you should know, we found the locker where Olga stashed the missing money. The count is nearly two million."

Parker couldn't contain his excitement. "Hold on a minute, Rucker." He turned to Judy and said, "I'll take this in the other room."

"I can talk now. That's great news! No wonder the syndicate was on my tail! Did Cougar lead you to it?"

Rucker laughed. "No, just dumb luck. A maintenance man at the hospital picked up the key and forgot about it."

"But that was months ago. Why did it turn up now?"

"The guy left after work for an extended trip to see his family in Venezuela. That was the day Olga came into the ER. When he got back, he heard we were searching for the key in the hospital laundry so he called us."

"Where did you find the money?"

"The key led us to the same storage facility where we first found the empty locker. Cougar's secret was that he rented more than one locker with different names. That way he could transfer the money he skimmed between lockers to throw off the syndicate. We finally found the two million in one of those lockers."

Parker felt his spirits rise. "Then I'm in the clear. But how will the traffickers know I had nothing to do with their money?"

"The press release to the papers will show Cougar and Carmella will get a free pass to Costa Rica. We'll also insert a statement that the cash was found in a locker. When the cartel learns that the missing money is in police hands, they'll put two and two together and forget about you."

"Then Cougar gets extradited without serving jail time?"

"That's the arrangement. He's promised he won't return to drug trafficking, but once he's out of the country, who knows?"

"Is that what you call justice? The guilty go scot free and guys like me have to obey the law?"

"Don't take it too personal, Doc. We're dealing in the real world. The tradeoff was worth it because he gave us enough leads to keep the department busy for a long time."

Parker understood why the scales of justice weren't always in balance. "What about Lindstrom and Trask? If you don't stop their counterfeit drug scam, I'm ready to blow the whistle."

"Don't confront them, Doc. We have most of the evidence and don't want them to become flight risks."

"What can I do to help?"

"Nothing," Rucker ordered. "Just don't get involved."

Parker snapped the phone shut and gritted his teeth. He wanted to crush those sons of bitches for all the hurt they caused and how they deprived Judy from getting the legitimate Procrit. All he wanted now was justice and if Rucker didn't do it, he'd find a way.

Judy heard the anger in Parker's voice as he entered. "What was that all about?"

"It's a long story and not important right now."

Parker's mood changed when Shawn appeared, wheeling himself into the room.

Shawn reached out and caressed the baby's head. "She's truly a gift, Judy."

"Spoken like a proud uncle," she answered, giving him a warm smile.

Parker stood by, taking in the heartwarming scene. It was amazing how much this hardened street-wise drug pusher had changed. The love that escaped brother and sister over the years blossomed before his eyes. All because of Kathy and baby Judy.

Kathy walked into the room with a questioning look. "Are you having trouble with the telephone?"

"No, why?" Judy replied.

"There's a telephone service man outside saying there's a problem with the inside lines in this building. He said we should expect someone will be coming into the apartment to check on it in a few days."

Fifty-five

Parker grew impatient waiting for Rucker to deliver on his promise to link Lindstrom to Trask's counterfeit drug operation. After the state dropped all charges against him, his animosity toward Lindstrom became unbearable. Certainly he was justified. If the blemish of professional misconduct had been sustained, what institution would have allowed him on its staff?

He walked the halls of MCA, reflecting on his situation. Although Lindstrom and Gold knew the state had exonerated him, they still couldn't be trusted. It was easy to trump up a host of fake charges again, so he knew he had to always be on guard.

As he approached the elevator, four men dressed in crisply pressed suits carrying attaché cases marched by. Parker decided they looked too neat to be doctors.

Lawton's voice came from behind as the chief of surgery moved toward him in green scrubs. "Keep your eyes on those fellas in black suits, Parker. They're on a mission."

"What kind of mission?"

Lawton smiled. "Sweet justice."

"Karl, come clean. Your grin has me curious."

Lawton burst out into a deep laugh. "I can't contain myself. They're federal agents checking MCA's books."

"For what?"

"For kickback payments MCA Corporation has been making to doctors to admit cases to the hospital. It's a nationwide investigation. They proved it in Texas along with Medicare fraud and now they're here in Florida."

"You mean the hospital actually pays doctors to admit patients to the hospital?"

"Yep, and they've already inspected a few offices, mostly family docs and internists. They're heading for the business office to audit the hospital books as we speak."

"It's unbelievable the depths businessmen will go to control their market," Parker replied.

Lawton gave him a broad grin. "Look at the empty halls. Right now the guilty ones must be in their offices burning records."

Parker laughed. "Since you and I aren't the anointed ones, we don't have to worry. But I'm not sure about Morty and some specialists on Executive Committee. Their contracts might look pretty generous to the IRS."

"You'r right, Parker. It's about time we see some justice around here."

Parker's face turned serious. "It's sad, Karl. Medicine used to be a profession. What should we expect when the bean counters take over?"

Without hesitation, Lawton replied, "More scandal, just like we're going to see."

Lawton's name sounded over the paging system. "Gotta go, OR's waiting," he said and walked away to enter through the swinging doors.

As Parker passed by the Executive Suite, he was startled to see the usually staid Carolyn Robertson rush out of Trask's office, franticly waving a letter in her hand. Before entering Lindstrom's side door, her eyes darted about to check whether she had been seen.

He paused in a doorway to avoid being spotted. Suddenly Lindstrom and Trask emerged with suitcases while Robertson followed, cuddling a bulky leather briefcase. The agitated body language of all three signaled something other than hospital business was up.

He quickly dialed Rucker on his cell and after repeated rings, the lawman's voice came on line.

He whispered in a hushed voice. "Rucker, it's Parker. I'm at MCA and something crazy's going on here. Looks like the unholy trio, Lindstrom, Trask and Robertson are in a hurry to go somewhere."

"Shit!" Rucker snapped. "The sheriff and I are on our way to meet with Lindstrom shortly. He said he couldn't meet this morning."

"They're leaving the building right now. Should I follow?"

"No, it's too dangerous."

"And let those crooks get away? I'm still wearing my GPS unit, so track me. Good bye!"

He raced down the hall, keeping the trio in sight and watched cautiously as they exited a side door to the doctors' parking lot. His breath was heavy with excitement as he followed into the daylight. Tracking them, he watched the three get into Lindstrom's white Mercedes. By the time he reached his car, they were out of the parking lot.

His pulse quickened when he thought he had lost them, but thankfully the traffic light at the corner slowed their flight. When the signal changed, he followed the Mercedes north onto I-95. The heavy traffic made it easy to go unnoticed. When they exited Indiantown Road in Jupiter traveling east, he followed, keeping a good distance away. He knew he had been spotted when the Mercedes began weaving in and out of the three lanes of traffic.

When the light turned yellow at the next intersection, the Mercedes made a sudden U-turn. Another oncoming car attempting to race through the red signal came to a screeching stop to avoid crashing into them.

As soon as the light turned green, Parker raced to make the same U-turn following the Mercedes west. His heart jumped when he almost hit an oncoming car as he crossed into its path. In the distance, he spotted the Mercedes speed back onto the I-95 North ramp. He followed, watching his speedometer clock nearly 90 miles per hour.

When Lindstrom's car exited onto State Route 714 in Palm City traveling east, he followed. By the time he drove onto the two lane country road, an oversize open-bed landscape truck loaded with tree clippings lumbered onto the road in front of him. Holding his breath, he made a quick left to pass, greatly relieved to see no car coming in the opposite direction.

In the distance, he watched the white sedan make a right turn onto a narrow side road. He made the same turn onto Boat Ramp Avenue and could still see the car in the distance. Trailing on the two lane asphalt road, he lost sight of them. He followed the bend in the road, buffered on both sides with dense foliage.

After a short distance, he reached a gated clearing with a posted sign. *"The Naked Lady Ranch, A Private Residential Airport Community."* He sped past the "Residents Only" gate which was still open and spotted the white Mercedes parked beside an airplane on the grassy field.

As he neared, he could see it was a push-pull craft with propellers spinning, one in front and one behind, ready for takeoff. The plane began to taxi down the runway, and he raced his car onto the field, hoping to crash into its tail to stop the flight.

Suddenly, he heard the staccato screeches of sirens, as two sheriff's patrol cars sped onto the field, intent on blocking the plane from getting airborne. The plane stopped and the cabin door flew open. A man in a white jumpsuit leaped out, running into the depths of thick bushes and trees beside the runway.

Parker vaulted out of his car and followed him into the lush greenery. Visibility was limited by the vines and bushes which provided a dark cover. He froze in place, hoping to hear footsteps he could follow.

Without warning, he felt a sudden blow to the back of his head that sent him reeling. He fell and when able to focus, he stared at the barrel of a gun held by the white-suited man who sported a flowing mustache.

Suddenly a shot rang out.

Parker felt the full force of the gunman's heavy body crumple on top of him. A rush of delayed fear coursed within his every fiber.

The next thing he heard was a voice call out, "Are you okay, Doc?"

He looked up to see the deputy standing over him. Relieved he was still alive, he suddenly felt as if some unseen power had lifted the weight of the dead man's body off his chest.

~ * ~

The burly deputy escorted Parker out of the foliage while speaking into a cell phone attached to his shirt. "We're coming out and Doc's okay. Just a little shook up."

"I can manage," Parker insisted as he limped through the dense brush with the officer's help.

Once in the clearing, he spotted Rucker with deputies surrounding the handcuffed escapees. Lindstrom's booming voice shouted obscenities, while Trask's head hung low as he trailed meekly behind. Robertson carried a glazed look as she was guided into the patrol car.

After the three were escorted away, Rucker waved to Parker, signaling him to approach the plane. He looked inside, pointing to the open cockpit.

"Smugglers are pretty slick nowadays, Doc. They buy aircraft made of composites that can escape radar detection. This one's called the Velocity."

Parker peered inside, astonished at the number of plump duffel bags squeezed into every available inch of space in the cabin.

"That's all drug money on its way to get laundered in the Caymans, Bahamas or wherever," Rucker commented.

Parker took in a deep breath. "Does all this belong to Lindstrom and Trask?"

"Not likely. Cougar arranged for Reliant money to be flown out with the syndicate's dough. Of course, at a price," he winked.

Parker shook his head in disbelief. "How much do you think is in there?"

"Must be over ten million."

"Holy shit!" Parker gasped, his eyes still glued to the tightly packed sacks.

Rucker gave Parker a broad smile. "We've done our homework. The computer we seized from Trask's house gave us the overseas banking numbers for him and Lindstrom. Once we show the money was gained fraudulently, the banks will have to open their records to us. After that, the IRS takes over."

Feeling lightheaded, Parker leaned against the plane to support himself. Everything had happened so fast, his mind was a blur. Even if he operated twenty-four hours a day, seven days a week, he'd never make the kind of money in front of him.

Rucker searched Parker's bleary eyes. "You don't look right, Doc."

"I'm okay, just a little out of shape for this type of play," Parker replied. "Before I got sucked into this mess, I never realized how wide hard drugs and counterfeits have invaded our everyday lives."

"Sadly, Doc, it's occurring all over the world. Even in our country. Many prescription drugs have been recalled recently and we've had our share of deaths from contaminated medicine. I'm afraid it won't end soon enough."

"You're making me feel very uncomfortable again, Rucker. So every time I write a prescription, I have to wonder if the patient gets the real thing?"

"Question everything, Doc. The FDA relies on physicians to alert them if a drug doesn't look Kosher.

Once a counterfeit is placed in the bottle, it's hard to prove where it came from."

Parker raised his arms to stretch his back. "I'm feeling better now." He ran his hand through his disheveled hair, smoothing it down and looked to Rucker.

"What about Robertson? Will she face the same charges as Lindstrom and Trask?"

"Can't say," the agent replied. "She's an accomplice, but that's for the courts to decide. You better go home now and get some rest, Doc."

He noticed Parker's unsteady gait as he limped to the car. "You're not right. Let me take you to the hospital to get checked out."

"I'm fine. I just need to call my office, and then there's someone I want to see."

A deputy approached Rucker. "The crime scene boys are on their way, the coroner's office has been notified and headquarters is sending a pilot to fly the plane to a controlled site. I'm staying to guard the scene."

Rucker nodded his approval. "Good, and I'm taking Doc to the hospital."

"I told you I'm okay," Parker protested.

"You're not driving alone. I'll take you anywhere you want." He paused and gripped Parker's arm. "I have to tell you what you did today was very dangerous and damn stupid. You could have been killed."

Parker felt his pulse quicken. "I just couldn't let those bastards get away."

"Guess I can't blame you," Rucker said, steering him toward the Honda. "Get in your car. Tell me where you want to go."

Fifty-six

Parker felt an increasing discomfort in his left hip as they drove to Judy's apartment. The pain persisted enough to make him decide to get an x-ray later.

When they turned into her condo's parking area, Rucker jammed on the brakes, making a sudden stop.

"Aghh..." Parker cried out, lurching forward.

A Bellsouth service truck careened past them with tires screeching as it raced out to the street and disappeared in the distance.

"Where in the hell is that idiot going?" Rucker snarled. He noted Parker's grimace and apologized. "Sorry, Doc, I didn't want to wreck your car."

"I'm all right, just pull in right there," Parker said, pointing to the empty space in front of Judy's apartment.

No sooner had they opened the car doors when they saw Kathy race out of the ground floor apartment, screaming, "Stop him, stop that truck, he's got the baby!"

Parker looked to Rucker in dazed amazement. "It must be the guy that nearly hit us." He rushed toward Kathy, reading terror written on her face.

Kathy cried, "He came in to check the telephone line. I

was in the kitchen for a second, and when I got back, the bassinet was empty."

Parker's heart sank. "Call the sheriff, Rucker. I'm going in to see Judy."

"Way ahead of you," Rucker answered, dialing his cell.

Parker hobbled into the apartment, oblivious of his pain and rushed into Judy's room. She stood over the empty crib, sobbing uncontrollably.

He held her and wrapped his arms around her. "We'll get her back, the sheriff will find her."

She pulled away and cried, "My baby, my baby!" and then collapsed to the floor.

He picked her up in his arms and carried her to the bed.

"No, it can't be," she called out, thrashing her head from side to side on the pillow. "Bring my baby back, I want my baby!"

He stared down in horror, wondering what motive lurked behind such a despicable act. His thoughts raced like wildfire. Could it be? Kent couldn't be that cold-hearted.

He held and rocked her gently, trying to reassure her that the baby was safe and soon would be in her arms again.

Rucker kept constant telephone contact with the sheriff's office, patiently waiting to hear news that the truck was located. Then the hopeful message came in. A Bellsouth vehicle meeting the description refused to stop after a patrol car flashed its lights. An all points alert was sent out and the chase was underway.

An hour passed and Rucker paced the floor with the phone glued to his ear. The stern look on his face only intensified Judy's worst fears. Suddenly, he broke into a broad smile. "They stopped the truck and the baby's fine."

Parker embraced Judy, who kept repeating, "Thank God, thank God."

~ * ~

The two men left Kathy with Judy to drive to the sheriff's administrative center. Rucker led the way into the building, waving at officers who recognized him.

They passed through the swinging doors and faced a heavy set deputy with a large holstered revolver at his waist, awkwardly cradling tiny Judy. The infant's intensified cries signaled a hunger alert.

"I'll take that little bundle," Parker said, reaching for the infant.

The deputy looked to Rucker. "Is it okay?"

"Sure thing. He's the baby's doctor and the kid needs a feeding and diaper change, which you can't do."

The deputy smiled and handed the blanketed baby to Parker, who rocked her gently in an effort to console her.

Rucker looked to the deputy. "Where's the kidnapper?"

"In the back, getting grilled," the deputy answered.

"I want to hear that questioning," Rucker replied. "Arrange a ride for the doctor and baby back to the apartment." He looked to Parker. "I'll get your car to you after I hear the questioning."

The baby again let out another piercing wail as Parker and the deputy entered the car.

"Let's get going, this kid needs to get fed," Parker said. After a few minutes of constant wailing, he pleaded, "Can't you drive any faster?"

"We're already breaking the law without a car seat,"

the deputy replied, "but I'll push it as fast as I can."

Parker's cell phone rang as he held the infant and he fumbled to answer it. "We have the baby and she's fine, Kathy. We're on our way so have the bottle ready."

On reaching the apartment, Parker thanked the deputy and dashed out of the car, holding the infant close to his chest. Once inside, he saw Shawn in his wheelchair with Kathy at his side holding the welcoming bottle. As soon as the baby's lips and the nipple met, a merciful quiet followed.

Judy struggled to rise from the bed when Parker walked the feeding infant into the room. "Thank God she's all right. I need to hold her, Parker."

He handed her the baby and gently guided the two back to bed. For one split second, he fantasized he was the father placing the child into the mother's arms. His heart melted watching the baby take strong gulps while tears of joy flowed down Judy's cheeks. He sat at the edge of the bed, kissing the top of Judy's head, her brow and cheek while she fed the child.

"I love you," she whispered."

Before he could answer, Shawn entered the room. His eyes swelled with tears. "Jesus, Sis, I thought we'd lost her."

Suddenly Judy's warm glow vanished. She looked up at Parker and Shawn. "Why? "Why did that man take my baby?"

~ * ~

It was 8 PM by the time a tired Rucker returned to Judy's apartment.

Parker could see the agent, who always looked

confident and in control, appeared troubled. "Did you have to beat the shit out of him for a confession?" he asked.

Rucker sank down on the couch and looked to Parker, Shawn and Kathy. "We didn't lay a finger on him. He was so scared he sang like a canary."

"Why did he do it?" Shawn snapped.

Rucker raised his hands in a calming gesture. "This telephone repairman is just a pawn. Claims he was in debt over his head after a bad business deal which led to a divorce. His ex's lawyer is pounding him for alimony and child support, so he agreed to the kidnapping for a big cash payment."

"How much?" Kathy asked.

"A hundred and fifty thousand. He was paid twenty-five thousand in cash by registered mail with the rest to be paid on delivery of the child."

"Delivered to whom?" Parker asked sharply.

"He doesn't know. After snatching the baby, he was to call a certain number for further instructions."

"What kind of instructions?" Shawn growled.

"He was told to meet at a remote parking spot at the Gardens Mall. That's where the transfer of the baby and money would take place."

"Did you trace the number?" Shawn asked.

"We did," Rucker answered. "It went to a cell registered to a John Smith. By now that phone is probably buried in a landfill."

Parker's voice rose. "And you have no idea who's behind this?"

"Not right now, but we're tracking all leads."

"Like what?" Shawn snapped.

"Like who's the baby's father? I need that information."

No one spoke until Shawn answered, "We don't know."

Rucker's eyes widened. "Oh, I see." Regaining his authoritarian composure, he continued, "We have to investigate the lawyer handling the kidnapper's alimony payments."

"Why?" Kathy asked.

"There might be a connection. His attorney knew this guy was in debt and desperate. He could also be representing a childless couple willing to pay any amount for a quick adoption."

The three sat in silence, trying to digest what Rucker had just told them.

Kathy jumped up on hearing the baby's cries. "Excuse me, she probably needs a diaper change." She left for the bedroom and within seconds, a shrill cry pierced the air.

All three rushed into the room to see her staring down at Judy's limp body, her arms still around the squirming baby.

"I think she's gone," Kathy said.

Parker approached Judy's wasted frame, studying the tragic scene of a crying infant lying on its mother's motionless body. He handed the baby to Kathy and placed his fingers on Judy's neck.

"There's no pulse, she's gone," he said softly.

Tenderly, he encircled her in his arms, rocking her back and forth. He couldn't hold back his tears, and his voice cracked as he looked up at everyone. "We should be comforted that Judy passed on knowing her baby was safe."

In his sorrow, he remembered his promise to Judy. Unless her baby needed help, he would never reveal the father's identity. But the kidnapping endangered the child and with Judy gone, it was now up to him.

In a firm voice he announced, "I know who the father is."

Fifty-seven

It was approaching noon when Parker drove through the cemetery gates. Thankfully, Kathy and Shawn had handled the funeral arrangements. Long rows of cars on both sides of the drive leading to the burial site forced him to park a distance away. Walking toward the crowd, he reflected on the many nurses who had stopped him in the hospital to convey their sympathies. He knew Judy was well liked and had touched the personal lives of many.

Before he reached the grave site, Rucker stepped out of a car and greeted him. "Hi, Doc. I wanted to be here and let you know we caught the kidnappers."

Parker gave Rucker a questioning look. "There's more than one?"

"Dr. Markman and his lawyer were at the bottom of it."

"I had a feeling."

Rucker continued. "Luckily, the repair man still had the envelope the twenty-five thousand was mailed in. The DNA from Markman's tongue when he licked it, along with his prints, provided the evidence."

"Did that make him confess?"

"Not exactly. We had to get a court order to open

Markman's bank account. Two hundred thousand in cash was withdrawn a few days before the kidnapping. Fifty of it was transferred to his lawyer, the same one handling the repairman's alimony payments. It all unraveled when we presented them with the facts."

"Why did Markman do it?"

"Because he was afraid DNA evidence would confirm his paternity and threaten his marriage. I guess there's big money involved and he didn't want to risk a hefty divorce settlement. By having the child kidnapped, there'd be no link to follow."

He gave Parker a broad grin. "Little did he know he would get caught in his own DNA trap when he put his tongue to that envelope."

"So what happens to him now?"

"He's in custody and the DA will decide about dealing with the attorney."

Parker shook his head in disbelief. "Great work, Rucker."

"Thanks for your lead, the sheriff provided all the help we needed."

Parker's eyes moistened as the scene of Judy's lifeless body lying in bed with the baby in her arms came to mind. Thankful the infant was safe and sound, he resolved never again to take the police for granted.

Rucker broke into his thoughts. "Let's go, Doc. We need to be there for the service."

~ * ~

The winter sun climbed high over the horizon as Parker and Rucker followed the mourners along paths separating grave sites. A heap of sandy loam lay piled beside the freshly dug grave shaded by a four poster canopy. Gwen and Paul stood beside the priest, whose purple sash lent the only color against a drab black suit and white collar. It had been Judy's request that Father O'Toole preside over the funeral.

Shawn sat in his wheelchair holding the baby while Kathy stood beside him. A needy cry from the infant brought a bottle to her lips, producing the only smiles on the somber faces surrounding the casket.

"Are we ready?" the priest asked, turning to Shawn who answered with a slow nod. Father O'Toole opened his missal and peered into the expectant faces before him. In a thick Irish brogue, he said, "Let us pray." He led the group into the Lord's Prayer and ended the reading with, "Ashes to ashes and dust to dust."

The quiet that followed was broken by coughs and soft weeping as the chubby-faced cleric cleared his throat to speak.

"It's not often one meets a stranger whose life is changed after a one hour meeting. I had that privilege when Judy walked into my church. I don't think there was a finer moment in her life than the day she made the decision to keep her baby. Now her legacy is this child which praises God's love for humanity."

Parker held back tears as he listened to the priest. He felt that no matter what the future held, his love for Judy would never fade. If only he hadn't turned his back on her. After those wasted years, who could have imagined this kind of an ending?

With his thoughts running wild, he looked to the baby as Shawn raised and kissed her cheek. Kathy responded by embracing them both. The moving scene brought back memories of his earlier days with Judy, a time when their future seemed so bright.

Father O'Toole's voice rose. "Today we say farewell to Judy and return her to God's hands. Thank you Lord, Amen." He closed his missal and gazed in silence as the casket descended into the ground.

Mourners wiped tears and slowly dispersed to their cars for the luncheon at a nearby restaurant. While Parker felt emotionally drained, he wanted to be there for Kathy and Shawn.

Gwen and Paul came to Parker's side, guiding him through the crowd. Nurses, a few doctors and an elderly hospital maintenance man stopped to share their sorrow. All comments ended the same. At least her suffering was over.

As they approached Kathy and Shawn standing beside the van, Rucker joined them.

Gwen turned to Kathy. "Are the Ackerlys here?"

Kathy smiled. "No, I didn't see them. They're not adopting the baby. We are."

"You are?" Gwen questioned.

Shawn beamed. "You're looking at the future Mr. and Mrs. Shawn Keller and their daughter, Judy."

Paul extended his hand. "Congratulations! You won't regret it."

Parker gave Shawn a thumbs up and hugged Kathy. "This is the best news I've heard in a long time."

Shawn nodded. "And we're asking you to be best man and godfather, Doc."

"Not a bad offer," Rucker broke in.

Shawn's eyes filled as he reached for Kathy's hand. "Raising little Judy was my sister's last wish before she died."

Gwen hugged Kathy. "I'm so happy for the two of you." Turning to Parker, she added, "Maybe now is the time you should give them your news, Dr. Dawson."

Karl Lawton approached through the thinning crowd. "What news?"

Parker sheepishly rubbed his chin. "I'm leaving. I've accepted a teaching position at the University of Florida medical school in Gainesville."

"Wow, that is news," Shawn replied. "You'll be missed, Doc, but I guess you have to get on with your career."

"I'll just be a few hours away," Parker answered, sensing how much he would miss his new friends and even Rucker.

Lawton grinned. "It was just a matter of time until you found your right niche, Parker. A philosopher once said, 'Success is a journey, not a destination' and I think you're on your way."

"And I have to thank you for saving my reputation, Karl. I couldn't have handled the hospital politics without you."

Rucker placed a hand on Parker's shoulder. "I wish you the best, Doc. Thanks to you, we broke Lindstrom's drug scheme, the local narco trafficking and even the kidnapping."

Parker's face softened as he looked to Gwen. "You were my anchor and hung in there for me. And Paul, thanks for trusting me."

Gwen's wet face touched his cheek. "It's been a hell of a year, Dr. Dawson, but in spite of everything, I'm going to miss that worried look of yours coming through the door."

High-pitched screeches of birds could be heard flying above. Parker turned his gaze to the billowy white clouds floating in a blue sky. Suddenly a white egret with its sharp yellow beak, brown buffed head and chest swooped down to land on the roof of the van. The bird waited for a long moment, flapped its wings, and then flew away.

With everyone's attention directed at the bird in flight, Parker smiled. "Could this be Judy's messenger letting us know she's still with us?"

"I think so," Shawn answered, waving to the bird as it glided toward Judy's gravesite. "It's a message of hope telling us life goes on. And with hope, there's always a new beginning."

Epilogue

One year later

With Danielle at his side, Parker drove south on Florida's Turnpike into Palm Beach County. This was his first trip back since leaving for the university. As they neared the exit ramp, his mood grew dark. Painful memories of Judy's suffering and the legal abuses heaped on him by MCA flooded back into his thoughts.

Over the past year, Gwen had kept him informed about the doctors and hospital administrators he left behind. Kent and his attorney were out on bail awaiting trial. With Sheila's divorce well underway, Mr. Glassman had cancelled all of Kent's HMO contracts. But none of this news gave him any satisfaction, even though these people deserved it.

Lindstrom and Trask were still in jail since the judge considered them flight risks. If the drugs they peddled caused any deaths, they would also face manslaughter charges.

Danielle broke the silence. "You're awfully quiet, Parker. What's on your mind?"

He returned a faint smile. "Just thinking about things."

"Good things?"

"Yes and no," he answered with a distant tone.

"Just tell me the good ones then," she laughed.

"Meeting you is the best, of course." He gave her a grin and planted a kiss on her cheek. "And I never imagined how positive my move to the university would turn out. I like my chief, my service and especially my research in melanoma."

Danielle's face turned serious. "Parker, I do have one question."

"Fire away."

"You told me about the medical dishonesty at MCA. Did you leave community medicine to hide in academia?"

His silence made her continue. "If it happened there, it has to be happening at other hospitals as well."

Parker's jaw tightened as he flinched inwardly. "Please understand, Danielle. Most docs work hard to do the best they can for their patients. It's just the few rotten apples that spoil the barrel." His brow knitted in thought. "The reason I left was because of the system."

"What do you mean, 'the system'?"

"Doctors have lost their independence. They're just employees of HMOs and corporate hospitals where profit is the bottom line. Unfortunately, the government works hand in hand with them. Together, their mission is to control costs by rationing care. While politicians don't treat people, they make the laws that affect the way doctors have to practice."

"But doctors are at fault, too. They rush patients through like cattle without giving them much time."

"Don't blame physicians for that. As I said, it's the

system. The expense of upgrading computers, hiring personnel to handle the overload of useless paper work and the escalating costs of litigation. All these demands in the face of lower fees force physicians to take on more patients. That's why they can't waste time on pleasantries."

"How can we change the system?"

He smiled and shook his head. "I've given that a lot of thought. It's bigger than the individual physician. It starts with the integrity of the physician working to regain the trust of patients."

"And how will you do that?"

"Although honesty is instilled at an early age in the home, ethics must be taught in medical schools as well. I have a hope. The local newspaper agreed to let me write a weekly medical column. As one voice, that's where I'll begin."

"Then you haven't lost your fire?"

"No, wait until you read my columns. You'll see."

The two sat quietly for a few moments, until he asked, "What are the good things *you* think about?"

She returned a bright smile. "My lucky day came when I met you at the Campus Club."

He nodded. "No, Danielle, I'm the lucky one. I was really down the night I drifted into the club for a drink. Then you appeared on stage and sang. Your words touched me, and I knew I had to meet you."

She held out her hand, staring at the diamond ring. "It's strange how things turn out. I wrote that song from my heart. It expressed the emptiness I felt after my fiancé died in that auto accident. Who would have thought it would lead me to my future husband?"

"We're nearly there," Parker said as they passed through the toll gate. "Kathy and Shawn are excited to meet you."

"So am I. They already feel like family to me."

Parker drove through the residential development of PGA National guided by his GPS and reached the Mediterranean-style home. Twinkling Christmas lights strung along shrubs and a pink flamingo with its Santa hat flipped to one side welcomed them.

As they stood at the front door, Parker took Danielle's hand, admiring her sleek ebony hair that accented the whiteness of her skin.

Her eyes met his. "Aren't you going to ring the bell?"

He smiled and pressed the button.

The door opened and Shawn faced them, standing upright with braces strapped to both legs. Crutches supported his tall muscular frame. Kathy stood beside him wearing a wide grin. A wobbly baby Judy with blond ringlets held onto one of Kathy's legs.

"You're walking!" Parker cried out, embracing Shawn.

Kathy's eyes sparkled with joy. "We wanted to surprise you."

As everyone moved into the house, Parker felt his spirits soar. With Danielle in his life, Shawn's recovery and a blossoming Baby Judy, it was a Christmas he'd always remember.

About The Author

Richard Berjian has practiced medicine in both community and academic centers. He served as senior research surgeon at a prestigious cancer center and also held the post of Chairman of the Department of Surgery at a major university medical center. He presently resides in Stuart, Florida with his wife, Sally, and is actively engaged in malignant melanoma research.